Pearces' Ocean

Pearces' Ocean

A J Pearce

PEARCES' OCEAN
First published in New Zealand in 2011
by AM Publishing New Zealand
www.ampublishingnz.com

Copyright © Tony Pearce 2011
The author asserts the moral right to be identified as the author of this work.

ISBN 1475099576
ISBN 9781475099577

To order copies of this book please contact Tony Pearce
tonyrose@ihug.co.nz

Cover image:
Douglas Horman
www.hormanfineart.com

Editing, proofreading, book design and layout:
Adrienne Morris, AM Proofreading and Editing,
Auckland, New Zealand
www.amproofreadingnz.com

Cover design:
Adrienne Morris

Dedication

This book is dedicated to the global Pearce family.

But mostly to Jack and Queenie Pearce, and Aunts Gladys and Ruby who brought up their cousins – Ernest, my father, Uncle Leslie and Uncle John (Cyril) – after my grandfather and grandmother died. From these now silent mouths came the basis of many of these stories.

It has taken four years to complete and was inspired by our family's history, which could so easily have been lost. I trust all of you will get enjoyment from it.

Special dedication is due to Aunt Barbara, Uncle John's wife; she encouraged me all my life in my search for adventure. Neither of these dear souls will see its completion. An editor herself, Barbara told me the first few chapters of the first draft were 'great' – a wonderful untruth, magnificent motivation.

The younger Pearce generations were my initial motivation to begin the journey. I hope you enjoy. I have no written research from before 1796, but these stories have rung in my head for half a century. They are in print partly for you to know those who have gone before.

To the rest of my readers, your families also lived through these difficult times. Could there be a smuggler or a pirate among them?

Acknowledgements

Thanks to Rosemary Picton who has endured reading more than one draft, and the other ten or so honoured draft readers, without whose critical input the finished article would be a shadow of what you now hold in, what is, I hope, fervent anticipation.

Thanks to my dear friend Ken Mells, who spent many hours helping me with the maps.

To Adrienne Morris – editor, proofreader and layout designer. That this book is here in any legible form is due to you. You have taught me so much – your patience with my mild dyslexia is the stuff of legend. Thank you, thank you.

To Doug Horman – artist extraordinaire. The front cover is from his voluminous, brilliant portfolio of Cornish and New Zealand villages, ships and seascapes.

Lastly, thanks to Napoleon Hill, and *Think and grow rich*: 'Whatever the mind can conceive and truly believe, we can achieve.' This has been my lifelong credo – it works.

In memory of Dorothy Roper
Thanks for the book,
The Blackwall frigates by Basil Lubbock

Preface

The Pearce family was but one of many who emigrated from Cornwall out of a desire to improve their lot, as did the Farmiloes mentioned in the story. My side of the family moved to 148 Winston Road, Stoke Newington, at the turn of the twentieth century.

After the Second World War, I was the only child of the family living in London. My four cousins – Rosemary, Alison, Simon and Peter, children of my Uncle Cyril – lived near Birmingham. Uncle Cyril married a Farmiloe, thus retying the family bonds of 250 years earlier.

Sitting in the scullery at '148', Uncle Jack, Auntie Queenie, and Aunts Ruby and Gladys would tell stories of Cornwall. The pirates, the wreckers, the smugglers – all seemed larger than life to me. The hanging of our men and their interment outside St Just's consecrated area is just one example of what I heard.

The rest of the book is fiction, except for the American connection, some of whom I met in 1973, in Daytona Beach, Florida.

Aged eighteen, I left London bound for the two most enjoyable summers of my life – on the Scilly Isles. I became involved in the search for the wreck of HMS *Association* – great fun. My part was very small but the lure of sunken treasure was strong. Others eventually secured the prize.

The Scilly Isles are situated at the gateway to the English Channel, just 28 miles off Land's End, the southernmost part of the English mainland. The islands are a meeting place for the currents of the English and Bristol Channels and their confluence with the Irish Sea. Driving the mighty Atlantic Ocean inexorably westward is the Gulf Stream, the spawning ground of England's weather patterns.

Scilly is a mariner's worst nightmare, protruding as it does off the toe of England. Measuring just eight by ten nautical miles, it is influenced, sometimes fatally, by all these forces. Not many ships survive during bad weather once tangled in her web of rocks, tides and islets. The people of Scilly have a long history of salvaging wreck – some legal, some not – and thus my lust for adventure, so prevalent in my forebears, was indelibly formed.

I became a yachtsman and have sailed all my life, a voyage to New Zealand 1972–74, and a circumnavigation of the world 1984–89 with two sons and a daughter, being the highlights. I have sailed all the ocean routes mentioned in the book apart from Carlos's voyage from Virginia to China.

John Pearce, our first protagonist, was the firstborn of ten children. Even after losing a brother and three sisters to sickness, there were too many mouths to feed. The press was at large in Falmouth, and John's father simply sold the boy to the navy. At least he would be fed: the navy, in one of its quirky rules, gave larger rations to boys who were freely apprenticed to sea than to pressed adults. With a rum ration to trade, he would have a far better life in the navy. In the Cornish seaport town of Falmouth, with a lowly tenant publican for a father, he would have little chance of anything. John's situation was typical for a man of his time.

Wars had wrecked the English finances. Taxes were high and sources of income few. Many people turned to smuggling, plunder and piracy as a means of survival. It is said that over 100,000 people were involved in these activities in the early eighteenth century.

This is a rags-to-riches story, a socio-economic history of the 1700s – with, of course, a large dose of artistic licence.

There are many parallels today, as governments still believe they know better how to dispose of constituents' incomes than the constituents themselves.

I try not to preach to you, but nothing really changes. The story is the most important thing. I have tried to move it quickly, dramatised where I thought fit. The historical facts are mostly correct, as are the sailing directions, winds currents, types of ship and the sailor's way of life.

Part One

1707–1747

ST MARTIN'S

BRYHER TRESCO

ST MARY'S

GARRISON HILL • • HARBOUR
• HUGH TOWN
• OLD TOWN

• CRIM LEDGES

• ANNET IS.

• ST AGNES

ISLES OF SCILLY

• WRECK OF "ASSOCIATION"

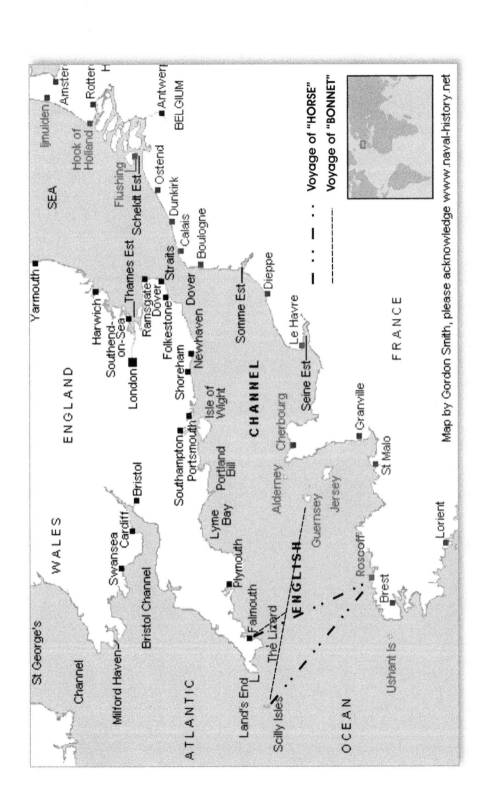

Voyage of "HORSE"
Voyage of "BONNET"

Map by Gordon Smith, please acknowledge www.naval-history.net

Voyage of the Maid of Aran

Chapter 1

A night to forget

It's the bastard Scillies after all; the admiral's done fer us. Bring 'er round to starboard. Look lively now or we're doomed. The flagship! She's dead ahead. She struck! We'll be on top o' her in a flash, and th' wind's increasing – every man fer himself. We're dooomed.

Eventually old John Pearce returned from his rum-induced dreaming. He noticed his young grandson watching him, wide-eyed in horror. Finally, his senses almost regained, he became aware of the screaming wind – no dream now, a howling reality.

Young Simon Pearce could hardly hear himself think. A thunderous, all-pervading cacophony of wind and breaking waves filled the cottage. Driven by 60-knot storm winds across 3,000 miles of Atlantic, foaming sea mountains – some 50 feet high – attempted to pound the Isles of Scilly into oblivion. Reforming after smashing into the Crim Ledges to the west, they finally expended their fury on the granite rocks of Garrison Hill, a hundred feet below the small cottage where Simon lay in his cot, feigning sleep.

The wind filled the living space ten-year-old Simon shared with his grandfather. The noise, as if insufficient discomfort, was augmented by a small trickle of water that had found its way through the thatch above, sharing his cot at the rear of the cottage. "Was it like this when the fleet struck the Gilstones, Grandfather?" Simon asked.

"'E should be sleeping, boy," John Pearce said gruffly. "It's a might late for tales o' the sea and her crossness. I like to forget 'em, not retell 'em. I've no wish to recall what being at sea on a night like this is for a sailorman."

Old John Pearce shivered as he reached for the pewter tankard from which he imbibed his daily grog ration. He refilled it from a stone gallon jar, his daily allowance now doubled.

"Old habits die hard, me handsome," he mused. "Once navy, always navy. If it weren't for the rum, no man would crew the Queen's ships, not as a volunteer anyhow. What with floggings and hangings and arrogant bloody officers. A hard life – hard but good – if 'e managed to get fair cap'ns and not get hit by a cannon ball, chain shot or flying oak splinters. To get out in one piece, ye needed the ear o' lady luck herself."

A squall more violent than the rest shook the tiny cottage. The boy, only his wide eyes visible in the eerie firelight, dodged a drip and pulled an old piece of oiled canvas over his cot in an attempt to keep himself dry.

"'E won't get no sleep this night," mumbled John to himself, his mind making the familiar journey back to that fateful autumn night – the 22nd of October 1707.

"What a sight we was! Thirty-eight ships – over half the Mediterranean fleet – was returning to England for a much-needed winter refit. We was loaded to the gunnels with the spoils of plunder and war. From our decks 'e could see 'em all. Close by was the bulk of the flagship – the 96-gun second-rater *Association*. Surrounding her, like bees protecting their queen, were other ships of the line – *Romney*, *Eagle*, *Indefatigable* and our own *St George* – who were in turn fussed about by a flock of frigates. Ships stretched in line to the horizon astern, and line ahead to the horizon in front.

"It were named the Wars of Spanish Succession. After the death of Charles the Second of Spain, the whole of Europe became embroiled in what were a struggle to keep a balance of power in Europe. England and her Dutch allies joined forces with the bloody Holy Roman Church and made war on France and their Spanish allies. They was trying to prevent these powerful nations from coming under the control of one monarch.

"In 1702, our Royal Navy won a huge sea battle at Vigo Bay – that were some fight, me lad. Our fleet, under Admiral Rooke, smashed a Spanish treasure fleet from which we took tons and tons o' silver. The following year Gibraltar were captured, giving us a vital base at the entrance to th' Mediterranean, right on their enemy's doorstep. It were a grand year – all us tars got a share of the booty.

"Our fleet had orders to harass and engage the Frenchies and Dagoes in the Mediterranean, their home waters. Their lordships of the Admiralty had given the job to the navy's rising star, Rear Admiral Sir Cloudesley Shovell. A fleet of 51 ships left England, crewed by some 30,000 souls.

"Sir Cloudesley had come to the attention of their lordships early in his career. 'E weren't of no high birth or nothin'; 'e were born to a yeoman family up Norfolk way. 'E loved the navy like it were his bride. He were very courageous, the sort of commander what led from the front. His men loved him, getting where he was by working his way through the ranks. He were an ideal 'ero for a country sick 'n tired of war and its massive cost to families in lost loved ones and over-taxation.

"The women of England outnumbered us men by near two to one – spinsterhood or widowhood were a spectre faced by half all women of the nation. The losses in manpower were great. Howsomever, life without war weren't a reality in England those days; heroes for the people were needed desperate. Their lordships of the Admiralty pinned their hopes on the dashing Admiral o' the Blue, Sir Cloudesley Shovell.

"Our 51 ships wreaked havoc on the French and Spanish with minimum losses to us. At Toulon, we left the town a blazing ruin with eight enemy ships destroyed. Sir Cloudesley left thirteen ships, under Sir Thomas Dikes, at Gibraltar; the rest o' us set sail for ol' England, the holds of the flagship full o' gold, silver and much rich plunder. My share alone, being a lowly bosun's mate, were near five years' navy pay. Enough to buy a cottage somewhere in Cornwall in sight o' the sea and a small fishing boat t' earn me keep. After 20 year in th' navy, I were the ripe old age o' thirty-three. I could afford me a wife. What a fine thing a good woman t' share me dotage with would be and, God willing, a son."

Simon noticed a stifled snuffle and ... was it a tear? His grandfather paused, far away in painful thought. The rum warmed him, chasing away ghosts his memory dragged up. Well lubricated, he recalled happier visions from the past.

"We weighed anchor at Gibraltar, known by the Greeks as th' Pillars o' Hercules, on the 10th of October, in the year of our Lord

1707. A fair breeze 'ard abeam from the sou'west, blowing at a steady 15 knots, gave us a good offing. Our course nor'west would have us in sight o' Cape St Vincent, 70 leagues ahead, in a day or so.

"The wind stayed fair as we rounded the cape, sailing full and bye, with a gently rolling, following sea. Being at sea, in weather the likes of this, makes a sailor's heart sing; even the officers, with their fancy uniforms and dandy ways, relaxed the iron discipline normal on Her Majesty's ships. Extra rations o' rum were issued to all hands; pity some never paid Neptune's toll – first drop of the extra tot gotta go over the side for him, or else!"

The old man's eyes rolled wide, his voice fearful. Simon loved this part. "We got a scent o' his displeasure right soon enough. A sea mist came down and lay over us and were to cover the fleet for most o' th' rest o' th' voyage.

"The admiral kept us well out o' sight of land, the mist just allowing any one ship to follow the one in front. Portugal, England's ally in the past, had been taken over by Spain. His Lordship didn't want to bugger up a fair voyage home by bringin' the fleet close to Lisbon. Little point in provokin' an enemy fleet to put to sea, fer to take a chance to get back wot we had stole.

"We doubled Finisterre. Our dead reckoning putting us 20 mile to the west, but no ship sighted land. Closing weather had the officers in a bit o' a quandary as to where us really was. The fleet shaped a course northerly, running up the channel to make landfall at Plymouth.

"Biscay, 'e bastard! I ain't never had a trip across yet that weren't no trouble. Finisterre to Ushant gotta be the worst 300 sea miles in the world. The wind backed and began to pipe. A signal to wear ship and close up flew from the flagship. This were then relayed from one ship to another. Topmen were sent aloft t' take in sail. The building gale were from the sou'east, offshore, and a fair quarter for Plymouth. Nerry no sight o' the sun was had to fix our position, nor no sight o' land.

"The building gale kept us busy. We was wet and cold with the October wind, rain and sea spray; still no undue concern was held by the old hands. Our officers be a stuck up bunch, walking the decks likes they had a ramrod up their arses, but they was the best seagoing commanders in the world. Unless you was unlucky enough to be under one whose family had bought them their commissions, but the likes o' them seldom made cap'n. Most, like our admiral, had worked themselves up from junior midshipmen the hard way, serving 15 or 20 year afore getting a command. Our cap'n on the St George were Lord Dursley. He had been pacing Her Majesty's decks all over the world, near 25 year, with no loss to his name. Much as we cursed 'em, 'tween decks us matelots knew we was in good hands.

"On watch it were thick with rain and driving spray, the October cold seeping to the marrow o' your bones. The nights were black as the inside o' a cow, and the wind played devil's tunes in the rigging. The only light to see being the stern light o' the ship a front, it were as if that light were the only thing leadin' us out of hell – which in a way it were – as long as it were on the right course.

"The officer o' the watch was bound to keep the ship a cable's length behind the one in front – any closer and us would have to slow down. If the light faded, us would have to speed up for to lose touch with th' fleet were one o' th' worst crimes a deck officer could commit. Us sailors was going aloft to reduce or increase the sail many times each watch. Climbin' slippery rope ratlines on a dark, stormy night put fear into the heart o' the most seasoned Jack tar. That be why most o' us never learned to swim – if 'e fell from aloft you'd drown quick; the swimmers just took longer to die. No ship could afford t' lose station lookin' for fallen mast topmen. Cannon would be fired to alert the ship astern, but once overboard a sailor was seldom found alive.

"Worse was off watch. Below, each of the gun decks was home to three hundred seamen. Here they lived, ate an' slept. A rolling, pitching and – with the hatches battened – stinking hellhole. We 'ad no room t' move – hammocks had an allowed space of nineteen inches per man. You could feel every movement of the man next t' you, the constant roll o' the ship would bang us together keepin' us awake. Night-times we was in pitch black, only a light coming from candles at the companionways cracked the gloom, and that was only there so us could move quick-like if all hands was piped. The deck were scarce five feet clear under the beams; we got used to bangin' our heads when the time come to move. The great guns lay beneath our hammocks – they was a soberin' reminder as to what we was really there for."

The cottage shook as another heavy squall raked the island. "When weather's as bad as this, prime English oak, hemp rope and stout canvas ain't naught before the will o' God and sea, lad. If the Lord was handing me a choice just now – to be on a ship to weather o' Scilly or give up grog forever – the grog would go!

"'Twas two bells, the mornin' of the 22nd, when our first lieutenant called the cap'n to the quarterdeck. I was doing my shift at the wheel, so I heard 'em clear. He said we was in a most unusual confused seaway, all worried like. He reckoned the log and dead reckoning put us on the approaches to Ushant, yet the seaway suggests deeper water, and our soundings found no bottom, sir …

"What of the wind, Mister Blackley?" the cap'n asked.

"Backed a bit, sir, east of south now would be close, blowing a half gale and rising, sir."

"Maintain station and keep the leadsman sounding. I'll take the next watch. Carry on, Mister Blackley." Lord Dursley retired below …

"At daylight the flagship signalled 'Captains an' sailing masters o' the fleet prepare t' board, soon as was practical, to attend t' the admiral's pleasure'. Us was all of a quandary; what were afoot?

"I were in charge of our cap'n's jollyboat. A cutter would 'ave been too 'eavy to get safely over the side with the present sea state; we hove to to launch the boat on our lee side. It were a trick and a half to row near half a mile to the flag, but in the lee o' the three-decker it were like the Solent on a summer's day, she were so vast.

"I went up on deck to supervise th' handling o' the jollyboat's lines. Sir Cloudesley was asking sailing masters their opinion as to the whereabouts of the fleet. *Holy Christ*, I thought, *some shit us are in – them don't know where the hell us be!*

"Sir William Jumper, captain o' the *Lennox*, were the only one who disagreed with the admiral. His calculations put the fleet 80 miles to the nor'nor'west, running down fast on Scilly. He reckoned the islands was but a few hours' sail away.

"A young seaman piped up in agreement with Sir William, sayin' the light they had seen afore dawn weren't that of a ship as the cap'ns had supposed but one o' th' fixed lights on Scilly. 'E were a Jenkins, a Scillonian – knew this water well. The brass ignored 'im.

"When 'e piped up a second time, Sir Cloudesley questioned the boy. 'Have you had the audacity to calculate the position of this ship, man? It is an offence against the articles of war for a non-commissioned person to do so, an offence that carries the death penalty.'

"The angry admiral called his master-at-arms and had the poor lad put in irons in the cable locker. Might as well 'ave hung him then and there, in the front of the ship – he would be the first to die. But who could blame Sir Cloudesley? He had 28 sailing masters agreein' with him and the same count o' captains, each with more than twenny years at sea. Howsomever the gatherin' changed its mind and put us closer to the coast of France, yet further from Scilly.

"Sir Cloudesley dispatched the quicker *Lennox*, *La Valeur* and *Phoenix* to Falmouth. Later us heard those ships got amongst the eastern Isles of Scilly – *Phoenix* were stranded on a shoal 'tween St Martins and Tresco; they was lucky no sailorman died. Th' other masters handled their ships magnificent, finding their way out of the maze o' rocks without a scratch, and they was able to anchor fer the night in Broad Sound under the lee o' St Mary's.

"Next day they sailed for Falmouth with the news of the fleet's true position, as yet unaware o' the biggest peacetime disaster in naval history!

"The rest o' the fleet were ordered to follow *Association*, thinkin' she was heading for Plymouth. We set sail, our course shaped for the north. The frigates that was usually at the head o' the fleet had been sent to Falmouth so the flagship was our vanguard, us on *St George* but a couple o' cables astern.

"I was watchin' as the flag stopped sudden-like afore us; a gun fired in warning. She broached beam to the seas, her press o' canvas heeling her over, pushin' her firmly on th' rocks, smashing seasoned English oak to matchwood. Looking at her were a sight worse than lookin' through the gates of hell itself. The *Association*, once pride o' the navy, were a mastless wreck in but a few seconds. Half under water on her beam ends, her wrecked masts and rigging snared men as they were thrown into the wild, foamin' sea.

"In an eye's blink, *St George* struck too! But a huge wave picked us up from aft and lifted us over the ledge. Cap'n ordered us hard on the wind, starboard tack, as us attempted to weather the Gorregan and St Agnes, which by the grace of God we was able to do. Men pumped constantly to keep the water from rising.

"Lookin' back, the *Association* was lit up by a shaft o' moonlight. Her was awash on her beam ends; men was, hangin' on to her rail for dear life. Them on deck – 500 men – was thrown to the mercy of wind and sea. Worse was for them off duty, stuck in pitch-black darkness below, with storm hatches battened and the waters rising to claim them. Them on deck had little chance in the violent sea, amongst sharp rocks, with tons of masts and spars falling all about them; them below, they had none. The mighty *Association* sank in but a few minutes, with the loss of most all hands.

"*St George* beat through to St Mary's Sound, the light on Peninnis Head just clear under our lee bow, showing us deep water. Us passed the Spanish Ledges, where a Spanish man-o'-war 'ad floundered after the Armada. We wore ship, turning to nor'eastward through North Channel, the Crim and Tearing Ledges well to leeward. Clear o' the dangers, we anchored. Dawn that morning we was in sight o' eleven sail a-sheltering in St Mary's Sound.

"Five ships were lost that fateful night: three ships of line – *Association*, *Eagle* and *Romney* – the frigate *Phoenix* and the fireship *Firebrand*. Near 3,000 men drowned. The admiral, his two stepsons and Cap'n Loades, commander of the *Association*, was all washed up at Porthellick Bay along with a part o' the admiral's barge. They had got away from the wreck. 'Tis said Sir Cloudesley was still alive when 'e was come across by a Scillonian woman. She finished 'im off and stole two of 'is rings, having cut off one of his fingers to get 'em. The admiral was buried that morning in the sand. Later they dug 'im up and gave 'im a state funeral at Westminster Abbey in London.

"Poor Lady Shovell lost 'er 'usband 'n two sons that wild October night. There was no courts martial, and the matter went quiet, except of course here on Scilly. The crimes o' the stolen rings were never solved; someone on St Mary's has got 'em hidden somewheres.

"Well boy, enough of an old seaman's ramblin's. 'E had better get yourself off to sleep. I'm turning in meself."

John snuffed out the candle, plunging the cottage into darkness; they were left with the noise of the storm, the two-foot thick granite walls of the old cottage softening the sounds sufficiently to allow a fitful sleep.

Chapter 2

Scilly

The great wind continued its malevolent song throughout the following day. John and Simon returned to the cottage soaked to the skin, having checked the moorings of the little yawl that provided their livelihood. The comely 24-footer was fully set up as a lobster catcher; however, her holds often held more than a lobster or two after what was, to the unwitting observer, an innocent fishing trip across the English Channel!

"Doubt as we be goin' to sea fer a few days yet, me lad," said John Pearce, as he removed the sodden oiled canvas jacket that served to protect him from some of nature's wrath. He removed his wet shirt revealing a well-built torso that suited his height of five foot nine – a very tall man for the times.

John produced a smoked mackerel and some bread, and he and young Simon sat down at the small, oaken table. The rude piece had been built from the bones of some luckless ship which had been among the countless wrecks caught on the rocks of the Scilly Isles throughout history. The simple midday meal was eaten in relative silence save, that is, for the sound of the driving rain and the ocean, as wave after wave smashed into the rocks below.

"How was it you came to live on Scilly, Grandfather?" asked Simon between mouthfuls of fish and bread, the Scillonians' staple diet.

"Yer flatter an old man, lad, a-wanting to hear me old stories – not that I mind the tellin', if ye'll excuse a tear now an' then. A good life at sea, then I finds a paragon of a woman that was yer grandma. Now I got you for company. I be a very lucky man.

"After the wrecking o' Sir Cloudesley's fleet, no prize money was to be had – the loot were mostly on the *Association* 'n that was now spread over the ocean floor a hundred foot down. I 'ad a few pound saved, not near enough t' set meself up proper. Howsomever the navy was good – the crews wot had saved their ships, they put us on half pay while the fleet were bein' refitted.

"Once the good ol' *Royal George* were moored safe at the naval dockyard in Plymouth, I packed me kit and took up lodgings at the Admiral Benbow Inn. A tidy place, not far from Plymouth Hoe, where Sir Francis Drake calmly finished his game o' bowls afore takin' out his tiny fleet against the mighty Spanish Armada.

"It were at the Benbow I first set eyes on Esther May. 'Tweren't what yer call love at first sight like, we just sort o' got together nice 'n slow. Esther had been a serving wench all 'er life, first in the employ o' Sir 'Enry Blackmore, cavalry officer, who 'ad used 'is 'trouser charger' in no polite way on 'is young parlour maid and got 'er wi' child. Dallying with th' household staff in fancy 'omes is a common occurrence – generally countenanced favourably by the lady o' the house who 'ad all the kiddies she wanted and were 'appy for her 'usband to let a serving lass take the wind out o' his sails, so to speak, as long as 'e be discreet about it. Howsomever when Esther May got with child 'Er Ladyship decreed she would not be so shamed as to live under the same roof as her husband's bastard. So Esther had to go.

"Sir 'Enry were good enough t' pay the innkeeper o' th' Benbow to take poor little Esther May in. She worked 'er keep and that o' th' child, a better lot than some unfortunates who ended up in a workhouse or worse. Esther 'ad a fine boy – his father kept a soft spot for 'im. At the lad's eleventh birthday Sir 'Enry paid for a midshipman's commission in the Royal Navy fer him. The boy did real well for 'imself. I 'ear tell that now 'e goes under the name o' Captain Richard Blackmore and commands a privateer in the isles o' the Caribbees.

"Life were rough fer a servin' wench in a seaport town in '08. Every man Jack would try to 'ave his way with her. Esther weren't one for an easy roll in th' hay like, a fact I was to find out for meself. She always said if I wanted my wicked way with 'er I'd have to wed her first."

John let out a loud guffaw at the memory of it. "That got me t' thinkin'. I were 34 year old, been in the Royal Navy since I were 10 – it were all I knew. There were but few ways a seaman could make a livin' out of the service. But if 'e 'ad a wife, a home and wherewithal to buy a boat, 'e could fish, maybe raise a family, and have a right fine life.

"Sundays was her day off, so I asked real nice-like if she would accompany me on a picnic excursion t' the Hoe the followin' Sunday. Ye should have seen 'er face; a tavern wench was used to a more direct and hardly so subtle approach from sailormen …

"A picnic, John?" she said. "What else are 'e after?"

"A picnic I says, and a picnic I means. Plus a few words in private yer might care t' 'ear," I says in the most gentleman-like way I could.

Esther curtsied all ladylike, and said, "Sir, I'd be honoured. After church - noon if it suits 'e."

"It do indeed, ma'am …

"No, it weren't no heart-hammering romance, us just sort o' talked of things 'n more things till I got to suggest we could 'ave a sort of future together …

"I'll 'ave t' go back t' sea fer a few year. I've got a bit o' cash saved, but not enough for the cottage and boat I want to own - not rent - so we ain't at the mercy of some miserly landlord."

"How much more does 'e need?" she asked all innocent-like.

"I've enough fer the boat," I says. "A cottage on Duchy o' Cornwall land can be 'ad for about 20 pound, 'n ground rent o' two shillin a year. Four year o' service pay fer a bosun's mate, less if there's prize or 'ead money to be had."

Her eyes went all misty like. "Now don't get me wrong 'ere, John. I like th' cut o' yer jib well enough; 'e seems like a decent man, but I'll not wed a navy man - not never!" she said. "Right now ye'r whole and hearty, and you've bin lucky. Four years more at sea with the wars not yet done, I might get back the leftovers o' the surgeon's knife, or worse - widderhood. Just leave it all for now, John. Let me thinks on it. In the meantime, if you 'ave a mind t' take me out again, I'll be mighty pleased for it. I'd kind o' like to tell 'e a bit about me life 'n all, that is, if ye 'as a mind to hear it?" said Esther.

"I'd be honoured."

"I were born in Dittisham, near Dartmouth. Me dad were a tenant farmer – there was seven o' us in all; five lived t' be old enough to work. I were the youngest and the only girl. Me brothers all worked the land with Dad. Me, I helped me mum washin' and cookin'. Wasn't much of a childhood. Funny, I don't remember really bein' a child – just chores, chores and more chores.

"I remember when I were six; it were me birthday – a March'nt, I was. It 'ad been a good harvest the year previous. As the family sat down t' supper, me dad 'anded me a parcel. 'Happy birthday, princess,' he said. I were all taken aback, but I was so proud o' me new dress, the only new one I ever 'ad! My brothers all fussed about me. I felt, for that one tiny space o' time, like I were a real princess. I rushed up t' me space in the attic an' put it on. It was all ruffles 'n frills, with a pink bow at me waist. I went downstairs and did a few turns, so me 'hole family could see. That was the only memory of 'avin' fun I recall from when being young.

"It were rent time again. I always knew when rent was due 'cause we had less and less to eat. We 'ad t' sell the best we growed so's we could stay on th' farm. Every year got a tad bit worse. Me dad called me to 'is chair; I knew something were wrong 'cause me mum left the room sobbing. 'Esther, I gotten 'e some other place t' live, me darling,' he said, all choked up like. I were eleven years old. 'Cept for church on Sundays I'd only known the cottage me eleven years had bin spent in. Why? were all I could think. I started crying. We had reached rock-bottom, 'n th' full rent could not be paid. My father 'ad indentured me into service for ten year – the rent would be paid with me wage. I was to be no better'n a slave. 'I'm sorry, princess, but this 'ere's a way us can keep the farm. With a bit o' luck us can put something aside fer the boys t' get a start.' Dad's eyes were bright, pleading-like. 'When yer done at Sir Henry's ye'll be well trained and get a paid job in any fine 'ome 'e likes.'

"So I enters Dittisham Manor as junior 'ousemaid. I was saved from the scullery 'cause I was pretty-like, and Sir 'Enry said I'd be wasted in th' kitchen. The first two year were good. I worked 'ard, but no more 'an I was used t' at 'ome. The 'ouse was warm 'n I 'ad clean clothes an' good food. Lady Blackmore seemed t' favour me, and I spent much o' my time fussin' over her.

"March come round again. It was three days after me thirteenth birthday. I was cleaning Sir 'Enry's study when 'e reached out 'an touched me bubbies ...

"It's a mighty fine woman ye are becoming, Esther. Mighty fine. Ye will make some man very happy when the time comes. That is, in eight years' time when your contract with this house is completed. If you could see your way clear to please me, lass, you could leave with sufficient dowry to get well wed."

"'E knows, sir, I want t' please,' says I, all innocent-like.

'E were kind of breathless-like, an' opened his pantaloons; his man-thing stuck out like a broom handle. 'E looked straight at me!

"Ye just need to learn ways to please this, my dear!"

What were a poor young farm girl t' do? If I didn't please him, I'd lose me job. At first all I 'ad t' do was rub it with me 'and, like – well, you've got one, so I 'spose you knows what 'appens. Later 'e made me do all sorts o' other things with it. It were amazing it took a full two year afore I got with child ...

"When she'd finished 'er story she 'ad tears runnin' down 'er cheeks. I vowed there 'n then I'd never let her cry again. Esther and me saw each other at meal times. I'd have me pint o' porter or half o' rum. She were real friendly-like; her made sure I 'ad my fair share o' vittles 'n a bit more besides. Nothing more were said about us hitchin' up. We 'ad a couple more outings with no more than a parting kiss between us. If I'd press her she'd just say, 'Give me time, John, give me time.'

"'Twas almost four weeks later, Friday dinner time at the Benbow, when Esther asked could she come up t' me room later – she had some news and were all flushed, excited-like. I could 'ardly wait. About eleven came a tap on me door. Her had gotten off early that night. I opened me door, and she rushed in clutching a letter ...

"Johnnie, me 'andsome. 'Bout that cottage 'e talked of. Would one on Garrison Hill at St Mary's on Scilly suit 'e?" she said, all of a fluster-like.

"Settle down, lass. A cottage on Scilly – what's the story?" I replied.

"My brother 'as done well for himself. He was left a cottage in his wife's grandfather's will. 'E said before that if I have need o' a place to go, I could live there. After our picnic I wrote him in London, and 'e said 'e would be happy t' give us the cottage as a wedding present. 'E's even sent a deed made out to Mr and Mrs Pearce to be signed by the pastor what weds us, so the cottage will be ours, all nice and legal-like …

"Us was wed soon as the banns were read. I bought the yawl 'n named her *Esther May*, in honour o' me new wife. Loaded t' the gunnels, we sailed her to Scilly, our new home, this same one us is in now. It were summer '08. It were just th' turn of our first year here that us was blessed with your father, Joseph. Your Aunt Elizabeth came along a couple o' year after that.

"Best 'e get outdoors 'n bring in some firewood, Simon, afore it gets dark. 'Tis a long winter's night we 'ave ahead, and that cursed wind's got a bit t' howl yet afore it gives us a rest."

* * *

As in any new place, particularly a small Cornish village on an island, newcomers were looked on as foreigners. It was difficult to obtain supplies and find the materials needed to repair the cottage. Much of the thatch needed replacing – what had not been ruined by rats had been at the mercy of the weather. In the windswept islands no thatch was available so after weatherproofing as best they could, they set off in the little yawl for the mainland to buy some.

The thirty-odd miles from Penzance to St Mary's is some of the roughest water found in England. Add fearsome tides, open Atlantic swells and rocky coasts, and only experienced sailors could attempt it. John required all the skills he could muster. He would hand over the helm to Esther so he might take an hour or two's rest, husbanding his strength for when it was needed. The couple worked hard to use the winds and tides effectively, and eventually slipped into Penzance Harbour 18 hours after leaving St Mary's.

What a hand she had on the tiller, and how quickly she'd picked up how to trim the sails. It was the most satisfying thing in John's life, showing his new wife the ways of the sea, and seeing the way she took to seafaring, like a pup seal's first swim.

The return voyage was almost the end for the both of them. Just south of the Seven Stones a violent squall hit the little ship abeam and lay her down. Piled high with thatch, she was top-heavy and threatened not to stand herself up again. John released the main and jib sheets and let go the main halyard, pulling the sail, now heavy with the water, up onto the heaving deck. Slowly *Esther May* became upright and turned neatly into wind, weathercocking on the tiny mizzen sail set in her after quarters. The wind eased, allowing the exhausted couple to hoist sail, making a safe home landfall. That night, after hauling the thatch up the hill on a borrowed hand cart, they fell on their straw mattress, exhausted – or not so exhausted, as it may have seemed, as John would tell later, that he reckoned that was the night that Simon's father Joseph 'got started'.

The local men soon recognised how skilful a seaman John was. Begrudgingly they began to respect the ex-naval sailor. He and the seafaring men of St Mary's swapped stories at the Mermaid Tavern on Hugh Town Quay, lubricated by rum, porter or ale. It wasn't long before they asked him if he was up for a 'bit o' the trade'.

As far back as anyone could remember, the men and women of Cornwall supplemented their meagre livelihoods by the time-honoured pursuit of smuggling. It was estimated that a hundred thousand English, Irish and Welsh men, women and children were involved one way or another.

To pay for the never-ending wars, Her Majesty Queen Anne had decreed that all international trade would be subject to customs and excise levies. Since then the traffic across the English Channel in illicit cargoes had been an integral part of Scillonian life, even in time of war, as the armies and navies of England and France were battering each other in bloody conflict. Small boats would run the gauntlet of weather and government excise cutters to trade in fine goods, wines and brandies only available on the Continent, where they were all readily available at a fraction of the prices they cost legally in Britain. Profits from the trade were all that saved many a family from starvation; it was an essential part of family income. All levels of English society were involved, as either procurer or customer. There were, however, considerable risks. A victory for the authorities could result in the death penalty being handed down to some poor wretch.

Government had become very alarmed at the success of smugglers, so they had begun to build large, fast, well-armed, sailing cutters for patrolling the channel. With a man at the masthead and a fore lookout, they would spot a suspicious looking sail from far off, run her down and apprehend her crew should all not be legal and above board. The least excuse would do. Boats of convicted smugglers would be confiscated and sold, the money realised becoming, in part, prize money for the crews of the cutter involved in the apprehension. The men of the trade on Scilly had long since forgone sail as the principal means to propel their craft. They had instead turned to channel pilot gigs to work the trade. Gigs could be away at sea for long periods, seemingly plying the legitimate business as pilots. They raised little suspicion when they returned from a 180-mile, five-day round trip to Guernsey or Roscoff, having delivered their illicit cargo to willing hands on some dark, deserted beach.

Pilot gigs were 32 feet long, more or less, with a five-foot beam, and carried six oars. They were very fast and seaworthy. A small 'dipping lug rig' was carried to ease work at the oars in a fair breeze in the dark. Gigs operating in the English Channel worked dangerous waters. A captain of a square-rigger making landfall, unsure of his position, could easily be cajoled into paying a pilot's fee. The crews were usually seven – a coxswain and six oarsmen, plus the pilot. Sometimes they carried extra men to spell the oarsmen, the norm on a smuggling gig.

If a revenue cutter were sighted they would row directly into the wind, a point that no sailing vessel could sail, while the cutter had to tack, beating upwind to catch their prey. At the time no Scillonian had been arrested for smuggling.

John clearly remembered the day that Brian Jenkins said the fateful words, 'What's 'er t' be, John? The moon 'n tides be right, me handsome; thar be a load o' brandy awaitin' us in Guernsey. I got a spare berth as Bart ain't comin'. Yer with us or not?'

He knew that to refuse would have dire consequences for him and his new family's position on Scilly. Scillonians were a fearsome bunch

– they would not take kindly to be turned down by a newcomer. It was considered an honour to be a gig crewman. His growing family needed cash. Though he caught his fair share of pollack, cod and bass, getting them to the markets on the mainland was difficult. He needed to salt or smoke them, then pack them carefully in boxes, sending them to Penzance on the island packet. The unscrupulous fishmongers would pay him a fraction of their true worth. Worse, if the fish were to spoil, he stood the loss. While he had also brought back the odd 'cargo' from his fishing trips, he did not have the contacts to profit much from these forays.

* * *

"Grandfather," asked Simon, "please tell me a story o' the gigs."

"Aye, lad … I were just now a-thinking o' me first channel run on ol' *Bonnet*." John leaned back taking a sip from his tankard. "Yer grandmother were a mite angry, what with me leaving her alone and 'er knowing what us was about. She were wi' child and her time was near. Knowing I had no choice in the matter, she packed some food for the journey. I kissed her farewell 'n made me way down t' the Mermaid where the lads was 'avin' a few ales with Sar'nt Bower and Corporal Brownlee o' the Garrison Guard …

"Well, me fine lads, you'll be away fer a bit, lookin' for pilot work I 'spose," said the sergeant, his florid features giving a conspiratorial wink. "These dark nights puts fear into 'em foreign-goin' captains – soon as they gets a whiff o' the land they'll happily pay yer pilot fee. Not bad cover for smugglers either. You lads keep a weather eye out for those rogues, won't 'e now – let I know if you sees anything suspicious-like? Her Majesty's gallows on Falmouth docks 'ave been empty for a while now, eh Brownlee?"

"Aye, sar'nt, they bin wastin' away these last few year," the rotund corporal answered.

"We'll keep 'n eye out, that's for sure, sar'nt," said big Brian, the smile on 'is face hidden by his full set of ginger whiskers. He kept smiling as he pushed another jug o' porter into the sergeant's hands.

"Th' ol' *Bonnet* had been carted over the Hugh Town spit to Porthcressa to save rowing round the island. We had a direct course t' France. All th' lads was there, Brian the skipper and Charlie Pender, the supposed pilot, his two brothers, Ben 'n Peter, took turns at stroke when Jack rested. There were the Hicks boys, Mike 'n Guthrie, and young Jimmy Barker in as coxswain - eight o' us, in all. Us'd do three-hour shifts at th' sweeps, restin' fer th' next one. It were 170 mile t' Guernsey - the trip would take about two nights 'n a day, if all went well. We needed to be well down channel afore daylight. With a good feed at the other end, the loading, then return, we should be home in a week. Any longer and suspicions would be raised at Garrison, givin' cause for Sar'nt Bower t' ask some awkward questions.

"A fair northerly breeze let us set the lugsails, easing the work at the sweeps, two oarsmen bein' enough to keep the boat moving at a steady five knots. 'Twas a fair an' easy run - beginner's luck, th' boys said it were. Us made landfall at dawn after just 30 hours. The northerly that'd helped us so much on our way was bone-chilling, mind - worse when yer was off the rowin' thwart. Good Frenchie brandy, 'n plenty of it, would soon warm us."

Chapter 3

The free-trade

Since well before 1700 the Channel Islands, and St Peter Port on Guernsey in particular, had been the main conduit of trans-shipment for contraband bound for the British Isles. Ships of all shapes and sizes, from the pilot gigs to custom-built armed cutters of 150 tons or more, came to St Peter Port to purchase fine goods at a fraction of their landed tax-paid cost in England.

By ancient charter, Guernsey was exempt from customs and excise levies; neither was it bound by excise laws in force on mainland France. The free-trade was a way of life for most of Guernsey's inhabitants in the eighteenth century, and it made many of them very wealthy. St Peter Port was a bustling town of warehouses, taverns, docks and wharves, offering everything their clientele - criminals in England - could require.

"Well, Simon me lad." Old John was back on track and soon got into his stride. "We hove up into St Peter Port be lunchtime, 'avin waited for the 35-foot tide to turn in our favour. Jack got the lads ashore for a meal and some grog. 'Ceptin' me o' course - as new boy I was left to guard the gig and her cargo o' tin, the currency what we was to pay for the return cargo with. I was bein' eyed up friendly-like by a few o' the locals but wasn't bothered by anyone. Brian arrived back with a couple of well-dressed men in tow ...

"Brian Jenkins," said a tall, lean man, his craggy features burned dark by a lifetime's exposure to wind and sun, "you know me as a fair dealing man. I'll give you a far better price for your tin than anyone else in the port."

Brian answered, his eye 'ard as flint. "Aye, Martin, we've 'ad some good dealings, but I'll not take the first offer I get without bein' sure that it's the best, not after the trouble we took to get it 'ere."

The second man replied as if he had been invited to speak. "André Monona at your service, sir. You will need to be secure alongside a ware'ouse wharf before dark or you will 'ave another long night watching over your goods. My 'umble establishmont is just to the right of Rosie's in the western end. We 'ave an arrangement with Madame Rosie that would make you very comfortable tonight, were we able to conclude our business satisfactorily."

"If you want to do business with a Frenchie, Brian, be my guest, but once an enemy, always an enemy is what I'd say," said Martin Polkinhorn.

André feigned hurt and replied, "Ah, Martin, your insult is perhaps to hide the not-so-good deal you have to offer this gentleman, eh? You Engleesh, you 'ave been in control 'ere for 'undreds of years, but the free-trade depends on the good, cheap products of France, no?"

"We've 450 pound o' the best tin 'e'll find; we want best brandy in return. Give me yer best offers, in private like, and I'll see if I like 'em. Maybe you can save me the trouble of askin' around," said our Brian to the Frenchie 'n Martin Polkinhorn. First André whispered into Brian's ear, then Martin took him to one side.

"Be that the best ye've got, boys, the whisper is I'll get a barrel o' the finest fer eight pound o' tin," said Brian.

"Let me see the tin. Ye are well over the top with yer price, but I may do a bit better once I've seen it."

With that Martin made his way down the long ladder into the gig. With 35 feet rise and fall of the tide, it was a long way down from the wharf at what was now low tide. Martin looked carefully and seemed pleased with the cargo.

"I'll take nine pound to the barrel, Brian; that's the best ye'll get on this island today," he said.

Brian looked to the Frenchman who said he would equal the offer and throw in a night at Rosie's fer the crew. A look in André's eye made John feel uncomfortable. He hoped that Brian would stick with Polkinhorn, the man that had proven to be trustworthy before.

"Thank 'e, André," says Brian, "but I'm not a man to whore around. Besides, my Dorothy would sniff another woman on me afore I'd got through the front door. It don't pay to annoy the likes o' she. We'll take your offer, Martin, as long as 'e'll find food, grog and a warm bed for the lads, as 'e has done afore ...

"I finally was able to get off the boat and join the rest of the crew in the tavern, continued Simon's grandfather. "Martin's men took the *Bonnet* to their own dock to unload her cargo on the high tide, replacing it with the agreed number of brandy casks. Brian had got us a good trade; he had paid a low price for the tin, and the agreement would turn a handsome profit. The split was half for them wot had put up the money for the tin, an eighth went to the Penders as they part-owned the boat, the rest was split between the crew. For me it would be equal to three months' navy pay.

"The King's Arms Tavern were in full flight when I arrived. My shipmates were well on the road t' a sore head, and it weren't long afore I was on my way t' join 'em. With Mr Polkinhorn's note in the innkeeper's hand, we was fed and watered the likes of which I'd not seen for a while.

"It were a sorry lookin' bunch o' drunks wot gathered at Polkinhorn's dock midway through the next mornin'. The only one missin' was young Jimmy Hicks, the cox'n; I'd seen 'im goin' out the back door of the tavern in tow with one o' the 'ladies' wot worked there. 'Where be that cursed boy?' said Brian. 'Us'll be leaving on the ebb. It'll be the first and last time 'e uses them jewels o' his if we miss the tide. John, you and Guthrie get about and find 'im.' Brian were in a thunderous mood.

"I went round back of the King's Arms and spoke to one o' the pantry girls. She reckoned young Jimmy was with Polly Prentice – she 'ad a room round back o' the fishmonger on Quay Street. The fishmonger, a huge man as round as he was tall, laughed good-natured like. 'Young buggers kept me awake 'arf the night. The boy won't be much good t' you men at sea t'day. Polly'll 'ave dun wore 'im out.' The fishmonger pointed to a small room tacked on to the back of his shop. 'They're in there,' was all he said, with another lewd laugh.

"I rapped on the door and yelled for Jimmy. 'You in there, boy?' I says. 'Jack's a-ready t' sail. He'll make a girl of 'e if us misses the tide.' Jimmy sort o' shuffled out o' the room with a grin from ear to ear and with no more than 'see yer next trip, Pol', we made us way to the dock.

"The weather looked fine, and at the top o' the Guernsey spring tide, us slipped our moorings, makin' way at a leisurely pace to the harbour entrance, taking our dipping rate from Mike Hicks at stroke oar. We charged past Castle Coronet - home of the island's governor and the main military barracks - sitting on its small island at the entrance to St Peter Port. Slipping under the silent, menacing cannon we thought o' the long row ahead. The next cannon we saw could well be on a revenue cutter pointing fair at us.

"The old *Bonnet* was heavy in the water. On the outward journey the tin was low in the bilges and had no bulk, making the boat stiff and stable. The casks of brandy we 'ad traded were everywhere space would permit, makin' it difficult t' row a full, flowing stroke. It were even 'arder for the off-duty oarsmen - they had to sit astride the cargo - no laying down t' sleep.

"All was well that afternoon, but there were a brassiness to the sunset with wisps o' purple in the cloud that bode no well for an overloaded gig in the middle of the English Channel. I finished me second spell at two hours to midnight when Brian called me to his thwart ...

"How'd yer see the weather, John? 'E have spent more nights at sea than the rest of us put together."

"A change is abroad fer sure, Brian," said I. "Yer saw the sunset. Since then, wind's veered to the west'ard, just where we want to go. Even if it only gets to force four or five we'll be takin' water over the bows and bailing to stay afloat."

"Aye, John, that's how I see it. At best we'd 'ave to ditch half the cargo, at worst turn and run back to Guernsey now, and that would 'ave us away from Scilly for too long. It would raise the suspicions of the good sar'nt."

"Us could head north," I says. "I've a cousin at St Just-in-the-Roseland; the 'hole peninsula is in the trade. Why the vicar at Gerrans was known to keep the congregation on its knees while he changed out of his robes t' get a head start when 'e heard o' a ship comin' ashore in his parish. It wasn't the saving of souls he had on his mind, I tell 'e.

23

It's only about fifteen degrees to the nor'ard off our present course and 'arf the distance than to Scilly if we reach the lee under the Lizard and rest while it blows itself out. Even maybe sell the cargo there, saving ourselves some trouble."

Brian pondered. "Yer right, John, but we'll be sailing into the thick o' the revenue men. I hear tell there's a new cutter at Falmouth, and the excise men keep watch over the bays and inlets during a blow, just fer the likes o' us."

"If we stays at sea we'll have to ditch the cargo t' stay afloat. If us head for a lee under the Lizard, if needs be we can net the cargo, put it over the side anchored and weighted, then head into St Mawes or St Just's where me cousin is the vicar's wife. We can then sit out the worst as an honest pilot boat taking shelter."

Brian gave his orders. "Right, lads, we're goin' to make a run for the coast. Break out the tarps and cover the for'ard quarter – let's keep as much o' the sea outta the boat as us can. Five and six oars come aft, move the high cargo for'ard, then row in pairs on three and four thwarts. Off-duty oarsmen bail. We've eight to ten hours to make a lee o' the Lizard. Us had better be at it quick-like …

"We jumped to the skipper's orders. Two barrels was lost as us shifted the cargo; sea tarps were lashed in place formin' a kind o' fo'c'sle that stopped the tops of the waves breaking into the boat. We changed course; the wind was now on our port bow making the distance between the tops of the wave crests a little further apart. We made headway, but terrible slow, every mile was wrung from our straining backs.

"Hour after hour we pulled fair into the teeth o' the wind, the only rest from the oars a brief off-watch hour, then us 'ad t' bail. It were the longest night o' all my years at sea. We was soaked t' the skin, and bone weary from hours at the oars and the motion o' the boat. Just before daylight, 'tween squalls, Jimmy got a sight o' the Lizard light to the west'nor'west. We was all but done for, me lad, but seeing the light gave us th' strength to row for four more hours. We made our way into a small cove, between the Lizard and the Helford River, edging our way past an evil group o' rocks called the Manacles.

"*Bonnet* anchored in a small cove, a mere dent in the deserted coast. Two men was left on board t' keep a watch, the rest o' us huddled together under the cliffs, out o' most o' the rain and wind. Finally sleep overcame us.

"After resting a while, we moved all but two barrels o' cargo above high-tide line into a natural cleft in the cliffs, covering it best we could with driftwood 'n stones from the beach. Mike Hicks, his brother Guthrie and Peter Pender were left in the cove with a brace of pistols apiece t' guard the loot.

"Reboarding *Bonnet* as dusk set, quick time were made o' the ten or so miles into St Just's cove. Rounding the small spit o' sand wot protects St Just's creek from the River Fal, we grounded on a small beach beside the wee church o' St Just-in-the-Roseland, pretty as a picture in the moonlight, at the head o' the cove. So far so good – we wasn't seen nor heard by no one.

"Me cousin Meg 'ad married a preacher by the name of Daniel Farmiloe. I hadn't seen her since before I went t' sea as a boy. Some years later, I'd 'eard that Dan was made vicar o' St Just's. I walked up to the vicarage where candlelight said that the household was not yet a-bed and rapped on the door …

"Who is it calling at this time of night?" a woman's voice called out. "'Tis John Pearce, lookin' for 'is Cousin Meg."

"John Pearce? How would I know you are telling the truth, man? What was my father's name?" the voice within questioned.

"Me father's name – your uncle – is Michael, his brother. Your father was Richard Pearce, and your mother was my Aunt Elizabeth," I answered.

After that Meg opened the door o' the manse and ushered me in. "Ye must 'scuse me manners, John. Me husband's away visiting the bishop in Truro. It's no best for a woman on her own to open her door to strange men in the dead o' night in these parts. Sit 'e down, and get the weight off yer feet. Can I get 'e a bite o' food, lad?" she said. "How long has it been, John! You was but a boy of ten or twelve when ye went t' sea with the navy. 'E must be 35 now. How, pray, did you end up on my doorstep out of the blue so late at night and with not even a note o' warning?"

Meg's questions flowed thick and fast; near an hour had passed before John could mention the true and delicate reason for his nocturnal visit.

"Well, luv, there's a bunch of us just rowed across the channel. We're on our way back to Scilly – we put in here to weather the storm. We have, how can I put it, done a bit o' trade on the way. I was kind o' wonderin' if you and your husband had any contacts in th' trade here? 'Tis well known the Roseland has many a fellow not keen t' pay the King's excise duty on 'is business dealins."

"Why, John! How on earth do 'e think a respectable Anglican vicar and his wife would have contact with smugglers and that kind o' folk? If you weren't family I think I'd turn you in," said Meg with a glint in her eye. "O' course one 'ears rumours in a small community like ours, but I'm afraid I can't help 'e. If you tells me where your boat is, I will bring some food for you and your companions early in the morning. I'll make a few enquiries on the way, that's all I can say."

John bid his cousin goodbye and went back to Jack and the lads, quickly passing on what he'd heard.

"Do yer trust 'er, John?" asked Jack. "Us is in your hands, and while we ain't got the goods here with us, we would 'ave some explainin' to do if the revenue boat showed up."

"Meg won't let on, least not t' the wrong folk. She's just being careful. Remember I've not seen her in near 22 year. I reckons us should wait till morning like she said and see what happens. Just hide 'em sample kegs away from the boat, and let's get some sleep," says I, full o' conviction …

"We woke to a rustling sound in the bushes, and three men came out of the trees, making their way towards us, real slow-like. A huge man, bigger 'an Brian and sporting a similar unruly set of red whiskers, called out my name, then smiled and held out his hand. 'I'm John Trefarthan.'

"It were so easy! An arrangement was made, and gold sovereigns changed hands. We went on our way, an honest pilot boat that had made port in the storm. After the cargo was safely stowed under false gravestones, we had a large tot with th' Roseland men and me brother-in-law, Dan Farmiloe, then left the pretty wee place. Afore long, us had rounded the Lizard, a light offshore breeze nicely fillin' the sail givin' us a fast, safe passage home.

"I were now in with the free-trading men o' Scilly. The St Just's connection had found a quick, safe way to turn contraband into cash without rowing it all the way to Scilly and then getting it back to the mainland again. I had become part o' things. As we landed, Nell Pender came up yellin', 'Get yourself home, John Pearce. Your son was birthed last night; all's well, as much as I can tell.'

"I was off home to this here cottage as fast as me legs could go. Soon I held the wee mite that were Joseph, yer dad, in me arms for th' first time. The tired eyes of me darling Esther May was a-brim with love for me and the squawking creature I was holding. It made I so proud to show her the eight gold sovereigns that had been my share of the profits. Eight gold sovereigns! Our money worries were over fer a wee while.

"'Tis late, Simon lad, get yerself t' sleep. Us'll fish tomorrow, I'm a thinkin'."

With that John started his pipe and took a noggin, his eyes turning misty with the memories racing through his mind.

Chapter 4

Joseph Pearce

It was a fine early summer's day in the year of 1729 as 19-year-old Joseph Pearce strode out of Hugh Town, St Mary's heading for Old Town, a walk of some four miles. His mind was full of how he was to impress the lovely young Jane whose father, the formidable Brian Jenkins, had just last week given him permission to call on.

Brian Jenkins was nearly six feet tall and weighed 200 pounds, his powerful frame carrying not an ounce of fat. Years of rowing gigs across the channel had left the aging seafarer a fine figure of a man. He wore the full set of deep red whiskers that were a badge of honour for Scilly's seagoing men, his whole aspect as if a throwback to his ancient Celtic origins. It would be easy to imagine him at Queen Boadicea's right hand as Briton tribes had their brief run of victories over the Romans nearly two thousand years before. While menacing to look at and somewhat gruff of speech, Brian had a fair and gentle disposition. He was often called in to adjudicate on local disputes, something the governor of the islands, Sidney Godolphin, was grateful for. The Scillonians were a proud and stubborn people; it was good politics to let them sort each other out on matters that had little consequence for the Crown, thus saving costly court trials at Star Castle.

Brian had been quietly pleased when the Pearce boy had approached him and asked if he could call on his daughter Jane.

"I know 'e is not o' a Scillonian family," Brian had said to his wife, "but he was born on the island, and his father is a Cornishman through 'n through and a good seaman t' boot. The lad's an asset on the gig; he's done three trips without trouble. His father's seagoing background be behind him, and 'e's fished these islands since 'e could stand. Our Janie could have worse than Joe Pearce - much worse, I tell 'e."

Dorothy Jenkins sighed; she had hoped her only daughter's striking good looks might catch the eye of an officer from the Star Castle Garrison or a naval officer from one of the many visiting warships. She knew her husband would not be at all pleased with her secret desires, albeit that Jane could have a better life away from the islands. He had, in fact, forbidden Jane to speak to foreigners, who had no Cornish descent.

Joe had known Jane all his life, as he knew everyone on the islands. Not more than a few hundred people lived on Tresco, Bryher, St Martins, St Agnes or the main island of St Mary's in the eighteenth century. It was after he had returned from his first gig trip to the now favoured supply town of Roscoff that Joseph began to see Jane as more than a childhood friend. The crew had put together for a local lady of the night to take away the boy's virginity, an experience he had enjoyed. It was also a right of passage with his fellow crew members – all first runners went through it. However, a realisation of what he truly wanted dawned on him during the long haul back to Scilly.

The girl Joe had once played children's games with on St Mary's had become a shapely, beautiful young woman. A slight problem for him was, of course, that she was the daughter Brian Jenkins, the gig's skipper who was in full knowledge of what had transpired on Roscoff, but hadn't mentioned the incident when Joe asked him if he could see Jane.

"'E's old enough, I 'spose, but if 'e be anything but a gentleman to her, lad …" he had said, not needing to finish the sentence. The lad fervently prayed his skipper couldn't see into his mind that day; if he had, the big man would surely have killed him.

Joe knocked on the door of the larger than average cottage that was the home of the Jenkins family, the first time he had called as a suitor for Jane's hand. As was the custom he handed Dorothy a gift, a simple bunch of flowers he had carefully picked on the walk over. "Might I talk to Jane, if it pleases 'e, Mrs Jenkins?" asked Joe nervously.

"Seems 'e might lad. You've fooled me poor husband as to your worth, but don't 'e and her get out o' me sight or I'll have Brian come a-lookin' fer 'e," with which Dorothy Jenkins waved imperiously for Joe to sit at the parlour table. "Wait there, Joseph Pearce. I'll see if Jane be ready t' see 'e."

After keeping him waiting just long enough to make him nervous, Jane entered the room. She had taken great care with her appearance without being too obvious; her hair was in light plaits woven into a knot at the crown. A simple cotton shift covered her completely, the gathering at her waist allowing the fullness of her hips and the abundance of her breasts to be shown to maximum advantage. Jane smiled demurely, with a glint in her eye. "Hello, Joe. Nice of 'e t' call."

Joe stood up and tried to speak; his mouth went dry, and his Adam's apple moved in his throat, but not a sound could he get to leave his lips, bar heavy breathing. He finally got a semblance of control and was able to offer a husky greeting. "Hello, Janie. 'E looks mighty pretty, if I might say so."

"Want a walk on the beach?" Jane asked.

"Aye, that'd be grand."

"Remember what I says, young man," exclaimed Dorothy Jenkins, the anger displayed in her manner hiding her inner thoughts. "If I looks over and can't see 'e, it's me husband 'e'll answer to." *A mighty fine lookin' boy though – they make a handsome couple, t' be sure.*

"Aye, ma'am," replied Joseph.

Joe opened the cottage door and the two young people walked the forty yards to the beach, a scuffle and sniggering behind a fence announcing that Jane's two brothers were enjoying overseeing the proceedings.

* * *

Six months later, dying gusts of the first of the westerly winter storms were battering Scilly. Jane and Joe were on Porthcressa beach making their plans for a May wedding. Holding hands, they were a picture of young love when the call went out.

"Wreck, boys. Wreck! Move yerselves to the boats; wreck on the western rocks."

Nothing put a glint in the eye of the men of Scilly more than the news of a ship running aground. As bow oar on the Jenkins's new gig *Horse*, Joe knew he would be required to put to sea with his future father-in-law. He also knew that if they were first to make a line fast to the ship, their boat would have first claim to salvage. A good wrecking could set him up with a cottage, or more. There were real risks in boarding a foundering vessel with the wind up and her planking being torn out from under her by the terrible, unforgiving rocks. "I gotta go, Janie luv, 'e knows that, don't 'e, me darlin'.'"

"Course I knows, luv. I seen me dad go out all me life, 'aven't I! You take care, Joey. I won't never forgive 'e if 'e gets hurt or worse. Yer life won't be worth livin', I promise 'e."

Jane Jenkins quickly turned her head after her beau's hurried parting kiss, hiding her welling tears. She knew many an island woman living alone, or with a young family, their husbands long lost to the raging seaways that surrounded them. Widows had little chance of remarrying, as women outnumbered men on the islands by almost two to one. They were fed and cared for by the community – part of each fish catch or profit from the trade was given to those condemned to a life of widowhood.

It was, in some ways, worse still for the wives of those men unable to escape the press gangs of the Royal Navy. These men were wrenched from their homes or taken from their boats when fishing. Not only did they face the natural dangers of a sailing ship at sea, the chances of death or serious injury in battle were very real for the crews of an eighteenth-century warship. With few letter-writing skills, and depending on literate shipmates, it was often years before details of what had become of their loved ones got back to the families at home. When a naval ship put into the islands there was always a group of Scillonian women to be found waiting for the tars to come ashore on leave, so they might ask if anyone had heard of their pressed men. If they had died, a curt notice would be posted.

The island's governor of the time was Colonel Sidney Godolphin. He had negotiated a truce with fleet officers that no men would be pressed on Scilly itself. He had reasoned that the serious shortage of manpower would reduce their ability to defend the islands. To provide defence was a provision of his family's lease on the islands, an onerous responsibility. However, as recently as a year before, a frigate of the King's service had pressed two men from a fishing smack returning up-channel, leaving 12-year-old Jimmy Nance with the job of bringing the 20-ton ketch back into St Mary's Pool single-handed.

Joseph Pearce ran to the beach in St Mary's Pool, where the gigs lay near high-water mark, sheltered by a small stone quay. Mixed feelings of lust and love were instantly replaced by the thoughts of the coming adventure. He knew also that he needed to get aboard before another man claimed his place; his future father-in-law had no favourites. It was a case of first come gets the thwart; the gig would put to sea with just six oarsmen and the coxswain – no need for relief rowers on a short local passage. As he reached the boat he found Brian Jenkins was already placing the long, graceful sweeps, which propelled the slim vessel so quickly, in their correct places. He also tied down the weapons, sealed in casks and ready loaded.

"Put the rollers underneath 'er, Joe, ready fer when the others get here," said the big man, every movement honed to getting the gig launched and away as soon as the crew arrived.

Hugh Town was abuzz with excitement, mingled with a little apprehension, as they watched crews race each other to be first away. The Jenkins's *Horse*,was a few minutes behind the *Bonnet*. Joe heard his father call out to him to get a move on, from his usual place at stroke. Harry Jenkins had taken over *Bonnet* from his brother, when *Horse* had been launched. John had stayed with his old boat at Brian's request. "They need yer knowledge, John lad," was all he had said.

Brian briefed his crew. "The keeper at Agnes light saw a brig touch the Crim Ledges and broach, losing her mainmast. From seeing her rig he thought she could be a foreign privateer."

A foreign ship, an enemy, was the best possible option for the Scillonians. They could take what they wanted without the need to care for her crew. She could be loaded with gold taken from a Spanish galleon, whose crew, in turn, had stolen the treasure from the people of Central America.

If she was a privateer under a British flag, or indeed any British ship, her crew would be of first concern. The Scillonians would work together to try and save first the crew, then the ship. If unable to do so, as much of her cargo as possible would be trans-shipped. Later a legal claim for salvage would be made through the official Receiver of Wreck.

This was a time-consuming process; the ship and the cargo owners would counterclaim against the salvors to minimise their losses. The thought of this ship being foreign spurred the men to greater efforts; she would be fair game without the troublesome bureaucracy.

"Us'll head to windward to the west'ard point o' Annet. With this 'ere wind and sea over the ebb, she'll hove up in Smith Sound or the rocks o' Agnes. I'm a th ..." Brian's last words were lost to the wind as the gig passed the end of St Mary's quay and shouldered the first of the waves, still large but not breaking too heavily in the dying westerly gale.

It was two hours' hard pull to cover the five miles to reach the point Brian was aiming for; no sign of the shipwreck yet. She could, of course, have sunk by this time, as nearly four hours had passed since the light keeper had sighted the stricken vessel in poor light. It was now four in the afternoon; light was fading fast. If they had to put into St Agnes for the night without making contact, the trip could be wasted. They were well aware that Colonel Sidney Godolphin would be being watching from Garrison Hill. His 50-ton cutter *Dragonfly* would be on the scene at dawn; her arrival would greatly lower the chances of a good return for the *Horse* on the day's work.

By agreement, and for a share in any salvage, the governor gave the islanders first chance at a wreck. This allowed him to make a modest profit without risking his boat or men. Besides, try as he might, the Scillonians wouldn't supply him enough local knowledge to allow *Dragonfly*'s captain to sail through the wicked rocks of Scilly in rough weather and poor light.

Joseph was standing in the forequarters of the gig when something unnatural caught his eye amid the rocks and foam at the south-eastern end of Annet – a mere glimpse of what looked like a mast rolling from side to side.

"Three miles to leeward, Brian. Southern tip o' Annet. I reckon she's stuck hard," he shouted above the wind, and leaping to his thwart as the men hauled on their sweeps.

Brian skilfully waited for some way to be built up before picking the smallest set of waves, turning the gig on a sixpence in the trough of the least dangerous one. A cry of 'proper job skipper' was shouted by all the crew. If he had got it wrong and the boat got to the crest of a badly breaking wave beam on, she would have broached, throwing all into the sea as the gig rolled her gunwales under.

With the wind and seas now from behind, *Horse* surfed down the waves at breakneck speed. Brian called the men to 'boat oars' as they were picked up by the oncoming wave. Keeping the wave dead astern, the crest foamed by, and then came the call to 'give way lively'. The men pulled for their lives to maintain enough speed to catch the next one safely. Failure to keep in harmony with the waves would mean the following sea would roll right over them. As they roared through Smith Sound, the waves began to lengthen between crests. The immediate danger had passed.

Joe shipped his oar and stood lookout. It was only ten minutes since the turn, and they had already reached the spot where he thought he had seen the stricken ship. Carefully quartering the milder following sea, they lay in the lee of the small, uninhabited island of Annet.

"'Tis mighty strange ain't no other boat in sight. Are 'e sure 'e saw her, Joe lad?" asked Brian.

"Aye, I'm sure, 'less she's sunk, or got blown off the rocks and gone away down to leeward. If she has, she's in open water and lost to us," replied Joseph. He scanned the area, standing precariously forward, eyes straining in the deepening gloom of a fast-approaching nightfall.

Suddenly a shaft of light struck a group of rocks more to leeward. It briefly lit a dismasted wreck held firm on a drying shoal. "She's on Melledgan, skipper, ain't no doubt about it; see her as clear as day, I did," he yelled above the moderating wind.

"Let's go. Us can be on 'er in minutes. If us leaves her till morning, she'll be broken up, or every mother's-son boatman in Scilly'll be on 'er."

The skipper was all concentration but visibly excited, the risk of boarding the sinking vessel in darkness but a shadow on his mind.

From the lee of Melledgan reef they saw their prize. She had been washed up on the top of the tide and loomed high now the ebb had left her. A grapnel and line was heaved aboard and made fast. She was a bark of 400 tons or so. Her flagstaff was gone, smashed away as masts and rigging fell. It was hard to tell what nationality the ship was; as yet no sign of life had appeared to identify her. An eerie quiet surrounded the site only broken by the waves now gently breaking on the rocks.

"I reckons she's 'n east-coaster, bin at sea some time, be the look o' th' fouling of 'er undersides. Take no chances now, me handsomes. Break out the cutlasses 'n pistols. Three of 'e board with me, the rest of 'e cover us. They ain't be British or them'll have hollered. If 'em be Frog or Dago, they'll know where 'em are. They'll be ready for a fight if there's anyone aboard alive," said Brian softly.

They manoeuvred the gig alongside and slipped up over the bulwarks. At first only silence, then a pistol shot, then another. As quick as lightning, men were swarming into the gig. Joe looked up just in time to see a great club being swung at him by a huge, swarthy, foreign looking man. He hit the water – then oblivion.

Mike Hicks gathered his wits, firing his pistol at the huge, club-wielding form ahead of him. The man's head disintegrated as the ball hit at point-blank range, and he went flying over the side.

Brian yelled from the rail of the stranded vessel. "Back the gig away, lads. The scum be tryin' to take her t' get away on. We can handle 'em wot's up 'ere. Keep an eye out fer me signal afore comin' back."

On the deck of the bark three men rushed the boarders; Brian sliced the arm off the first with a mighty swing of his razor-sharp cutlass. Charlie and Ben shot the other two. Other crew members were found but they had no fight in them. They were injured or exhausted fighting the storm. Brian called from the poop deck that the ship was theirs.

Bonnet hove into sight and came to the aid of *Horse*. After a brief scuffle that threatened to capsize both gigs, the foreign boarders surrendered.

Soon as the gigs were secured to the wreck, John Pearce anxiously called up to the deck. " Brian, have 'e seen young Joe?"

"Saw 'im get hit 'n go over the side, John. I got the bugger wot hit 'im," shouted Mike Hicks.

Hearing this, all attention was focused on looking for Joe, a job made difficult by the deepening twilight. It was with a heavy heart that John moved to *Bonnet*'s bow. All thoughts of plunder put aside, they started a search to leeward of Melledgan and the wreck, carefully ensuring they missed nothing, that every piece of ocean, wreck and rocks was covered.

Many hours had passed since they had left. Exhausted, the two gig crews pulled into St Mary's Pool at midnight. Three women had maintained a lonely vigil at the end of the quay, as many had done before them. Dorothy, with one steadying arm around her daughter, the other comforting Esther May as they looked down into the boats as they came into view. When they saw Joe was missing from his place in *Horse*'s bow an inhuman wail came from deep inside the younger woman. It was as if her very soul was being torn from her.

"Joe, Joe, oh my Joe, where in God's name are 'e?"

Brian, real dampness in his eye, ran up the steps and said to his wife and daughter and Esther May, "Nothin' more to be done tonight, my lovelies. Us ain't found no body, so there's still a fair chance. I'm sorry; we'll 'ave another look on the morn – 'im what hit Joe won't ever hit no other, that I can promise 'e."

Over at St Agnes lighthouse, Fred Nance the keeper was readying himself to trim the wick when he saw a light flickering to the west'ard, on Annet. *Must be some o' the lads stayed over fer the night,* he thought.

Bill Pender called in at the lighthouse after the *Golden Eagle* had been beached. "'E saw a light on Annet, Fred?"

"Aye, I did."

Bill Pender went to rouse his tired crew. A one hundred to one chance was better than none.

No sleep was to be had in the Jenkins cottage that night. The candle on the parlour table was about to flicker out when Brian heard loud voices coming from the beach. He had just stirred himself to make for the door when Bill Pender of the Agnes boat appeared in the doorway. "Us have 'im, Brian," said one of the men. "'E be mighty poorly-like but he's still with us."

"Dorothy, Janie, get yerselves down 'ere; we've just had a miracle performed on Scilly. As God is my witness, I'll no longer a doubter be." With this simple statement of relief Brian cleared the table and motioned for the men of Agnes to put young Joseph upon it.

"'Ow in the name o' God did 'e get t' Annet?" Brian asked the men of Agnes.

"Damndest luck ever, I reckons," said Charlie Mumford. "When 'e went over, 'e landed on a 'atch cover that had come loose in the lee o' th' wreck; out cold 'e were. A back eddy sets there, running opposite the ebb tide. It carried 'atch cover with Joe on it agin' the wind to th' south beach o' Annet. 'E must 'ave comes to long enough to gather some kindling and light a fire. 'E knew it would be seen by the light keeper, so he's still got 'is wits. Us rowed over, found 'im and brought 'im straight here; 'e come to now, but he's in a bad way, me handsome."

"Thanks, Charlie, Bill and all you lads. We owes yer," said Brian.

"'E would 'ave done same fer us, Brian," said Bill turning to leave.

One neighbour ran to tell the Pearces and another to fetch the military surgeon from Star Castle. Dorothy Jenkins took control of the scene; Janie stoked the fire to boil water.

"The boy's brain has been badly shaken, though it seems his skull is not cracked," said the surgeon. "Lay him comfortably and stop his head moving as much as possible. Once he's awake keep him awake. A little spirits will help ease the pain. I'll call in the morning."

The women were fussing around him when, without warning, Joe's eyes opened. He grimaced with pain but smiled when he felt Jane's hand in his. "Better us have that weddin' brung for'ard some, me love, while me luck's still a-running," said the exhausted young man, attempting to smile.

The wreck was found to be a pirate. Brian's assessment that she was British-built with a brig rig was correct. She had been taken from her moorings in Yarmouth two years before by a gang of European mercenary soldiers attached to the British Army, disgruntled because they had not been paid. The men, a mixture of all nations, were led by a ruffian named Benjamin Browne, the eldest son of a well-known smuggling family from Devon. Ben was on the run for having killed an excise man in a fight during the landing of contraband from France.

Little in the way of saleable salvage had been brought from the wreck, a fact the crew of *Horse* were bemoaning over a pint of ale at the Mermaid when the governor's lieutenant entered the bar.

"Ha, Jenkins – just the man. The governor has asked me to inform you that the man Browne has a price on his head of 50 guineas, subject to his formal identification by the sheriff in Plymouth. We are sending him on tomorrow's packet under guard. We know it's him; one of my men knows him from the past. We should receive the money within the month. As skipper of the *Horse* the bounty will be paid to you – less of course costs and the governor's commission – the balance for you to distribute as you see fit."

"That'll be worth a crack on the head, I reckon," said Brian to Joe, and he ordered a round for all in the bar. "Still, I pity the poor bastard Browne. It'll be the end o' a rope fer 'im."

"So what's the split, Brian?" asked George Hicks. "Is it the usual – a third for the boat, a third for the skipper and a third for the crew?"

Brian thought for a few minutes. "If it 'adn't been fer Joe here spottin' the wreck, no one would get nothin'. If it 'adn't been for Mike 'n *Bonnet*'s boys holdin' Browne, he might 'ave overpowered 'e in the gig and got away, boat 'n all. I reckon the share will go four ways, an' some t' *Bonnet* wi' a bit fer Frank Nance wot saw Joe's light. The rest t' Joe 'n Mike. The final share be a split between th' rest of 'e."

As usual Brian had dealt with the situation fairly and wisely, to the extent of taking a smaller share than he himself was entitled to; all were satisfied. He had also ensured his daughter and future son-in-law would get a start in life, with enough to buy a small cottage of their own. With this and the part share in the *Horse* he would give them on their wedding day, they would start married life in a far better position than most young couples on Scilly could dream of.

Joseph Pearce and Jane Jenkins were married on the 20th of May 1729. Joe was twenty, Jane just seventeen. They moved into a modest, newly built cottage on the hill above Porth Mellon. Jane had made it a condition of their marriage that Joe took work ashore, where he would be home nights, not at risk of wind and wave. Master Gunner Abraham Tovey was in charge of building a great fortified wall around Garrison Hill. This massive undertaking had been a work in progress for 15 years and was as yet only half finished. Most of Scilly's sons preferred a life at sea to the hard manual labour he offered, so Tovey was pleased to be able to employ Joe.

Chapter 5

Changing fortunes

In the beginning, 1736 promised to be a good year for the Pearce family on Scilly. George Hicks had returned to the islands after nearly ten years away as an apprentice at sea with the East India Company. He had risen to the position of first officer and could expect a command within a few years, such was the growth of the grand 'John Company', as it had come to be known. He had promised Joseph's sister Elizabeth that when he had reached this position he would return to Scilly and they would be married. So at the age of 27, when most young women of the day would have expected to have already had their children, George and Elizabeth walked down the aisle.

Elizabeth's father, John Pearce, was 56 years old by this time. He was happy that his daughter had married such a fine, up-and-coming young seaman, but he had difficulty with his being a senior officer, albeit from the merchant service. All his time in the Royal Navy, officers had to be treated with awesome respect; they had the power of life and death over even a senior non-commissioned officer, as he had been. Officers were hated for their hardness, and although not navy, George was still an officer. John had boxed the boy's ears on more than one occasion while he was growing up.

Try as he might, John couldn't help himself. Esther May, his dear, ever-loving wife, was beside herself because of it. Even at the wedding he did it! Whenever he encountered George in uniform he would doff his cap, embarrassing the whole family.

His new son-in-law was seriously embarrassed, so it was with some relief all round when George went back to sea. As was customary with the John Company, a mate's wife was allowed to accompany him on the first voyage after their wedding. It was a red-eyed Esther May who waved the young couple goodbye as the packet sailed out of St Mary's Pool, the ebb tide and fair westerly rapidly getting her under way.

A pall seemed to descend over the cottage on Garrison Hill. John would still fish and occasionally work with Joe on the fortifications of the Garrison, but to his wife's annoyance he would spend a lot of time at home. She would go on long walks, occasionally visiting Dorothy Jenkins at Old Town. The bustle and busyness had gone, as was usual when the household's children left home – usual, but hard for a woman to deal with. George had promised Esther May and Elizabeth he would apply for a position on the island packet once he had a command. This, however, would be several years hence, and Esther had reached that time in life when things for a woman changed. She found she could no longer have her hopes so far into the future. A nagging pain in her head had developed; it would come and go but sometimes it was unbearable. Along with this illness, of which she had spoken nothing to her husband, was a belief that it was sent by God to punish her. She began to lose interest in the things she once held dear. The vicar advised prayer and suggested she keep out of strong sunlight.

Joe was working six days a week, ten hours a day, with Abraham Tovey on the Garrison fortification. Jane had three-year-old Simon, named after her grandfather, to care for and was again with child. It wasn't that she could not use her mother-in-law's help around the cottage or in the garden, she simply didn't trust her with the young boy.

Recently Esther had taken Simon to Porthcressa beach for the afternoon. Closing her eyes to block out the glare, she had fallen asleep in the shade of a rock outcrop. The boy had been amusing himself, paddling at the water's edge, when he trod on a sharp stone and fell headlong into deeper water. It was high tide, and the beach shelved steeply; a wave sucked him out of his depth. Some men building a new fishing boat above high water on the Hugh saw the boy fall and ran to his aid. Dripping, he was returned to his grandmother unharmed, but she had to be roused to receive him. The men thought it strange that she did not seem to be very alarmed by the situation and spoke to Janie about the incident.

When Esther returned Simon to his mother she was in no way prepared for the tongue-lashing her daughter-in-law subjected her to.

The boatbuilders had made Janie realise her son could easily have died.

Angrily she turned on her husband, shaking, saying, "Yer mother ain't never to be left with our children alone again. Never, never, never. Her's unwell, can 'e not see it?"

Joe tried to calm her and stamp his authority, as man of the household, on the worsening situation. He could not accept that Esther May could be suffering an illness. "My mother is my children's grandmother; you will treat her with respect. With whom could they be safer?"

"Darlin', yer mother's sick in the head. Since Elizabeth went away 'er's bin getting worse. Would 'e really have me risk your son on 'is own with 'er again?" pleaded Jane, the height of her anger now passed.

"Reckon not, me bonny, but let's not make issue o' it. Us'll just kind o' see there's always someone's with 'er when she has Simon," Joe answered, taking his wife in his powerful, bronzed arms. She melted. Joe was tall – near five foot nine – and strongly built, his muscles hardened by three years working the stone. Yet he could be so gentle! He picked up his wife as if she were no heavier than a pint of ale. Laying her on their bed, she slid out of her undergarments quickly, as did he. Joe knew he was a big man; he knew how to prepare his wife for his entry into her. Waiting for her full arousal, Jane still gasped as his manhood entered her. Their coupling was blessed by a tremendous climax. When he finally came to his senses he said mischievously, "Us had better fight some more, lass."

"Joseph Pearce, yer the best man a woman could hope for," answered the misty-eyed young mother.

Just then there was a rap on the door. It opened to reveal John Pearce. "Joe, lad. I just gotten back from a drink at the Mermaid. She's gone! Door were left wide open – 'er shawl be gone from its hook. I'm right afeared as to what she's at, son."

The young man took charge. "Janie, take up Simon, and get yerself down to the Mermaid. Have the men search Hugh Town, Porthcressa and out to Peninnis Head. Get someone to check she ain't gone to yer folks at Old Town. An' get someone to go to the church, 'n get help from the vicar. Da, take the Garrison track west about. I'll take it to the east. Here, take this tar-torch. It'll be as black as the insides of a cow out there when the sun's gone."

As the folk of St Mary's turned out to search for her, Esther May Pearce turned her eyes to the westward. She could see St Agnes in the fading light, the faithful light flashing its warning to mariners twice each minute. She reached part of the wall that was still under construction, massive granite stones made square by the skill of the stonemasons. The tradesmen, with her son's help, had created a stairway for her to descend the newly built ramparts.

The terrible pain in her head had grown in strength over the last few months; it now seemed to leave her and fly heavenward. She no longer felt as of this earth. She smiled at a line that danced in her mind: 'Pain to the sky, peace in the sea; the pain in my head will soon cease to be.'

The stunted trees prevalent on the headlands of the Garrison had been removed so as not to provide an attacker with cover, thus Esther May was unimpeded as she walked towards the outermost rock on Woolpack Point. She loved the peace of the place. Often she had watched a magnificent sun set over the western isles, those very rocks that had so nearly claimed her son all those years ago. She thought of John and their life together. A small tear rolled down her cheek. Her mind was now completely clear.

"Better this way, love. I'll not wait in agony while the Lord decides if 'n when t' take me, nor'll I put 'e through the waiting and the watching me fade. Us has had a grand life, 'e 'n me, but my time's at an end, as one day it will be fer 'e. Then with God's will, us'll be together ferever."

She stood on the outermost point of the rock, a light groundswell rising, breaking, whispering and calling her to enter the depths. She raised both her arms, dropping her shawl, when a shaft of pain carved its way through her consciousness. As if hit with an arrow loosed by a far-off archer, her mind lost control of her pain-racked body. The moon retired behind a cloud bank as Esther May dropped down into the waiting icy water. Now at full run, the ebb carried her away from her loved ones and her home. As her skirts became saturated, she slowly sank into the bosom of the sea.

On this occasion the sea chose not to give up its dead. All the next day the islanders searched until a tired old woollen shawl was found on Woolpack rocks.

The Pearce family, unsure of the circumstances of Esther May's passing, and with no body to grieve over, became dysfunctional. John took to drink and would not be consoled. Jane, believing she was responsible in some way, isolated herself in the cottage, became remote and was seldom seen.

Joseph got into a fight with Gunner Tovey's corporal and would have killed him if he hadn't been stopped. It was only when the fair-minded Tovey found out that the corporal had been bad-mouthing Joe's mother did he reduce the charge of assault on a King's man, which carried the penalty of a flogging with the cat-o'-nine-tails to the much lesser charge of insubordination. For this he lost his job building the Garrison fortifications.

Joe caught a few fish, and the family eked out a meagre existence using money Jane had saved from past wages. Jane grew gaunt, and Joe worried for her and the child she was carrying. "Janie, me darlin', 'e gotta eat more. We've plenty; your mother brought over a sack of cornmeal today."

She said nothing, just looked through him as if he wasn't there.

The young woman who just a few months before had been a picture of health and youthful vitality barely smiled, her features as one 30 years older than her true years. Joseph needed to get his wife in a good frame of mind. He had to tell her he was about to break his promise to stay away from seafaring. His father-in-law, Brian Jenkins, had approached him that day, offering him stroke position back on *Horse*. They were bound for Roscoff for a bit o' the trade. Jane hardly raised her head when Joe told her of his decision to return to smuggling.

The gig *Horse* was rolled out of her boathouse at Old Town. In the dark of the moon other gigs of Scilly were being readied for the 90-mile haul across the channel to Roscoff. *Czar of Tresco* and the old *Bonnet* of St Mary's were in the pool, pulling on muffled oars. *Golden Eagle* had Jack Pender still in command, even though he was the wrong side of sixty.

The crew of *Horse* settled to their task. Brian Jenkins had given up the coveted position of stroke – the aftmost oar that set the rhythm for the rest of the crew – to his son-in-law Joseph Pearce. Brian would control the course of the gig as coxswain and skipper.

Roscoff is a small Breton town on the western side of the peninsula that has the great seaport town of Brest on its southern flank. The famed island of Ushant is to the west, known and feared as the northern entrance to the Bay of Biscay. Roscoff, while protected by Île de Batz and its myriad rocks and reefs, is subjected to exceptionally high rise and fall of tides. Tidal streams could run as fast as a gig could be rowed by six strong men. The harbour would be dry at half-tide so timing a vessel's arrival was extremely important. Should the tide window be missed, a seafarer would have to anchor and await the next tide 12 hours later.

Black, oily swells rose to meet *Horse*. The lugsail flapped giving a small advantage in the light south-easterly breeze. Rowing four men on, two off, the gig was making four knots – not enough to be in Roscoff by the following nightfall.

The wind rose, backing nor'east. With the dawn they were in sight of the French islands.

Bowman Bert Nance suddenly shouted, "Sail to windward; heading to intercept."

Brian instantly recognised her as the new revenue cutter *Vigilant* out of Falmouth – they had met before. "We've no chance o' outrunning her from 'ere. We've nothing t' hide; we're outward bound 'n no trade cargo. Better drop the mainsail and wait fer 'em. We're an innocent pilot gig looking for channel pilot trade. They ain't got no cause to 'old us."

"Ahoy there! What is your vessel, home port and your business?" was the call from the cutter.

"Pilot gig *Horse*, St Mary's, about us own piloting business," returned Brian.

"Who's the pilot?" The cutter's captain was being thorough.

"Charles Pender of Agnes, and 'e knows 'e's a registered pilot," returned Brian.

"Why are you so far to the east?" The persistent excise captain was beginning to annoy the red-bearded Scillonian.

"Us headed to the coast for a night's rest; back out at first light. There's an East Indiaman 'omeward bound. She's due soon. We're looking t' put our pilot aboard 'er," Brian replied.

"We'll be in these waters for a while," returned the cutter captain. "It wouldn't pay for us to see you heavy laden, scurrying home. I've had my eye on you Scillonians for a while. I'll check records to see how many ships you've actually put a pilot on when we get to port."

With that, the cutter hardened her sheets, tacked and made her way back to her station mid channel. Brian gave the order to make sail, and the gig raced eastward.

A low coastline rose over the horizon, and the unmistakable silhouette of Ushant hove into view confirming the gig's position.

"We'll be in afore nightfall with this breeze," said the skipper, a statement that was to prove a little optimistic. As darkness fell, they had just made the channel between Île de Batz and Roscoff. With the full ebb tide against them, the gig was beached on the island. The crew made themselves as comfortable as they could for the night. A hundred miles at sea in an open boat and sleep soon claimed them.

After a hastily taken meal of bread and salt pork the bows of *Horse* were once again headed for Roscoff. The few remaining miles took only minutes to cover now the tide was fair; the gig was beached right in front of the town. At once the traders descended making their offers of comforts to the crew; the skipper was soon negotiating for cargo. These days cash was used instead of trade goods, as it returned a better deal.

The wind had backed to the north and rose, which suited Brian Jenkins well; he was in no hurry to leave, with an excise cutter cruising between him and home; besides he was having a good time. He had done well; with several French traders bidding for his trade, he had secured several tubs of fine lace and perfumes, as well as the usual spirits. These would make the gig lighter on her return voyage as well as achieving much higher returns per pound weight carried.

The burly skipper had found comfort in the arms of an attractive although slightly older prostitute named Natalie. She delighted the crew in the telling of her 'fantastic' nocturnal experiences with their leader while she drank glass after glass of red wine at breakfast the next day. His father-in-law made no protest when Joseph found comfort with Natalie's cousin Justine. In his normal, fair-minded way Brian reasoned that his daughter would not be fulfilling her wifely duties during her sickness. He knew a man, once used to a passionate woman, found it mighty hard to be without, so it was a bawdy few days the crew enjoyed in the little French seaport.

The wind finally eased and veered southward. *Horse* was loaded, farewells made, then at the top of the evening tide the tiny ship made her way out into the Atlantic Ocean.

Brian Jenkins reasoned that the revenue cutter would cruise mid channel as several big cutters, well-armed ships owned by the notorious Cater family from Cawsands, were in port. These famous smugglers would shape a more northerly course for home. He decided to head as westerly a course as the gig could hold, a heading well south of Scilly. By sailing all night they would make as much ground as possible before shipping the mast and rowing by day, to make themselves less visible. From a masthead, a lookout would be doing well to spot them from four miles. With the wind in the south and a revenue cutter likely to be well to leeward, the excise men would have to tack many a time to reach them, the tacking effectively halving the speed they could make in a direct line. As the sun rose, anxious eyes cast about them.

"Sail ho! Due south and coming on fast," called Bert Nance at lookout in the bows.

The crew strained to identify the oncoming ship.

"She's no excise cutter – too large, of that I'm sure," yelled Brian.

Yet it was tense on board the gig until the vessel made a course alteration and showed three masts, those of a full-rigged ship. She flew past the gig not three miles distant yet showed no sign of seeing them. Several other sail sightings were made that day, each adding to the tension on board; none, however, reached hailing distance.

That evening the masts were stepped once again and a course shaped to the north. It was the skipper's plan to slip into the River Fal under cover of darkness, landing in the Roseland before daybreak. This required a steady nerve, as they would have to sail within half a mile of Royal Navy ships at anchor in the roadstead. They would then rendezvous with their people, unload and make for Scilly the following night. Not for the weak of heart was seafaring in the free-trade; profits made were hard earned. In those desperate times it was the difference of life and death for some families; the risk had to be taken.

For every seagoing smuggler there were many landsmen accomplices; the seafarers, however, were given hero status. In the old days there were few prosecutions. Even if a smuggler was brought to trial, a local jury would usually acquit the defendant, or an important witness would go missing for a while. The early eighteenth-century citizen, while fiercely patriotic and Christian, seemed to think that smuggling was not a crime, merely a way to get back at a greedy, oppressive king.

The authorities had lately stepped up their efforts to break the smugglers, building fast, armed cutters, of which *Vigilant* was one. Platoons of armed excise men scoured the coastlines seeking out rendezvous places and hunting sympathisers. Smugglers in turn armed themselves and devised cunning schemes to avoid apprehension. Escalation in policing caused pitched battles to be fought; inevitably, casualties were suffered on both sides, and prosecutions made by the Crown became more frequent.

They sighted the Lizard light in the early evening and were rowing past the warships at anchor in Falmouth roads after nightfall.

"Quiet-like, lads. Let's no' give the navy the pleasure o' a chase at this hour. Break out the pistols, Joe lad, just in case our welcome is not as we'd 'oped for," whispered Brian.

The arrangements started by John Pearce all those years ago had blossomed into a thriving business. John's brother-in-law Daniel Farmiloe was still rector of St Just's. Farmiloe, having a sense of adventure, had been as keen as any to be part of the free-trade. It was one of the most successful smuggling rings in the West Country, the point of entry being the beautiful little church of St Just and its extensive graveyard. Running as it did right down to the water's edge, a small boat like a gig could discharge its cargo straight into opened vaults that had never held a corpse. To an unknowing observer the hiding place looked like any one of hundreds of graves at the site.

There had been some form of church at St Just-in-the-Roseland for centuries. The mystique, beauty and peace of the place were a perfect backdrop to the tales whispered in the cottages and farms of the Roseland. During the reformation, after King Henry VIII decreed himself head of the Church of England, many a persecuted Catholic priest was hidden from the bishop's men in the very vaults now used for hiding goods of the free-trade.

All went well. By daybreak the goods were stowed, money changed hands, and *Horse* safely hidden away from prying eyes in the woods by the churchyard. Soon the crew was eating a hearty breakfast in the parlour of St Just's rectory. After the meal tired men went down into a concealed basement to sleep. Later, under cover of darkness, all but Ben, who had broken his leg on slippery rocks while unloading, would make the run out of the River Fal where, once again in the open channel, *Horse* would become an innocent pilot gig returning home.

Horse slipped out from behind the sand bar in St Just's creek. Peter Pearce, a local sixteen-year-old farm boy and second cousin to Joe, had taken Ben's place. Peter was wild with excitement; at last he was free of the drudgery of farm life – a life at sea beckoned.

They were grateful for the gentle headwind that blew the sounds of their passage astern, mingling with their silvery wake. Brian shaped their course close to the eastern side of the Fal to be as far from the anchored ships as possible. Now passing St Mawes Castle, just hidden by the trees, they were close inshore, giving the crew cause to worry. Once they had left the cover of the shoreline and headed on into the open water of St Mawes estuary, they were at their most vulnerable. Only a couple of miles rowing and they would be safely in open sea, home a night's sail away.

"Halt and be identified." The shout came from the riverside where the warships were moored. "Halt in the name of the King."

"Can 'e see 'em, Joe?" called Brian.

"No, nothin'," Joe whispered back.

Just then a musket shot rang out. *Thwack* was heard by all as a lead ball hit the water, astern but very close by. Joe instinctively pointed his pistol at the flash; later he couldn't remember firing. "'Er just went off like, all by itself,' he would say.

A cry of pain was clearly heard by the crew of the *Horse*. "For the love of Christ," exclaimed Brian, "he's 'it one of 'em. Row fer yer lives, lads; row like 'e 'ave never rowed before!"

It was near midnight. Torches were lit from braziers set on the decks of the warships highlighting the lofty spars in an eerie glow. Masters-at-arms were being roused, angry, from their warm hammocks. The red coats of the marines showed clearly in the glow. The clamour grew as the navy geared itself for action.

"Get the cutters ready to follow them; quickly now or the row will be harder. They must be apprehended at all costs," came the unmistakable voice of an officer, floating over the water.

"We'll sneak around the Lizard and then 'ead seaward. They don't know who or what us is, with this 'ere onshore breeze, no sail can be set t' follow us. If us get to mid channel we've a chance," said Brian. "I'll spell an oar later t' give 'e a break. Fer now, row. I've a feelin' firing on a navy ship be 'n act o' treason. Yer don't have to think hard what they'll do if us gets caught.

"We're getting well ahead," he continued. "With the gig light she's makin' six knots 'n 'em cutters be near four, us have t' be out o' sight afore daybreak. Pray for a mornin' sea mist – 'tis all that'll save us." The skipper moved forward to relieve the second oar, behind Joe on stroke.

It was an exhausted crew that finally raised *Horses*'s masts and bent her sails to the light sou'easterly. Another few miles and they would be in the shipping lanes, an innocent pilot boat plying her trade once again.

"Weapons over the side," called Brian as the sea mist burnt off in the morning sun. It was then he spotted a topsail, not two hundred yards abeam, above the thinning mist.

"Halt. What vessel are you?" It was a familiar voice, and no happy coincidence. The hailing vessel was awaiting the dawn and a breeze to carry her into Falmouth safely. "Drop your sail. We are the revenue cutter *Vigilant* and will board you. Do not try to run, our guns are trained and loaded."

"Aboard the cutter smartly if you please, Captain Jenkins. I'm sure you can explain why the *Horse* is on a course out of Falmouth and not in mid channel looking for honest trade." Captain Richard Menzies knew he was too late; any cargo the gig may have been carrying was now safely ashore on its way to the market so he was not in a happy frame of mind when Brian Jenkins boarded *Vigilant*. Brian was well aware that the breathing space the speed of the gig and the fortuitous mist had given them was being reduced by the second.

He faced Captain Menzies nervously.

It was not long before *Vigilant*'s masthead lookout called out to the captain. "Boats, captain, 'alf a dozen of them. Navy pinnaces and cutters by the looks, all makin' straight for us, sir."

"Well, Jenkins, what mischief do you be up to, eh? Half the navy pulling boats in your wake, and this far offshore? Most strange! Shall we await them and see if we can be of assistance?" The wily captain's suspicions now fully roused, he was sure he had a prosecution to follow his morning's work.

The first boat came up to them in a very short time and pulled alongside *Vigilant*. "Lieutenant Richardson of HMS *Sovereign* at your service, sir, although I believe it is you who have been of great service to the navy this day." The lieutenant recounted the story of the previous night and requested the *Vigilant* put *Horse*'s crew in irons and transport them to Falmouth.

"My great pleasure, lieutenant. Perhaps you and the other boats' crews would care to come aboard for the short voyage. We can tow your boats and offer some food and drink after your hard chase."

Captain Menzies, now in great humour, gave the necessary orders to get the cutter under way. *Horse* was hauled on deck for safety, the prize money for the gig, while modest, would keep him in wine for a good while.

When searched, Brian's stash of gold sovereigns was soon discovered.

"Honest pilot boat, are ye? Be damned if ye are. Your life as a smuggler ends here, Jenkins. Your own miserable life will shortly end, swinging from His Majesty's gallows – not to mention injuring a naval rating. Maybe they'll draw and quarter ye? Your crew will look grand, swinging beside you."

Captain Menzies had Brian chained to *Vigilant*'s mainmast. He continued to taunt him the four hours it took to work the cutter back into Falmouth in the light and variable breeze. Brian never flinched, staring straight back, unblinking, eye to eye.

Chapter 6

Falmouth

There was considerable disagreement between the Royal Navy and HM Coastguard – as the customs and excise enforcement department was then known – as to which service would hold and prosecute the case. The navy maintained that, as one of their non-commissioned officers had been brutally shot by 'pirates' on the 'high seas', the prisoners should be handed to them for military courts martial. The coastguard, however, maintained that the crew of the *Horse* had been under surveillance by the coastguard cutter *Vigilant*. The said ship had made the actual capture of smugglers, not enemies of state. These facts made it a civil case to be prosecuted by them, in a civil court.

"My dear admiral," began Richard Braithwaite, commandant of Coastguard Southern England. "May we not, as gentlemen, finally decide this matter? I have a suggestion that may be acceptable to ye, sir; a compromise."

"Of course, commandant, we are career officers. We must settle the matter for the honour of both our services. These villains have lived on His Majesty's pleasure far too long – near six months. Should have been hanged long ago," said Rear Admiral Sir George Bing. "What is your suggestion?"

"My superiors are adamant, sir, that the prisoners are dealt with as smugglers, in civil court. We must make an example of them – show 'em our service has teeth. I understand the navy's main concern is that a civil court may be too lenient. The offence being in some respects an attack on a King's ship means only a death penalty would be sufficient. Is this a correct assumption, Sir George?"

"Yes. Frankly, their lordships have concerns that any lesser penalty would suggest a weakness in naval discipline and that the navy was subject to influence out of its control. It is well known that smugglers in the west are deemed heroes by most of the populace, not as the pirates they truly are. Many of your prosecutions have failed because of public – and, in no small part, official – sympathy," answered the admiral.

"In this we are as one, sir. It is essential that the leaders and the man who fired the shot, at least, should hang. My suggestion is simple, and one that would ensure a satisfactory result. I recommend that the navy prosecute the case before the civil court – my superiors have already agreed to this; cooperation between the services will look good to the politicians. Our fledgling service will benefit from a show of strength and be a lesson to others in the smuggling community. We will also benefit politically – the new ship *Vigilant* will be seen as a success, paving the way for more to be built. Last, but not least, the navy will get its wish. The need for naval ships to be involved in excise matters will diminish as more cutters are built to patrol the coast. More navy ships will be available for the wars against the infernal Spanish and French."

The commandant could see his final words strike home with the taciturn admiral: a naval officer needed war for advancement and the taking of enemy ships as prizes to increase his fortune.

"An excellent suggestion, commandant. I see your reputation as an intelligent officer is well founded. Pity you are not in the navy. If you desire a change, sir, I could guarantee you excellent prospects," offered the admiral.

"My sincere thanks, Sir George, but I have committed myself to the new service. Lord knows we need all the help we can get – smuggling today is epidemic," replied Braithwaite respectfully.

"Quite right, commandant, quite right," puffed the admiral. "It's a worthy if mucky job that must be done and done well. I will inform the Admiralty today of your suggestion, along with my personal recommendation that we proceed with it."

The commandant left the naval dockyard at Falmouth well pleased with himself; his career would do well after a successful prosecution – the service would too. He walked the short distance to his small office near the inner harbour, let himself in and locked the door. He reached under his desk for a polished piece of timber, in the shape of a boat cut down its centre line. It was a half-model of a 150-ton cutter he dreamt of building for the Falmouth division of Coastguard. The model had sleek, beautiful lines. Designed purely for speed, with none of the bulk required by cargo-carrying vessels, she would carry 14 guns, thereby able to outgun all the smuggling vessels afloat at that time. *Yes, he thought, one step nearer to getting you built, my beauty.*

* * *

John Pearce and Dorothy Jenkins made their way to Falmouth from Penryn. They had left Jane with the two children at the inn they had moved to; courthouses were no place for children of the accused. The family had left St Just's to be closer to the courthouse for the duration of the trial.

The courtroom was packed. The prosecutor, no less than a naval captain, had presented a clear-cut case. All Joe and Brian's defence counsel could do was throw his clients on the court's mercy and await the jury's decision. John and Dorothy knew the chances of Joseph and Brian being returned to them were slim; however, if the sentences were for transportation Jane could at least hope to join her husband at some future date. But that awful naval captain had asked for the death penalty for all but the pilot, Charlie Pender – because of his skills he would serve the rest of his life on His Majesty's ships.

"What is the verdict of the jury, Mr Foreman?" the judge asked.

The foreman of the jury had been brought from London for the trial, and his foreign accent was the only sound in the now silent courtroom. "On the charge of smuggling we find the accused not guilty. On the charge of the attempted murder of a member of His Majesty's Navy, while operating a vessel in a suspicious manner, we find all the accused guilty."

The foreman sat down amid sighs and groans from the public gallery. An almost inaudible high-pitched wail escaped the lips of Dorothy Jenkins.

The judge reached down and put the dreaded black cloth over his immaculately powdered wig and looked sternly at the dock. "You are all found guilty of most heinous crimes. The jury has dismissed the charge of smuggling. I wonder, however, what a pilot gig from Scilly was doing leaving Falmouth Harbour at night, breaking curfew. Interesting also was that the captain did not inform the harbour authorities of the gig's arrival in the first place! Brian Jenkins, as skipper, and Joseph Pearce, the man who fired the shot – you clearly carry the greatest responsibility. I sentence you to death by hanging."

The crowd was silent; a sob escaped Dorothy's lips – she had just lost her husband and son-in-law. Old John Pearce silently took her hand in his.

"Charles Pender. The navy has requested leniency in your case and offers you a life in the navy where your piloting skills may pay in some small way for your crime. However, you may, if you wish, join your skipper on the gallows. How say you?" The judge's eyes bored into Charlie's as he shuffled uneasily beside Brian in the dock.

"I choose the navy, Yer Honour," said Charlie, his eyes cast down, not wanting to see the reaction of his shipmates.

"It's the right thing ye did, Charlie," whispered Brian.

"Charles Pender, you may step from the dock and go with the naval escort." The judge removed the black cloth and addressed the *Horse*'s remaining crew. "As for the rest of you, it is decided that you had a lesser part to play in this affair, so I have adjusted all your sentences accordingly. You will each be taken from this place and put into prison until such time as the next convict ship leaves for the colony of Virginia, in the Americas. You will be transported from England and work the land as prisoners for ten years. After that time you are to be freed but are not to return to England for the rest of your lives."

The judge's gavel came down ending the proceedings.

John Pearce and Dorothy Jenkins made their way the three miles back to the Prospect. Jane Pearce didn't need them to tell her the news; it was written all over their faces.

"Sorry, lass, they wasn't never going to let the boys go. It was decided before us entered that cursed courtroom. At least it ain't be all of 'em." John reached forward to hold his shattered daughter-in-law in his strong, shaking arms.

The two women burst into heavy sobbing; the desperate sound wrenched at the heart of the old sailor who had seen some fearsome things in his years at sea, but nothing could have prepared him for the awful sound coming from the two women sitting before him. Young Simon burst into tears also, although not quite knowing why; he had yet to be made fully aware of the terrible fate that awaited his father and grandfather.

At this moment a man in the vestments of the clergy and his wife arrived at their table. The woman spoke first. "Oh, John, we have been praying for better tidings. St Just's was full last Sunday, and Daniel said a special prayer for the children, Jane my dear." Margaret Farmiloe took each of their hands in turn as tears ran down her cheeks. In her mind also was the fate of her cousin Peter Pearce – he was just a boy of sixteen, bored with life at Penpeth, the family farm on the Roseland's northern boundary. Peter had dreamt all his life of adventure and going to sea, but as the family's eldest son, he was destined to run the farm when his father retired.

Peter had been the first to volunteer to replace the injured Ben Pender on the gig's return trip to Scilly. He had broken his leg while pulling the gig into hiding in St Just's creek. His father, Michael Pearce, had reluctantly allowed the lad to go, saying, "Maybe it'll be a rough voyage 'n it'll get the urge t' go t' sea out of the boy."

Young Peter had got his wish. He would never have to become the patriarch of Penpeth Farm now, spending the rest of his life in that peaceful place. Instead he faced life as a convict in the American colonies, thousands of miles away, where he knew no one.

Daniel Farmiloe took control. "We cannot have all of ye, all waiting here in a public house for two weeks; the cost would be severe and torture for ye. I assume ye wish to stay until after, ahem ..." Daniel coughed as he struggled to find the right words. "... I mean you will want to see Brian and Joseph as much as possible. Margaret and I would be pleased if you would stay with us in the rectory at St Just's – its only an hour or so across the harbour to Pendennis Castle where they are being held. Our parishioners are very much on your side; they will be pleased to ferry us across the harbour and help in any way they can."

In his usual efficient manner the Reverend Farmiloe had an oyster boat waiting at the quay. The tide was rising and a fair breeze blowing as he urged the grief-stricken family to gather their belongings and board the boat. They soon covered the few miles across the River Fal and docked on the sandspit at the head of St Just's creek. The boatman then rowed them over to the beautiful little church of St Just-in-the-Roseland. They entered in silence, and Daniel offered prayers for the two condemned men.

Later, at the rectory, John Pearce was reminded of many a clandestine visit to this peaceful spot – happy times spent with smuggling crews and the people of the Roseland who assisted them. He said in anguish, "What did I do? It were I what started all o' this. If I hadn't brung the *Bonnet* in 'ere all 'em year ago, this would not have happened."

"Shush yourself, John," said Daniel. "For years ye and the Scillonians have run trade into St Just's; the people here have had a reasonable life. Had ye no shared the trade with us, many would have starved to death. Times are harsh. Tin mines be only workable summertime, and the Duchy of Cornwall takes all the profits from them, so His Lordship can live like a king in London. Farmers barely make a living, the crippling rent 'n taxation keeps them so poor."

"We aren't the only clergy that helps the trade," said Margaret Farmiloe. "We do it out of desperation, because of the poverty of our parishioners."

"It's said there be 10,000 folk involved in Cornwall alone – what wi' Devon, Somerset, the Home Counties, Wales 'n Ireland, a hundred thousand are at it, they say. The trade could be stopped overnight if them in power reduced the duties to fair levels, stopped their wars 'n made taxes reasonable."

Margaret Farmiloe had years ago used this argument to get her husband to agree to participate in the venture with the Scillonians. The Farmiloe name had become something of a legend in the area, St Just's rector regarded as a hero. It was whispered that the Bishop of Truro himself was quietly aware of the help his flock were giving the seagoing trade. The tithes gathered from the seaside villages were far greater than those from the landlocked ones. *The lord moves in mysterious ways,* he thought, never enquiring as to the true cause of the anomaly.

Making their way to the rectory through the old church grounds brought little peace to the troubled family. Walking past the decaying gravestones, they were reminded that a Christian institution had been on the site since 550 AD and pagan worship had taken place for centuries before that. It was rumoured in hushed tones that Jesus himself had sailed into St Just's Pool and landed at the church site with Joseph of Arimathea, a tin merchant wishing to do business with the Cornish tin miners. The sanctity and the beauty of the site was little salve to the families' shattered minds.

Once at their home it was clear that the invitation to stay with the Farmiloes was not a spur of the moment one. Meats, pies and foods of all kinds were ready for the family as they entered the parlour – the people of the Roseland wanted to show sympathy to the Pearces in the most practical of ways. They too loved the men who had risked all, from which they had all benefited.

After a meal, of which the adults partook only out of respect for those who had provided it, Jane tried to put young Simon to bed. The boy knew of course something was amiss and couldn't help but protest. "I want to see Father and Grandfather before I go to bed!"

This was too much for the boy's mother, and she collapsed to the floor, howling. Margaret came into the room saying, "Come with yer auntie, Simon. I've a grand story to tell ye. I know it's not the same as your father telling it but he be unable to be here tonight."

She took the boy to a tiny room on the first floor of the rectory, laid him gently in a cosy bed and began telling him the story of Robin Hood and the men of Sherwood Forest. They stole from the wicked King John who had usurped the throne from his brother, King Richard, who was at the Crusades.

"Yer see, Simon, yer father 'n grandfather be like Robin Hood, only the bad sheriff has captured them and they have to be away awhile."

With his aunt's hinted-at assurance of his father's return the boy closed his eyes and slept.

The Farmiloe children were at the breakfast table early the next morning, eager to hear of the previous day's happenings. They were soon made to be quiet as the adults planned the coming day.

"John and I should go to the castle today and see if we can make arrangements to see the lads. I think it unwise that the ladies accompany us until we are sure of the regime. We will be able to make a time for ye to visit. Please pack some food as there will not be much for our kin to eat in that gaol."

The exhausted women were only too pleased to allow Daniel to organise the immediate future.

Once back on the Falmouth side of the river, John and Daniel made their way up Quay Hill to Castle Drive; from here it was a mile of hilly walking to reach the gate of Pendennis Castle. They asked to see the condemned men; the sergeant of the guard told them to wait. Some considerable time elapsed before they were informed that they would not be able to see their kin that day and that only one visit would be allowed before the execution in eleven days' time.

"I wish to see the castle commander, sergeant, and quickly if you please. I'm sure the Bishop of Truro would be displeased if I am denied," said the Reverend Farmiloe.

The sergeant, not wishing to upset so senior a member of the clergy, motioned them to enter. After a brief interview with an untidy captain, Daniel was shown back to the castle gates.

"Thank God 'e are here," John said to Daniel. "I wouldn't 'ave got t' see the commander."

"The good captain has desires of the flesh that involve young girls. I simply made him aware of my knowledge of his nocturnal visits to certain houses. After that he wasn't hard to convince that our request to see the lads daily was reasonable. At least they will be well fed and cared for," said Daniel.

Later, Brian and Joseph in the dungeon far below were relieved to receive the basket of food. They ate in silence in the dark, damp cell, very much aware of the atrocities perpetrated in the name of the King in this dark place, so full of foreboding.

When they had been taken to their cell they went down a narrow spiral staircase, downward from the castle keep. They had passed through a chamber with a rough table with awful looking instruments hanging from it on iron hooks – there was little doubt as to their purpose.

The gaoler, seeing their concern, had laughed. "Don't fret none, me handsomes. We ain't about to use them pretty little tools on youse all. We got bigger plans for ye – a good hemp rope 'n ye swinging at the end o' it. The whole town'll turn out; nothin' like a double hangin' to entertain 'em."

They were shoved roughly into a cell carved out of the living rock. It was just eight feet by six; a pale shaft of light entered from a tiny slit in the ceiling. Two piles of straw were the only furnishings, the stench from the smaller indicating its use as the sanitary area, the second making a sleeping place large enough for one man at a time.

"If youse 'ave got money us'll improve things a bit, like. Talk t' yer family," said the gaoler as he slammed the door and turned the large iron key. The two men were left in the gloom, their own private fears playing heavily on their tortured minds.

"Oh, Brian, what a mess I got us into this time. I'm real sorry. I fired the shot; you shouldn't be here, and what of Jane and the young 'uns. I only want t' get it over with," Joseph wailed.

"Don't go on lad. I been running the channel in the trade fer near 30 year 'n have gotten away with it - had my fights with the excise too. Between the sea 'n the excise, I been lucky t' live this long." The skipper's stoic reply did little to ease Joseph's anguish. "Best get yer 'ead straight afore the womenfolk visit tomorrow, lad. It's they that'll 'ave t' cope with everything after next Saturday week. We don't want t' make it harder fer 'em."

That Sunday Daniel bribed the serjeant-at-arms to allow him to perform a service in the keep yard. It was a bright sunny day as Brian and Joseph were led from the dungeon. In the harsh light they were unable to see the small family gathering at first. Jane and Dorothy ran to embrace their menfolk. The service was brief, so the families could spend the time allowed them together.

Joseph could only look away when his son said, "When is 'e coming home, Da?"

Had he spoken, he would have given way to the welling tears.

"Janie, luv, I wants 'e to know you're the best wife a man could 'ope fer. When 'e gets all this behind 'e, take another man t' be dad t' Simon 'n Mary. Yer don't deserve life alone. Stay 'ere in th' Roseland, better chance than Scilly. I already spoke t' Aunt Margaret 'n Uncle Dan 'bout it."

"Oh Joe, 'ow can 'e say such a thing! I loves 'e - only 'e. No man can take yer place." Jane broke down as her husband and father were led away, her anguish hidden until Joe was out of sight.

It was Saturday the 27th of November 1736. Brian Jenkins and Joseph Pearce were led out of their cell into the courtyard for the last time. The gaoler gave them each a bucket of water, a washcloth and a change of clothes, brought the day before by the family. They stood on a small cart and began the journey to Packet Quay, the site of public execution.

The gallows were set up with a wide cross-beam. Two nooses of heavy hemp rope dangled from it; it seemed they were to die together, thus sparing one from watching the demise of the other. They were led up the scaffold steps, and after a last handshake their hands were tied behind them, and their legs were bound together to prevent them flailing about as they choked. They were made to stand on a high stool as the noose was tightened around each of their necks.

Joseph looked into his father-in-law's eye, heart pounding, unable to speak. "See 'e up there, lad," was the last thing the big Scillonian said.

After a few brief words from the preacher, drums rolled and the stools were kicked out from under them. The two men kicked and bucked at first, then as the nooses tightened, they slowly strangled to death. Falmouth's populace watched in morbid silence; all sense of the earlier festivities vanished as they watched the slow, agonising deaths. Many a hand went to its own neck to remove a phantom itch.

Daniel Farmiloe had been busy; it was the last wish of both men that they be buried at St Just, thus escaping the indignity of being dumped in a pit of quicklime, the usual fate of the executed. Daniel used all his influence with the bishop to obtain a letter to present to the Garrison commander in support of the men's last request. So it was that the two bodies, necks twisted and faces blue, were passed into his care.

The vicar of St Just had come well prepared; the inert forms of his kinsmen were put into two simple coffins, which were loaded quickly onto a waiting oyster boat moored on the outside wall of Packet Quay. The crowd, for whom the gruesome deaths had been the high point of their weekend entertainment, began to disperse, mostly into the many public houses and inns that catered for the seaport. *Flame's* gaff mainsail was hoisted. Solemnly the family – the living and the recently deceased – made their last journey together.

The gentle southerly bore the mourners slowly across the River Fal into St Just creek. A silent crowd waited, eager hands took *Flame's* lines as she reached her mooring place. The men, honest farmers and fishermen by day, who would become smugglers by night, bore the coffins through the sacred churchyard of St Just-in-the-Roseland, passing through the famous gateway outside the fence then along the path bordering the churchyard.

The Bishop had been adamant. 'You push me too far, sir,' he had shouted. 'I have acceded to all your other requests with regard to this ghastly affair, but in this you will hear and obey me! Executed men may not in any circumstances be interred in consecrated ground. You may, however, bury them outside, on the boundary of St Just's. Now be gone!' Daniel had known better than to argue further and with a 'Yes, Your Grace,' he left Truro Cathedral.

The party reached a small glade near a sacred spring where two graves were prepared and ready. More than a hundred friends and colleagues of the two men, including gig crews from Scilly, formed a circle around the graves as the coffins were placed on planks over gaping holes, dug just outside consecrated ground.

Daniel took his place at the head of the graves and began the service. "Lord God Almighty. We ask you to receive these two poor sinners into your care. Thee, who knowest all things, know that your sons that lie before us did things that were offensive to the laws of our land. And the wounding of another human being is against your commandments and sacred laws. We beseech you, O Lord, to take the souls of these men, Brian and Joseph, who have paid for their sins here on earth, grant them the grace of your boundless forgiveness, and accept them into heaven. Dust to dust, ashes to ashes, in the name of the Father, the Son and the Holy Ghost, we commend their earthly shells to the ground."

The two coffins were then lowered the six feet to their last resting places. John Pearce took young Simon's hand to lead him away as the Roselanders began to fill the graves.

The boy pulled back, crying. "Why are we leaving Papa and Grandad Jenkins in the ground, Grandfather? I want my papa, I want my papa."

"I want 'e to go back to Scilly with yer grandad," said Jane Pearce to three-year-old Simon. "Mary 'n me will come back for 'e; ain't be nothing more for 'e to do here. Take him away, John, please. He's seen enough trouble fer one so young; take him home while I gets me 'ead straight."

It had been decided that Jane would stay at the rectory. Margaret saw how the loss of Esther May, and now the awful death of her husband and father, had unhinged her mind. She would need constant care if she were ever to return to normal. Dorothy was also asked to remain, as she could assist in the care of her daughter and have a time of adjustment before returning home. The women could not bear to go back to Falmouth, so they said their goodbyes at the landing on St Just spit.

Simon, now in the guardianship of his grandfather, sailed from the Packet Quay for St Mary's and home.

Chapter 7
Scilly 1746

Simon enjoyed his life on Scilly but vowed he would never be a gig's crew, a choice he kept well hidden from his kin. He aspired to greater things.

Although Jane Pearce's mother returned to Scilly, Jane herself never did.

A year later Dorothy Jenkins and John Pearce were married – it seemed the natural thing to do; they had been through massive trauma together. Everyone on the islands was delighted that these two well-regarded people found love out of their recent losses.

It was a perfect July afternoon. John Pearce looked up from repairing the thatch roof of their cottage on Garrison Hill to seaward, out past the Crim and Tearing Ledges that had ripped the bottom out of the *Romney* back in '07. He squinted as he looked into the setting sun. His sixty-year-old eyes had not been mistaken. It was definitely a sail making good speed in the 15-knot south-westerly. At about half past four he looked again and saw a fine brigantine wearing ship, safely inside the reefs of the western rocks. Once the turn was made and the wind was now on her starboard quarter, she settled on to her new course for St Mary's Pool. Her topsails were furled, then her forecourse, till only her mizzen spanker remained to spin her into the wind as her anchor crashed to the seabed. *A fine piece of seamanship*, thought John.

The ship, some 400 tons, was well armed with a dozen twelve-pound cannon a side. A fine pair of long-barrelled bow chasers showed in her fore quarters, giving testament that she had been designed to fight. A sight to behold, at first John thought she was navy; however, no naval ensigns fluttered from her mastheads, only a red ensign from her poop aft declaring her to be British. A puff of smoke followed by an explosion some seconds later erupted from a swivel gun on her poop deck as she saluted Star Castle, formally announcing her arrival.

"What ship, Grandpa?" said Simon Pearce as he looked longingly at the smart vessel lying peacefully at anchor beneath them.

"Dunno, lad. Reckon she be a privateer, back from th' Caribbees. Bin, hammerin' French 'n Spanish treasure ships most like; back 'ere t' refit 'n pay her dues," John speculated.

A privateer was a freelance warship with a warrant from the Crown to plunder ships of an enemy nation, taking prizes and cargoes as it pleased. The privateer had to pay a part of his plunder to the Crown for these rights. The Royal Navy would also offer protection if they were pursued, an arrangement in place since before the time of Sir Francis Drake, the most famous privateer. The Royal Navy, always short of manpower, eyed the privateers' crews with some envy. It was, however, an unstated 'gentlemen's arrangement' that the press gangs would not touch these experienced, freelance warrior sailors.

John went back to his thatching. "Pass us up some more thatch, Si lad, 'n give a hand – me ol' fingers is getting too stiff fer this 'ere job."

"Be 'em comin' ashore, Grandpa?" asked Joe excitedly.

"Aye, the cap'n 'll be payin' his respects t' th' governor. It's the law. See the yella duster flyin' from her main yard? That's be sayin' her's fresh in from overseas 'n so bein' needs t' show clearance papers from her last port."

The man and boy finished on the roof and went inside the cottage, thoughts of the fine pollack they had caught early that morning uppermost in their minds. Dorothy was a fine cook, and they knew the food would be good. They would be eating alone as she had gone to visit her aging aunt, a widow in Old Town. Free from his wife's disapproving eye, John went over to the battered old sideboard and brought out a bottle of navy rum, pouring himself a good measure. Settling down in his creaky rocking chair, he took a deep draught, closing his eyes, savouring the powerful spirit as it made its way from his mouth via excited tastebuds to warm his stomach.

A few hours later, just as the summer sun was settling over the western rocks, there was a knock at the door.

"See who that be, lad," said John Pearce, mellowing.

Simon opened the door to a most impressive looking gentleman – he fully filled the doorway. He was tall for the times – some six feet – and broad of shoulder, with curling black hair rolling down his shoulders from under his tricorne hat. His deep red coat with gold trim and toggles were the finest the boy had ever seen. Across his shoulder was a wide black leather strap held together by a shining silver buckle. Attached to this was a curved sword in an engraved scabbard. The man's black leather sea boots rose to the underside of his red frock coat. In all, it could be said he was awesome to behold.

"Don't stand there with yer mouth open, boy. Ask th' gentleman in, fer God's sake," bellowed John Pearce.

"Captain Richard Blackmore at your service. I presume I am at the house of Mr John Pearce?" said the cultured visitor.

"Aye, sir, indeed it be, an' what've us done fer this 'ere pleasure," stammered John, removing his wool cap as he stood up so quickly he knocked his rum tankard over in the process. "Come into our 'umble cottage, sir, please. Simon, wipe that there chair so Cap'n Blackmore can 'ave a seat. Hurry now, boy, don't keep the cap'n awaitin'."

"I assume you know who I am, sir?" enquired the seafarer.

"Aye, sir, I believes I does; 'e be Esther May's first son, if I ain't mistaken." John was bemused by the sudden appearance of his dead wife's first son, who had been sent to sea before they had married, and whom – before now – he had never met.

"Yes, sir, you are correct," said the captain. "Having established that you are my stepfather, we can now abandon formality, can we not? You will call me Richard, and I shall call you John, when in private, that is. The boy is, I assume, Simon, son of my stepbrother Joseph?"

"Aye, cap'n, 'e is right enough," replied John, as yet unable to break the years of deference he had been imbued with, to men of rank. "'Is sister Mary is with 'is mother in the Roseland. She hasn't been able to face coming back t' Scilly, not since the loss of Joseph 'n her father."

John's eyes cast down uncomfortably, the tragic events of ten years ago rising vividly in his memory – things that had not been talked of since he and Simon had returned to Scilly.

"Please do not pain yourself now, Stepfather. I am appraised, if scantily, of past events, as well as the fact that my mother also died tragically. I intend to remain in port for some days, and while I am anxious to hear all the family history in more detail, that can wait for a more appropriate time. Let us for now have a drink together." Richard produced a bottle of the finest Cockspur Barbados rum from a pocket in his coat. "To this, a man of your experience will do justice, I am sure," and the captain poured an ample tot for each of them.

"I 'ave never 'ad a drop o' the likes o' this. Thankee, cap'n, er, Richard," stammered John.

"Perhaps you and Simon would care to visit me tomorrow on board the *Maid of Aran*. I will arrange for a boat to be at the quay at noon, if this is suitable to you?" Richard sat back and toasted the family in the finest golden Caribbean rum available on earth. "I must pay my respects to the governor, so until tomorrow …" Captain Blackmore drained his glass and stood to leave.

"Aye, that'll be grand," said John as the handsome figure bent deeply to clear the lintel of the cottage doorway and was gone, leaving the bottle to be finished and a dozen questions to be answered.

A sea captain; his father's stepbrother – this could be the opportunity he had dreamed of. The young fellow had made a decision – although he could not quite remember when – that he would leave Scilly. Largely to avoid the pressure to follow in his father's footsteps and join a gig crew, he dreamt about a life at sea. All his friends were busting to get aboard a gig. The old hands had set up races for the young men so they could learn about the boats and become strong. Simon himself was due to start his training soon.

He had spoken to his Aunt Elizabeth about a seagoing apprenticeship. His Uncle George had been a captain with the East India Company – could he not help? She had spoken to her husband, and he had made enquiries on the lad's behalf. In true British manner the company had turned the lad down flat, even with the recommendation of one of their ex-captains. The sins of the fathers were to continue being paid for by the sons.

"Employ the son of an executed man, a smuggler, a pirate? Not a chance," said the honourable John Company.

The boy lay in his bunk, dreaming himself to sleep. He woke early to the usual sounds – the gulls screeching overhead and his grandfather snoring. There was little wind and what *was* about was coming through the cracks in the old door. *Easterly*, he thought; *the* Maid of Aran *will be safely in the lee of the land.* He suddenly panicked and rushed outside to make sure the ship was still at her anchors, which of course she was. Simon sat on his favourite rock on the hill behind the cottage; from here he could see the breaking waves on the western rocks – Sampson, Bryher, Tresco and most of St Martins. Nestled in the midst of this protective ring of islands lay *his* ship – the *Maid of Aran* had become his daydream.

They were sailing in uncharted waters; he was at the foretop keeping watch. Was that a reef ahead? Yes. He called to the deck 'Reef ahead, some three miles and breaking!' Then he saw it, a deep blue channel through the line of reefs that were waiting to tear the bottom out of his beloved ship. 'Channel three points to larboard, captain. I can con from 'ere.'

The freshening breeze on his back momentarily broke his reverie; he looked at *his* ship ridding snugly at her anchor and dreamed on.

As he called each turn to the deck, Maid *altered her course accordingly. After an hour of tense manoeuvring they were past the breaking water. He had brought the ship safely out of danger.*

Simon smiled to himself. *If only, if only.*

He had sat on the rock most of the morning, only leaving his perch for a brief breakfast. He felt as if he was the guardian of the ship. From his position 150 feet above sea level, he kept his watch, dreams ebbing and flowing in his mind as the tide below ebbed and flowed.

John Pearce called the boy in. "Best clean 'eself up, lad. Y' can wear yer Sunday best. Might as well give Cap'n Blackmore a good impression of 'e. I can 'azard a guess as t' what 'e have been thinkin'."

"Sorry, Grandpa. I knows 'e'll miss me, but if I'm going t' get t' sea, this'll be me best chance. The navy won't 'ave me other than as a powder boy, nor will John Company, because, well, us both know why. Ain't be nothing more I could want fer than t' sail with th' *Maid of Aran*, if they'll 'ave me," Simon said with passion.

"Aye, lad, I'll miss 'e, that's for sure, but I've just about 'ad my three score years and ten, so don't 'e be worrying 'bout me. Besides, I got ol' Dorothy to nag I to death, ain't I. Yer a bright boy, yer know yer numbers 'n letters too. Don't 'e worry none. I'll do all I can t' get 'e aboard that ship. Just give us time with Cap'n Blackmore 'n don't be too hurried likes; things can take time," and John spat on his hands and smoothed Joe's hair for the third time. He chuckled to himself. "Esther May and yer da would be mighty proud of 'e today, boy."

A longboat pulled away from the ship as they walked the half-mile to Hugh Town quay. The bosun smiled and politely showed John to the after quarters of the longboat, the captain's thwart. It seemed his exploits in the navy and the trade were well known to the *Maid*'s crew; still, it felt strange - his place was with the men at the oars. This time, however, he kept his wool cap firmly on his head. The time had come for him to show pride, if only for the sake of his grandson.

Richard Blackmore was at the companionway to greet them. Although dressed in less formal attire he still cut a most imposing figure. "Mr Pearce and young Simon - welcome aboard. I suggest, Simon, you explore the ship while your grandfather and I talk. Is that to your liking?"

"Aye, sir. I bin watching 'er all mornin'. It'll be grand to get acquainted personal-like," answered Simon.

Richard Blackmore laughed in a friendly fashion and ordered one of the on-watch crew to keep an eye on the boy. "Bring him to my cabin at two bells for some lunch, Jones, if you please. John, come below and let me hear of my family here on the Scillies."

By that afternoon it had been decided that Simon would sail aboard the *Maid of Aran* as an apprentice, learning the trade of a seagoing officer. He would become fully acquainted with all facets of seafaring.

Richard Blackmore had been frank and open in his discussions with John Pearce. "My father made a provision for me in his will, much to his wife's disgust, sufficient to purchase the *Maid of Aran*. As I have never married and have no children, I would be happy to train Simon to run the ship so I can have income in my retirement. On my death Simon will inherit the ship, his little sister Mary and he will share the rest of my modest fortune."

Simon was stunned; the boat's crew returning them ashore had already started calling him 'Mister Pearce'. In the space of just one day his expectations had gone from spending his life as a smuggler and fisherman on Scilly to - if he worked hard - a sea captain and ship owner trading all around the world. His imagination ignored the fact that he would also be a licensed pirate, fighting for his living. He saw no reason to worry about that; he was becoming as strong as his father had been.

Once ashore he rushed around the island telling all his friends. Dorothy heard the story on her way home from her aunt's. It was an angry woman that confronted a well-satisfied John Pearce, sitting with the dregs of the Cockspur rum on his favourite chair in Garrison Cottage.

"What in the name o' the Lord have 'e concocted 'ere, John Pearce, 'n why wasn't I asked? Not so much as a by your leave. Me, who brought the lad up like her own, yet yer don't see fit t' let me in on 'is future!"

"Dot, love, 'e wasn't here. Besides, would 'e 'ave said no to a chance like this fer th' lad?" asked John.

Simon came in and settled it. "Grandma, I be goin' with yer blessin' or no. This is me chance to have all me dreams come true. Please give me yer blessing. I'd like it better, it be wi' it."

Dorothy saw the determination in the boy's eyes, hugged him and said, "Better 'n rowin' fer the trade, I 'spose. Ask yer mother first, mind."

"Aye, I will," he replied.

Chapter 8
Bristol

His life had been a whirlwind since the arrival of Richard Blackmore. Simon Pearce had left Scilly just a week after the *Maid of Aran*. She had sailed for Bristol for repairs and to load a cargo for the settlement of Norfolk in the colony of Virginia. Simon was told to join the ship in a month, so he took the time to visit his mother, sister, aunt and uncle at St Just's.

John Pearce looked hard at his grandson, his heart a-turmoil. He knew that the lad's expectations had advanced dramatically with his stepson, Richard Blackmore, offering to provide a career path for him; however, he couldn't avoid the selfish thought: what of me! The look in the boy's eyes spoke volumes. *Aye, this is enough,* John thought, *and I still got a wife t' be home fer.*

"Have gale on yer first trip, fer luck, Simon lad," John had said. "Look after yerself, boy. Give me luv t' yer mother for I, will 'e?"

John hugged Simon but neither could find the words - goodbye - fare thee well - be good - be kind - be strong. What is to be said when a grandfather, who has brought up his grandson for much of his life, knows they may never meet again.

At thirteen years of age Simon Pearce walked up the gangplank of the Scilly packet into his new life. He waved to Dorothy, his stepbrothers and friends. John waved from the familiar old stone quay as the ship was towed from her moorings into St Mary's Pool. A brisk sou'westerly filled her sails, powering her through St Mary's Sound and towards the mainland.

George Hicks, Simon's unhelpful uncle, was the packet skipper that day; he had few kind words for his nephew. "I 'spose 'e don't have much chance 'cause o' what happened, but 'e'll end up like yer dad, at the end o' a rope, if it's the pirate's trade 'e chooses."

Simon ignored his uncle's jibing; he just watched the islands that had been his home slip into the packet's wake. Two days later he was at his mother's home on the Roseland.

Jane Pearce had remarried just two years after the execution of her Scillonian husband. It had been a simple, if orchestrated, twist of fate; Daniel Farmiloe had introduced Jane to his second cousin Michael, without thought of a possible union, at the family Christmas gathering the year before.

Esmeralda Farmiloe, Michael's first wife, had always thought herself a station above the other Farmiloes, being distantly related to a Lord Somebody-or-other. But as she was plain and penniless her father had accepted Michael Farmiloe's proposal gladly, as the best prospect his daughter could hope for – Michael at least owned a small farm on the Roseland. As number three female of an irritatingly large brood of girls, Esmeralda brought no dowry to her husband, who had expected none.

After a brief, formal courtship the couple was wed. A respectable twelve-month passed before the sickly girl was delivered of a son. After a protracted birthing, the attending midwife suggested that further children would be a considerable risk to the mother's life, a prognosis which proved to be correct, as poor Esmeralda died giving birth to a daughter two years later.

The wedding of Michael and Jane was sanctified in St Just-in-the-Roseland Church, beneath the beautifully carved medieval ceiling. Officiating at the ceremony, Daniel could hardly believe his clever wife had not planned the whole thing! Perhaps indeed she had, was his final thought as he took the couple's vows. This ready-made family of three boys and a girl was an admirable solution for two single-parent families of his parish.

With Michael Farmiloe now his stepfather and head of the family, Simon spoke to him directly as to his prospects. "I'm right pleased 'e 'n my mother 'ave wed, sir. 'Tis nought bar the best o' health 'n happiness I wish fer 'e both. I want to do me best fer the family 'n show me brothers and sister us Pearces can do well. With Captain Blackmore, I reckon, be the best chance I'll get, sir."

"Yes, lad, I agree, if it's a life at sea 'e wants; howsomever there be many a danger in your proposed career, more 'an the navy. I could use your help on th' farm, 'e knows that, and 'e would 'ave prospects of owning part o' the farm after my time." Simon's stepfather looked to his wife for support.

Jane had lost her pallor and apathy and regained some of her natural love of life which had so attracted Simon's father. The healthy, rosy complexion for which she had previously been famous had returned, much due to the loving care provided by Margaret Farmiloe, along with kindnesses the folk of the Roseland had bestowed upon her. The greatest leap forward in her recovery, however, had been made since Michael had suggested they weld their two families in wedlock; what had begun as a practical way to care for the children was turning into a deep, growing respect for each other, the type of respect that is the breeding ground of a true and enduring love.

"Son, I know 'e sees this as a great romantic opportunity fer 'e, but 'e must know I could not bear to lose 'e. Seafaring 'as taken too many o' us's kin. Yer father promised me he'd not a sailor be; look what happened to 'im. As if the cruel sea in itself weren't enough o' a danger. Captain Blackmore's trade be more or less piracy, albeit a piracy condoned 'n encouraged be the King. It is a warrior's trade you will be in. Live by the sword, 'n ye'll die by the sword – it's a saying that you should heed afore 'e starts this adventure. I beg 'e think hard on it, son. I won't forbid ye in this, as I could 'cause o' yer tender age, but should ye not return I shall be inconsolable," said Jane, using the age-old mother's tool – emotional blackmail – to try to change her son's mind.

Simon Pearce looked at his mother with contempt. In the week he had been at the Roseland farm he had tried to get to know her again. She had been distant, not unwelcoming but distant, as if her new family brought her enough promise of happiness leaving no room for him. It was as if he had brought the demons of the past back into her new home. His youth was not prepared for the turmoil he now felt. His little sister and half-siblings were in awe of his prospects, as were the men of the Roseland he spoke with. They well remembered, when they were young, their dreams that were never to be realised because of family ties.

One John Trefarthan, the oyster fisherman who had ferried the family to and fro over the River Fal during his father's imprisonment, was most emphatic. "Go for it, me 'ansome. Cornwall be one o' the finest places in the world, but the world is growin'. Get 'e out there any way 'e can; make a place fer 'eself."

Simon could not understand why his own family wanted him to be a subsistence farmer for the rest of his life. Better a risk and a chance of advancement, than guaranteed subservience. *I can do more for them by going to sea than staying here,* he declared to himself, his resolve now firm.

"Mother, Stepfather," implored Simon. "I tell 'e Captain Blackmore be entering a different business than before. When the ship leaves the repair yard her's loading with goods for the settlements in Virginia. I 'ope t' find me Cousin Peter there – 'is ten year will be up b' then. If all be well us'll be back next spring with cotton and tobacco. I knows the farm needs 'ands, but 'e have three more sons a-growing to fill that place. If I takes the farm, it'll be they what'll have t' leave home. It'll be them'll 'ave t' find a way in the world, like as not with a lot less prospects than wot I have now. Please, let I go wi' yer blessings."

The couple were stunned with such considered eloquence from the thirteen-year-old.

"Let yer mother 'n me talk some on it, lad. Ye 'ave a mighty persuasive way with words, I tell 'e." With this Michael motioned Simon to leave them to ponder more.

* * *

So it was that Simon Pearce left the Roseland as many a Cornishman had before him, to seek his fortune on the sea and in other lands. Michael had taken Simon to Falmouth and fitted him out at a seaman's store; his outfit included a tricorne hat, though it was not nearly as grand as the one his captain wore. He sat on the top of the post coach in his new finery. He had four days to ponder his exciting new future as they rumbled towards the 'river city' of Bristol, at that time Britain's largest seaport after London.

The stagecoach clattered its way through Redcliffe, an outer suburb of the city of Bristol. It approached the ancient bridge over the River Avon with its five-storeyed terraced timber-built buildings hanging perilously over the water by at least a yard. These were houses of wealthy merchants whose businesses operated out of the lower levels, their living rooms on the levels above. These worthies had a major advantage over their fellow citizens – they had no need of the council's night cart services or the public privy! Their 'water closets' were situated in that part of the house that overhung the Avon – all garbage, including human excrement, was simply dropped straight into the river.

The tidal range at the bridge was a convenient 30 feet. When on the ebb, the mass of human detritus was conveniently washed out into the River Severn, some eight miles away, roughly north-westward. Naturally, on the flood tide, the seething morass that had made its way as far as the Severn was washed at a rate of knots upriver, north towards Gloucester. On the ebb, much returned seaward; the muck which had not made it to the great waterway was simply washed back up the Avon to be deposited on the glutinous mudbanks of the upper river, producing a powerful stench for which the seaport was famous.

The city centre, Queen Square, was situated at the confluence of the Avon and the River Frome. The stench, particularly at low tide, was overpowering to all but native Bristolians. It was said the merchants of Bristol would arrange to meet unknowing clients at the square during the ebb, just as the mudbanks of the two rivers were freshly exposed. The clients, kerchiefs firmly pressed to their noses, would often conclude their business in an imprudently speedy manner, much to the advantage and amusement of the locals. 'The foreigners' would then be seen rushing up Hill Street, climbing briskly up Brandon Hill to reach the elite suburb of Clifton. Here, the malaise of the town below would be cleared by the slightest breeze, and they could breath freely again.

Simon, relieved at being off the bucking stagecoach, was directed from the coaching inn on the High Street, along Small Street to the old stone bridge near Key Heads. There lay his love, tugging strongly at her mooring warps in the fast-flowing tide; the *Maid of Aran* was moored on the outside of a motley group of vessels. She was hardly the picture of serenity etched into his mind at St Mary's Pool. The tide was on the ebb; it seemed the infamous Bristol mud had got everywhere. He stepped gingerly over the shoremost ship, a virtual derelict that had not seen salt water for years, over three others that improved in condition as he neared the *Maid*.

Calling to the deck, he identified himself to the ship's bosun, a Welshman named Bryn Thomas, whom he recognised from Scilly; Bryn returned his hail. The lad was welcomed aboard in a voice that sounded like singing. "Welcome, young fellow. I'll show you where to stow your gear, then come on deck and we shall get you to work ..." adding with a chuckle, "... the captain's away till morn, I suspect."

Bryn Thomas roused him at first light. "Look lively, lad. Captain wants to see you in half an hour."

At the appointed time Simon entered the captain's cabin, which was laid out in a most comfortable manner and many times the size of his own.

"I want first to let you know what your position of apprentice on board this ship means, Simon," opened Richard, now looking his 50 years after a night of frolic with an absent army officer's wife. "As you are in training to be a ship's officer, you will be addressed as mister by all hands, including officers, the same courtesy accorded to a midshipman in the navy. This does not in any way give you any authority whatsoever over any of the ship's crew - even Michael Douglas, our ship's boy, with two years at sea under his belt, has much to teach you.

"You will look to Mister Thomas for instruction as to your duties and then any other seaman he may delegate this responsibility to. Ye must see, Simon, it is your place to learn everything about the ship, sailing her, maintaining her in good condition, loading, stowing cargoes and yes, fighting for her if need be. I suspect that you're a bright boy; if ye are and ye work till ye drop each day, ye may become a captain yerself in ten to twelve years or so - double your present age! Are ye up for it?" asked the captain.

"Aye, sir, I am. I've dreamt of a chance t' go t' sea since me father's death. There's nay prospects fishing and runnin' gigs out o' Scilly! I'll do my best t' make 'e proud o' I, sir," answered Simon.

"Another point, lad. No disrespect to your background, but as a modern ship's captain you will be entertained by society and need to deal with tiresome government officials, not to mention gaining the respect of your crew – all of which will be easier if you speak with a more neutral accent. Listen to me and the ship's officers, and gradually learn to speak as they do. Do I make myself clear?"

"Aye, sir. I think so, sir," answered Simon, somewhat puzzled.

Richard looked sternly at his new apprentice. "This ship is run on similar lines to the Royal Navy, the main exception being that we do not flog or hang miscreants. They can earn many times the wages of their counterparts in that glorious service, so we simply fine them. Loss of earnings is a far more efficient, humane and less messy deterrent. The men, as you will be required to do, sign documents to this effect. There will be no favouritism on this ship. From this moment, only at family gatherings, or when invited to in private, will you acknowledge or allude to the fact that we are related. You will address me as either sir or captain, all other officers as sir, or their rank, or mister and then their surname. You will find the crew will defer to you initially, because they all know of our relationship. You will, however, need to prove yourself to them by your actions, to become fully accepted. When the time comes and you are in command of men's lives, you will find that the officer whose men respect him will achieve a hundredfold more from them than the officer whose only hold over his men is rank and fear. This type will often be driven off their ships by the very men they are purported to command. Actions do truly speak far louder than words, Simon – mark my words.

"Today I have a treat for you – your first lesson, not in seamanship, but in commerce, another skill a freelance captain must master. I am in search of weapons as trade goods, and a wily vendor as any we are soon to meet."

After a hasty meal Simon accompanied his captain ashore. They both coughed and spluttered as the disgusting odours rising from the Frome invaded their throats and nostrils.

"Only the indigenous of Bristol ever get used to it, lad," Richard said with a grimace.

They proceeded along Broad Street to near the old city wall. Here they turned into a large yard; they entered a decrepit looking building that was the establishment of one Josiah Epstein, the famous Jewish gunsmith. He was waiting in the grimy lobby to greet them.

"Welcome, captain. Welcome to my 'umble establishment. I have samples of each of the weapons we have available, primed and ready for you to trial, sir."

They were ushered into an enclosed courtyard at the rear of the building. There waiting, were two of the old Jew's sons standing by a table on which was laid out a dozen or so firearms. "Please allow me to introduce my sons – Abraham," he waved towards the larger of the two, "and Job," a surly looking fellow of fifteen. "Boys, this is Captain Blackmore and his nephew Simon."

The fact that the well-known captain had taken on board his relative was a matter of public knowledge to the merchants of the bustling seaport. It paid to know your clients as well as your enemies.

"Now the guns, captain. Please fire each one at your leisure. We shall be very interested in your opinions. As I said, each is primed and ready. Please, use the bottles on the shelves at the far end of the yard as targets." Josiah waved graciously towards the line of glass containers.

Richard first hefted a standard military musket, known universally to soldiers and sailors alike as the 'Brown Bess'; he raised the gun to his shoulder, aimed and fired. Simon heard a sharp click as the flint struck the pan, then an explosion that echoed round the courtyard, the enclosed space amplifying the sound many times. He felt pain in his ears, which he covered with his hand, a little too late.

"As usual, Master Epstein, a fine piece," said Richard as he saw, to his satisfaction, the first bottle disintegrate. "We could be interested in 20 cases of these should we be able to agree on favourable terms." Richard observed Epstein lean slightly towards him involuntarily as he anticipated the profits that were possible from this customer before him.

"I am most interested in pistols, Master Epstein. In the New World they are the most sought after. What have you here?" Richard exclaimed, eyeing the array before him.

Josiah Epstein drew in a deep breath. Lovingly picking up a beautifully finished cavalry pistol crafted in the French style, he let out a sigh. It was as if the weapons he produced were each a child of his loins, not the killing machines they in fact were. "This piece, captain, is becoming very popular among seafarers. It is smaller, lighter and has a smaller bore than you would be used to. It is thus possible to carry considerably more ammunition than the standard navy 14-inch barrel weapon we have to your left. Please, sir, test fire each one and see for yourself."

Richard hefted each pistol in turn and fired at the targets. With the larger pistol he was used to, he hit the target at 25 paces; with the smaller weapon he missed. "The French gun has much less recoil than I expected. Why is this?"

"Slightly smaller bore, less powder, but with the same range, equals less recoil. Job, please reload so the good captain can get her true feel. If you are looking for stopping power, try this, a .45-calibre Kentucky style with a rifled barrel, accurate and a real killer. As you are considering resale in the Americas I strongly suggest you take some of these. They were designed there and are very popular." Josiah handed the weapon to Richard to test fire.

An opposite reaction to the French gun, the recoil was massive, but Richard observed with satisfaction the large piece of brickwork the ball had dislodged from the wall behind the targets. "Puncture a foe's body anywhere with that .45-calibre ball of lead, and he will be no further threat to you," the master explained, almost gleefully – after all, he wanted his customers to win their fights and return to buy more.

Richard then took hold of the French-style gun for the second time. Carefully adjusting his aim to compensate for the reduced recoil, he fired.

"Excellent shot, sir," said Master Epstein as a green bottle shattered.

"What be 'em, sir?" asked Simon, indicating iron balls with necks, also a strange looking bottle made of exceptionally thick glass.

"Grenades, young sir," answered Epstein. "Devastating at close range. A slow match is inserted into the neck of the grenade with a tight-fitting plug after the body has been filled with black powder, prior to boarding an enemy ship. If several grenades are thrown onto a deck much damage can be wrought with little danger to one's own side."

"As long as the length of fuse does not give the enemy time to throw it back on one's own deck!" interjected Richard Blackmore.

"Indeed, captain, skill in setting up a grenade is essential. May I draw your attention to this, our newest innovation – the glass grenade? Where the conventional iron weapon will generally cause more damage to structure and be lethal at close range, its new glass counterpart will shatter into a thousand sharp shards, wounding many more people at a far greater distance from the blast than its brother of iron," said the gunsmith.

"I could be interested in the purchase of 200 of each, Master Epstein."

Simon watched and listened, intrigued, as his captain sparred with the gunsmith. Giving compliments, suggesting he was able to place a large order but not appearing too eager, giving no firm commitment. He had noticed the Jew had let his keenness for the deal show on a few occasions. He was unable to see that Josiah was biding his time for the right moment to close the deal. Being vastly experienced in the art of selling, the gunsmith knew that if he let his customer leave without giving him an order, his chances of success were reduced by half, as his customer would be free to look elsewhere. The wily trader, having timed his move, played a final ace he had up his sleeve.

"Your potential order is indeed large, captain. I have given you the best prices you will find in the land, which I am sure ye have checked before coming here. Should you confirm now, before you leave, I have a small gift for you and your protégé. For the boy, this!" Josiah produced a beautiful, small double-barrelled over and under pistol made in Italy. Simon's eyes opened wide with delight as he took the weapon in his hands. "It is not loaded, young sir. Please allow Abraham to show you how, and you may test fire at the far end of the range."

The boys went off leaving Josiah with Richard Blackmore's undivided attention.

"Captain, for you something of a work of art a man of your taste will surely recognise and appreciate." Josiah handed a polished mahogany box to Richard and watched with a mischievous glint in his eye as he opened the box.

Richard gasped when he saw the contents. The two pistols were undoubtedly the finest he had ever seen, each gun matched in its style and immaculate standard of finish. They were, however, totally different in bore and weight.

One resembled the French-style weapon he had tested earlier with a longer rifled barrel for better range and accuracy.

The second was a masterpiece of the gunsmith's art – a triple-barrelled gun designed for close-range combat. It had but one trigger and dog head, but each barrel had its own pan and frizzen, allowing each to be loaded, primed and ready to fire before a conflict started; it was, in effect, three guns in one. The user simply fired the first barrel, turned the nest of barrels to engage the trigger to the next primed and loaded barrel, and he was then ready to fire again in a mere second or two.

Richard knew he had been won over; he had to have the pistol set. He had, as the gunsmith had suggested, checked prices before this visit to Epstein and Sons and knew the deal he had been offered was indeed competitive. The gifts had made doing business with Epstein and Sons irresistible.

Simon was delighted when his captain shook the master gunsmith's hand, as he desired desperately to keep hold of the double-barrelled beauty he had just test fired.

"Please bring the consignment to the ship tomorrow, Master Epstein; we can conclude our business after each weapon has been inspected. If you have no objection, sir, your gifts we will take with us."

With effusive goodbyes from the three Epsteins, the pair headed back to the ship.

The next days were a mass of activity in preparation for the voyage. Loading trade goods, ship's stores, powder and shot, also fine rum, brandies and cloth for gowns for the ladies of Virginia. Livestock was boarded for fresh meat, along with bales of hay to feed them. Sacks of potatoes and vegetables, barrels of salted beef and pork, also ship's biscuits and flour, the seaman's staple diet, followed. It was with some regret that Simon waved goodbye to Bristol, having not had time to properly explore the old seaport town.

Chapter 9

So to sea

Just before the start of the ebb, the *Maid of Aran* was warped to the end of Key Head then towed the length of the Avon by two large clinker-built punts, each with six oars, into the open water of the River Severn. Wales could be seen clearly to the north, a woodsmoke haze over Cardiff being a most obvious indication. On her way down river she passed over a hundred moored ships of all types and condition, along with the thousands of seaman who manned them.

The huge tide, the second highest in the world, with spring tides reaching an incredible 42 feet, had turned. Richard Blackmore's timing was perfect. With a moderate easterly behind them and the Severn's spring-tide ebb under them, they should make over 65 miles before the flood tide began its inexorable return run, attempting to bear them back towards Bristol.

Mister Partridge, the *Maid*'s first officer, lowered his eyeglass. "Minehead is four miles ahead, and two clear to port, captain, just where it should be." Looking to Simon he added, "Once past the headland the channel triples in width, much reducing the speed of current against us. We've made a good offing!"

"Thank you, Mister Partridge, I believe the wind will stay offshore and in the east a while yet. Once Minehead is abeam, make our course two and a half points to port, west'sou'west. By staying inshore we can miss much of the opposing flood. Simon! To the foretop with you. Keep watch; hail the deck when you have a light in sight – it should be on the headland Mister Partridge pointed out, and fine on our port bow."

Kin the boy may be, but the captain had no favourites on his ship. Richard had seen the lad's face gradually turn white as the ship made her way towards the Atlantic Ocean swells. In sending him to the topmast, Richard had made a point to his crew.

The ship made good speed, doubling Land's End before the following day. Simon's birthplace - the Scilly Isles - was slipping slowly by on the starboard beam as they headed for the open sea.

It was his third watch aloft; at first it had been agony. That first night at the foretop he had just hailed the deck that Minehead light was in sight. The concentration of lookout was slackened for a moment. His stomach violently turned over; only just in time he removed his new hat as his dinner retraced its steps back up through his mouth. It pained him greatly to throw up into his beautiful hat, but anything was preferable to the shame of showering his captain and shipmates with puke. It was a baptism of fire, but tough methods soon found Simon his sea legs; his hat, however, took weeks to lose the smell of its erstwhile contents, no matter how often he washed it.

The next morning they were clear of the Bishop Rock and in the English Channel, heading south-west on course to pass the archipelago of the Acores, or the Azores, as the Portuguese islands were known in English. Richard wanted to make use of the fair but infrequent easterly to bear them on a course well clear of the infamous Bay of Biscay, where strong prevailing westerlies blew over force seven for half the time, at this time of year. A ship caught inshore in a westerly would have no option but to beat north, then south across the bay, praying for an angle on the wind that would allow her to clear either Ushant in the north, or the dreaded Cape Finisterre in the south, a distance of 360 miles. Should she not get clear, she would be inexorably driven onto the lee shore, the shallows of eastern Biscay, somewhere between Saint-Nazaire and Bayonne.

Richard explained to Simon, "The trick, lad, is to gain sea room. If a ship has sea room - that is, as much distance between her and the lee shore as possible (the shore the wind is blowing on to) - she has time. At sea, time is of the essence; sea room gives a master time to react to changing conditions. In time, all sea conditions change from a howling gale to a frustrating calm; everything changes, eventually - if you have time, you are in control.

"There is always an optimum time to be in any one place on the sea. While things change, they can remain more constant in a particular place, according to season. We have written logs of thousands of past voyages that help us learn these constants. The greatest boon to pilotage and navigation is knowledge of the ocean's winds and currents. All this you must know before your time comes to become a captain.

"We intend to head west across the Atlantic to Virginia, which lies at a latitude approximately 37 degrees north. On our ship, at noon today, we were a little south of 49 degrees north. Captains know, from tens of thousands of observations over hundreds of years, most of the wind patterns of the world's known oceans – and more importantly, that they blow in a circle. So I know that if I should head directly for Norfolk, arguably the shortest distance, I would be heading into a prevailing pattern of headwinds. If, on the other hand, we travel south, once past Finisterre the wind will back northerly, and at around 30 degrees south latitude the prevailing wind will be east to sou'east. The current will also be with us. Thus we sail more miles, but travel more quickly and comfortably. The shortest route is not necessarily the quickest!

"When we return to England, we simply head north from Virginia until we reach the westerlies, then head east, the prevailing wind and current both with us again. Remember, the closer we are to a coast, or an enclosed area of sea, the land affects the prevailing wind; this can be useful to the knowledgeable captain.

"Now we are at the most difficult part of any voyage – passing out of one prevailing wind pattern into the next. We have been most fortunate in this area of prevailing west and south-westerly winds to have made such a good offing, or departure from shore; the prevailing wind has been absent."

The captain looked into the west and frowned. "The setting sun is a great indicator of change. See how that sun turns the sky to the colour of brass as it makes its way to the horizon?"

"Yes, sir, I see the underside o' the clouds 'ave gone the colour o' purple, 'n the sky like shiny brass. It's the same at Scilly, sir! A brassy sunset be strong wind coming and backing t' the west," answered Simon proudly.

"Well said! And I fear you are right, lad. Methinks we'll snug her down for the night." Richard called out, "Bosun, get your men aloft. Furl topgallants and reef main topsail, if you please." As he spoke the wind backed towards north and piped up, the force five pressing the ship a little harder, but still on course.

The *Maid of Aran* was designed for speed so she would be the fastest in her trade; she could run down any freighter and outrun many a frigate. In the current conditions, with force five wind over her starboard quarter, she was off like a greyhound. The reduced sail area had allowed her to stand more upright as her stern lifted to the rising northerly swell, a bone of white foam roared at her bow. Simon was entranced and exhilarated as the ship flew southwards.

"Enjoy now, lad. This is as good as it gets! By tomorrow we'll be up agin it. Get ye some sleep while you can. Mister Partridge, take the watch, if you please. Keep her more to the west while we can, course west'south'west. Those off watch get some hot food, then to your hammocks." The captain departed to his great stern cabin under the quarterdeck.

With some regrets Simon left the excitement of the deck as the ship charged south-westwards through the Atlantic. He received his dinner from the cook and then made his way to the small cupboard of a cabin situated aft under the captain's quarters. It was made for two to share, but for now it was his alone. He quickly closed the small scuttle that opened out of the transom, the only source of air into the six-by-four-foot space he occupied. He moved to the lower bunk, reversing an earlier choice made when the ship was not moving so violently. *I'm glad I don't have to share the cabin this trip,* he thought.

Simon was, of course, by the standards of the ordinary seaman, in luxury. While less cramped than the navy issue of six feet by nineteen inches within which to swing their hammocks, these 'free sailors' – all forty four of them – still had to bunk together on the gun deck, swinging their hammocks over the lethal cannon. The senior ratings had the luxury of privacy in the fo'c'sle in the bows of the ship, but here the motion was at its worst. The officers – Mister Partridge, Lieutenant Thomas the second officer, and David Trevellen the third – each had a small cabin. The other apprentices – Smith and Langton – shared a cabin similar to Simon's. Captain Blackmore was well known to look after his crew; he knew very well that to attract the best men, he had to offer the best conditions as well as pay.

Morning brought a purple tinge to the sunrise; Captain Blackmore eyed the malevolent scene with some trepidation. "Long foretold, long last, eh, Mister Partridge."

"Indeed, sir. This one's going to stir us up some. The wind is a point further to the west and a steady force six. I have our dead-reckoning position at 48.20 north and 6.30 west – about the latitude of Ushant, sir," said the first officer.

"Thank you, Mister Partridge. We need another hundred miles of westing to safely clear Finisterre when the gale comes. The wind will continue to back, if I'm not mistaken, putting us at some risk. Harden up, furl the foretops'ls, and point as hard to windward as she will go."

The captain's orders were quickly carried out. The *Maid of Aran*, her head now put to wind, buried her lee rail taking the building seas hard on her starboard fore quarter, as she clawed for the open Atlantic. The noise level increased dramatically from earlier, when the wind was from astern, her forward velocity now added to the wind speed. She shuddered, her timbers shivering as each Atlantic roller crashed into her, showering her decks with salt spray from stem to stern. Simon was called down from the foretop and sent to a platform just above the forecourse yard and told to lash himself down. Richard was not one to take the unnecessary risk of a close encounter with another ship. He would obey that fundamental law of good seamanship: keep a good watch, as long as you can.

The ship was a magnificent sight from Simon's position 30 feet above the heaving deck – rising to a crest, smashing through its foaming top, before dropping into the following trough in a stomach-twisting dive, the performance repeated with the next wave a few seconds later – the never-ending dance of a ship at sea, swirling to the tune of the wind.

Exhilaration banished all thoughts of seasickness. Simon was feeling that old salt's feeling of a deepening love affair with his ship. He now knew why his grandfather had mentioned something that had seemed strange at the time as he said his goodbyes on St Mary's old stone quay. 'I 'ope 'e gets a gale early on, Simon, me handsome. It'll give 'e faith in yer ship 'n crew, as she sees 'e through.'

The wind continued to rise, and worse – in line with Richard's predictions – backed westward, forcing them towards the coast. They were making good ground but not in the right direction.

The captain passed an order to his second officer. "Get that boy down, Mister Thomas; no point in risking him after dark, and it's going to be a long night. Furl the forecourse, and set the storm staysails, if you please."

"Aye, sir."

Simon joined five men on the forecourse yard. He was the furthest away from the mast on the leeward side with nothing but the yard's footrope between him and the heaving ocean beneath. "One hand fer yerself an' one fer the ship," yelled ordinary seaman Bert Smith on the yard beside him.

As the sheets were eased, the men on deck hauled on buntlines, lines that collapsed the wildly flapping sail. The crew aloft, with superhuman effort, gathered in the heavy, sodden canvas, lashing it to the yard with gasket lines. Twenty minutes of extreme effort and danger later, five men and a thirteen-year-old boy returned to the relative safety of the heaving deck. The staysail became a demonic, uncontrollable force before it was sheeted in, using only the muscle power of the deck crew, aided by block and tackle.

It began to rain; freezing drops of water flew at them like bird shot from a discharged shotgun, stinging bare flesh and further reducing the air temperature. Seamen from the main mast, who had been performing the same tasks as Simon's team but on the larger spar, also returned, exhausted, from aloft. The rest of the deck crew were busy trimming the newly set sails to their captain's satisfaction.

The crew's efforts were instantly rewarded; the helmsman reported that the ship was now handling as well as could be expected. He could now point her higher into the wind, further away from the deadly distant coastline. With smaller sails set, the *Maid* had slowed slightly but stood more upright.

"What do you think, Mister Partridge – is she snug enough?" Captain Blackmore asked of his first officer.

"Aye, sir, she's settled well enough for this, but as you said, there'll be more to come," Partridge replied.

"Keep her as she is for now – we need as much speed as we dare.

Call me before dark. We'll reduce sail again then if we have to," yelled Richard over the building gale.

The entire on-watch crew were soaked to the skin, their oiled canvas greatcoats no match for the biting wind, spray and rain, their bare feet blue with cold. Cook Billy Davidson had tried valiantly to produce hot food from the open fireplace in his galley, protected only by timber framework and a canvas awning on the forward end of the main deck. He was only able to offer lukewarm stew and ship's biscuits to the freezing, complaining men as they came off watch.

Cook was the toughest job aboard; with just the boy Michael Douglas to assist him, he was required to produce three meals a day for close to 50 men. Only the off-duty watch – half the ship's company – were available to eat at any one time, the cook had to be on duty from early morning till the first dog watch began at eight pm. The only benefit he had over the seamen was that he was able to get a full night's sleep – he was the only crew member, apart from the captain, not required to keep a night watch.

The off-watch members of the ship's company settled down below in their hammocks and tried to sleep. The constant noise of the ship beating into the gale, combined with the *Maid*'s violent motion, made this very difficult. Some dropped off from pure exhaustion. The older hands, thinking of all that could go wrong on a night like this, dozed fitfully, as the four hours before their next watch in the cold, black night ticked inexorably by.

Two and a half hours after the port watch had turned in came the dreaded call, "All hands on deck," from the first officer. He had raised the alarm as the wind had increased to force nine – a strong gale – and backed further. The ship was now travelling fast toward the southern arm of the Bay of Biscay, 50 degrees off their intended course.

Richard Blackmore came on deck taking command. "Bosun! Get your men aloft and double-gasket all square sails. We shall lay to on the starboard tack, Mister Partridge. Let's try to point up, hold our position and limit our drift to leeward."

The violent night wore on. At eight bells, starboard watch was the on-deck watch; Simon was part of the port watch. He struggled to shake off the tentacles in which his deep, exhausted sleep held him.

Surely it wasn't time to get up already? he thought. The lad dressed as best he could in the darkness, on the steeply heeling, pitching cabin sole. He was glad now that his cabin was so small, its confining walls preventing the violent motion from throwing his battered and bruised body too far.

A bleak dawn rose just as four bells were rung, indicating the port watch was halfway through. Just two hours and Simon could tuck himself once again into the imagined safety of his bunk, blotting out the horror of the freezing, wet, shrieking world on deck. A loud crack sounded, like a pistol shot – the clew of the main storm staysail had torn out. The heavy triangular sail simply disintegrated thread by thread as the sail, released from its tether and goaded by the wind, vibrated at hundreds of oscillations a minute, disintegrating before their eyes.

Maid was now unbalanced. With too much sail forward, she fell off the wind and gathered way towards Biscay. A new staysail was brought to replace the shattered one; it took twelve strong men on the halyard to haul it into place, and another ten to sheet it in. Tired men, working without thought, other than that their turn off-watch would surely be soon.

"Mister Partridge, to my cabin if you please," shouted Richard over the din. "What do you think our position is?" he asked.

"My calculations put us mid-Biscay but well enough to seaward for now, sir. We should hove to on port tack and head slowly north-westward, more or less back from where we 'ave come. We must be making a knot or two leeway in this sea, so we are slowly being pushed into Biscay. The southern tack would be worse as Finisterre projects further west than the parallel of Ushant. No way we would weather that cape from here," summed up the first officer.

"Yes, Mister Partridge, I agree. We are safe enough for a while yet, as long as we do not sustain any serious damage. Should we lose a mast or spring a leak, God forbid, we would be blown helter-skelter to the shores of France," Richard pointed out with a degree of impatience. "We need a wind shift, damn it! Even with a sou'wester we can sail nor'west and weather the Scillies – albeit the wrong direction for our present endeavour. This infernal west wind has us like a rat in the mouth of a trap, the door about to spring shut!" The captain made his decision. "Put her about to maintain just enough speed so we can steer. If the wind is still west this time tomorrow, we will run back up the channel for the shelter of Dover while we still can and start out again with a wind fair."

"I agree, sir. I'll take the watch till noon, when perhaps we will get a sun sight. It would be best if we both took an independent sight, for accuracy, don't you think, captain?" added Mister Partridge as he left the stuffy cabin.

Noon had come and gone without a sight of the sun, which could have confirmed their position. The starboard watch was about to come on deck as evening turned to night. Port watch was taking what shelter it could, with little to do but relieve the helmsman. The men just got wetter and colder.

Simon put his head up to take a last look over the weather rail before he went below. Walls of water were racing towards them in a wild act of self-destruction, but the sky had lightened. Behind the ship a dark line appeared and seemed to be coming towards them. Simon called his captain's attention to the now distinct line astern.

"It's a front, Simon; as it passes the wind will increase, then, if it pleases God, we'll get our wind shift, and about bloody time too," Richard answered and smiled a worn, tired smile.

The front passed over, and the wind shrieked again, but this time from a more favourable direction. They set main topgallant and foretopsail; the ship was taking a real hammering now. Great combers that had been building up from the west, across the Atlantic, for the last three days were now being harassed by a gale from the opposite direction, standing on end, like horses galloping in one direction being suddenly reined in and turned to another.

The captain did not set full sail until late the next morning, when the wind and sea had lost their vicious edge. "Set a course for Madeira, Mister Partridge. A little of that island's famous wine will be a great addition to our stock-in-trade. Not to mention the recuperation a stay there will afford our men. We will check the rig for chafe and repair as necessary before the Atlantic crossing."

"I had presumed, sir, that you would at least wish to sight the island as a navigational check; the course is sou'sou'west, sir."

"Excellent, Mister Partridge. Four days sail in this wind, I suspect, Simon."

"Aye aye, cap'n."

"You will begin navigation lessons with Mister Partridge today. Heed him well; he is one of the best."

Richard Blackmore, satisfied, left George Partridge to manage the ship.

Chapter 10
Madeira

It was, in fact, five days later when the *Maid of Aran* anchored in the roadstead off Puerto Funchal, the capital of the Portuguese island of Madeira.

Simon woke early the following day, the ship's motion having taken on the gentle roll associated with open roadstead anchorages in the lee of islands or promontories. What caught his attention, once the effects of his deep sleep had faded and his normal senses were restored, was the sweet aroma brought to the ship by the gentle offshore wind. The sweet, somewhat sickly smell was associated with sugar cane which, along with the famous fortified wine known by the island's name, was among the reasons the island had prospered. More sinister was that Madeira was a centre for the Portuguese slave trade.

Eight bells sounded. Simon quickly dressed and made his way to his station on deck.

Dressed in his finest uniform, the captain was giving orders to his officers; he was mostly concerned that they prepare a list of the damage that would need repair before they set off across the Atlantic. Mister Thomas the bosun was organising the ship's jollyboat to be swung over the side. The *Maid* was abustle with activity. Simon was ordered below to change into his number one uniform.

"You will accompany me to the governor's office where we shall present our papers and ask to be officially entered as visitors to Portugal," said Richard Blackmore.

Later, Simon and his captain were walking briskly along a stone jetty not unlike the one on St Mary's he knew so well. They walked the short distance along the Avenida Maritima towards an impressive, white-plastered building with an orange terracotta tiled roof. They entered a spacious, lofty hallway with a desk at its far end.

A young officer stood smartly to attention and spoke in English with a heavy accent. "Senhor Capitão, plees 'xcuse. I will inform 'Is Excellency the Governor of your arrival." He returned immediately and ushered them into an imposing room, painted white with an intricately plastered ceiling.

The subaltern closed the door after them, as a dark, red-faced, heavily jowled man in his fifties rose to greet them. "I am Diego Gonçalves Mendoza at your service, Capitain Blackmore. You, your crew and your ship ees welcome in Puerto Funchal. Plees join me in a small glass of our island's fine produce, then tell me 'ow may we be of assistance?"

"Thank you, Your Excellency. It is an honour that you receive us in person. After a stormy run here, a glass of the famous Madeira wine would be most welcome." The captain bowed deeply. "Please allow me to present Simon Pearce, a young relative on his first voyage."

Simon answered the governor's short, stiff bow with a deep one of his own, following Richard's example.

Once the wine glasses were drained, Richard presented his papers, including his Letter of Marque. Seeing this, the governor lifted his eye from the page and looked at Richard with renewed interest. The Letter of Marque was his licence from the British Crown to attack and plunder its enemies. Spain was at the top of that list, while Portugal was a long-time ally.

Portugal and Spain are neighbours, co-occupiers of the Iberian peninsula; there was, however, little love lost between the two countries. Portugal and England, on the other hand, had enjoyed a long history of alliance going back several hundred years. A hundred years ago the alliance was strengthened when, in 1662, Charles II of England married the Portuguese Duchess Catherine of Braganza. Catherine brought Charles a huge dowry, part of which was the Indian city of Bombay, giving England her first legitimate foothold on the subcontinent. Soon after the wedding, the Spanish were forced by a Portugal backed with Britain's sea power to accept Portugal's independence, after over 80 years of Spanish rule and domination.

The governor handed Richard back his papers adding, "I trust your voyaging will be successful. I hear the rewards from your, um, occupation are harder to come by these days, Captain Blackmore?"

"Indeed, sir, they are; we are ever looking for new opportunities. As you see from our manifest we are more interested in trade with the American colonists than our previous exploits. Business for the privateer has been diminishing steadily since its peak in the '30s. The Spanish are sailing in convoy with powerfully armed escorts. I shall be investigating opportunities for the future while in the Caribbees. We intend to purchase a good supply of your excellent Madeira wine to augment our stock for trade. I trust that is acceptable, Your Excellency?"

"Yes, of course. We live in a changing world, do we not?" replied the governor. "Perhaps you would care to join me for dinner? You will meet some of the island's more prominent people from whom you can make your purchases. Possibly we can also discuss some information that has just come to our attention, which may be of interest to you. It is, as you know, our custom to eat late in Portugal. Shall we say nine?"

Richard was effusive in his acceptance.

"Excellent! I will have my coachman meet you at the wharf. As for the young man, if you can spare him for the day I will have my son Juan show him our humble island. Perhaps also he would be keen to learn of our country's seagoing feats?"

Simon looked eagerly at his captain.

"Most educational for the lad, Excellency; he is due some shore leave."

"Good! It is settled." The governor instructed the young officer to take Simon and introduce him to Juan Mendoza.

A few hours later, two boys lay on a clifftop some ten miles west of Funchal, having ridden there quickly on two magnificent ponies. Waves crashed into the rocks a dizzying 2,000 feet below them.

"So, fisherman, I show you the 'ighest sea cliff in the world! What do you think of that!" Juan Mendoza continued the disparaging manner he had displayed since the first moment they had been introduced.

It had been easy for the educated and confident Juan to dig quickly into Simon's origins, his accent still broad, though he was trying hard to shed it. In the typical manner of educated, adolescent offspring of government officials, the thirteen-year-old took delight in his companion's discomfort. "You Engleesh, you t'ink you own the world and are the greatest seafarers, no! But it is Portugal that 'as opened the

93

trade routes to Brazil, Africa, Ceylon, India and the Spice Islands of the East Indies. You people merely followed in our wake. It was that lousy Spaniard Columbus who discover the Caribbean and Americas your England so proudly call its own!

"We Portuguese 'ave inhabited these islands since João Zarco discovered them in 1418, over 300 years ago! The great Prince 'Enry, known as the navigator even though 'e seldom went to sea 'imself, immediately colonised zis place. Now Madeira makes a variety of wine zat is unique in the world. We also control a large part of the slave trade, a most lucrative business. Negro slaves 'ave been taken from Africa and sold for great profit for years – it is their labour that produces much of Portugal's wealth," explained Juan.

"'Enry sent expeditions to all corners of the world. Thanks to 'im a new ship was designed for ocean travel. The caravel is much more 'andier than the square-sailed buckets you Engleesh sail. Its triangular lateen sails can sail three points 'igher to the wind than your square rig."

Simon thought how great an advantage 37 degrees higher pointing ability would have been as they were being pushed towards Biscay in the recent storm. He had seen caravels in Funchal harbour, and he decided he must find out their secrets. "Can you get me aboard a caravel, Juan? They sound superb."

"Suppose I could," said Juan, adding, "Bartolomeu Dias, Vasco da Gama and other of the greatest names in seafaring will never be forgotten. It is thanks to these men and 'undreds like them that we Portuguese 'ave the empire we 'ave now. From Brazil we have gold, silver and diamonds. From India tea, a most valuable commodity, most sought after in your northern island. You were our best market for the stuff before Catherine bought your King Charles with her dowry and opened the door to India for you. From the Moluccas come the spices that make our food so tasty." The young Portuguese was rightly proud of his tiny country's achievements; Simon was in awe of Juan's knowledge and understanding of worldly matters.

"As ye 'ave said, my background 'n knowledge be most ordinary," said Simon candidly. "I didn't even know that Portugal had a trading empire before England even started! Us 'ave two things in common:

our countries are both small compared with their achievements and we 'ave been allies for hundreds o' years. Cap'n Blackmore 'as said I'll be his heir if I do well in my learning of the sea and the world. I shall be ever in your debt, Juan, if ye can instruct me more." Simon was trying to follow Richard Blackmore's instruction to lose his thick accent.

His guest's forthright plea struck a chord in the proud and pompous young Mendoza. He was ambitious and wished to impress the apprentice seaman. His father had taught him one of the most important factors in getting ahead in life was to have as many contacts as possible, people who would remember and admire you. If they are in your debt, all the better. He had a feeling this ship's apprentice was worth cultivating.

"If only I could take you to our Lisboa! She is the finest city in Europe; there I could really show you things. No matter, we will do what we can. I will see you each afternoon you are 'ere, after we each 'ave performed our daily duties. Will that suit you?"

"Oh, Juan. Thank you. I shall request a change of duties and start at four am, the second watch which no one likes. I'm sure Captain Blackmore will approve," answered Simon with delight.

That night, after a sumptuous dinner at the governor's mansion, the ladies left the room. Diego Mendoza poured Madeira into small crystal glasses. "One 'undred years old, captain. Thankfully my predecessors had the foresight to build large cellars into this 'ouse. It has been a tradition ever since to set down the best of each vintage for the pleasure of successive governors, each replacing that which he consumes. An equal number of bottles is gifted to our most saintly monarch." Mendoza put the crystal containing the precious maroon liquid contents to his nose. "I believe this could be the best yet."

Mendoza addressed the glittering company. "I trust you will all excuse us. I wish to speak with Captain Blackmore on a matter of business, which I am sure would bore the rest of my guests. Captain, if you please." The governor ushered Richard into an anteroom off the main salon.

"Your exploits in the field of seafaring and sea battles go before you, sir. You 'ave long been an ally of my country; your business 'as been much to the detriment of our respective countries' common adversaries

– Spain and France. I note that you have taken a sensible decision – now these countries protect their shipments from the Americas. It is dangerous to attack ships with armed escorts, is it not?" The governor looked knowingly at Richard. "I wonder if the circumstances were suitable, and of course the rewards adequate, that you might consider another foray into your old business?" asked Diego Mendoza, in a conspiratorial manner.

"Indeed, Your Excellency, a freelance shipowner is always on the lookout for ways to earn a profit from his investment, as is any investor. Do you have something specific in mind?" asked Richard, his heightening sense of interest well hidden from his host.

"What I 'ave to say," began the governor gravely, "is a matter of the utmost secrecy for our country. I must ask for your word as an officer and a gentleman that nothing said in this room will you ever repeat, should you decide not to become involved with the, ah, project."

"You have my word, Excellency," answered Richard, further intrigued.

Diego Mendoza offered Richard a fine handmade Cuban cigar, which he politely refused. Lighting his own, he puffed great clouds of aromatic smoke, which slowly billowed from his nose and mouth. Leaning back in his luxurious leather wing-backed chair, he took his time, sensing his guest's growing sense of anticipation. "You know well that our neighbours, Espanha, 'ave reduced the Inca and Aztec nations to slavery, removing tons and tons of gold and silver from Central and South America in the process. It is a commonly 'eld belief that the source of these streams of riches 'as all but dried up. Apart from mining relatively small amounts, there is simply little gold available for plunder."

"Indeed, that is in line with my understanding; it is why my endeavours have, out of necessity, changed focus," agreed Richard.

"What would you say if I could prove to you that Espanha 'as discovered a new source of plunder and that they are planning to transport a large amount of treasure across the Atlantic this coming season?" said the governor, trying to sound casual.

"I must say you have my interest, Your Excellency. You say you have proof? With the greatest respect, it will take something very special to change my present plans, if that is what you have in mind," said Richard, suspicious of the governor's motives in telling him this fantastic story.

"For many years it has been rumoured in Brazil of a civilisation that supposedly lives 'igh in the Andes Mountains. They worship their gods in temples of gold. Several Portuguese expeditions 'ave set out from Brazil, up the Rio Amazonas to the foothills of the Andes in search of these people. Many did not return; those who did suffered hugely. No treasures were found. You will 'ave 'eard, I'm sure, of the Espanhol settlement of Maracaibo?" asked the governor. "It lies about 600 miles west of Grenada, on the South American mainland."

"I have heard of it, sir, but know nothing in detail," replied Richard.

Diego Mendoza inhaled deeply from his cigar, slowly exhaled a cloud of smoke then continued. "Let us understand a simple geographical fact. Maracaibo is approximately 11 degrees north latitude, yes? The Rio Amazonas roughly follows the equator, yes? The Rio Amazonas as explored so far is approximately 1,200 miles from 'er mouth, westward. Were we able to fly as a bird due north from the end of the river we would end up at Maracaibo, a distance of approximately six 'undred miles, not far on the sea but a very difficult journey through jungle-clad mountains, yes?

"We believe the Espanhóis 'ave found the golden temples! They 'ave sailed south, through the Bay of Maracaibo, passing through a narrow strait into a 'uge lake. This lake has taken them close to the temples, which we understand are very 'igh on a mountain ridge. Below this ridge is a valley that runs to the lake, a simple march from their ships. It is easy to see 'ow the river people of Brazil 'eard of these rumours – the temples are due north of the source of Rio Amazonas, an area hunted by Brazilian Indians!" Diego Mendoza puffed some more as the man before him absorbed his story.

"A delightful story, Excellency," Richard said, with as much conviction as he could muster. "I congratulate you on your understanding of geography and latitude and longitude; indeed, the picture you have so eloquently painted has an air of probability. Yet, Excellency, you said proof. And how am I to fit into the equation? Surely this is an affair for your government, not a private agent of a foreign power?"

"You Engleesh, so impatient, no?" The governor chuckled at his own small joke and continued. "I shall answer your last question first, captain. My country and Espanha are enjoying a period of cautious peace. Even should we make the near impossible journey to the temples through Brazil and take treasure, we would be declaring war. The same outcome would occur if we attack the treasure fleet on its journey home. So, you ask what it is we want? While it would be very nice to 'ave an unexpected treasure trove in our possession, the possibility of achieving this goal without war is unrealistic. Can you see our allies, England, supporting us in such a war? No, we know they will not, why should they? We do not expect to 'ave the treasure for ourselves, but we do not wish our cousins, the Espanhóis, to 'ave it either. Backed with this equity, they would almost certainly attempt to recolonise Portugal and take control of our overseas possessions. A most delicate situation, no? But if a group of enterprising but in no way aligned seafarers were to 'ear of the fleet and shall we say 'assume possession' of the cargo …?"

"Spain could not point the finger at Portugal," interjected Richard.

"Sim, sim, most adroit of you, captain," said the smiling governor.

"That just leaves the proof, Excellency," said Richard, his interest now fully aroused.

"Ha, yes, of course, el proof!" said Diego Mendoza, enjoying himself. He reached forward and inserted a key into a lock on the bottom drawer of his elegant desk and withdrew a folded piece of paper. "I see in your eyes, captain, you are thinking, ''e is not showing to me a treasure map, no?' "

"Well, er, yes, that thought did cross my mind," returned Richard trying not to sound flippant.

The governor withdrew a chart of an area between the parallels of fifteen and zero degrees north. Clearly shown and well known to Richard were the English possessions of Barbados, Trinidad and the Grenadines. Further west was Isla Margarita and west still further, a line of smaller islands leading to a peninsula followed by a deep gulf, which bore the name Golfo de Maracaibo. At the gulf's southern end was indicated a narrow strait of 20 or so miles, which opened into a huge, inland sea that terminated 150 miles south at the foothills of the

Andes. It was just as the governor had described. Most interesting to Richard was that the notations on the chart were in Spanish. He was looking at a stolen, highly sensitive national secret.

"I presume you would wish to interview the person who passed this document into my possession, captain, would you not?" asked the governor. "I 'ave prevailed on Capitain Da Silva to attend on us later tonight. For now, let us rejoin my guests. We 'ave left them long enough."

The last guests left the mansion at one thirty in the morning; Simon was already abed, dreaming of the marvellous evening. Richard and the governor went back to the anteroom where they had been previously. Sitting in the seat Richard had occupied before was a tall, dark man in his early forties who was introduced as Captain Roberto Da Silva.

"A pleasure to meet you, Capitain Blackmore," said Da Silva.

"The pleasure, sir, is mine," said Richard bowing deeply.

Governor Mendoza, pleasantries completed, got straight to business. "Gentlemen. I believe I 'ave been able to interest Capitain Blackmore in the proposed venture. I 'ave also shown 'im the chart which you brought with you. I now ask you, Roberto, to inform the capitain as to the circumstances that put the chart in your possession."

"Certainly, Excellency," began Da Silva. "I was in command of a small squadron of caravels returning 'ome, carrying goods from Brazil to Lisboa. We were between Madeira and the ilhas de Açores, not 500 miles from where we are now sitting, when we came upon a badly damaged, dismasted Spanish ship. The crew were in poor condition – they 'ad been at sea three months. They were dismasted in a storm ten weeks earlier and were desperately low on water and provisions. The capitain, after his first words of gratitude, became surly and began to demand that I dispatch 'im on one of my ships direct to Espanha, as 'e were on a mission of great importance. 'E guaranteed a good payment for the chartering of one of our ships and allowing 'is ship to be escorted home – a salvage fee he thought would be appropriate.

"My suspicions were aroused. What ship's capitain would make such an offer? 'E knew that to lose 'is ship would mean 'is career was over. Why such a rush to get back to 'is country? I stalled him by saying I would consult with the capitains of my flotilla, as to agree to 'is

99

request would be a breach of our orders. Meanwhile I instructed my most loyal crewmen to make friends with our guests, in order to obtain information as to the reasons for their voyage. We quickly found that they 'ad departed from Maracaibo, not Santo Domingo, as the capitain had first told me. They were returning to Espanha with a request for a fleet of galleons to be dispatched as soon as possible." Captain Da Silva paused briefly to allow his words to have their desired effect.

"The Spanish capitain carried an attaché case with a strap on 'is shoulders at all times. I asked him what it contained. 'E was silent, so I reached for the strap. 'E drew a dagger and threatened me, but 'e met with an unfortunate accident – the ship rolled 'eavily, the Spaniard fell out of 'is chair, impaling 'imself through the 'eart with 'is own dagger. It was so quick I could do nothing to save 'im."

Richard Blackmore smiled wryly and said, "How unfortunate for him, but, ahem, most fortunate for you."

"Indeed, Capitain Blackmore. As you say, most fortunate, for I was able to examine the case without further need of persuasion. In the case was the chart you 'ave before you – also these strange gold coins and ornaments." Da Silva laid a pile of gold pieces in front of Richard before he continued. "We examined the 'olds of their ship, 'undreds of golden artefacts were found 'idden among the cargo. Those before you are but a small sample.

"During the voyage 'ere, we put together the story you 'ave 'eard by interrogating the crew. From Espanha no armada of galleons will sail to assist in bringing the treasure back, as neither the messenger ship nor any of its crew reached a port. The dangers of voyaging, eh, capitain," said Da Silva with a sly wink.

"We know there exists a contingency plan to use whatever ships are available to sail from Maracaibo laden with as much gold as they can carry, should the fleet of larger ships not arrive. A much more attractive and less dangerous target than an escorted convoy, yes, capitain?"

Richard weighed his next words carefully. "I, of course, have a considerable number of contacts in the trade; however, to assemble a battle fleet of non-Portuguese in the time frame we are talking about would be challenging to say the least. I am assuming here, possibly incorrectly, that you would like me to arrange the, ah, 'disappearance' of the Spanish treasure fleet for you?"

The governor beamed. "We 'ad not dared to 'ope you would take on such a task personally, Capitain Blackmore, but if you were to consider the possibility, it would be a most expeditious way to successfully conclude the enterprise. Some conditions, of course, would 'ave to be in place for the security of both sides. No? Let us sleep on it, as you Engleesh say. We will meet again at noon tomorrow, 'opefully to proceed to an agreement."

"Agreed," answered both captains.

"Goodnight, gentlemen," concluded Diego Mendoza, feeling justifiably pleased with himself.

Richard and Roberto Da Silva left the mansion and made their way back to their respective ships, each man full of thoughts as to how to make the best of this most interesting operation.

Once again at sea, Richard reflected on the unique opportunity he had been offered. It had not taken much to convince his crew of the possibilities this diversion from their proposed voyage could offer. Each man would become wealthy in his own right, should the business be concluded successfully, notwithstanding they would have to fight for it.

The governor had insisted that Captain Da Silva and six of his top fighting men would accompany them – to look after Portuguese interests, he had said. Richard saw this as a benefit – with the esteemed captain aboard, it was less likely the whole thing was some kind of trick. Roberto Da Silva's presence would assist greatly in convincing some hard men Richard knew he would need, to join the venture, if it were to get to the starting line.

Chapter 11
Atlantic crossing

The north-east trades blew their steady 20 to 25 knots; Simon fell into the rhythm of the seas. He had never been happier in his life, or more confused. He had parted firm friends with Juan Mendoza, a practical young man who saw advantage in a friendship with the quick-witted Cornish lad. Simon had absorbed all the learning Juan offered like a drunk absorbed wine. His enquiring, agile mind impressed his peer.

It was for this reason that Juan had taken the unprecedented step of introducing Simon to his sister Isabella, whom he had met briefly at the first night's dinner. At thirteen, she had the dark, stunning looks of her race. She was tall, haughty as a young mare chafing at the bit. The girl possessed the passion of a much older woman, and acted as one. How she had laughed at Simon's efforts to join her in her native tongue.

For all Isabella's attempts to hide it, a fatal spark had been struck within her heaving young breast, a fact easily observed by her brother, but unnoticed by Simon during his adolescent attempts to impress the young woman - he failed to recognise the signs. Simon had implored Juan to take him to the house again, but instinctively the budding beauty's brother had sensed the first smouldering passions his sister had felt for the tall, handsome Englishman. He had made every conceivable excuse to foil - for now at least - any fledging romance, while thinking what a fair couple they would make. No, Simon was a common sailor, not of sufficient breeding for his beautiful sister.

A day or two after leaving the island Richard Blackmore ordered Simon to his cabin. "Pray sit, Mister Pearce. Perhaps you would be good enough to share the origins of this with me," he said with no little annoyance, passing a piece of expensive vellum across the table to his young subaltern.

Simon looked at the piece of parchment that had his name written in a perfect copperplate hand upon it. He answered his captain cautiously. "I think I can guess, sir. It may be from the Lady Isabella; may I read it, please?"

"May be from that young lady, boy? Of course it is, and well you know it. And no! You most certainly may not read it." Richard Blackmore was as angry as Simon could remember.

"This is a matter of the utmost seriousness. Should Señor Mendoza get to know of it, he would be furious, and our plans could be destroyed. Thank God the servant charged with its delivery was wise enough not to pass it to you. You are hereby ordered not to seek Isabella's company or write to her ever again without the governor's express permission. Is all this understood?" demanded Richard Blackmore.

"It will be as you say, sir. I will not put the mission in jeopardy," answered Simon sadly.

Prior to their departure Diego Mendoza had invited all the participants of the venture to a fête on the mansion's lawn. Here the lovely young Lady Isabella cornered Simon and spoke most harshly to him. "So! Simon da Engleesh. You avoid me, no?"

"Indeed not, my lady," answered Simon, doing his best to perfect his way of speech. "I have tried most hard to get your brother to bring me into your presence again," he prevaricated. "Indeed, it is my most ardent wish to spend time with you, but we sail tomorrow. I shall not get ashore again."

"So! My brother tries to control me! I shall 'ave to be cleverer than 'im, yes?" replied the girl imperiously. She added with a devilish grin, "Is my fence so 'igh you could not 'ave climbed over it one dark night if you truly wished so much to see me?"

They had had but a few heated minutes to speak, but it was enough. Simon was totally smitten; the fire in the beautiful, young woman's eyes issued a lightning bolt that shattered his senses, his thoughts as a puppy, naked before her. He had to have Isabella for his own. Nothing he could do would get her out of his mind.

Later that evening he had taken a huge risk, managing to find a quill and paper in Dom Diego's anteroom office. Upon it he had fashioned his first stumbling love letter. 'I will wait for you forever. I will return.' Carefully he passed his missive to his love as they said their goodbyes at the evening's end.

The next morning the *Maid of Aran* came alive as hands and feet urgently performed the tasks required to get the ship under way.

To Simon, lovesick and aching, the situation seemed unreal; he was sailing away leaving Isabella! At the white mansion was another forlorn pair of eyes, watching tearfully until the horizon was void of sail, naught but miles of rolling ocean waves.

A firm, kindly hand rested on his shoulder. "Plenty of fish in the sea, boy," said Bryn Thomas; he had seen it all before.

Eight bells was his call to watch, only to find he would spend far too much time buttoning the flap of his pantaloons, in a vain attempt to hide the first adolescent stirrings of his manly parts. Off watch, in his berth, his life was a private agony. *If only I shared the cabin,* he thought, *maybe it wouldn't happen.* He just could not leave the beauty of Isabella in the proper and correct place, that of his memory. Pictures of her floating across the mansion's lawn, adorned in her flowing pink gown, her ankles clad in ghostly white stockings – superb in the sunlight – would waft from his subconscious to taunt him.

One night, in a fit of angry frustration, he grabbed the uncontrollable thing with his hand in an attempt to beat it back into its normal state. His hand suddenly became all wet and sticky; he felt he might pass out. *At least,* he thought, *the wretched thing has gone back to normal now.* That was, of course, until the next time he was trapped by his mind. He found, as Isabella floated across his subconscious, the degrading process would repeat itself, leaving him swooning and confused, but mercifully able to sleep for a short time.

He looked for extra work so he would exhaust himself before turning in, a positive by-product of which was that it made him most popular with the bosun and the ship's officers.

Not so, however, with Michael Douglas, the ship's boy, who found himself being compared unfavourably with the new apprentice. Michael baled Simon on the 'tween deck and told him, "Slow up, yer shit'ead, if 'e don't wanna be beaten to pulp." The burly fifteen-year-old then punched him hard a few times to show he meant it.

Bruised and confused Simon retired to his cabin, where his thoughts once again wandered onto dangerous ground. Wretchedly he clambered out of his cosy bunk and climbed aloft and tied himself securely into the crow's nest where he slept fitfully.

The ship roared across the ocean, like a stallion jumping fences, leaping from wave to wave, revelling in the perfect conditions. They were sometimes accompanied by birds, many making their annual migration to their winter feeding grounds. Simon wondered most of all at the tiny stormy petrel, no larger than a sparrow, a thousand miles from any land. The hardy ball of feathers would take shelter in the rigging for a night if the trades were unusually boisterous.

He never failed to be amused by those most wonderful of God's creatures, the dolphins, as they frolicked in the ship's bow wave. Occasionally he sighted their huge cousins, the whales, cruising past the pressed ship overhauling her seemingly without effort. Fluffy trade-wind clouds whisked over them warmly, in a steady sou'easterly progression. 'The sailors' wind' remained comfortably off the starboard quarter, with nothing more than a shift from force five to seven, demanding an occasional reef or sail trim. The largest workload was repairing cordage chafed with the constant motion. The entire crew was in high spirits as the *Maid of Aran* made for her next landfall, the exotic Caribbean island of Grenada.

The only person not on a high was Simon. After two weeks at sea and more than halfway, he should have been on top of the world but he wasn't – a fact noticed by his watchful captain and guardian who, on a pretext of wishing to advance the boy's knowledge of navigation, ordered him to his cabin for instruction.

"What ails ye, lad?" asked the captain when they were assured of some privacy. Seeing the boy's uncomfortable state, he probed some more. "Sick, are ye?"

"No, sir. Well, sir, I really don't know, sir," said Simon, his face turning deep cherry red.

Richard remembered that blush when he had spoken with Simon about Isabella's letter. At the garden party he had seen the young pair out of the corner of his eye while engaged in conversation with a sugar cane grower. "Ye ain't a-pining for that Mendoza lass, are ye lad?" he said softly.

Simon's embarrassed silence answered his question.

"Well, I suppose you were never instructed in the ways of life by your grandfather. I think we can relax the rules a little, eh? The girl's far in our wake, out of harm's way. I had better take the role of parent for this interview at least." 'Uncle Richard' proceeded to inform Simon of the facts of life. But he did not relent in the matter of the letter – Isabella's passionate outpourings had even the hardened sea captain break a sweat.

Bolstered by the knowledge that he was in fact a normal, healthy boy passing into manhood, Simon immediately began to enjoy the voyage. A quick mind and willingness to perform any task with passion and delight made him a favourite with all aboard. His problem with the ship's boy disappeared after Michael was seen beating up on him by Sean Finnegan, the huge, Irish leading seaman.

"So a bully it is yer a-wantin' t' be, Michael, is it now? Let me show ye what 'appens to all bully boys sooner or later," said Sean picking up Michael, as if he were no more than a rag doll, and throwing him across the 'tween deck into a bulkhead. "I wouldn't punch ye 'cause yer not worth the effort, yer shit-stinkin' pig's carcass, 'e. Lay a hand on young Simon here again, I'll knock yer inta next week, t' be sure I will."

Michael scurried off like a bilge rat. He wasn't about to argue with the angry six-foot, broad-shouldered Irishman.

Sean turned to Simon saying, "Ye need t' learn to fight better'n that afore we hove alongside a Spaniard, lad. I'll speak t' Mister Thomas 'n arrange a bit o' training, if ye 'ave a care to."

"I would sure be grateful to 'e, Sean, if 'e would," said Simon. So began a friendship that was to last a lifetime.

What a sight she was! Every stitch – including stunsails – set on extensions at the ends of the course yards, driving the *Maid of Aran* through the sparkling, foaming sea. She had taken on the air of a giant bird – dipping, gliding, ticking off the miles inexorably to her exotic destination. Routine shipboard life in subtropical latitudes was a far cry from higher latitudes, where a seaman's life was harsh in every aspect. Even the food was looked upon in a new light – ship's biscuits, salted meat and cabin bread seemed less awful when eaten on a bright, sunny, dry deck.

What luxury when an oceanic fish – dorado or wahoo – was hooked and fought aboard. It was Michael who caught the first, a delicacy of the tropics, a dorado. The boy had fashioned a lure from some musket shot drilled and threaded onto his line above a large hook. The whole thing was covered with strips of coloured cloth. With the ship travelling at seven knots, the initial strike almost pulled Michael over the taffrail. Sean Finnegan, being close by, took a turn of line around his huge forearm and tied it to a handy belaying pin. Miraculously the line held. With the immense pressure of the ship's momentum dragging it through the water, the fish gave up its fight and was easily pulled in as it bounced, flat on its side, across the water.

The catch made Michael very popular; Cook prepared a feast of fried, white-fleshed fish for the evening meal. There was plenty for all, washed down with a liberal ration of rum.

"That was a fantastic catch," said Simon to his tormentor of the past.

"Aye, thankee, Simon. I'm sorry for what I did t' 'e," Michael Douglas said with true humility. "I'm glad Sean sorted me out."

"Don't think of it. I 'ad some things on me mind and was actin' strange. I would like it if we could be friends," returned Simon.

They raised their pewter tankards, banged them together and drank a hearty toast to each other – the two young sailors solemnly declared their friendship in watered-down rum.

The next day at dawn a call came from the foretopman, a skinny fellow named Peter Drake, who was considered by the crew as the ship's ancient mariner, at 36 years old, being alive after his 25 years at sea, aloft amongst the miles of halyards, sheets and braces, a testament to his agility. "Ahoy, deck below. Land cloud ho, three points o' th' starboard bow, 30 mile off." Peter had the sharpest eyes in the crew; Captain Blackmore relied upon him totally.

"All hands to the braces, get the stuns'ls off her; be quick about it, lads. We will eat on an even keel tonight."

The raft of orders given out by the captain were carried out in next to no time, the crew eager for landfall that evening, leaving the rolling Atlantic to its lonely self once more.

Chapter 12
The isles of the Caribbees

The twenty-two days they had been at sea seemed but a wink to Simon, when land was sighted just three points off their current heading. A true feat of navigation, as no way to calculate longitude had been perfected, at least by Europeans, at this time. The loss of Sir Cloudesley Shovell's fleet had been the catalyst for the Longitude Act of 1714, from which the Board of Longitude was formed. It was not until Captain Cook circumnavigated the globe, from 1772, that John Harrison's chronometer was proven beyond doubt and accurate time longitude could be calculated. Only then was that patient man, Harrison, able to claim the full £20,000 prize proffered by the board.

They had a few anxious moments as they sailed passed Point Salines, the southern-most, shallow tip of Grenada. The two leadsmen in the ship's eyes called the depths every minute or so.

"By the mark twenty, by the mark fifteen, by the mark twelve and one half fathoms."

They were wearing ship to round the point when a 30-knot katabatic gust heeled the ship, down to the port-side gun ports. The captain ordered the topgallant sheets run to release the pressure. As usual, *Maid* quickly regained her composure, and the helmsman was back in control. The topgallants were furled for the short beat into deeper water and up to St Georges Harbour, one of the best anchorages in the Caribbean Sea. Richard knew the anchorage was a frequent haunt for many a British privateer; it was the company of these colleagues he sought.

Richard's plan was to sail northwards along the line of the Lesser Antilles, stopping at each anchorage he knew might well be occupied by one of the ships he was seeking. He wanted to recruit as many more ships as possible to join him for the attempt to relieve the Spanish of some of their ill-gotten gains. As the anchor was lowered he was somewhat dismayed to see only British men-of-war and a few desultory merchantmen. Where were the fine, lean private ships whose captains carried the Letter of Marque – those who could be up for a chance such as he had to offer?

A visit ashore gave him an answer. His Britannic Majesty's governor of the Grenadines was none other than Sir Archibald Swank, a retired general who did not understand the ways of the sea. A stickler for protocol and correctness, he greatly disliked the privateer whom he saw as a thief and brigand, definitely not a military man, such as himself, who fought for his country for honour not mercenary reward. Being born into privilege he could afford to dedicate his life to the service of his king. Most other Englishmen had to claw their way from poverty and serfdom to achieve a decent livelihood.

When presenting his papers, Richard was seen by the general's aide-de-camp, one Lieutenant Dewey, also from the upper classes. Dewey spoke with an affected lisp. He asked Richard his business, and on discovering that some of his cargo was of a military nature, the foppish boy then showed some serious interest.

"I see from your manifest that you are trading in weaponry, Captain Blackmore. We have need of some of your goods here. I trust you have no objection to selling to His Majesty's armed forces?"

"Indeed not, lieutenant. I would be most pleased to oblige. Choose what you require from the manifest, and I will offer you a price," answered Richard, pleased to be able to sell some of his cargo, thereby replenishing his cash reserves and defraying the expenses of the new venture. However, he did not wish to sell too much, bearing in mind the mission on which he was now embarked. It required some delicate negotiation to convince the general that the part of his cargo he wished to keep was pre-ordered for the garrison in Antigua.

Another stroke of good luck was that Richard was able to sell the majority of his non-military cargo to the island's general store. They were delighted to be able to purchase luxury goods destined for the wealthy tobacco growers of Virginia. These could now be sold to the families of traders and officers who garrisoned the British West Indies.

Maid of Aran beat her way northwards to the famed English Harbour of Antigua, after a stop at Bequia and St Vincent, where none of the ships Richard Blackmore sought were to be found. They cautiously sailed far enough offshore to avoid the French islands of Martinique, Dominica and Guadeloupe and their powerful warship bases.

They lay into the outer bay of English Harbour and anchored. To Richard's delight he saw several ships he knew would carry Letters of Marque. Early next morning the ship's boats were lowered and the *Maid* was warped into the inner bay, well known as the best hurricane anchorage in the Lesser Antilles.

Richard asked his apprentice to step ashore with him. They had barely reached the bottom of the gangplank when he was hailed in a booming bass.

"Blackmore, ye are a sight for sore eyes, ye are fer sure." The voice belonged to a huge, barrel-chested man, at least six feet tall and possibly the weight of two normal men. Simon thought he might even be larger than Sean Finnegan. Benjamin Gunn strode over and pumped Richard's right hand, making as if to remove it from his body.

"Ben, you old rascal, I thought you were dead. I heard somewhere that your ship had been overrun by Indians in the Orinoco Delta. Were not all but a small boatload lost?" asked Richard, both amazed and delighted.

"That's what was said by those bastards that mutinied and took off with the ship's boat after they saw the Indians coming for a second time," replied the giant man. "We was down to hand-to-hand combat, all powder being spent. Most of my men had been killed by spear or arrow. I was alone on the quarterdeck when their leader put up his hand to stop the fighting. There were a dozen arrows on the string ready to fly at me when the leader simply looked me fair in the eye and pointed to the horizon. It seemed he wanted me to go, and have me tell my kind not never to come back."

"Ben, it is really good to see you, and more, our meeting could be very much to your advantage. Do you have a new ship? I don't see the *Black Swan* hereabouts," said Richard.

"Aye, laddie, the *Swan* is 'ere. That be 'er over yonder, careened on the beach. Some planks got eaten by the Teredo worm. Some o' the buggers were 20 feet long and an inch thick. Another two weeks and we'll be off again, though," said Captain Gunn.

"The lad here is my apprentice and son of my stepbrother. Allow me to introduce Simon Pearce," said Richard.

"I be mighty pleased t' meet ye, sir," said Simon.

"Grand t' meet ye too, lad. 'E sounds as if 'e're from the West Country, same as I," said Ben.

"Yes, sir, I be that," said Simon, embarrassed. He looked at his captain to gauge his displeasure, if any, at his slip back into his vernacular.

"Come aboard the *Maid* for dinner tonight, Ben. I've some fine Madeira wine, and we've much to talk about. How about sundown, it will be cooler," said Richard.

"Sundown, t' be sure. I'll bring some old Cockspur rum," answered Ben as he turned to walk away, his spheropygian form displaying its owner's propensity for overindulgence in food and drink, as he disappeared into the hot, dusty noontime.

* * *

Could it have been so ridiculously easy?

Now, just six weeks from that meeting in early February, Ben had returned to Antigua, four weatherly privateers and two schooners following him in, all well armed and keen to fight. It seemed that business had definitely turned for the worst. Governors like Archie Swank had restricted the mobility of freebooting privateers by introducing more and more bureaucracy. Where in the past captains carrying Letters of Marque were given the freedom they needed, new restrictions appeared each time they entered a port. The group that assembled in the *Maid of Aran's* great cabin were possibly the last of their kind, the ten captains drawn by the same thought – one big win and retire. Richard's Portuguese-backed plan was just the thing they desperately needed.

"Gentlemen, please allow me to introduce Captain Roberto Da Silva. He is the original source of the information I have relayed to you."

Richard motioned for Da Silva to speak.

By the end of the evening, after the consumption of much rum and wine, Richard laid out a chart of the Caribbean and outlined his plan. "We know that a fleet of galleons will not arrive in Maracaibo. The officer in charge will not adopt the fallback plan until the last moment, as he would much prefer to send the gold in company with the larger, better armed vessels. They will, I believe, leave Maracaibo early May to be clear of the Caribbean before the hurricane season, beginning in June. We don't know what kind of ships they will have commandeered to transport the treasure; there could be several men-of-war from the Spanish Caribbean fleet among them; only time will tell. As we all know, they do not sail close to the wind therefore they have but two choices of course available to them.

"The first is to sail as close to the wind as they can and attempt the Mona Passage between Hispaniola and Puerto Rico, both territories of Spain, therefore safe. The prevailing winds now south of east, the fleet can head north into the open Atlantic, safely passing to windward of the reefs and dangers of the Bahamas. Their second choice is to use the Windward Passage between Cuba and Haiti; this entails a dangerous piece of navigation and brings the fleet into close proximity with Jamaica, a British possession. Having passed through the Windward Passage they must then navigate through the outer Bahamas or head west through the narrow channel that separates America from the Bahamas. This adds great distance, and danger from American privateers – but the benefit, a fair wind and current.

"I do not believe they will attempt the Sombrero Passage as they would be sailing close to British territories; besides, they wouldn't get that far to windward. Any comments, gentlemen? Yes, Captain Gunn."

"I agree the Mona is most likely," began Captain Gunn, "but as you say, each side is Spanish territory. The commander at Maracaibo will have sent a scout ship to inform the governors of each that a fleet is coming through. If it were me, I would also have ships scouring to the south looking for any opposition. Where do you plan to attack them?"

"We must get to them before they get to the Mona Passage. We will sail line astern with the wind just forward of abeam across their course. With ten ships we can cover almost 70 to 80 miles of ocean. I shall be in the vanguard at the start of each sweep. When we wear ship, the *Black Swan*, in the rear on the westward tack, will be the leading ship on the eastward. We will reach across the treasure fleet's path until we sight them; each ship must remain within signal range of those closest to her. Any more questions …? No …? Good."

"We have six weeks to be in position and seven days sail to reach our cruising position. Prepare your ships. We leave in three weeks; use this time to train your crews. The Dagos will fight to protect the gold. Once we make contact we will choose a target and proceed to engage independently. It will be up to each ship to secure its own target, unless some of the smaller units wish to work together. This option will be the best if the Spaniards' vessels are large and well armed. That is it for now."

Richard closed the chart as the captains finished their drinks and prepared to leave.

The mood on the *Maid of Aran* was no longer that of a carefree tropical cruise. Just yesterday Simon was introduced to cannon fire as Richard began a programme of rigorous training. Some of the men had been with him though the halcyon years of privateering and were well experienced in the deadly art of fighting a ship at sea. The ex-navy men well knew the cannon's roar.

For the others like Simon it was all new and rather frightening. He was port-side powder boy while Michael was assigned to starboard. Running from the magazine deep in the bowels of the ship up to the gun deck carrying barrels of black powder was no easy task as the ship rolled and bucked to the recoil from a full broadside. As he watched the shot fall the lad realised that in action the enemy's shot would be falling on them.

Working with Sean Finnegan each day had hardened the ship's apprentice; he began to have an assurance, a confidence about him. Daily he would wrestle with Michael, the bouts overseen by a watchful Sean Finnegan. While the ship's boy was the stronger, Simon was quick of mind as well as action. Michael would lunge in an attempt to get at close quarters where his weight would be an advantage. Simon would feint, counter attack and send his attacker sprawling, carefully using his attacker's weight to his own advantage, much to the delight of his tutor.

"To be sure, lad, I don't know how much more I can teach ye."

Richard was pleased with his motley fleet's preparations; it was a huge advantage that the crews in the enterprise were there from choice – no pressed men or slaves to deal with. He rightly asserted that one free man was worth ten slaves.

He ordered all captains and sailing masters aboard the *Maid* for a final briefing. "Time to sail, gentlemen. The Spanish await us. The brig *Tyrant* that passed through yesterday with mail confirmed that a larger than usual gathering of Spanish ships has been seen at Maracaibo; as best as I can say, it is for the trans-shipment of the gold. They saw two quite large ships; these will most surely be deployed, one in the van and one at the rear. It will need two of our ships to take on either one of these. We need to take the leading vessel so she is not free to raise the alarm in Hispaniola or Haiti. Good luck and piles of gold to each of ye."

The fleet of buccaneers reached the designated cruising area – to windward of Hispaniola and the smaller island of Puerto Rico. Between these two islands lay the Mona Passage. The privateer fleet maintained a distance of 100 miles south of the islands so they would not be discovered by coasting ships, or worse, an enemy man-of-war. Each twelve hours, at dawn and sunset, the fleet would go about then retrace their courses of the previous twelve. After a week of this sailing in a disciplined fleet, the captains used to being masters of their own destinies grew restless.

A call from the *Maid's* masthead alerted Richard that the nearest ship to them, the schooner *Brilliant*, was making more sail so she could overhaul them.

Damn McArthur, thought Richard. *He wants to talk and it's time to close up for the night and go about.*

Just then a second call came from the masthead. "Sail ho, abeam to windward!"

Richard himself went aloft; there was no mistake – this was the fleet they lay in wait for. As he had predicted a large ship was leading, her topsails just visible on the horizon.

Richard was furious with the feisty Scot. They sent signals, but the little schooner was now almost out of view, hove down under maximum sail.

Once he had understood the situation James McArthur had needed no further encouragement. He immediately went about in order to relay the sighting; he signalled that he would be on station to assist the *Maid* next morning as arranged.

Maid's topgallants and topsails were lowered and furled, allowing her to be closer to her quarry without her sails being seen. She maintained her course to be west of the convoy of Spaniards by morning. Richard was pleased to see other vessels of his fleet lower their topsails and bear away so the enemy would not spot them before nightfall. The plan was to reduce speed in order that the convoy would catch up with them by daylight. The *Maid*, being the closest to the enemy, crossed their path and hove to.

"I want to be sure we have the right target before dawn," Richard said to his officers and senior crew. "Prepare the yawl for launch, if ye please, Mister Booth. Mister Trevellen, take four men and sail as close as ye can get to the target without being seen. Include Sean Finnegan. He can speak some Spanish – the Dagos held him prisoner after an unsuccessful raid some years ago. Voices carry well over water, and the yawl will be to the lee. A shouted order or a glimpse of her flag will tell us all we need to know. Take young Simon as well; he's a good oarsman and small boat sailor. Arm yourselves, men, but only fire if fired upon. If their ships are allowed to scatter, our work will be much harder."

He handed a cavalry officer's sabre to Simon saying, "This will be better for ye than that hanger ye have been training with. It was once my father's; it will serve ye well."

"Th-thank you, s-sir," stammered Simon.

"Take care, boy," was the gruff reply.

The 20-foot yawl looks tiny bobbing up and down beside her mother ship, Simon thought with some trepidation.

David Trevellen, the third officer, went over his captain's instructions in his mind as they headed towards their enemy, the yawl bucking sharply as she was brought hard on the wind. '*Sail towards their path at four knots. With them ten miles away from our present position and doing the same speed on their current course, ye would hove up a mile or so to starboard of them. If ye sails for half an hour then heave to on the other tack. Ye'll see them in the light of the rising moon. When they are close, lower your* sails so no moonlight reflects off them. When ye have confirmed who she is and her speed, make back on the reverse track ye sailed out on. After half an hour turn downwind heading 025 degrees. We'll be here awaiting.' The captain had ended his instructions to the five face-blackened men with, 'Godspeed.'

A little under an hour later sails were furled and oars shipped. They had been muffled with sackcloth and the thole pins, the oars' pivot point, had been greased with pig fat – a squeaky oar could give them away. Tension mounted as the four men and a boy waited. Simon saw them first, as the large ship floated eerily into the light of the rising moon. "Thar' her be, Mister Trevellen! What a sight her is, like a ghost ship, like as not."

"Quiet boy," whispered the third officer, who was but 18 years old himself. "We're too close to her path. Pull, lads, pull away."

"Steady, Mister T. I kin 'ear voices; ship yer oars," said Finnegan.

They could hear 'Keep your course steady; you are worse on the helm than a bitch in heat' issued in Spanish, from the ship.

"That be 'n officer abusin' th' helmsman – 'er be Spanish, right enough. Time fer us t' get away, sir," said Sean.

The Spanish ship slid slowly by; she was under reduced sail so the fleet following would not struggle to keep up.

David Trevellen turned the little yawl on a reciprocal course to their target, ordering the bowman to drop a knotted line from the bow; he timed it passing the stern. He estimated their speed at three and a half knots. The mainsail had just been rehoisted when he heard another call, this time from a Spanish lookout.

"Over to port, all eyes!"

"Bring her to port," came from another voice, probably that of the officer of the watch.

Simon instinctively dropped the yawl's mainsail as oars were reshipped and they pulled away from danger, at right angles to the Spaniards' course.

Shortly another curse was heard from the ship. "Antonio, you arsehole, you saw nothing. Helmsman, resume course."

It was not until well past midnight that the yawl was safely back in her chocks aboard the *Maid of Aran*. After the debriefing Captain Richard Blackmore asked his officers to remain in his great cabin.

"Finnegan, remain with us, if you please. We have found in you a fine seaman, with obvious leadership qualities. We sailed short one bosun's mate, thinking to elevate someone from the ranks to fill the position, and we are unanimous in this company that you would be the best man for the position. How say ye, Sean?"

"'Tis not I be ungrateful, soir," said the humble giant looking very uncomfortable, twisting his seaman's woollen hat in his hands. "T' be sure now 'tis not, soir. Just I bin a gun deck man all me life. I'm used to a-taking of orders, soir, not a-givin' of 'em. T' move t' the fo'c'sle is kind of a leap t' the moon fer the likes o' me, soir. Asides, I got kind o' fond o' young Simon. I kind o' like t' watch 'is back, so t' speak, when the action starts, if that be okay, gennelmen?"

The Welsh bosun piped up, "With yer leave, captain."

"Please proceed, Mister Thomas."

"Sean, I've sailed with ye for nigh on ten year now, 'n no finer seaman has there been aboard. Ye are a natural leader, hell man! The men follow ye anyway without the rank. With it, they will follow ye with confidence. Ye know what it is to have a dullard doin' the orderin'. Ye'll give the men someone to respect. I'll give ye the mainmast as bosun's mate; that's where the captain's kin'll be. Ye ken keep an eye on 'im from thar."

"Indeed, Sean, a great plan. Just follow the bosun's directions; if unsure ask one of us. Will ye do it, lad? Oh, and by the by, the pay is twice your current stipend," added Captain Blackmore encouragingly.

"Er, thankee soirs, 'n all ye gennelmen fer yer kind words. I'll not disappoint 'e," said Sean, grinning widely.

"Cochran!" The captain called his aging steward. "A flagon o' Cockspurs and glasses. A toast to our new colleague, Bosun's Mate Sean Finnegan."

"Now gentlemen, to business, if you please. This lead Spaniard must not be allowed to pass us and raise the alarm at any of the Spanish settlements otherwise we will have difficulty passing through the Mona Passage ourselves after the action, and with any damage we may carry we may have no choice but go through.

"*Brilliant* is on the target's starboard hand; we are to her port. At first light, both ships will attack simultaneously. The rest of the fleet should be able to attack the ships behind with ease having the weather gage. It will be just as we have planned. They are at liberty to choose their targets but it will be up to us to prevent the alarm being raised ashore. Once this leading ship is subdued I shall put a prize crew aboard, leaving *Brilliant* as escort. *Maid* will then be free to intercept any stragglers. Any questions …? Good. Abed be thee all; action stations at five am – that's but two and one half hours. Use it well, we'll all need to be our best when we face the Spaniard this dawn."

All hands were at their stations as the captain addressed the ship's company in the balmy, tropical predawn darkness.

"Master gunner, aim for her spars with the long bow guns loaded with chain shot. If we can slow her while presenting the small target of our bow to her guns, things will go mightily more easily for us. We should be able to fire three or four salvos and hurt her before we get into her range and receive her return fire. Our accuracy at this time will decide our success.

Brilliant will be attacking from her starboard quarter; she carries but a single bow gun. Due to the enemy's more powerful broadside she must avoid close contact until her target is weakened. Once this has occurred we shall grapple and board. Remember, the Spaniards have stolen this treasure; we are simple relieving them of it to assist our great ally Portugal and to become wealthy men! Good luck and Godspeed. Roberto Da Silva has a few words to add."

Da Silva stood; the cabin became quiet. "First I geeve to you the best wishes of my king and country. May you all fight bravely and be unharmed. Our neighbours, Espanha, have enslaved us in the past and would do so again if they believed they could. If thees treasure finds eets way into their exchequer they will 'ave money aplenty to take action against us. They may yet consider another attack against England! They still smart from the defeat of their Armada, and they desire to depose your church and return England to the Roman Church. So, my friends, the outcome of thees enterprise cannot be in doubt. My fellow countrymen and I will fight alongside you disguised as English seamen. Should we fail, we shall not be taken alive, and you must never speak of us. Godspeed, *amigos*. Forward to victory and riches!

Chapter 13

Battle at sea

A glimmering, peaceful, tropical dawn lit the eastern horizon. At the *Maid of Aran's* maintop Simon could see the Spanish ship's dark hull clearly, as well as her rigging spars and sails silhouetted in the first light of a new day. *Is this to be my beloved ship's last moment in perfect, seagoing condition?* he wondered.

The Spaniard was much larger than his first impression during the subversive mission of the night before. He called to the deck that she had 20 guns aside, more than a match for them, he knew. As he watched he saw hurried movement on deck and in the rigging of the oncoming ship.

"Deck, ahoy!" he called. "Enemy making sail; they've seen us."

And yes! A second sail to starboard of their prey. Captain James McArthur of the *Brilliant* had closed during the night and was in a good position to attack the enemy. The Spaniard was trapped, with a highly manoeuvrable aggressor at each beam.

Simon fervently hoped that maybe she hadn't the manpower to man her 40 guns at the same time.

Another sail was now clearly visible astern of their target and sailing about three miles away. He could see the brig *Defiant* harden up a couple of points to intercept her. All this Simon reported to the deck 70 feet below.

The privateer fleet followed Commodore Blackmore's instructions to the letter. Simon saw the attacking ships peel away to intercept their individual targets. In the enemy fleet, the alarm was fully raised; the vessels astern of the leading ship turned in an attempt to evade the pack yapping at their heels. With the wind now dead astern they slowed while their attackers were on their fastest point of sailing. Simon could see they had little chance of escape. Seeing the enemy the night before while remaining unseen themselves was a huge advantage to the pirate fleet. It allowed their smaller, more lightly armed ships to be perfectly positioned for the chase at dawn. They had achieved a position of superiority, roughly equivalent to taking an opponent's queen in the opening moves of a chess game.

"Bring her wind a point abaft the starboard beam, if you please, Mister Partridge. Rig the nets overhead," ordered the captain. "I believe she will run from us towards *Brilliant*. The Spaniard will surmise that *she* is an easier apple to bite than us. He's not yet met our crazy Scot." He laughed, revelling in the battle scene as it unfolded as planned. "Gunner, your bow guns, engage as you bear."

"Aye aye, sir. Bring her a couple of points higher, captain, if it pleases ye, so we can ease back off the wind for firing on an even keel," requested the master gunner. "It'll gain us 50 yards in range."

"As you say, Gunner. Mister Partridge, sail to Gunner's commands during the long range engagement," ordered Richard.

"Aye, sir," answered the first lieutenant, whose duty was to sail the ship during battle, allowing his captain to concentrate on the unfolding events of the engagement.

Jonathan Connery was a man in his early forties who had been press-ganged to sea at the age of 16 and stationed on the gun deck of a fast Royal Naval frigate. During action some years later, having being a gun captain, he had taken command of his battery after a huge splinter had killed the gunner's mate. Not without some luck, the fledgling gun layer's first salvo turned the engagement around for his ship, taking out her antagonist's maintop and foremasts, making it a sitting duck for his guns. He was soon made chief gunner as it was found he had a natural rapport with the flaming monsters that allowed Britannia to 'rule the waves' – no enemy could reload and fire faster. His name had been all but forgotten – he was respectfully known simply as 'Gunner', by seaman and officers alike, that handle being a far higher honour than any rank or title could confer.

After 20 years in the navy, and during a period of peace when many an officer and seaman were wasting away ashore, Connery was enjoying a pint of rum in a public house in Plymouth. Richard Blackmore was recently returned from a successful sortie in the Caribbean. Knowing the man's history, he worked hard to convince him to join the *Maid of Aran*. He knew that to have Connery behind his guns could be decisive in battle. He did not beat around the bush; straightway the captain offered him a share equal to that of the first officer, potentially many times navy pay. Gunner Connery also knew that Richard was one of the finest privateers afloat, and he accepted gratefully; he had been a member of the *Maid of Aran*'s crew ever since.

"What do you call as the range, cap'n?" shouted Gunner.

"Fifteen hundred yards is my estimate, Gunner, as I think she's bearing away from us towards *Brilliant*. She'll offer a fine target as we close. Her captain will think he's safe, him being unaware of our 18-pound forward chasers," said Richard.

"Ease 'er t' port now," called Gunner. "Ye lubbers be ready t' fire on command. Fire! Reload! Fast as ye likes," Gunner's commands stirring the gun crews to their best.

After the cannons' first salvo, Simon could hear an eerie whistling as the pair of twin cannon balls linked with chain flew to their target. "Only one water spout, one must've hit!" he called from his perch at the topmast.

"Next shot full elevation," ordered Gunner. "Let's get among 'er rig!"

As the nimble *Maid of Aran* began to overhaul her enemy, her salvos began to take effect. The enemy's mizzen topmast fell to leeward just as *Brilliant* began her attack. She raced forward of the Spaniard at an angle, as if to cross her bows. Her cunning captain kept out of the firing arc of the Spaniard's 20 powerful cannon, while opening his own broadside. He raked the closing ship on what was near a collision course, firing twice in quick succession, causing damage but still not able to be fired upon in retaliation.

Just as it seemed the two ships must collide, James McArthur spun his ship's stern across the wind. With an audacity combined with commensurate skill, the cunning Scot headed his ship directly at the larger vessel just as the Spanish guns began to bear – thus presenting a smaller target to the enemy – at the same time firing his bow cannon. The recoil from the grotesquely oversized piece seemed to stop *Brilliant* in her tracks. With his first shot laid at maximum depression he hit the gun deck forward taking out several loaded cannon, at least one of which exploded causing a fire – deadly on a wooden ship in the heat of battle.

The Spaniard fired a ragged salvo at her aggressor, but the hissing balls passed over the low-wooded *Brilliant* due to the close range, causing but minor damage to her sails. Once again *Brilliant* fired after the fastest reload imaginable, the ball again smashing into the gun deck in the region of the captain's quarters, now stripped for action. McArthur turned back onto the starboard tack. Now just behind his enemy, the *Brilliant*'s bow gun continued to bombard the Spaniard's unprotected stern.

In the meantime Gunner's deadly accuracy had damaged the Spaniard's rigging – she was making only half her previous speed. "Slow 'er down, sir. I'll drops a few explosive shells on to 'er deck to shake 'em up a bit. Gun captains, prepare the broadsides."

The long guns again belched smoke and flame; this time explosions could be seen on the larger ship's deck.

Weary of being battered without hitting back, the Spaniard turned to bring her port broadside to bear on *Maid*. To Simon's eye she seemed to erupt in flame as she fired; the explosion was deafening. The salvo was laid to straddle the *Maid*. Several holes appeared in her sails, and Simon heard at least one ball hit the hull. Then the *Maid* answered her attacker with her own broadside.

"Get 'e away down 'ere, Simon lad. 'E've done all 'e can up thar," shouted Sean Finnegan above the din.

Simon reached the relative safety of the main deck, oh so different now battle had commenced. Gun crews, sweating profusely, raced against time to fire, reload and fire, each man well aware that the ship that inflicted the first major blow would suffer the least casualties, winning the encounter.

Gunner paced the deck assisting his gun captains in their aim. As they were to leeward of their foe they had a range advantage because they heeled away from their enemy, raising their firing side. The enemy, however, was larboard side to them, the wind pressing that side down, thus her firing side angled downward; even with her heavier broadside she was considerably disadvantaged, lacking range. However, a cannon ball spinning and hitting the water just right could bounce several times, hitting their enemy about the waterline.

Richard took maximum advantage of the situation; using the Maid's superior speed and manoeuvrability, he shaped his course to intercept the Spaniard. It was a risk grappling a larger ship and attempting to board so soon. *Brilliant*, guessing what Richard had in mind, was overhauling her, aiming to grapple the opposite side at the same time Richard came alongside her larboard.

Maid staggered as several bouncing cannon balls from the Spaniard hit her fore quarters. Now at close range, the effect of a 20-pound ball hitting the wooden topsides was devastating. Simon was ordered below to assist Bryn Thomas in caring for the wounded.

"Take your sword and pistol with 'e, lad," yelled Sean Finnegan amid the din.

Nothing could have prepared the boy for the mayhem on the 'tween decks. Only one ball had fully penetrated and that in the fo'c'sle. Amid the clearing smoke lay several men, some groaning in agony, others silent. Body parts, hardly recognisable as human, lay casually around. The ball entered by the forward starboard gun; its crew were showered at high velocity by a hail of oak splinters. All four were dead. Big James Smith was hanging hideously from the bulkhead, pinned by a huge splinter that had passed through his body and into the timber behind. Next Simon saw a headless torso, impossibly crushed, wrapped hideously around the gun carriage.

"Thank God the 'it was in 'ere," said Mister Thomas. "The for'ard bulkhead 'as taken most of the blast, protecting the main gun deck."

"Arrrr, 'elp me."

Simon heard a weak cry from forward. Cautiously he moved in the direction of the sound. It was then he saw the pained face of his old antagonist, Michael Douglas, in the gloom. He was momentarily distracted by the crash of iron balls on the hull behind him, as several more shots hit the poor *Maid of Aran*. These bounced away because of the angle of the ship to the angle of fire, but not before dislodging more deadly splinters from shattered timbers. The screams of men impaled by these wooden missiles could be heard behind the bulkhead, above the din of battle.

How much more of this can she take? Simon wondered, refocusing on Michael.

His face white from shock and loss of blood, Michael looked like a man of 60, a far cry from the strapping lad of 15 he had been but moments before.

Michael weakly held his hand towards Simon, who took it gently saying, "Where does it hurt, Michael? What can I do?"

"I-I-I don't reckon thar's much t' be done for me, Si," Michael gasped from bloodless lips, as he lifted his hand that had been clutching his side.

Simon involuntarily shuddered; it was as if a monstrous fish or animal had bitten a chunk of flesh from the boy's body. Parts of his gut were visible poking through the gory mess. "I'll go get 'e some cloth," he said moving away, shaking.

"Nay, it won't do no good. Stay with me; I don't want to die alone," Michael whispered. "'E do forgive me fer what I did, don't 'e?"

Simon turned back to his dying shipmate, a tear in his eye. "Course I do, Mickey, in the name of God I do. If it hadn't bin for 'e I'd not have had Sean t' train me. Reckon I'm gonna need that trainin' sooner than later."

"Ye'll do grand, Simon Pearce, I know ye will. Wish I could be there t' see it ..." Michael's eyes rolled in his head as he quietly died, his soulful words spoken with his dying breath.

"There's nothing more we can do here, Simon lad. Best we get topsides for the boarding. Ye are to stay on board *Maid*, stick close to Sean, and keep the bastards off our deck." Bryn Thomas's voice hardened as he pronounced the uncharacteristic expletive.

The men were assembling in sheltered spots on deck. The last deafening salvo had been fired by each of the three ships. The Spaniard's had whistled harmlessly overhead, her guns placed higher in the much larger ship, but the salvos from the *Maid* and *Brilliant* had had devastating effect, shattering the enemy's hull just a few feet from the waterline.

"Cease fire. We don't want to sink her. Loose the grenades; muskets, aim for those in the rigging," barked Captain Blackmore. He sensed the tide of battle was in his favour, the familiar rush of adrenalin, along with his growing lust - natural in all men - to kill.

Grenades swept the Spanish ship's decks in a hail of iron and glass, Master Epstein's creations killing and maiming, as they were designed to do. The two ships came together with a sickening, grinding crunch. Grapnels were thrown and made fast as the boarding parties swung onto the enemy ship's deck.

Several heavily armed men had dropped from the yards of the Spanish ship in counter-attack. Sean was engaged by two of them as a third charged Simon. Instinctively he pointed his little pistol at the running man; he cocked the hammer, aimed and coolly fired. The man stopped in his tracks, a small red hole appearing where his Adam's apple should be; his forward momentum propelled him to Simon's feet where he lay twitching, drowning in his own blood. The boy, stupefied, calmly watched the man die. He, Simon Pearce, 13 years old, had killed a man.

A yell came from one of the men attacking Sean, who had been too quick for him – he was now impaled on the Irishman's sabre. While Sean struggled to remove his weapon from the man's quivering flesh, the second attacker was upon him, slashing wildly with his heavy curved sword. To avoid the blow, Sean had to release his hold on his own weapon; he stood before the grinning Spaniard unarmed. Simon revolved his pistol barrel to put the second loaded barrel before the hammer and aiming at the middle of Sean's adversary's back, fired. Sean smiled, giving Simon a gesture of thanks, as he dislodged his weapon from the groaning body of his first attacker.

"Shelter under the poop and reload, Simon, me lad; methinks this fight be all but over."

The boarding combat had lasted but 20 minutes, but in that short time many men had died. And a 13-year-old boy had killed two of them. Richard ordered all the captives to be locked in the forepeak whilst their prize was searched. Soon cargo was being transferred from the *Concepcion*, the captured ship, to both the *Maid of Aran* and the *Brilliant* – a difficult task, as the three ships, still locked together in the moderate seaway, ground and swayed against each other making the most awful grating sounds. With some of the bullion transferred, the order was given to part company.

Richard organised a prize crew to remain with the Spanish ship, one of whom was Sean Finnegan, because of his knowledge of Spanish.

The leading seaman of yesterday was now second-in-command of a Spanish man-o'-war, her prize captain a proudly grinning 18-year-old third lieutenant.

Simon looked astern where another battle was in progress. *Defiant* was engaged exchanging broadsides with the next Spanish ship in the convoy. She had been damaged. The *Maid* altered course to assist. Hard on the wind she positioned herself to hit the Spaniard on her unprotected stern, as *Brilliant* had done so effectively in the battle with *Concepcion*. The result of *Maid* entering the fray caused the Spanish ship to strike her colours, the crew's promised share of her cargo insufficient incentive to risk the devastation they had seen on their flagship.

More sail was seen to the south as the following fleet, realising what was happening, came before the wind in an attempt to outrun the pirates, several of whom gave chase. Ben Gunn changed course on *Black Swan*, chasing the rearmost and largest Spanish ship to the Windward Passage. He had the advantage of sailing towards friendly, British waters. His superior speed, he knew, would allow him to overhaul and pounce on his prey before they escaped to relative safety – the channel between the Bahaman islands and the mainland coast of America.

Each of the ten ships of Richard's fleet had its own bloody story to tell. That is, with the exception of the brig *Highlander*. She took on a much larger vessel alone and was demolished by accurate cannon fire. She exploded, with the loss of all hands, as a shell from the Spanish reached her magazine before she herself could inflict any harm.

Simon looked at the chaos about him. His lovely *Maid of Aran* was a mess; however, apart from the hole forward made by the shot that killed Michael and a few shattered planks above the waterline, no major damage was sustained to her rig, nor were any spars damaged.

Richard had a strong argument with Roberto Da Silva, who wanted to kill the surviving Spaniards.

"It is a matter of security," Da Silva said. "The King of Spain must never even suspect Portuguese involvement in the destruction of this treasure fleet."

"I will not kill in cold blood, sir, and there's an end to it. Do not try my patience, please. I will have enough to answer for when I meet my maker. Your men were not recognised; we will interrogate fully later to prove that. As of now, sir, we need to prevent any of the Spanish fleet from making landfall to ensure the security you desire."

And with that Richard ordered *Maid* on the chase of a small, fast brig making full sail to pass them. The smaller ship was soon overhauled and sunk by superior tactics and firepower. Preoccupied, Richard was unable to search for survivors.

A raft formed mainly by the brig's main hatch cover eventually hove up on the shallow eastern coast of Hispaniola. Only three men from a crew of 40 had survived. On the raft, one Carlos Jesus Horta, a 16-year-old middy, vowed revenge.

Sean watched as *Brilliant* rode the waves on their starboard hand. They would head for the Caicos Islands in the outer Bahamas to do repairs and allocate each ship's share of the treasure; it was here that the fate of the Spanish prisoners would be decided. The *Maid* would carry the Crown's share back to England and pay off her soon-to-be wealthy crew, for whom life would never be the same.

Chapter 14

Hero returns

Simon Pearce was feeling exceptionally pleased as great news had reached him. Richard Blackmore's prize agent had been in discussions with the Crown receiver. All indications were that the officers and crews of the ships that had taken part in the Battle of the Mona Passage, as the action had been named, were in for a larger than expected payout. Once an agreement with the receiver was finalised, he would be a wealthy young man.

The *Maid of Aran* was in the shipbuilding yard of Blackwall and Co. on the Thames; she would be under refit for three months. Urgent repairs caused by the action and all maintenance that had been deferred would be attended to, including a full re-rig of both standing and running rigging. All her armament would be completely overhauled by Epstein and Sons, who would replace her 12-pound cannon with the latest, longer range sixteens. The long-barrelled bow chasers were also to be replaced with larger twenty-fours and the greater firepower required her gun decks to be reinforced to take the extra loadings. The rapidly growing colonies of the Americas offered new opportunities for the wily ship's captain. Richard Blackmore was keen to participate.

The King had been impressed by the accolades the Portuguese ambassador had privately showered on the *Maid*'s captain, not to mention the Crown's share of the booty presented to him. He took the unprecedented step of conferring a knighthood on Captain Richard Blackmore who was now and forever Captain Sir Richard Blackmore.

Simon was in awe at the ceremony, where the King had congratulated him personally on his contribution and made him an attractive offer. "There's a naval commission available at any time, young man. That is, if Sir Richard can spare you, which I sincerely doubt. With me as your sponsor, a rapid rise through the ranks would be assured."

"I thank you, Your Majesty, but I cannot leave the *Maid of Aran* at this time," Simon said confidently to the King of England.

"Would this decision have some bearing on a certain young woman of Maderia, where next, Sir Richard assures me, you are to sail?" asked the king, smiling.

As his carriage made its way from Truro through the Cornish countryside, Simon was at peace. After this visit to the family farm at Roseland he would return to Scilly to see his ailing grandfather. He was not due back in London for two months when recommissioning of his ship began. Simon's carriage rolled into the wide entrance at Penpeth Farm.

"Is that you, sister?' asked the young seafarer. "How you've grown."

"Aye, brother, 'n 'e ain't stood still none, 'ave 'e," answered a blooming Mary Pearce.

Simon jumped from the carriage and embraced his sister, of whom he had seen very little. She had been born in St Just's after their father's execution and had remained with her mother.

"How old are ye now, sister?"

" 'leven."

"That's almost the age I first went t' sea," beamed Simon.

"Simon, me 'andsome, what a sight fer these ol' eyes 'e are, for sure," said Jane Farmiloe, delighted.

"Mother, ye look so well an' right pretty. You put on your best frock, I see," exclaimed Simon, trying not to slip back into his Cornish vernacular, even though he was no longer under the watchful eye of Sir Richard Blackmore.

"Michael's in the fields with 'is young Davie. Ernest here made some excuse or other to work 'ere. 'Twas just so as 'e could greet ye first, scallywag that 'e is," Jane said ruffling the hair of a twelve-year-old boy. "Jennifer, come 'ere, don't 'e be shy; greet yer famous 'alf-brother right now," she continued with mock anger.

A pretty blonde girl of nine came out from behind a barn door and timidly shuffled forwards to greet Simon. "Pleased, I'm sure, sir," was all she said as she drove her face into her stepmother's skirts.

"What a young beauty! And less of the sir, if ye please, sister," answered Simon laughing.

"Come now, girl, a kiss for yer brother," said Jane.

Simon hugged his blushing half-sister, who beamed with the fuss he made of her.

After a simple lunch Simon sat with his mother. "There's more I have to tell ye, mother. I 'eld back the best for last. I've met the girl I intend t' marry. The loveliest thing on earth - dark hair, slim, and flashing brown eyes; 'er name's Isabella."

"Yer a mite young t' be talkin' marriage, son, ain't 'e? Where, pray, did 'e meet this paragon?" asked Jane warily.

"Isabella's Portuguese and lives on the island of Madeira. Her father, Dom Diego, is the governor there; they are very well t' do. Since I am now wealthy I have a chance t' win her," answered Simon.

"Am I t' unnerstand 'e 'aven't spoke t' the father about askin' fer 'is daughter's 'and?"

"No, Mother, I was far too young before and had yet to make my fortune. Now I 'ave and am a man o' position - I even spoke t' 'Is Majesty the King - I can ask confident like."

Jane was seething; not wishing to show her emotions, she spoke carefully. "I s'pose 'er is Catholic, 'er bein' Portuguese 'n all. What does 'e think 'er family'll think o' that? Fer that matter, what'll y' stepfather an' uncle think o' it, what wi' being churchmen 'n all? Catholic 'n Church o' England don't mix too well, son. Us, we're Chapel, 'e knows that."

"I know Isabella loves me. That's all I care; we'll sort it," said the boy hotly.

That evening Michael Farmiloe sat with his stepson in the parlour, both of them with a pewter tankard of beer in hand. Once they were alone he began to tell the true story of the family's situation. "Things 'ave been a bit 'ard o' late, lad, though we're better off 'n many. The farms a bit small, like. I'd like t' send the boys t' school at the abbey in Truro, but ain't enough income t' pay fees, and none fer labour t' replace 'em."

"I stopped a few days in Truro," said Simon, "an' I went o'er to th' parish to seek news of land for sale on the Roseland. I reckon it's good land hereabouts an' a good investment. Cap'n Blackmore advised me to buy some land if I can get it worked. I found two farms next to

Penpeth here are t' be sold up – the Bainses an' the Browns can't make ends meet. If their acres be added to Penpeth's, would that be enough, sir?"

"Aye, indeed it would, lad, but where would we find th' money for that," answered Michael, guilelessly.

"As I said, sir, I bin advised by Sir Richard that an investment in good English farmland is th' best way t' secure some of the returns of our recent adventures. What better than t' invest in land for our family? If ye agree, I will purchase the farms! The three can then be run as one. Y'll need t' sign the papers as my legal guardian," said Simon, somewhat breathlessly. "Plenty o' income for both David and Ernest to get schoolin' and th' girls good dowries so as t' be wed well. I would have a home t' come back to 'ere in England for when I gives up the sea."

"I'm overcome, lad. Be 'e sure that's what 'e wants t' do?"

"Sir, y've made a good home for my mother 'n sister; it'd be an honour t' make things better for all o' ye. Besides, I will still own part of the total farm; it'll provide a pension for me, in me dotage," replied Simon.

It was not as easy doing, as saying. Sir Richard had to become guarantor until the cargo and prizes had been converted to cash. He was keen to assist, as he believed the 220 acres of prime Cornish farmland to be a very good investment for his protégé. So he arranged with his bankers to loan the required funds to complete the purchases so the land was safe.

Whilst on the Roseland, Simon met George Pearce, Peter's father. It had been eleven years since the trial that sent Peter as a convict to Virginia, the same trial that had condemned Simon's father and his father-in-law.

"Aint 'eard nuttin' o' th' lad since 'e were shipped away. 'E cain't read nor write. I'd be mighty pleased if 'e can make some enquiries when 'e be over there, like? Peter should be free by then, 'n 'e might even be able t' bring 'im 'ome."

"I will indeed look for him, if I can. As ye know, we didn't get to Virginia on the last trip. Give us all th' information 'e can – the transport ship's name would be a big help – 'n where 'e were sent. I'll do the best I can to locate my cousin, sir," said Simon, excited by the challenge.

"Thank 'e, lad, thank 'e. Me ol' missus still turns a tear when she thinks of 'im." George suddenly looked old, even though he was but a man of forty-five.

St Just-in-the-Roseland's congregation filled the small church to overflowing on the day of the special service Daniel Farmiloe had arranged for his great-nephew. The local womenfolk had turned it into a fête, providing a great array of food and drinks for after the service.

No lesser personage than Sir Henry Bickerton, lord of the manor, attended. He wasn't going to miss a gathering honouring a local hero who had, it was said, the King's ear. Even if it was a gathering of the lower classes.

Soon it was time for Simon to leave. He felt well pleased with himself. He was now a Cornish landowner; he could legally vote when he turned twenty-one, as only landowners could; and his half-brothers had left the farm two days earlier to begin their education at the cathedral college in Truro. With his family's future secure in the hands of his stepfather, he boarded a carriage that would take him to Penzance, then the Scilly packet to see his grandfather.

George Hicks greeted his nephew somewhat less coldly than before when he arrived on board the Scilly Island packet George still commanded. He still felt the disgrace, because of his wife Elizabeth's father having been executed. "What's this," he exclaimed, "an officer's uniform, and a might fine 'ne too! Some lads get things easy. I s'pose y' grandfather will be pleased enough t' see 'e," and George proceeded to become busy supervising loading his ship's cargo.

Simon tried on several occasions to engage his uncle in further conversation but met with polite coldness. No semblance of warmth would he display to his kinsman.

"Ye'll be a stayin' with yer grandfather, I presume," asked the packet captain, suggesting he would prefer Simon not lodge with him and his aunt.

"Aye, Uncle, I wish t' spend as much time with Grandfather as I can. I'll be away for a year on the next voyage. I understand, sir, he is not well?"

"Aye, 'e ain't good. 'E is seventy this year – not 'ad an easy life, 'ad 'is three score year 'n ten." George excused himself and went below to his private cabin, not offering to share its comfort with his nephew for the short but difficult voyage to Scilly.

The winds were variable and light, a mariner's curse in the dangerous waters between the mainland and the Scillies. It took the packet eight hours to cover 28 miles, which would have been achieved in four if conditions had been favourable.

In contrast to her husband's attitude, his Aunt Elizabeth was effusive. As she hugged him as he strode off the gangway, his hat was almost lost to the sea. "Simon, oh Simon, how well 'e looks! So grown, so much a man. T' thinks 'e left 'ere but a slip of a boy just a year 'n 'arf ago."

"You look right well, Aunt. 'Ow are me cousins?" he replied.

"Ye'll see for yerself soon enough. I've arranged a bed fer 'e in the sitting room, fer while yer 'ere, said Elizabeth, unaware of her husband's earlier discussion with Simon.

"Thank 'e, Aunt; ye'r most kind, but I'd prefer t' stay in the cottage with Gran'father, if ye don't mind. I've fond memories o' th place, and wish t' spend as much time wi' the old man as I can, seein' as it could be the last, God forbid," said Simon. But seeing disappointment in her eyes he added, "Perhaps a night or two when Uncle George is at sea?"

"Very well, Simon, I'm sure that's fine. Jason and Anne would be broken'earted if their famous cousin weren't t' stay wi' us fer part of 'is stay at least. Dad 'as most of 'is dinners wi' us – after 'e's spent a couple of hours at the Mermaid, that is – so we'll see 'im some days," agreed Elizabeth.

Simon walked his aunt to her door in Hugh Town, promising to return for the evening meal, when his cousins would be home from the parish school. Turning left before the Mermaid, Simon began the short climb up Garrison Hill towards the familiar cottage he had occupied for nine years with John Pearce.

Memories of his childhood flooded into his mind. A wave to Sahara Jenkins; a slap on the back from Charlie Pender; grins all round. Would he ever get used to his new status in life?

By God, I'm beginning to like it, he thought immodestly.

133

"Simon, lad, 'scuse an ol' man fer not waitin' at the quay fer 'e; getting a bit old fer 'anging around, I be. What a sight fer these old eyes 'e is!" John's eyes watered a little underlining his emotion. "Tell it t' me slow like, lad, all o' it; a gran'son o' mine met th' King, by God! That'll get us a few free rounds at the pub," John said grinning hugely.

The Mermaid had a full house that night; short of a wreck to plunder, a night of celebration was the best entertainment on the islands. A few sly digs like, "'E comin' on the run t' France t'morra?" from Frank Pender. "Best not get beer on 'is uniform, eh lads."

It wasn't till late that the two men, one very young and one very old, somewhat three sheets to the wind, arrived for the evening meal prepared by Elizabeth Hicks.

George, a teetotaller, was fuming.

The next day Simon, nursing a sore head, found another reason for his uncle's aloofness. John had something to say.

"Simon, me lad, I've left it t' ye. 'Ere's a copy o' me last will and testament. Esther May brought the cottage with 'er when we was wed; it's in the name of Pearce, an' that be 'ow I want 'er t' stay. George be a stiff ol' stick; good enough, I s'pose, to y' aunt but he don't like me, an' me 'im. So she's yorn, lad, when I'm gone that is."

"But Grandfather, I have my own fortune now. What of Jason and little Annie?" Simon replied.

"They ain't Pearces, lad; they be 'ickses. It's fer 'e t' decide what 'appens yonder. 'E'll be 'ead o' the family when I'm gone. There's y' sister t' think o' too. Now no more of it; I'm decided." John poured two glasses of rum. "Seal 'er wi' a tot lad, then 'er's done."

Although Simon tried to speak with his uncle on the matter, saying the cottage would be at their disposal at all times – he even suggested that another more permanent arrangement could be made when John passed on - still George Hicks remained cool.

Elizabeth made up for her husband's standoffishness, being the eternal aunt. "George 'as a right chip on 'is shoulder, lad. Being born Scillonian in the first place 'e reckons all else be lesser bein's. But it's cause o' y' dad an' Brian leavin' this earth the way they did; reckons us all are criminal stock, so t' speak. He's not just a bit jealous of 'e, neither; what wi' yer expectations an' all. I'm not minded t' leave

Garrison Cottage in 'is 'ands. Ye'll do the right thing when th' time comes. Let's speak of 'appier things. Tell us more of y' lady friend."

"Hardly a lady friend yet, Aunt 'Lizabeth, but that's what I dreams of. Isabella must be the most beautiful girl on this good earth. Y' should 'ear 'er laugh, like a bird singin'. It's a grand family she comes from, well known at court in Lisbon."

"'Er sounds mighty fine, mighty fine indeed. I s'pose bein' Portuguese 'er's, ah, Catholic like?"

"That she is. I know what you're goin' t' say, that the family'll not accept 'er her. I know I am young, but if Isabella would 'ave me, nothing on this earth would stop me marrying her. I would do anything, even convert."

"Aye, lad. I think yer uncle's attitude is more 'cause o' this – 'e's Wesleyan an' staunch. That's chapel like. 'E knows if 'e marries Isabella ye'll 'ave ter convert t' papism; 'e'll never speak ter 'e again, lad, nor yer offspring. Others in the family'll think th' same. But ne'er's the mind, ye'll follow yer heart, ye're determined. Methinks the family'll be worse fer it."

The talk was the beginning of a new closeness with his aunt.

It was with a great sadness that Simon took leave of the Scillies, he knew that his new life would keep him away for a long time, possibly forever. It was with a deep feeling of sorrow that he took a final hug from his grandfather, whom he knew he might never see again.

A coaster out of Falmouth delivered Simon to London docks and the premises of Messrs Blackwall and Co. The *Maid of Aran* looked magnificent, her new paintwork sparkled in the summer sunshine. A new gold stripe had been pressed into her gunwales, and she looked like a royal yacht. Once aboard, Simon was absorbed with shipboard life. He worked himself to a standstill on all manner of tasks. Sir Richard had promised to visit Madeira on the outward voyage, so he reasoned the quicker the ship sailed, the sooner he would see Isabella again.

It was Easter 1746 before they were ready for sea, loaded and deep in the water. The ship was warped to an outer quay to await favourable wind and tide to leave. Simon was able to celebrate his fourteenth birthday on an even keel prior to her departure.

Part Two

1773–1786

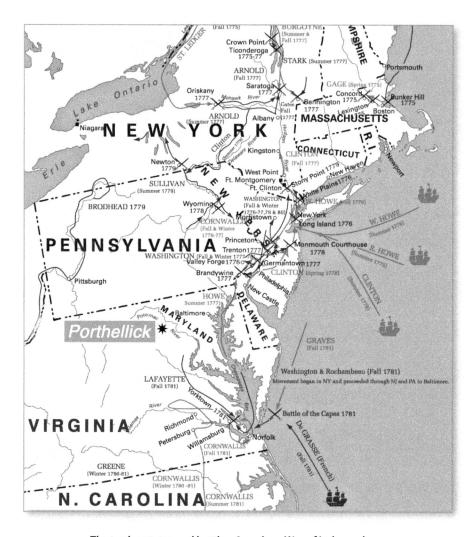

The twelve states and battles, American War of Independence

Chapter 15

The *Esther May Pearce*

Captain Simon Pearce stepped onto the quarterdeck of the new three-masted schooner, *Esther May Pearce*. It was just before the change of watch at eight bells – eight o'clock on a cold, blustery Bristol Channel morning. He nodded to the officer of the watch then spoke with the ship's sailing master, Sean Finnegan, with the rare rapport – almost familiarity – of men who had spent years at sea together.

"How is our offing, Mister Finnegan?"

"'Tis looking well, cap'n. We're full and bye, with Land's End a point and an 'alf off the port bow. Only an hour till change o' tide, but force five on the quarter should have us well clear o' the Scillies afore nightfall. The Seven Stones be six miles t' windward, out o' harm's way."

"Thank you, Mister Finnegan. Fine work as ever."

Simon took time to reflect on the first time he passed between the English mainland and Scilly. He hadn't anchored in the islands of his birth since his first command, the old *Maid of Aran*. His uncle, George Hicks, made it clear he was unwelcome at their home, having become 'a papist idol-worshipper'. The last time he had seen them was at his grandfather's funeral. John Pearce's will was read out to the mourners, as was the custom. When they found Garrison Cottage had been left to Simon, the Hicks family left the room in silent protest. He hadn't spoken to any of them since.

Sir Richard Blackmore had promised that on his death the *Maid of Aran* would become Simon's. A musket ball had hit him in the shoulder during a skirmish at sea while delivering illicit cargoes to America. He came close to death through infection and lost his arm. Then in his sixties, he had finally retired from the sea and passed ownership of his beloved ship to his stepbrother's son; Simon then owned and commanded the ship he had fallen in love with in St Mary's Pool all those years before, aged just thirteen. Now at 40, with 27 years of seafaring behind him, the *Maid of Aran*, well past her prime, had been sold and replaced by the *Esther May Pearce*.

Simon had invested the rest of his share of the Spanish treasure taken at the Battle of the Mona Passage well. His most pleasing purchase had been the freehold of Penpeth Farm, along with two neighbouring smallholdings in the Parish of St Just-in-the-Roseland. Ably run by his stepbrothers, the farm was some 220 acres, a very large property in England at the time. The income was more than enough for the family's needs and sufficient to send his nephew and stepbrothers to public school. The family had been elevated to the ranks of yeomen farmers and employed labour for the hardest work. A house befitting their status had been built on the property. Jane Farmiloe, now a healthy 64, was content living in the bosom of her family. She been widowed a second time – Michael Farmiloe had died of consumption during the particularly cold winter of '72.

Captain Simon Pearce eyed the set of the sails of his new ship critically; he found no fault and was deeply satisfied. Her builders Blackwall and Co. of London opened their yard in 1611. Builders of the famous Blackwall frigates of East India Company fame and dozens of ships for the Royal Navy, the master shipwrights had done him proud. It had taken a lot of persuading to build and rig her as their client instructed. Old Philip Perry, Blackwall's patriarch, was eventually convinced by his son John, recently returned from his schooling at Harrow and Oxford, to see the advantages of the new style of ship. Simon had seen the agility and swiftness of the American schooners; they simply turned hard on the wind, and pointing near four points higher, they sailed away from their cumbersome square-rigged naval pursuers.

"It's the new age, Father," young John Perry had said. "Besides, do you want our customer to give the order to the troublesome American shipbuilders on the Hudson?"

Eventually Philip, the master shipbuilder, was persuaded to build the ship to his client's exact design and specifications.

The *Esther May Pearce*, named in memory of Simon's grandmother, was rigged in the American way as topsail schooner. She was square-rigged on the foremast only for efficiency downwind. Carrying a coarse, topsail, topgallant and royal, an array of staysails and jibs forward of and between the main and foremast, she could point high to windward. Main and mizzen-carried gaff headed fore and aft sails; she could also set topsails above the gaffs on jack-yards. This amazing rig required far less crew and was less dangerous to sail than a full-rigged ship, as most of the fore and aft sails could be set from the deck.

The ship was 175 feet long on deck – the length of a naval frigate – and 550 tons berthen. Carrying eight 12-pound cannon and six twenties each side, as well as two 10-foot long toms at the bow and stern, she was very well armed – a power to be reckoned with. Letters of Marque had become outdated, so the ship's wily owner-captain needed a good excuse to arm her so. She was initially leased to the navy to protect supply ships carrying goods to the British forces in the Caribbean Islands and American colonies. Simon was able to argue that this amount of protection was required to prevent his ship and cargo from being taken by American privateers who harassed shipping in western waters.

American rebels were a cautious lot. Never offering the chance of a sea battle, they constantly harried the British supply lines, stretched as they were by the need to carry everything across the Atlantic Ocean, some 3,000 miles. With the French threatening war at home, the British Admiralty was loath to send the ships needed by the admiral commanding to keep the seaways safe. The supply route was south into the trade winds, across the Atlantic skirting the treacherous Caribbean and Bahaman islands, to New York or Boston. A voyage could take two or three months in good weather, even more in the hurricane season from May to November, when winds of incalculable strengths sent many a ship to her doom.

The *Esther May* was more than a match for the rebels and privateers. The ship was very fast, being fine forward and with a fair straight run aft, her deep-ballasted keel gave her the ability to point without giving much ground to leeway. Most ships of the day were built to carry maximum cargo at the expense of sailing ability – this ship was built to fly.

Simon watched the creaming line of foam pass from the ship's forefoot, along her sleek topsides, to end up as if icing on a cake, adorning the quarter wave rising many yards astern. He had learned to judge, by the size and shape of this wave, the rate of the ship's progress. The officer of the watch worked out the speed using the time-honoured method of dropping an object such as a knotted piece of cordage from forward, timing it as it passed the stern, thus producing via simple calculation the ship's speed in nautical miles per hour, commonly known as knots.

Once an officer had made his calculation and written it in the deck log, Simon would pass a note to him with his own estimate written upon it; they would then compare notes.

"Nine and one quarter," he said to himself.

Looking at the log he found the figure nine and a half. *Not bad*, he thought, *not bad at all.* At this rate Madeira will hove up in four to five days. He would have two glorious months at his plantation with beautiful Isabella and his children.

Thoughts of his wife and family warmed him so, that even the cool September nor'easter could not chill him. He remembered the days before he married Isabella and the difficulties he had in securing her hand ...

Over the years, Sir Richard Blackmore's deeds and those of his protégé had become well known on the Atlantic grapevine. The Mendoza family, who now lived permanently on the island, had warmed to the once outrageous idea of an Englishman marrying into the family. Juan Mendoza had succeeded his father as governor and had finally considered Simon a suitable suitor as his friend's list of exploits and wealth grew.

Because of their services to his country, the Portuguese monarch had waved a strictly observed decree that foreigners were not to own land on Portuguese territory, and he secretly granted both Richard and Simon freedom to purchase property on Madeira. On each voyage, from then on, the *Maid of Aran*'s holds would be loaded with fine Madeira wine, which was traded with the many large estates of the Carolinas and Virginia for tobacco or cotton. Well-to-do English military officers and colonists were also good customers, being hungry for luxury goods and weapons – it was a very profitable business for both men.

The two lovebirds developed a magical trust between them. Isabella knew well that any man she married could be away making his fortune for much of their younger life. She could not bear other foppish, spineless young men that would arrive on the island from time to time to court her, at the behest of her father. The suitors' lineages and family wealth made the chore of earning a living unnecessary for them. They had little to talk of other than intrigues at court – who was doing what and with whom. These wastrels offered no competition to Simon in Isabella's eyes; they were dismissed out of hand, no competition to her dashing sea captain.

To Simon, Isabella was simply a goddess to be worshipped.

On the return from the *Maid of Aran*'s sixth voyage to the Americas, George Partridge had retired and Simon had been promoted to first lieutenant. The petty officers, including Sean Finnegan, had paid for a high-class courtesan to take away what the crew thought to be Simon's troublesome virginity. After an embarrassing introduction to this apparently well-to-do lady ensconced comfortably in his room, he became aware of her purpose. Quietly but forcefully he told the lady of his love for Isabella. The simple revelation was made with such passion that the prostitute broke down in a flood of tears.

During the story the courtesan composed herself; she suddenly smiled and spoke. "Truly, sir, your Isabella is a most fortunate woman. Not many men would turn me down as you have. But I could still be of service to you without betraying her trust. What do you truly know of the ways of love and how to enrapture and please your lady beneath the covers of your marriage bed?"

"Frankly, madam, my knowledge is cursory to say the least. It is a fact of no little cause of concern to me," replied the young ship's officer, now at ease as the woman before him had seemingly evolved from whore to teacher.

Josephine went into great detail explaining the processes of lovemaking, especially from the woman's point of view. She lifted her voluminous skirts and petticoats so as to actually show him the areas of a woman's anatomy to which he must pay special attention. Nearly fainting with embarrassment as he stirred to what his manhood must have thought was to be its first full-on engagement.

"I am somewhat mollified, sir, that you find me not totally undesirable," Josephine jibed with a lurid smile as she casually brushed his appendage. "You may yet practise that which I have tried to impart, sir, should you have had a change of heart."

"Madam, I can honestly say that I have a strong urge to do just as you say; however, how am I to look into Isabella's eyes and ask for her hand in just a few months' time if I were to do so?" He sighed, thanked Josephine and, when she was ready, gently ushered her from the room.

Diego Mendoza sat stiffly on a gilded chair in his drawing room, his carefully prepared words flown from his mind, as the young ship's officer before him pleaded for his only daughter's hand in marriage.

"There are difficulties, yes, many difficulties - more than you can ever imagine - to this union you propose," he said firmly. You are a fine young man with a good future before you; you have participated in deeds that have made you well thought of in high places in my country. While my son and I cannot fault you as an honourable suitor, we are a Catholic family in a Catholic country. Isabella is a *Catholic* - do you understand just what that means? Dear God, man! You have stated that your own family is less than pleased at the prospect. Is not your uncle not a Protestant clergyman - what does he think of this?" The ex-governor was now red-faced and not a little angry at the problems his headstrong daughter had brought him - why, she could have had her pick of the best in the kingdom.

He waited for the young man to reply.

Simon composed himself and began the speech of his life. "All you have said is true, sir, but you must understand my point of view. I know Isabella is a Catholic but first she is, as I am, a believer in the God of all men, a good and caring God that sent his only son to die on the cross so we may be saved. My own family are Protestant, yes, but what you do not know is that, while we are Church of England, my cousins are Wesleyan and attend a small chapel on the northern boundary of the Roseland. The people of each branch of the family seldom speak together. This is solely because of a different interpretation of what Isabella and I believe are the same basic facts. I see only dogmatic and political differences between all Christian denominations - the ideals and way of life told by our Lord remain the same in each.

"As a sailor I have seen some wild, wondrous and terrible things at sea. I have fought some bitter battles against an enemy who prays to the same God as I do, for salvation in the same battle, yet we fight on opposite sides. I cannot believe that this one God, that all claim as their own, can only be worshipped within a church of a single denomination and that this merciful God, whose son spoke so much of love, will send to eternal damnation all those souls who worship Him in a church of another denomination.

"I understand, sir, that the Bible was first put to paper some 400 years after the death of Jesus and that Christians have been fighting about the interpretation of the gospels ever since. One thing we all seem to agree on is that there is one God. And that his son was sent to earth to save us from sin. The finer details frankly, sir, do not interest either of us; they are in fact little more than political expediency.

"Isabella and I have discussed the problem at length; there is, we believe, but one solution. In order to be accepted by society here I must convert to Catholicism. As I have said, I have no favour for any faction. This appears to be the only course we can take to be married and live together with our union sanctified in God's name.

"These views are ours and not known by any save you, sir, and Juan. We know many would consider us heretics; they are therefore dangerous. I trust you can see that your daughter's happiness is of paramount importance to me. I will do anything honourable to achieve that happiness for her. We have waited near ten years, sir; by your leave, we shall wait no longer."

Diego Mendoza was stunned. Yes, his thoughts had run on similar lines. Dangerous thoughts he had uttered to no one - the Spanish had left inquisition fervour among many of Portugal's clergy.

"What will your family think of this, er, conversion?" he asked, seemingly swaying in his resolve.

"When I told my mother of my decision, she was at first shocked, but she soon realised I was committed to my course and would not be deterred. She has agreed to come to Madeira as the sole representative of our family at the wedding - apart from Sir Richard Blackmore, of course, who has agreed to perform the duties of best man," said Simon forcefully.

Mendoza rang the small bell on the table beside him; a servant appeared at the doorway. He instructed him to bring Isabella to the room.

She made a magnificent entrance, again putting her father in a position of discomfort.

"So, my dear, this impudent young man has asked for your hand in marriage. What say you to the matter?"

"Father, there is nothing more I would wish for in my entire life than to 'ave Simon as my 'usband," the young woman answered, with a passion that her father knew would not be denied.

"Pearce," he said with a smile. "An odd name for a Portuguese family, is it not?"

Thus concluded Diego Mendoza's contrary discussion on the matter ...

"Scillies t' weather, cap'n. Wind steady, nor'east by east freshening some; we will feel the bite of channel swells in a few hours. Reckon it would pay to reduce sail afore nightfall," hailed Michael Johnston, the ship's American first officer, his words finally dragging Simon from his reverie.

Not long now, my darling, not long now, Simon thought, as he brought his attention to the tasks of the present.

Eyeing the scudding clouds to weather and the brassy look to the setting sun, the captain replied, "Quite right, Mister Johnston. Furl the forecourse, and the gallant. Let's get the main and mizzen topsails off her as well; we'll remove the foretopsail before dusk, I think. Have the heavy weather staysails bent as a precaution."

With all square sails now furled the ship was close-hauled and making her course steadily, the wind six points off the starboard bow, sailing far higher into the wind than any square-rigged ship could hope to.

As the glass began its inexorable fall, the wind changed to the sou'west. How often did this happen? A ship just clear of the channel, and the lee shore of France and Biscay beckoning, the wind would turn against her. Again Simon marvelled at the way his new ship handled the growing wind and wave height, yet point so high to weather. Reduced now to heavy staysails and double-reefed main, she plugged into the building head sea, each wave showering her with spray and burying her lee scuppers in foam and green water. Yet with the building gale she was comfortably on course to weather Cape Finisterre. All night she plugged southward. More sail had been taken in, the crew were tired, cold, wet and hungry.

A dreary dawn greeted the change of watch; the captain anxiously awaited the time he could obtain a sight of the sun to fix his position. With the heavy cloud cover, only an occasional glimpse of the heavenly body was to be seen, making the chances of obtaining the traditional 'noon sight' improbable.

Simon had purchased a chronometer before the previous year's voyage. This he meticulously calibrated and formed an error table. With an accurate timepiece a navigator could find his ship's longitude. At noon he would take his customary noon sight, thereby ascertaining their latitude. He gave the precious machine its precise eight turns of the key, its spring fuelling it for the next 24 hours of accurate timekeeping. Being conversant with the equation of time, and with the aid of the current year's nautical almanac, he could now take a sun sight at any time of day. After working through a tortuous set of calculations, he would be able to draw a line on his chart, on which – somewhere – was the ship's position. He would then move the noon latitude across the chart using parallel rules, along their course, the distance they had sailed. The earlier line would be at a different angle, as the sun's declination changed during the day, so the lines would cross. The point at which the lines crossed was a fixed position at the time of the second sight – a firm position. To a navigator of the old school, that cross on the chart was better than a pot of gold – they could now fix a position out of sight of land! Assuming the clock was accurate – because but four seconds error would produce a one-mile error – a navigator's calculations had to be accurate. Needless to say, a parallel set of dead-reckoning calculations and deck log was kept in the old way by the sailing master, for comparison.

It was well known that Master John Harrison's chronometer was not yet fully approved by the Board of Longitude, and of course that hard-working, long-suffering man had not yet picked up the £20,000 prize money offered by the King at the time of the wrecking of Sir Cloudesley Shovell's fleet. Notwithstanding this fact, many an enterprising private ship's commander who could afford it was using one.

"West'sou'west, cap'n, an' a-risin'; 'ard to keep 'er to course. We must be makin' a point o' leeway at least," said bosun's mate Matt McGellygot as he fought the bucking wheel.

"Better us 'ave second man at the 'elm, fer safety's sake," said Sean Finnegan with growing concern.

The *Esther May* plunged into another deep trough, burying her bows and sending a wall of cold seawater racing aft along her decks as she lifted her defiant head to the next foaming crest. The sun made an occasional if somewhat obscure appearance between the racing clouds. It was enough, however, for the captain to snatch an observation, all be it with great difficulty. Observing the sun through his sextant's telescope, he had to bring the mirror bar of the instrument down to place the lower limb of the sun so it just kissed the horizon, which looked now like a jagged mountain range – a difficult procedure in the gale.

"How does it look, cap'n?" the first officer asked nervously. He had been taking the exact time of each sight as Simon called 'now'.

"Well enough, Mister Johnston. I will average the three sights; being morning with the sun east of us, the resulting position line will be between us and the lee shore. This will give a good indication of how much sea room we have. If you and Mister Finnegan would join me in half an hour we can compare my results with the dead-reckoning position." Simon then went below to reduce his sight to a line on the chart.

He called 'enter' to the courteous rap on his cabin door. "Gentlemen, please be seated. I have been able to obtain a position line that puts us clear of Ushant, but I believe we are headed well inside Finisterre. Please plot your dead-reckoning position, and let us see what we have."

"I have us 20 miles to the south and east of the Little Sole Bank, sir. My mark is but 10 miles short of your sight. I think we can assume that we are within a circle that encompasses both our positions. Our present course will be a little east of south, allowing for leeway. Should we continue as we are, we would hove upon the coast of northern Spain in 36 hours," said Johnston.

At thirty, Johnston was old for a first lieutenant. The custom in the Royal Navy at that time was that no loyalist Americans ever rose to the rank of even the most junior captain. He had jumped at the chance to join a private vessel when the *Esther May Pearce* was in need of a first officer after her own had been killed in a dock loading accident. The naval port captain had offered Johnston to the new ship to ensure that Simon could leave on time, to carry out his difficult naval charter.

It had not taken long for the *Esther May*'s captain to value his new second in command; it seemed he was an accomplished navigator as well.

"Yes, Mister Johnston, I agree. Sean, what do you think?"

"I agree, cap'n, an' we'll make a sight more leeway as the seas steepen, the water shallows and the wind increases. I believe we should maintain this tack till either the wind goes further south or until nightfall, then go onto port and make some sea room."

"Mister Johnston?" asked Simon.

"Aye, sir; that would be prudent. It would be mighty handy to pick a noon or afternoon sight as well; a fixed position now would be right handy," said Johnston, his lazy drawl masking his seaman's underlying concerns.

It was the beginning of the first dogwatch. All hands were called to put the ship about onto the port tack. The sun had not shown itself again, and the wind had moved further south. Simon glanced at his sailing master and said, "When in doubt, stand out, eh Mister Finnegan!"

"Indeed so, soir," he answered.

The ship plugged through the night heading at almost right angles to her preferred course, well away from the direct line to Madeira, but also away from Biscay's dreaded shoreline. The foretopsail's gaskets had loosened during the night, and the officer of the watch had ordered his top men aloft to secure the wildly flapping canvas that threatened to fill and take the topmast out of the ship.

It is doubtful any landsman could ever fully comprehend what was involved in carrying out that order: at deck level, handholds were required just to be able to stand; at the topsail yard, seamen were suspended, hanging onto the spar, their feet clinging to a footrope underneath – all this 80 feet above the heaving deck, the mast describing an arc some 90 feet wide every minute or so. The seamen had to securely tie the heavy canvas sail to the spar; nails were torn from fingers. Wildly flapping canvas was ready to knock them senseless or send them spinning into the sea below. Topmen were a breed of their own.

It was of some considerable concern to the captain that Michael O'Flaherty, the foremast's bosun's mate, had gone aloft with his men. A veteran of 20 years at sea, he was leading his men from the front; however, at 33 years of age he was getting a little old to be aloft in those conditions. Simon watched, heart in mouth, as the foretop yard described its arc through the gloomy sky, when she suddenly plunged to leeward as a particularly steep sea rolled the ship more than usual. As if in slow motion, she just recovered from the first steep sea when a second thundered into her bows. The men aloft had been braced for the first, then expected a gentler roll to weather, the sails full of wind counterbalancing the ocean's attempts to roll the ship from beam to beam. Two of the five figures aloft had the obdurate canvas, filling with the power of the gale, ripped from their hands. As the ship crashed into the next wave, the topmast became a whip staff, flicking two men from their precarious perch. They fell head over heels, like rag dolls, into the foaming sea. O'Flaherty and young Tommy Philips simply disappeared – erased – gone – as if they had never been.

Simon came out of his trance-like state. "Sean – Michael – get sail off her, put her about. We can drift down to leeward and find them."

Big, wise Sean Finnegan put both hands on the captain's shoulders, partly from affection, partly to steady them both on the heaving deck. Shouting to be heard against the howl of the gale he yelled, "We could maybe find their bodies, but we'll roll the rig out o' her tryin', ye knows that, soir. I've known Michael since 'e were a boy; he'd not 'ave 'e risk the rest of the crew for little or no chance o' findin' 'im. Anyhow, like most of us, neither 'e nor the boy can swim; 'es with God, cap'n. Let it be."

Simon allowed Sean to see him to his cabin once the remaining three foretopmen had cut away the sail and regained the safety of the deck. The weight of command suddenly too much to bear, he fell into his bunk and slept fitfully, his crew tending the ship as she made her way to the relative safety of the wide Atlantic Ocean.

"A full three-dayer, sir," said the first officer to his captain, eight bells signalling the end of his night watch. It was midnight.

"Aye, Mister Johnston, and a long, slow beat to windward if I'm not mistaken," answered Simon, all traces of the intimacy of the last evening gone as his authority as sole arbiter of his men's lives returned.

Chapter 16

Home on Madeira

Captain Simon Pearce had the jollyboat loaded with his personal gear, along with a number of conspicuous parcels destined for his wife and family. The *Esther May Pearce* had anchored off the small town of Machico, on the east of the island of Madeira. Simon had handed temporary command to his American first officer, Michael Johnston, for the final few miles to Puerto Funchal, the island's vibrant capital. Machico had been the landing place of the original settlers of the island; Funchal, however, was soon preferred as capital, being more sheltered from the winter gales.

Isabella was at the quay waiting with three of their children – Juanita, Carlos and Isabellita. Juan, the eldest, was studying medicine in Lisbon.

It had been ten long months since Simon had seen his family, and he struggled to keep the tears from his eyes as his lovely wife greeted him.

"You look well, 'usband. We 'ave all been counting the days until your return."

"For ten months of lonely nights I have dreamt of this moment. Carlos, my son. 14 years old now, eh? It will soon be time to come to sea, my lad. Ah, Juanita, you look so like your lovely mother and so grown-up in that beautiful dress. And Isabellita – eleven already."

Simon addressed his family with a casual formality, as if he'd not been away for more than a few weeks, carefully complimenting each in front of the villagers assembled to greet him. More informal greetings would wait until they reached the estate in the cool hills just an hour's carriage ride to the south of the tiny but thriving town.

Having acknowledged all those who had come to greet the popular sea captain at the quay, the Pearce family escaped, making their way home to the estate at the foothills of Madeira's impressive northern mountains. They drove along a beautiful driveway lined with shady fruit trees coming to a springtime crescendo of blossom. The end of this shady lane opened into a broad area of cobblestones upon which stood their large, two-storeyed house.

Built in the traditional manner of the Madeiran vineyard, it served two purposes. The entire ground floor was given over to grape presses and storage of maturing wines. Those of the finest vintages were stored in cellars hewn from the cool rock by the hands of many slaves, Madeira being the centre of the Portuguese slave trade in the seventeenth and eighteenth centuries. Many an unfortunate Negro was used on the island while awaiting shipment to the markets in the Caribbean, America or Brazil.

Upstairs the luxurious accommodations had a magnificent view – hundreds of tidy lines of vines cascaded down the hillside towards the bay, culminating in an amazing vista of the sea. From the house, young Carlos Pearce had spotted his father's ship, still 40 miles offshore, through a telescope received on his last birthday.

"So, my 'usband, 'ow do you think of it?" Isabella asked excitedly as the family walked through to the new dining wing built during his absence. The roof of the structure was specially strengthened to bear the weight of two long 12-pound cannon and four 18-pounders. These Simon would install to protect the family and 30 of the estate's retainers from attack by French pirates. These violent, desperate men had become troublesome of late. Simon's first job would be to properly install the guns and train his people to use them. Gunner, the *Esther May*'s master gunner, now in his sixties, would arrive in a few days, along with Sean Finnegan, to attempt to turn Madeiran farmers into disciplined gun crews.

"My darling, you never cease to amaze me. I had fully expected to return to tradesmen everywhere, dust and an incomplete structure. You have achieved a miracle," exclaimed her husband.

"I 'ope you remain so 'appy when I give you the final accounts to pay," returned Isabella mischievously.

After a sumptuous dinner with meats, fowl and wine that would have satisfied the king himself, Simon's father-in-law, the ebullient

Diego Mendoza, sallied forth entertaining the company till well past midnight. Eventually Simon and Isabella were alone.

"I think, Captain Pearce, it is now a time in our life for us to practise, 'ow you say, restraint, eh? You come 'ome for but a few weeks a year and leave me to bear you yet more offspring. The priests are 'appy, but my bones grow tired," the twinkle in Isabella's eyes giving away her attempts to fool her husband.

"Restraint, madam! D'ye not think that near ten months living as a bachelor is restraint enough? Perhaps you would have me take a young 'tottie' to sea for comfort along the way, and maybe a mistress here to save you any trouble?" Simon retorted, engaging in her playful game.

Then joking was put aside as their long-awaited moment of intimacy was upon them. Isabella let go the last clasp of her beautiful golden gown, to which had been cleverly attached the many undergarments worn by women. A woman of 20 would have been proud of her looks, but she was a mature matron of 40, who had borne four children. Clad in but a light, Florentine silk chemise her smouldering brown eyes looked over a perfectly shaped shoulder, her crooked finger beckoning towards a large bed at the far end of their chamber, her meaning unmistakable. "What you think, we forget I said restraint, eh, captain? Besides, I 'ave received instructions from a Chinese doctor on ways to be careful, just at particular times each month."

Simon undressed quickly, shaking with urgency. Eyes moist with tenderness the handsome couple fell onto the sparkling sheets as one.

Casa d'Ouro came alive, with the return of the master of the house. Not that Isabella was unable to see to the affairs of her household - on the contrary, she ran the estate most ably, also overseeing the children's education and dealing with the servants. But the estate was not the same when he was away. While she said nothing, Isabella longed for the day her husband would retire from active seagoing life, something she knew was some years away yet - Simon would not retire until their son was able to take over the seafaring part of their business.

Juan had already left home to study medicine, against his father's wishes. It would fall to Carlos, their third-born son, to go to sea, thus beginning the long journey to qualify him to fill his father's ample sea boots. She had, however, begun - as women do - to formulate a plan.

She would wait for the right moment to begin the process of getting her husband's agreement.

Breakfast was served; the family sat at a huge mahogany table in the newly built dining room enjoying a feast of fresh fruits. Simon noticed Isabella appeared distracted and obviously concerned about something.

"What is worrying you, my dear? You seem preoccupied this morning."

"It is the guns," she answered. "For years the pirates attack. We 'ave the two forts in Machico Bay that 'ave always given us time to 'ide in the mountains. Sometimes the pirates get past the soldiers and steal from the vineyards but the peoples they return; so we lose some wine and some animals, but we are still alive, no? Our people are farmers not fighters. I fear many a good *senhora* will be made a widow by these guns you bring among us."

"I understand your concerns, sweetness, but consider this. The next time pirates attack, they will find us ready. They are cowards; they will be far less inclined to return once they find we are prepared for them. They need to get in and out quickly. If we make a stand they will not be able to attack and retire with the necessary speed. This may give us enough precious time for our ships in Funchal Bay to get to sea and engage them. Should we, God willing, prevail, other pirates will hear that Machico is too tough a nut to crack and leave us alone." Simon was optimistic – men who had fought for their lives and livelihood needed to be.

"It is always the same. Mens tinks only of fighting; women tink of giving and saving life. I tink maybe if you open up the nest of the hornet, he no 'appy till 'e 'as stung everyone in the town." Isabella left the table, not wishing her children to see her discomfort.

While pirates were an ongoing menace, it was in fact partly due to a sixteenth-century pirate – one Bertrand de Montluc, who raided Funchal and stole much gold and wine – that the island's products became more widely known. The pirate's customers, in the highest echelons of French society, became legitimate customers of the island, paying a premium for Madeira wine's powerful flavours.

Antonio Fernandes stood solidly outside the estate office, situated at the entry to his master's apartments on the villa's ground floor. In each hand he held the bridle of two fine bay mares. At forty-five, as general overseer of the estate, he had proven himself a trusted, clever and loyal retainer. Antonio had been on Simon's staff for 16 years, ever since he had purchased the property. "I give praise to *Dios* for your safe return, master. I 'ave taken the liberty of preparing the 'orses so you can inspect the property," he said.

Simon took his servant by both shoulders, answering him with affected anger. "What have I told you many times, Antonio, you old fox! Don't call me master ..." and with affection in passable Portuguese, "... you are too old a friend."

The heavily moustached man replied quietly, "It is not good for the peons to see us too familiar, sir; it distances them from me. To serve you best I must hear what is going on under the surface of the community."

"As usual you are right, Antonio. Call me captain then if you must; master smacks too much of slavery for my liking," returned Simon.

"As you wish, captain. We begin the inspection now, if you please?" requested Antonio.

They mounted, Simon riding in the uneasy manner of a seafarer, while Antonio was in his element. It was noon before Simon was able to convince his head man that he was totally satisfied with the condition of the estate – Antonio had insisted on showing him every corner. He carefully discussed improvements he wished to make to the picturesque, triangular stone and thatch workers' cottages that were a unique feature of the island.

As Simon rode into the courtyard, he heard Carlos calling. "Father, father! A whale has been caught; it is being brought to the beach this moment. I see it through my telescope. Can we go – pleeese." Carlos's spoken English was as good as any country squire's son, thanks to the English teacher Simon had brought to Casa d'Ouro three years previously.

"Slow down, my lad. What does your mother say?"

"I 'ave no wish to see the beautiful creature dead an' 'acked to pieces on the beach," she exclaimed with indignation. "'Ave your pony saddled and go with your father if you must. I will 'ave Rosa bring some food from the kitchen to eat while you ride. Eating may slow you ruffians down a little," Isabella added with a smile.

"Can Pedro come too, Senhor Antonio?" asked the boy, in perfect Portuguese, his good manners pleasing his father.

"*Sim*. If he has finished his work, it will be fine."

Pedro Fernandes was a pleasant boy, a year older than Carlos. The boy had dark olive skin which told of many generations of ancestry on the island, whose amazing climate was generally about 24 degrees. Pedro was the family's youngest child, his father's favourite among his brood of five sisters and older brother, Manuel. Pedro had intelligent eyes and his father's ability to assess people quickly while at the same time putting them at their ease. He had overtaken the other children in the class Isabella taught for the children of the estate, to the extent that he attended extra sessions she, along with the English teacher, provided for her own children.

Pedro and Carlos were firm – no, best – friends.

Weeks flew by, and the time drew near for the *Esther May Pearce* to load her cargo and once again take Isabella's beloved Simon away. She became restless and irritable. She had lowered her usual reserve to reply angrily to the wife of a wealthy sugar cane grower who had commented about her not being a true Catholic – her with a foreign husband who only converted from the heretical English church to have his way with her. While the males of the island's top families welcomed Simon into their community, their womenfolk, being more devout to the Catholic Church, held Isabella at arm's length when their husbands were out of earshot.

One Sunday afternoon as the Host was being performed at mass in Capela dos Milagres, the oldest church on the island, a lieutenant in charge of Machico's two small forts burst in. He strode towards the pulpit and spoke to the priest in hurried, whispered tones. The congregation shifted uneasily in their pews.

"Thank you, my son, now go and attend to your business. Godspeed!" said the priest.

Then as he addressed his flock, Father Domingo's demeanour became grave. "My children, it appears that God has not heard our prayers; yet again the devil prevails in our small town. There are unrepentant sinners in our midst who have allowed Satan's minions, the French pirates, to seek us out once more. Go quickly to your hiding places, and prepare later for a full confession of your sins once the danger has passed."

Isabella was organising the people of the estate into groups – women and children into one group, and the men who would return to Casa d'Ouro and rejoin Gunner and Sean Finnegan to defend the property, in another. Fortunately she had allowed Carlos to ride his horse to church that day. "Ride home quickly, my son. Inform Senhor Finnegan and Gunner of our danger. Take food and water and make your way to Puerto Funchal. Inform the governor and your father. Take the mountain road."

"Yes, Mother, but surely the coast road is much quicker?" replied the lad.

"No! The coast road is quicker, yes, but in the past the *bastardo* French 'ave landed a party to stop our riders getting through. The pass is longer and dangerous but you will not 'ave to fight to get through."

Isabella knew that Carlos was a good rider; he had travelled the pass many times. It worried her that he was still a boy, but her instinct was to get her son as far away from the firing line as possible. "Take Pedro with you, my son, do you understand?"

"Do not worry, Mother. Pedro and I will get through," the boy answered bravely over his shoulder. Pedro climbed onto the mare behind him as he spurred the beast into an urgent gallop.

As a general might marshal his forces, Isabella split her household into two groups. The women drove their own carts with the children and old folk. Their destination was Los Roques del Diabo, high in the *cordilheira*, a region of volcanic peaks in central Madeira, an area of ravines and caves never yet found by an invader. The men were given the family carriage and spare horses to get to Casa d'Ouro as quickly as possible to prepare. With some misgivings, Isabella was complying with her husband's plans to defend their home.

Shortly after Carlos and Pedro had left for Funchal, the estate men arrived, lead by Antonio Fernandez. The teachings of Sean and Gunner had ignited a flame in these simple landsmen; they had had enough of the wild pirates raiding their town at will. They believed their English teachers. It was God's will that they defended their homes, and they believed in their own ability to fight.

Sean was less optimistic. "'Tis well enough them peasants know how to load and fire cannon, Gunner me lad, but as we both well know, the whistle of shot around their ears could well turn their anger to bile. We must hit hard 'n quick when they come."

"Indeed, Sean. It must look to the Frenchies – if they arrive – that Casa d'Ouro is just another estate left empty for them to plunder with ease. We'll 'ave all the men 'ere on the ramparts, 'idden like. We'll need a scout at the entrance o' the drive t' let us know that them's on their way. When they gets into the open we'll let 'em 'ave it with chain and grape. We must 'it 'em 'ard with the first two salvos or they'll wait till dark and pick us off." The veteran of many fights looked unconcerned, but he was used to fighting at sea; the land was strange to him – too many places for an enemy to hide.

Sean nodded agreement at Gunner's plan but added, "There's Antonio's son, Manuel, and a couple of other youngsters I bin trainin', if you can spare us. Us could do much t' discourage a counter-attack by sniping at 'em from behind, after ye 'ave given 'em a maulin' with cannon. We need to fool 'em into tinkin' us's better'n we are. "

"Risky, but t'would give us more of a surprise. I got 'nough men t' man the guns for a couple o' rounds. Go to it, Sean, and Godspeed."

The shipmates of two decades shook hands and went about their own preparations, each immersed in their own pre-battle thoughts, fears and misgivings.

With about 150 estate workers and villagers, Isabella reached the point where they must leave the wagons and head up the valley that lead to the ravine of Los Roques del Diabo. As the name suggests it was an awesome place; huge boulders littered the valley floor giving the valley its name, 'the rocks of the devil'. They carried water skins, food and blankets – it became quite cold at night in the caves where they would shelter.

As Isabella led the people through the boulder-strewn ravine a bigoted woman, overweight, in her forties, muttered that God was displeased because their community harboured heretics, indicating the Pearce family. Had not Father Domingo said so? Why else would the pig, French pirates come to their town?

An eerie quiet followed the rumblings of distant cannon fire.

"The western fort's ceased firing, the eastward's out o' range. Methinks the lieutenant's stayin' put in 'is cosy fort. We'll 'ave visitors afore too long, Antonio," said Gunner to the nervous estate manager. "Ye 'ad better keep yer 'ead down; you're the only one who can translate me orders to your people. A mistake at the start could be fatal. Make sure everyone stays outta sight and quiet. We're aimed 'n as ready as we'll ever be." The veteran seaman, with more battles and fights behind him than he could remember, waited for the enemy, the waiting, as usual, the hardest part of a fight.

With help from Carlos's telescope, Gunner spotted a group of armed men making their way up the dusty road towards the gates of Casa d'Ouro, the first estate out of Machico. A stand of trees hid the entrance so his next sighting would be over the sights of his beloved cannon.

In the fading light the man who had seen a hundred fights first heard, then saw, about ten heavily armed men approach the house from the gloom of the driveway, not suspecting that any resistance awaited them.

"That's it, me beauties, stick together like that an' I'll 'ave 'e all," Gunner said under his breath.

Taking a slow match he put it to the touch hole of his cannon, while signalling his three gunner's mates to do likewise. A deafening roar made the newly trained gun crews cower in fear. Recoil shook the building, sending pictures from their hangings and plaster from the walls.

The Madeiran farmers looked on in awe at what they had done. Chain shot had cut three men in half, while the grape had killed or grievously wounded the rest of the advance party. Not a groan escaped a lip, so effective was the pattern laid by Gunner. The earth of the driveway was red with gore and the air filled with the moaning of dying men.

"Don't gawp, ye lubbers, reload. There's more be'ind this lot."

The sound of small arms fire spurred the gun crews into action, preparing their charges to unleash another murderous rain of iron and lead. As the small arms fire died away, Gunner spotted movement behind the carnage caused by the first salvo.

"Steady now, lads. Wait ..." His words were drowned by the cannon furthest from him, just as he identified Sean and Manuel walking casually into the fading light. The boy was cut to pieces before his father's horrified eyes. Sean fell, clutching his left shoulder. Gunner raced down the staircase and ran to his friend's side.

Sean was kneeling over Manuel's shattered body, a tear in the veteran's clear blue eye. "Pedro, Marcelo, Diego – are ye hit?"

His question was answered as he saw two of the young men helping the third along the drive. They had been far enough behind to miss the main force of the blast – only a ricochet off a rock had unluckily redirected a ball into Marcelo's left leg.

Antonio had remained on the roof. Having picked up a ramrod, he swung it at the unfortunate who had fired his gun in haste. Had it not been for his companions, a second farmer's death would have occurred. They pinned their boss to the rooftop until his anger turned to tears. Antonio didn't need a closer look to know that his son was beyond any attention a mere father could give.

"Come, lad, let's get t' the 'ouse. I'm no surgeon but I'll need t' 'ave a look at that," said Gunner indicating Sean's wound.

"It'll take more 'n this to do for me, matie."

The Irishman walked slowly away from the bloody scene, his good hand stemming the flow of blood from his shoulder. As he walked away he muttered, "Cover the boy up. Don't want Antonio seein' 'im like that. Poor bugger – and 'im soon to be married."

"Do 'e reckon any o' the lubbers got away?" Gunner called after Sean.

"Not as I seen, but if any o' the bastards did, we mayn't 'ave seen the last of 'em this night. Better be ready if they come a-lookin' for their shipmates."

Watches were kept throughout the night, both at the gate and the house. The men rested uneasily knowing that they would not have the advantage of surprise in another attack. Sean's shoulder was badly lacerated; no bone damage was evident to the makeshift surgeon. Likewise fortunate was Marcelo – the ball had passed nearly through his thigh. Gunner made a small incision after the young man had been rendered comatose with the rough brandy brewed from the dregs of the wine presses. The ball, half an inch below the surface, was quickly removed.

Several fires could be seen in the village below, more alarming to the occupants of Casa d'Ouro; several more were evident higher up the road. The arsonists had to pass the estate gates on their return – this large group of pirates knew where the richest pickings would be.

As dawn broke cannon fire was heard in the bay. Two caravels were heading towards the nearest of the French ships, bow chasers strafing the anchored vessel. A square-rigged ship would have had to be content with blockading the bay until a wind shift allowed her to engage. Just rounding the headland, behind the Portuguese ships, Gunner could clearly see the *Esther May*, her gun ports open at the ready, her course directly for the second pirate ship, which was in the process of getting under way. Seeing the danger, she cut her cable.

A cheer was stifled in Gunner's throat as he thought of the numbers of pirates that may still be on shore. *Let's 'ope the soldiers from the forts will come out and get amongst 'em*, he thought.

A greater uneasiness yet dawned on him – if the scum could take Casa d'Ouro, with its fine cannon, and bring hostages here, they would greatly increase their bargaining power.

"Antonio," Gunner called loudly. "Reckon we may 'ave a bit o' a problem."

The offshore breeze quickly gave the pirate brig steerage way, expecting the oncoming *Esther May* to come about to engage her port side. With her crew greatly reduced by the shore parties, they had loaded and run out the starboard battery only.

Simon saw this and chuckled. "Load our port side but run out starboard," he ordered. "Bosun, have your men ready at the sheets. I intend to bear away, cross her bows then come hard on the wind and blast her port side as we pass. They'll not be manned both sides. I'll wager we will not receive a single shot in return. Bow chasers, fire at her as you bear. I will give you a point blank first shot. Make it count, reload speedily and take a second."

"Mister Johnston, what do you make her speed?" asked Simon.

"Three knots, sir, but getting quicker. About two minutes till we hit, captain," replied the excited first officer.

"Helm down and ease away. Keep the sheets to hand; be ready to harden quickly on my order," called Simon.

With the wind now on the beam, the *Esther May* shot forward like a horse heading for its barn. The enemy captain saw Simon's ploy too late and tried to get his slow-moving ship to bear away, her jibboom sweeping away his adversary's jack yard, flag and all. The *Esther May* passed but 30 feet from the Frenchman as she fired her broadside; the effect was devastating. Swivel guns and musketeers in the rigging laid down a leaden curtain of fire on French gun crews, sitting ducks on the open decks with no bulwarks to protect them. It was all over in two minutes after a single broadside swept the brig's decks and punctured her hull. Her mainmast toppled gracefully into the sea bringing her foretopmast with it. The crippled pirate lost steerage way; they were at the mercy of their attackers.

Simon realised the dilemma of those ashore. With their avenues of escape taken from them, the pirates there would be doubly dangerous. "Mister Johnston, prepare a fully armed landing party. I shall lead it myself. Take us as close to the shore as you can. Let the caravels see to the other ship; you take this one as our prize."

"Aye, captain," Johnston replied.

Once ashore Simon sought to appraise himself of the situation. Sporadic small arms fire told of pockets of resistance, but he saw no one he could gain information from. He organised his men to follow him along the road to his home. During the short row to the beach he had ascertained that none of the three hillside fires was Casa d'Ouro. Now he wanted to secure the estate, his home. The governor would arrive shortly with reinforcements from the ships to carry on mopping up the invaders still in the town.

Gunner watched with pride as his ship was handled so brilliantly by Michael Johnston – the man was indeed a fine sailor. As the landing party headed for the beach, he could see his captain in the stern sheets of a gig. *The lad's read me mind; let's 'ope he makes quick time*, he thought.

About 40 refugees from other estates had made their way to Casa d'Ouro, hoping to gain refuge under its guns. They told stories of pillaging, looting and killing. Sean interrogated them carefully with Antonio translating; he was able to deduce there may be as many as

40 pirates in and around the various estate grounds. They would have seen the events in the bay; it was only a matter of time before they joined forces to plan extrication from their predicament.

Evidence of the massacre the night before had been cleared; Sean had insisted that sand was brought to cover the dried blood on the drive. Once again, to the casual observer it looked as if the estate had been abandoned, its occupants hiding in the hills.

Gunner had carefully fitted timber shutters, painted to match the walls of the house, artfully covering the gun ports. Thus the parapet line was unbroken, unthreatening.

"What do ye reckons, Sean lad? Ye knows the lay of the land better'n me," said Gunner.

"We must 'ave men in the trees each side o' the drive and entrances. Be sure we must hit 'em hard again with the first strike. These lads are brave enough behind a loaded gun; they'd 'ave next to no chance 'and-to-'and fightin'. The men'll need to be well out of the cannons' arc of fire, then move in after two salvos. I've got 20-odd ready to be on the ground but they're afeared of a repeat o' last night," replied Sean.

"When do you think they will attack, Senhor Gunner?" asked Antonio.

"Dunno, lad; mayn't come at all if they 'ave their 'ostages already; if not, they'll come soon. Best we get 'ot food into the men and be at stations. I seen the captain start t'ward us not long ago; 'e'll need two hours t' make it on foot. Let yer men know 'e's comin', it'll make 'em feel a whole lot better," said Gunner.

The thirty-odd pirates that entered Casa d'Ouro's drive were far more cautious than the first attackers; they advanced slowly under cover of the trees. Sean's platoon was able to account for several Frenchmen with sniper fire, withdrawing, as had been previously planned, before the guns at the house opened their murderous fire. With no bunched target this time, the damage caused was minimal; the enemy, however, regrouped and deciding discretion was the better part of valour, began a cautious retreat, firing at the ramparts as they left. Simon had found some horses and a cart and arrived on the scene in time to prevent the pirates' escape.

They were lining the pirates up in front of Casa d'Ouro when a shot rang out – a last frustrated attempt at some gesture of revenge.

The sniper had picked his target carefully; the ball struck Gunner in his chest. Sean and Simon rushed onto the roof.

Simon held the dying veteran of a hundred fights as he whispered his last. "I got a will o' sorts wi' me gear on board, cap'n. All my owin's goes t' me niece what lives in Shoreditch wi' three young 'ns; 'er 'usband was killed – navy yer see."

"Worry not, old friend. I will see she is well looked after; the pension I'd planned to go to you will go to her," answered Simon.

Gunner grimaced with pain, rolled his eyes and died.

Chapter 17

The new world

Isabella eyed her husband from across the table as he entertained their guests. Simon was a hero to the menfolk of the island. He had beaten the French pirates, and he was well known to the kings of both Portugal and her ally, England. All the important members of the community were in attendance, with the notable exception of Father Domingo, the disapproving priest for the district of Machico.

She had been ill at ease since returning from hiding in the hills and wondered how she was to broach the subject again. The year before, Simon had listened with some annoyance to his wife's pleas for them to move from Madeira to America or even England. He failed to see why she would wish to leave their profitable estate where the weather was always fine. Was not Portugal her homeland, the birthplace of her children? He had, however, failed to grasp the undercurrents abroad in their small society; how could he understand? He returned for but six weeks each year.

He put his wife's unnatural request down to her missing him during his long periods of absence, dismissing the subject by suggesting she could join him on a voyage in a few years, once the children were older and the new governess, knowing them well, could look after them. It would have to be, of course, after the coming American rebellion was finally decided.

The solitude she felt when he was away, why did men in their stoic way not see it? The way the womenfolk shunned her as having married a heretic. It did not matter to them that he had converted to Catholicism. They knew it was the only way he would be allowed to marry her and stay on the island – they had seen through that! To them and to Father Domingo they were heretics, and their children heretics by association. This was clearly proven as she had insisted on schooling the children at home, away from the guidance of the priest and his small school. How could they be devout Catholic, with an English, Protestant governess overseeing their education?

Besides, they spoke in conspiratorial tones among themselves. Was not the grand Senhor Simon Pearce little more than a pirate himself?

Then of course there were the infernal French pirates. Fine for him to fill her house with guns and show her people how to shoot them. Had not the most recent incursion proved that the Madeiran farmers would be incapable of mounting an effective defence without the leadership of seasoned warriors like Sean and Gunner (God rest his soul).

England, of course, would not be much better than here. Catholics were a tolerated underclass, never to be accepted into society. Simon's immediate family was Wesleyan, or Church of England, so there would be little camaraderie there.

No, America was the place. Keep away from those puritans; buy land where their children could be in control of their own futures, free of bigotry.

As if the mood of the evening were to reflect Isabella's musings, her brother, Juan Mendoza, swung the topic of conversation to politics. "Surely our good captain could contribute much to the running of our country? A career at home would allow my poor sister to see more of you, Simon."

After a short but pregnant silence Dom Frederico Ferandos, one of the most influential growers on the island, coughed and added, "Indeed, Senhor Mendoza, but is it not true that His Majesty will allow only Catholics, born Portuguese, to hold office in his dominions?"

Simon grasping the innuendo moved the conversation on. "Indeed, I am flattered, brother-in-law, but my future is in commerce. I cannot picture myself behind the desk of an administrator."

Later that night Isabella was careful to wear a nightgown much favoured by her husband, but when it seemed that Simon's ardour might be somewhat blunted by wine, she prudently postponed the pursuit of her quest till morning.

The sun was streaming into the bedchamber windows as the master of the house finally stirred.

"What hour, my love? Have I slept through the day?"

"Indeed, I thought you might, 'usband," she said with a smile. "I 'ave coffee to ease the pain in your 'ead, the pain you 'ave poured in through your own mouth, no."

"Thank you, darling. Most considerate. I believe I will stay abed a while longer, if you don't mind," he said closing his eyes in an attempt to get his wife to leave him alone.

"Simon! I must talk with you. We must leave Madeira and move to America, for my sake and the children," Isabella uttered breathlessly.

"Please, my dear, do not press me now; I have indeed heeded your concerns raised last season. I have purchased some land on the Potomac River, at the top of Chesapeake Bay, that is uncommon lovely, as insurance against unforeseen circumstance. Now be a good girl and leave me to my self-inflicted agony," with which Simon rolled over in an unmistakably dismissive gesture.

A little angry, yet elated, Isabella left the bedchamber, joining her children for their morning lessons. *Why has he not told me of the land before? What does it matter?* she thought. *He has taken my fears to heart and acted.*

"So you have kept from me a secret, 'usband, no?" Isabella stated once they were alone again after luncheon.

"You know, dearest, I do not bother you with details of my business," he said with a hint of condescension. "I have for some time sought an opportunity to purchase a quality block of land in the Americas. That opportunity presented itself last voyage when a merchant I was dealing with was a little short of cash, and he offered me land in exchange for the goods he had ordered. You see, I do listen to you. Once at sea I thought about the things you had said. When the deal for the land was on the table I thought it would please you if I took it."

"Yes, yes, I am well pleased, but why did you not tell me before?" she answered hotly.

"Because I didn't wish to get you all het up and ready to leave when I believe we will have to wait quite a while before we can live in peace there. Open warfare is the state between England and the American rebels. Thirty thousand Redcoats are on American soil. England taxes the Americans to pay for European wars, and they, not unreasonably, object. The Royal Navy is blockading American ports; American schooners are running the blockades and getting through, but the rebels barely hold their own against the British. And so, my love, we have a considerable dilemma. Do we enter America as British subjects - loyalists - or as Americans, and therefore rebels?" Simon's question summed up their delicate situation.

"The *Esther May* is under charter to the British Admiralty. Should we become rebel Americans and assist in what, I believe, is a rightful struggle against an oppressive colonialist government - a struggle that the rebels could win with help from Spain and France? Or do we go to, say New York, a British stronghold, and fight for the Crown? If we act for the rebels, with whom I sympathise, I will have committed treason against the Crown. The Royal Navy will spare no expense to hunt me down. We will know no peace; we will not be able to return here. As criminals in the eyes of the English, Portugal would be obliged to extradite us, as their allies. Our land here would be forfeit.

"Should we, on the other hand, move over there and live as British citizens, we will be at best second-class citizens if the rebels win and probably be forced to move north into Canadian territory - a land of ice and snow that I fear will not suit our family, who has known only the balmy climes of Madeira and Portugal. But if I continue as I am now, purely as a guard vessel for the navy and acting belligerently only if attacked, there is a good chance we may be able to enter a free America after the war, as welcome immigrants. Not the most honourable course, but the only safe one I can see for our family."

Simon paused to see the effect of his words.

"What would you do, 'usband, were you not encumbered with de children and me? Sit safely in de middle, or declare for the side you believe is right?" asked Isabella, cutting deftly to the chase.

"You ask me, dearest Isabella, something I cannot answer; our situation is as it is. We are married, we do have four wonderful children," he retorted, attempting to put his wife off her mark.

"I see I am right," she said seeing the complete picture. "Also it is that you are right. What are we to do?" she asked.

Simon held his wife's shoulders and looked into the fathomless pools of her eyes. "For now, my love, we must do as I have said. You must remain; be strong, for here you and the children are safe. Your brother and father still have much influence. I will sail as soon as we can ready the ship and quietly plan for the future. Not a word must be spoken to anyone, not even family, especially not the children. Do you understand?"

"Yes, I understand, but for 'ow many years will it be so?"

She answered herself, "Many, I fear."

Once at sea Simon was again in his element, but he couldn't shake the vision of his brave wife and children. Her beautiful dark brown eyes looking into his as they parted at the quay, filled with resignation, tinged with not a little admiration.

"I will start thinking and planning for the adventure, in my 'ead. *Adeus*, my love," she said, kissing him goodbye.

No other course was safe; this he knew. How could he bring his family into a war zone? However, with each passing day he became more convinced that their future lay in the New World.

Following their normal course south to 20 degrees, the latitude of the trade winds, then due west, until eventually the turn was made to the north-west, to make landfall, sighting the Turks Islands, north of the treacherous Silver Banks. Having verified the accuracy of their navigation, they sailed with the prevailing sou'east winds until entering the full force of the Gulf Stream which assisted their passage northwards by some 40 miles a day. It seemed no time at all had passed before they found themselves off Sandy Hook light. The lighthouse had been completed just that year and was already proving its worth in reducing seagoing incidents and shipwreck. Having reached New York in a record time of 28 days, Simon and his crew were looking forward to some shore time.

After presenting his credentials to Captain Grenville on board HMS *Resolution*, Simon was ordered to sail for New York harbour. Here he was to unload his cargo at the wharves of Lower Manhattan and to report to Admiral Howe's flagship, HMS *Eagle*, anchored with the rest of the North American Squadron in Hudson Bay.

"Have you heard, sir," said the young lieutenant to whom Simon reported as he climbed aboard the huge, two-deck *Eagle*, a third-rater of 64 guns, "we were attacked last night by a submerged vessel! Yes sir, I know it sounds impossible, but ye must in truth give it to these rebels, they are nothing if not most innovative. Fortunately our copper sheathing prevented the underwater craft from attaching the bomb to our hull; it exploded some distance off. One of our lookouts saw something under the hull, thought it was a whale," he said with a laugh. "No real harm done, shook us a bit though, I can tell ye. I'll inform Captain Mortimer, the admiral's flag captain, that you await him, sir."

At the interview with Captain Mortimer, Simon was informed that there were no orders for him at that time and that he should report back in four weeks when he would be informed if his charter with the Admiralty was to be renewed. With the highly unsatisfactory possibility that his ship may become unemployed, he had taken his leave to see to his own affairs.

It seemed somewhat incongruous to Simon that his king and government could lay claim to the vast lands and peoples of the North American continent, much of which remained undiscovered. The English had defeated the French in Canada and driven them out of the Missouri River Basin, where for a while they had controlled the constant procession of development westward. *How*, he thought, *do the British ever think they can retain control of this vast growing land, having to supply their forces and report to a government so far away? It would be six months at best from a courier ship leaving New York with dispatches for London, to return with fresh orders.*

Here, walking the streets of Lower Manhattan, although everyone spoke English it seemed to Simon he was in a foreign land, as different from any English town as he could imagine. As he made his way along East River Drive to an address in East Village he felt the vibrancy of the place, the bustle, the purpose. The British may think they have control of these New Yorkers, but in reality the colonists were biding their time; an economic giant was creating itself, awaiting its time to wrest control.

Many long years ago when the gig *Horse* had been seized in Falmouth Harbour, a young Roseland lad had been sentenced to 10 years hard labour in the colony of Virginia. The man's name was Peter Pearce; he was Simon's third cousin. Simon had been trying to locate Peter for years. When last in New York, he had instructed an investigator to try and find Peter. He was on his way to a meeting with the investigator now having received a note saying that good news awaited him.

Gerome McTavish was a stoutly built Scotsman whose Gaelic heritage was revealed by his accent and a set of fiery red, mutton-chop whiskers, his head crowned by an unruly mop of greying auburn. He had arrived in New York in the thirties, seemingly loyal to the Crown, but he was secretly convinced that America's future was as a totally independent entity from Britain.

"Well, captain, it seems we have had a touch of good fortune in the search for your cousin. It would seem that Peter ran foul of the law in the town of Norfolk, Virginia, on the Chesapeake, and had been incarcerated in the town gaol in '69. Our investigations have since turned up an address where he is employed as a farm labourer, not far from Norfolk. In this envelope is the address. And, er, the account for our troubles. We would be obliged if this account could be settled before you depart our fair town, sir." McTavish pushed the envelope across the stained leather desktop towards Simon.

Simon read the short report and eyed the account, which at $68.00 was, he thought, a fair price for the information. "I am happy to pay you half the amount now, McTavish, the balance once I have verified my cousin's whereabouts. We will sail for the Chesapeake next week, subject to fair weather. This note presented to my bank for the second portion will be honoured once they receive notification from me. I trust this is to your satisfaction, sir?"

"Not our normal terms, captain, but in your case, I agree," replied McTavish, noting the firm disposition of his client, showing he would not easily be persuaded from his course.

The *Esther May* had taken advantage of a moderate nor'easterly breeze and lay at anchor off Norfolk, just nine days after Simon's interview in the investigators office. It was a simple matter of visiting the town gaol to verify that the report he had been given had substance. Having organised the final payment to be made to McTavish, Simon made arrangements to be conveyed to the farm where Peter worked.

On arrival at the farm the next morning, Mable McCormack, the portly wife of the farm owner, greeted him graciously. She saw the captain was a man of substance and offered him refreshments while Peter was brought in from the fields.

"If 'e would care, captain, we could bring Peter to the port after Sunday service so you can 'ave more time to get acquainted. This being a workin' day 'n all, Peter'll need to be getting away back to the fields afore too long."

"Most kind, Mrs McCormack. I would be very pleased if you and your husband would join us aboard ship for Sunday lunch? I will arrange a carriage for you all," suggested Simon.

The man standing before him appeared older than the 52 years Simon had calculated him to be. "You are Peter Pearce, once of the parish of St Just-in-the-Roseland, near Falmouth?" he asked.

"Aye, sir. I be 'e. I was transported 'ere in '37, I were," said Peter.

He was tall for the time – he would have reached five foot ten had he not been bent of back from years of hard work in the fields. His gaunt frame was gnarled from work, his sun-browned skin stretched like old parchment over his bones.

"Do you know who I am, Peter?" asked Simon.

"Aye, sir. I unnerstan' us'r related, like," answered the older man, his West Country accent obvious, with an overtone of a southern drawl.

"Indeed, I believe you to be my cousin," answered Simon. "Would you care to come aboard my ship in Norfolk on Sunday? It would be grand to get to know each other a little better."

Simon recalled a time when a sea captain had entered his house on Scilly. Could this man's life change because of this meeting?

A glance at the indomitable Mrs McCormack confirmed that he had permission to proceed. "Y'all be the first relative I seen in more 'an 30 year," Peter said, his eyes showing a sparkle at the prospect of the reunion.

After a sumptuous luncheon on the *Esther May* on the Sunday, the McCormacks stood to leave. "We'll be pleased to leave Peter with ye for a day or two, captain. Y'all 'avin' come this far, y'all will 'ave much to talk aboot," offered the burly farmer.

Peter stood, cap in hand, offering thanks to his employers before they left.

"What can ye tell me of the situation in these parts, Peter?" asked Simon.

"While Virginia and the Carolinas still 'ave British governors, they 'ave no soldiers to back 'em up; all is not well for their side. A group callin' 'emselves the Regulators 'ave been rioting in the towns. They ain't declarin' out and out for the rebels, but them 'r demonstratin' agin the stamp duty and other British Government taxes. Not 'avin' no forces to command, the British 'ave given commissions to leaders in the communities an' ordered 'em t' raise a loyalist militia t' put down the rioters. These men 'ave little t' say on the matter, as to refuse service would be treason, their lands and lives then be forfeit. There be a large group o' Scots in the mountains – they like as like would join the rebels afore the British. But they raised their militia quota as ordered – 'em don't do nothing but wave sabres. I was in a militia afore I were in gaol."

Peter continued with an eloquence that was most enlightening to Simon; there was much more to the man than he first imagined.

"Ye seem to be well versed in the politics of our time, Peter," stated Simon.

The older man became guarded as if he had entered a minefield and couldn't remember the way out. "I c'n read 'n 'ear what's said around. Keeps it t' meself, safer that way, see."

"Let me be frank with you," said Simon. "My own sympathies lie with the Americans; I cannot for the life of me see how the British Government can manage this vast land from 3,000 miles away. The people here are far too knowledgeable and capable to live as vassals of a far-off, rapacious king. Yes, I know I'm in the employ of the British Navy, but that is solely an excuse to ply these waters legally. It is my intention to settle with my family in a free America."

His audience was somewhat taken aback as Simon swept onwards, the kernel of an earlier idea now taking shape in his inventive mind. "I have purchased a fine block of land on the banks of the Potomac River, not more than a hundred miles upriver from where we are anchored. It is on this land I intend to establish my family. I plan to wait until America is independent then bring Isabella and the children here permanently. In the meantime many preparations need to be made. I shall require the services of a trustworthy person – who could I trust more than a kinsman! – to get these works under way. If you were to take this position a 100-acre block of land will be yours, freehold. A reasonable stipend will be paid to you for your troubles in the meantime. What say ye, Cousin?"

"Indeed, sir, I am honoured that ye could 'ave so much trust in me after so short a time. I can't say I 'ave all the skills ye requires, but I c'n read and know numbers. I c'n purchase the expertises I lack. It'd be grand to be part of the family again," Peter answered modestly.

"It's decided then, Peter. We'll settle with the McCormacks and sail for the Potomac on the next favourable tide. Mister Johnston, would ye be so kind as to join us for a toast."

It was a startled but pleased first officer who drank his captain's toast: one solemnly stated word – America.

The *Esther May* retraced her course carefully down the Potomac River, having established Peter in a small shack on Simon's landholding. They left Chesapeake Bay and headed northward once again, rounding Sandy Hook to anchor with the British fleet at the mouth of the Hudson River.

During the voyage, Johnston had opened up to his captain: he was in fact no loyalist. His strong feelings, no longer bound by the belief he was a spy in an enemy camp, spilt from his lips like a torrent following a spring thaw.

"John Paul Jones and other American captains are creating havoc with British supply lines. More than a hundred ships have been seized since the war began. Have ye not wondered, captain, why the *Esther May* has never been attacked by any of the American Congress ships or privateers we've sighted?"

"We've had some close encounters, but now as you come to mention it, no, we've never been attacked," answered Simon, questioningly. "yes, there was that time an American schooner had the weather gage of us, yet she let us be, as if so ordered ...?"

"The reason is, captain, you have been earmarked as a possible convert to our cause," stated Johnston. "This ship is one of the finest privately owned afloat in her class. My orders are to secure you and the ship, one way or another. Isaac Hopkins himself made the arrangements to get me posted on board to see if you would become an ally, bringing the ship with you, of course. Should this not be possible other ways would be found to secure the ship for the cause. The Congressional Navy is desperately short of men with your skills. If ye do not wish to join the navy, congress-sanctioned privateers make a grand living in these waters, as well you know. You have been planning for your family to have their future in the Americas. Why not join us now? Soon a declaration of independence will be made, the line in the sand firmly drawn. What do ye say, sir?"

Simon's initial reaction was that of anger at the treason being promulgated in his stateroom. Then the simple logic of the situation dawned on him. His first officer had secured his position to subvert him to the American cause; the Congress had seen he was an outcast from the British system.

He was in no way the first ship's captain to be approached in this manner. Many an American privateer once flew a British flag; many a captured ship and crew had changed sides for what they believed to be a better life, away from Britain, a country where government was in the hands of those whose birth was fortunately 'high' enough, to put them in a privileged class, regardless of skill. Would justice American-style have executed his father and grandfather, have transported his cousin? They were simply making a living opposing unjustly harsh taxes, as the Americans themselves were now doing. The King, nobility and Parliament had an insatiable demand for money; they got it from the bent backs and skills of their subjects.

Simon felt strangely relieved. He had made his feelings known with his toast; he had tacitly decided to cross the line of allegiance, and he knew in his heart he had to follow his inner beliefs, regardless of cost.

"Ye have touched a nerve that's been raw for some while, Mister Johnston; let me think awhile, if you please. Leave me now, and send in Mister Finnegan. I'll need to have his support in this to win over the crew." Simon was stalling yet planning his next move.

"Well, me lad," said Sean Finnegan addressing his captain in the diminutive for the first time since his promotion to sailing master. "I bin a-tinkin' to meself; to be sure, America would be a fine place to lay up these old bones when the time comes. Lord knows I got no love of the British; 'em 'ave done terrible tings t' the Irish people. But I'll not be the one t' change the way it is over there. Shakin' 'em out of

America'll hurt 'em 'ard enough. I got a sister and two nephews. I'd like for them t' have a chance, an' be around in my dotage."

"We'll bring them with us, Sean; I've land for a dozen families! I am not sure the navy will want to renew my contract. If they do, I'll demand too high a price, and they will release me to trade on my own behalf, for sure. We will sail to Ireland – let go any crew that isn't with us there. Then we head to Falmouth as I have family business to attend to. Then load cargo that we will need in America and on to Madeira to pack up my family. I shall hand the estate over to my brother-in-law Juan; he will quietly find a buyer. Once our men's families are settled on the Potomac, we shall declare for America, our new land – one that will allow our families to grow without oppression, without bigotry."

Simon held out his hand to his old friend.

"Well now, I followed 'e in many tings, soir. Why not this?" answered Sean.

The two friends shook hands to settle the matter.

Chapter 18

Voyage to a new life

Michael Johnston was as good as his word. Before the ship left America on her last voyage as a British registered ship, Simon had been introduced to several senior members of the rebel government and military, including the legendary John Paul Jones. Once they were assured of his commitment to their cause, doors began to open, all bureaucracy quietly dispensed with.

Peter Pearce had been able to secure materials and labour to begin the task of constructing a house adequate for Isabella and the family until a larger accommodation could be constructed after the coming war. With less than a year to complete the building project and to prepare and plant fields of crop, he was a very busy man. A skill in organisation and getting people to work well for the modest man was again allowed to flourish.

When alone his mind was taken back to when he was first imprisoned on a floating hulk in Plymouth, awaiting his transportation to Virginia, his punishment for being part of a smuggling gig's crew, Peter had worked on ways to slowly improve the lot of the prisoners in his work gang.

Peter and nine others had been assigned as 'scrapers' in the naval dockyard, their job to clean the bottoms of men-of-war. Once they had been lightened, topmasts and guns removed, the ships were beached then winched over on their sides to expose fouled underwater sections. The scraper's job was to scrape them clean and repitch them, a messy, arduous task; the men received many an infectious cut from the clinging shellfish it was their job to remove. Once clear of fouling they were recoated in pitch. Or if the ship was destined for a long mission overseas, she could be sheathed in copper, the only permanent if costly solution to the voracious Teredo shipworm. The creature would enter a ship's planking, growing longer and fatter as it ate its way along the grain, living inside wooden ships' timbers, making them unseaworthy in a few short years.

The guard in charge of their group received an amount of money for their labours if the job was completed well and on time. Peter had said to the gang, "If us works 'arder, Jamie Smith the turnkey makes more money. I reckons if us do well fer 'im us can get a share o' th' money – c'n buy better food, even an ale or two."

"Why in 'ell's name do we want to work 'ard fer the prick; 'e only beats us," said Gerry Tomlinson, a burly tin miner from the Helford River who was being transported for stealing a sheep to feed his starving family.

"If we don't get 's some decent food us'll end up sick or dyin' o' the cold. If us makes it worth 'is while, ol' Jamie'll look after us. Shall I talk to 'im?" he asked.

After some discussion the men agreed to give Peter's plan a try.

Some four months later the scraping team, led by young Peter, was the best fed and most warmly clothed of all 500 souls awaiting a ship to take them to the cotton or tobacco fields of Virginia where, once landed, their transportation sentences would begin. Near three dozen men and women had died or been flogged to death on the hulk since Peter's incarceration.

A large ex-slaver had anchored in the roads; it was rumoured she would be taking the transportees across the Atlantic. When the time was right Peter approached Jamie Smith to find out what he knew. "Is this it, Jamie? Are we finally to get away from this piss 'n shit-ridden 'ulk?"

"Well, maybe ye do 'n maybe ye don't, so as t' speak," answered the turnkey, with a conspiratorial glint in his eye.

"What in God's name d'ye mean by that?" returned Peter.

"What about if I can get yer sentences to start from the day you boys got 'ere? What if you boys missed a few transports, spent a couple of years 'ere like. The navy's decided that they want to copper sheath all their ships that be careened from now on. That means lots o' work, 'n they 'aven't got the labour. Seems like you boys are well thought of by th' dockyard brass. If ye was all free ye'd make a right packet. Seein' as 'ow ye ain't free, that ye're convicts, ye need me to be in the middle, like. 'Ere's 'ow I see it. Do two year in the Plymouth dockyard workin' fer me, I'll give 'e twenty-five per cent o' what I makes. T' boot, I'll get 'e passage t' Virginia on a navy ship as seamen, now that's 'n 'hole lot better'n bein' in the belly of a slaver fer two months. What do ye say, lad?"

"Twenty-five per cent 'n we do all th' work – 'ardly seems fair, do it?" said Peter warily.

"Ain't no fairness fer convicts, Peter. Y' scum 'ccordin' t' the law. I can give 'e nothin' if I likes," was the gaoler's terse, calculated reply.

"Does us 'ave t' live on the 'ulk, Jamie? I don't reckon any o' th' lads'd do it if we 'ad to do that," answered Peter. "If 'e can get us a berth ashore, they'd do it, I'm sure."

Jamie Smith had no idea how he was going to provide the terms he had negotiated with Peter Pearce. What he could see in his mind's eye was the little pub in the Home Counties he and Beth had dreamed of for years. With the convicts' labour sold, he could see the dream coming true. The dockyard post captain had assured him that the work was there. He would try to meet his part of the bargain. *They be only convicts, all said 'n done,* he thought.

Two years passed quickly. To a large extent Peter and his men were well treated, and Jamie Smith paid the twenty-five per cent he had agreed. The money Peter and his men received, however, was only just sufficient to pay for their accommodations in the naval dockyard and their food and drink, but they were in many ways lucky. Then came the time Jamie Smith purchased his public house in the Home Counties and was no longer interested in the dockyard work.

"Y'all be boarded on a king's ship bound for Virginnie in a couple o' weeks, lads. Ol' Jamie 'as done 'is best by 'e," the turnkey had said when leaving.

The last ship Peter and his men had careened, scraped and coppered was the frigate *Audacious*. The dockyard shipwrights were busy working on ships of the line, in preparation for the coming war with France. *Audacious*'s first lieutenant was a man called Martin Blake, an officer who had risen through the ranks – a good, fair-minded man. Peter spoke with him regarding his men's plight.

"I am much impressed by the work your men have done on this ship, Pearce; we would still have been waiting had you not been able to complete our refit. Please explain your situation to me," said Lieutenant Blake.

Peter told the officer their story. "We was promised delivery t' Virginia as crew on a king's ship once us 'ad done two years 'ere. Now the turnkey 'as vanished, got what 'e wanted like and dumped us. All us men are convicted to 'ard labour in America, sir. We've worked dawn till dusk fer two long years – 'spose t' come off our sentence. Can ye 'elp us, sir?"

Blake was a man of honour; he had made his way in the navy by hard work and sheer skill. He was every captain's ideal first officer – hard, fair and a superb seaman. The only reason he was not a captain at his advanced years of 39 was the circumstances of his birth. He thought a while. It was the first lieutenant's responsibility to find the manpower to crew *Audacious* and he saw a possibility.

"The ship will be off the beach on the tide tomorrow evening. I will continue to engage you and your team while she completes her refit and is prepared for sea. I need to obtain the approval of the provost marshal; he will then need to apply to the civil authorities for their approval. In the meantime, you and your men report to Captain Ferguson, *Audacious*'s marine contingent commanding officer. It will be his responsibility to keep you under guard. Do not let me down," said Lieutenant Blake sternly.

"We won't, sir, I promises 'e," answered Peter, delighted.

Lieutenant Blake did all in his power to assist Peter Pearce and his men. He had them transferred to the frigate for the duration of the voyage to America; this was the good news. Not good was the cold hard fact of the law of transportation: a sentence began when the convict arrived. The two years' hard work in the dockyard had brought them no closer to freedom.

As gash hands on a king's ship, and convicts to boot, the dockyard men were treated with the contempt that only a community hierarchy in the cramped quarters of a naval warship could produce. They all knew that as convicts their word would never be accepted over that of a free seaman – even if half the so-called free seaman were either the product of the press gang or had made the choice to go to sea rather than swing at the end of a rope.

Audacious was to sail directly to New York with Admiralty dispatches. It was a time when each of the ten men prayed to God that they could become invisible; the work was hard, the food was terrible. All this paled into insignificance when the men were below decks. Peter being young and a handsome lad was the first to suffer. A huge gun captain from Liverpool sat in front of him at the mess table, first having pushed his messmates opposite him out of the way. His gun crew stood behind him, waiting, knowing what was to unfold.

"Ben's me name, pretty one. I reckons ye'd look mighty fine warming the cannon, convict boy," he said with a lurid grin. "What do 'e reckon, me fine lads?"

Ben Black's gun crew made incoherent, lustful noises of agreement.

Peter's scrapers stood to defend their leader, but they were muscled out of the way by other gun crews, anticipating the forthcoming entertainment. The gun captain simply lifted Peter, a man of 160 pounds and laid him across the 18-pound cannon he was in command of. Black's crew quickly tied Peter's hands and feet. Then a huge gunner, sweat pouring from him in his anticipation, ripped off Peter's trousers, reached down to the gun's wheel to find some grease which he applied to his rigid manhood, then with a primordial grunt, he began Peter's torment.

"'Ow are 'e now, m' dear?" asked Black with mock concern. "Next time we'll dress 'e up a bit girlie-like, make it more real." The big man turned away laughing.

Buggery was a capital offence in the Royal Navy, as was rape. Not so, it seemed, if the complainant was a convict – after all, a convict was not human, his life forfeit until his sentence was completed.

Lieutenant Blake was made aware of the events at the gun deck and had consulted his captain.

"Ye know well where we stand, Blake. As I said from the start, the convicts, not being committed to the navy, should be kept apart from the gun deck. I have had discussions with the bosun's mates of the deck; there are no witnesses that will speak out against Black, apart from the convicts, and as you appreciate, their word does not count.

From now they will live under guard in the cells forward over the cable locker. It's the only way, Martin, wretched though it is. Black will get his comeuppance, the men will see to that."

"Aye, captain, you are right. I'll see to it," said Blake.

"Oh, and number one, let's douse the galley fires afore the noon watch change – give the cook a rest. Let Black get some lower-deck justice from his hungry messmates. May as be they'll make him warm the cannon, eh?" Captain Jerome St Clair-Barclay had not looked up from his writing, but Blake was sure he saw a grin on his captain's face.

Six weeks later, after an event-free passage, the 40-gun *Audacious* was making her turn to the north-west to clear the eastern Bahaman islands, her new heading nor'nor'west to New York. They had made good time. While a couple of Yankee schooners had been sighted from the masthead, they had turned away from the powerful frigate, leaving her unimpeded on her voyage north.

Peter Pearce had not spoken since the incident with Black. He responded to orders, did just enough but no more, his silence keeping his humiliation in the forefront of the crew's mind. Black's men missing their evening meal had been damaging to Black's prestige – had he been flogged for the offence, he would have become a hero.

Another big man worked the deck in silence, but this one had a plan. Gerry Tomlinson, the miner from the Helford who had worked with Peter in Plymouth docks, waited. Waited for what he knew would be the last act in his life, waited with revenge on his mind. His time had come.

"Reef topsails, get the topgallants off her," called Martin Blake, officer of the watch, as a particularly vicious squall ripped through the ship. "Square your helm, brace your yards; quickly now or ye will be ducking broken spars."

Gerry was on the lee braces easing the heavy hemp bracing line, while Black was on the weather deck hauling the windward brace. Because of his bulk he was the last in the line. Gerry waited while Black belayed his brace, his back to Gerry, who timed his short run across the deck perfectly. A wickedly sharp knife appeared in his hand as he crashed into the gunner, the knife opening up his right side and lower back, spilling guts and organs on the deck. The momentum of the fight carried the two men to the rail; in a final embrace both men disappeared, as if in slow motion, over the weather rail. The first lieutenant, his mouth open in silent horror, looked over the quarterdeck rail to the boiling wake astern. He thought he saw a smile on the convict's face as he disappeared beneath the waves. *Thank God we won't have to hang him,* was the first thought that went through the fair officer's mind.

The convicts were quickly trans-shipped in New York for the voyage to Norfolk, Virginia, and the start of their penal servitude. For Peter Pearce the sentence was ten years with hard labour. It had already been three years since he had been convicted, but ten years in Virginia he would still have to serve.

Martin Blake had known some American landowners and had spoken favourably of Peter Pearce and his men. They were split into three groups of three and handed over to the landowners in chains, the usual whips and ropes end not employed.

Peter spoke only rarely, generally in response to a direct question. To Davy Martin and his brother Samuel he was but a shadow of the man who had led them at the dockyard in Plymouth. Two years into his sentence Peter was about to turn twenty-one – he looked forty. Convicts were not permitted personal possessions; however, the American plantation boss had allowed the brothers to give Peter a present on his birthday. It was a beautifully carved whalebone gig, complete with sweeps and steering oar. The young but old man had cried; he sobbed and gasped for breath as the events of the past five years flooded through his tortured mind.

Even the rough plantation boss was touched. "Hell, boy, stop yer blubberin'. Y'all c'n work the home garden instead o' the tabaccy fer a month."

Peter became a very good gardener. His slight frame was always to be seen bent over in the vegetable garden, or on the drive leading up to the house where the flower gardens were exceptional. The lady of the house, Mrs Fitzsimmons, was from a prestigious family and knew a good servant when she saw one. Being born of old Virginian money she was used to her status and never used the expedient of belittling a servant to reinforce it. On the estate she looked upon her senior loyal workers much as highly valued pedigree dogs – she fussed and flitted around them, putting them at their ease. None, however, was in any doubt that he was an outside dog. Any meeting between the lady and her people was in her office close to the kitchen at the rear of the great house. The only servants who entered the inner portals of the great house were domestics, most of whom were despised by the estate people.

She had observed how tenderly Peter cared for her beloved flower gardens and had requested that he be put to work permanently on them. She also had his leg irons struck off. "Them ol' irons will wreck m' plants," was what she had said to the boss when he objected.

"You won't run, Peter, will you?" she asked him compassionately.

"To where would I run, ma'am?" was Peter's simple yet honest reply, at which the boss agreed to have the irons removed.

His life passed quietly, season following season. Peter was not quite sure how long he had been on the Broadridge Estate, until one day the plantation boss came up to him saying he was free.

"Free; can I go home now?" he said.

"I guess y' can, but y'd need money to pay yer passage. Mrs Fitzsimmons has asked if you want a job, as a free man, with pay and yer own cottage. She's planning some new fancy garden and wants you to be in charge of it. You'd have niggers under yer for the hard work. What do yer say?" asked the heavy-set man.

"Er … yes. I guess this is my home now," answered Peter.

As the years went by, thoughts of home faded. Peter became a respected member of the Fitzsimmons household; Davy and Samuel worked with him for a while. One day they up and left, lured by the stories of gold from out west. He was now the estate under-manager and was responsible for all lands excepting the plantations. He married Dorothy, a quiet Scots woman, the same age as him. She was from the Appalachian Mountains, in the Carolinas. The couple were well suited and enjoyed a simple yet childless life. They were completely settled until the day he was called to the big house. The first thing he saw was a group of soldiers.

Mr Fitzsimmons called him over saying, "The Honourable Mr Dinwiddie, His Majesty's Governor of Virginia, has ordered me to raise a militia company. It appears a group of nationalists calling themselves the Regulators are rioting and threatening action against the Crown; many a loyalist property has been razed. You are British so you had better be one of them. The slaves can keep my wife's garden while you are away; you have taught them well."

Not knowing anything about the political situation, Peter did as he was told, kissed his tiny, red-headed wife goodbye and marched away with the ragged column. Because of his position at the Fitzsimmons Estate he was given the rank of sergeant, an honorary position until he had been trained.

Captain Ebenezer Hardy, an American who had been trained in the British army, was Peter's commanding officer. 'Big Bad' Bill Morrell was the company sergeant major, a more violent, foul-mouthed man, Peter decided, it would be hard to find. A shiver went down his spine as he remembered whom Morrell reminded him of – the evil gunner, Ben Black.

"Pearce, ye son of a whore, ye'll be no fuckin' good t' me till yer knows a bit about soldiering, but as yer got yer numbers, an' can read 'n write, ye'll be the company's quartermaster sergeant fer the meantime. Now quartermasterin' is a fine job where, if yer careful, ye c'n make a shillin' or two fer yerself, if y' gets my drift. Now this ye'll share fifty-fifty with me, got it!" said the red-faced sergeant major menacingly. "'N if I catches yer a-cheatin' me, ye'll lead the first action an' each action till yer gets yerself killed, got it?"

"Aye, sar'nt major," said Peter snapping to attention badly.

"Now fuck off, whore's spoor, 'n make an inventory of all the food 'n equipment we got. I wanna see it tonight, so as I c'n makes a few adjustments like, afore I shows the captain." Bill Morrell thereby assumed control of Peter's destiny.

That night Morrell came to Peter Pearce's small tent; it had been a parting gift from Mrs Fitzsimmons. She had taken Captain Hardy aside and using her feminine qualities had persuaded that worthy to look after Peter and allow him the privacy of the small tent she had provided.

"Good, Pearce, very good," said Morrell, who was not without some understanding of the written word. "You 'n me'll get along fine, just fine. I'll get the cap'n's signature an' he will pass out the sovereigns fer ye t' buy what's needed. Y' can start yer creative accountin' from then. Keep on like this 'n ye'll never 'ave to fight," said Morrell, having worked out how much money he could make.

While Peter was made to train with the other conscripts he was never ordered to take direct action in the few skirmishes that occurred with the Regulators. He had simply made himself too valuable to Morrell and the captain, for whom he acted as a company adjutant, minus the usual commissioned rank. He found he had become quite adept with a sabre and enjoyed the small notoriety he had achieved in the company. He demonstrated his skills in practice swordplay during the mock fights Captain Hardy arranged in an attempt to relieve the tedium of waiting for action. It was the waiting that caused the most serious breaches of discipline and could totally demoralise a fighting unit, a fact the good captain was well aware of.

In 1765, the Crown imposed the Stamp Act, the British Government's first attempt to exact a taxation regime on her American colonies. A prominent colonist, one James Otis, had said that this one single act had set more people thinking of succession in six months than ever before. The Stamp Act greatly deepened the rift between loyalist, separatist citizens and the Crown. Other acts were passed to further impose on the freedom of the colonists, as well as their pockets. King George III was adamant that America should pay for its own defence. The money raised by taxes, however, hardly covered the costs of collecting them. The divisions in both British and American society made the taxes very expensive and, politically, very destructive.

The Stamp Act had been followed by the Declaratory Act, designed to entrench the authority of parliament and its right to tax the colonists, which resulted in further antagonising the Congress, which was now stockpiling arms and secretly building an army.

"Sar'nt major," called Captain Hardy.

"Sir," replied the NCO.

"Parade at 8 am, if you please. I have news to impart." The ageing, bespectacled, overweight officer had thought of retiring, but only briefly. He had no urgent desire to submit himself permanently to his wife's bitter tongue before it was absolutely necessary.

The captain strode from his tent across a makeshift parade ground to address his men. He had dressed carefully and portrayed the very image of an infantry officer of the British Army. "Stand easy, men! We have been given the honour, by the House of Burgesses, to provide escort for three of their number who are to make an assessment of militia capabilities and report back to the house. None other than Brigadier General Retired George Washington is to lead the group. I have had the pleasure of serving under the general when he was commander of the all-Virginia force. He's a stickler for good order, and while he is now in the position of a civilian, he is to be treated as if he still holds his commission in the King's army. The three arrive tomorrow. This camp will be spotless and ready for a general inspection. Don't let me down.

"There is another matter I am ordered to inform you of." Drawing himself to his full height the captain continued. "Early March, this year of 1770, some British soldiers were confronted by a group of workers at a ropewalk in Boston. They had apparently been looking for part-time work and were humiliated by the civilians. It appears our soldiers had gone to get reinforcements as pieces of timber and rocks were viciously hurled at them. On their return some hothead ignored his captain's order and fired on the then considerable crowd, at which other soldiers opened fire. I am given to understand that a group called 'the sons of liberty' had orchestrated the event for political purposes. The result was that five of their number were killed, a dozen suffering lesser wounds. I understand that the soldiers involved, including their captain, are to stand trial.

"Men, I urge you to consider that disobeying their officer was likely the cause of their current predicament. Bear this in mind when we become confronted, as no doubt we will, by malcontents and rebels. I do not wish to have this sort of event in my command. United we stand, divided we fall. Stand easy, men. Dismissed." The captain turned and marched back to his tent.

"It be obvious that this review o' the troops be to assess the colonial members of the British Army's loyalty to the crown – men like us." Peter was speaking to a group of NCOs who had been meeting recently to discuss the political situation.

"There be 'ardly a British trained soldier 'ere – 'part from the captain 'n sar'nt major. We was all brought to this by the governor's edict to raise a militia. I wonder if Mr Washington may not be 'ere to assess things on behalf of America, not the Crown," said Peter.

"Them's dangerous words, Sar'nt Pearce, mighty dangerous. But I guess we were all thinkin' along th' same lines."

"Are we wearing the right coloured uniforms?" The speaker was a tall, wiry, tenant hill-farmer named Jeb Mason, who had been forced to leave his land and family by his landlord, to comply with the governor's order. They all had much the same story to tell.

"We needs t' keep our ears open an' see which way the wind's a-blowin'. Now let's get this 'ere place tidy for our esteemed visitors on th' morrow," said Peter, striding away deep in thought.

Washington and his entourage arrived at noon; the company was called to attention in the midday heat. The tall, muscular man had a wide mouth and very prominent eyebrows, beneath which hid a pair of blue-grey eyes. It seemed to those who met him that he could see right through a man, searching out his truths, looking into the depths of his soul. The skilful horseman sat astride a fine black stallion, which would have given much trouble to a lesser horseman. "Stand at ease, men. Captain Hardy, good to see you again. Fifty-eight, wasn't it? You were in the Lancashires, as I remember."

"Indeed, general," said the captain, delighted that the great man had remembered him.

"Mr Washington now, captain. Just another nosy civilian to bother you," he said, laughing, his eyes silently penetrating. "May I introduce my fellow Burgess men, Mr Michael Collins and Mr Benjamin Richards?"

The three men dismounted and shook the captain's hand.

"Let's get your men out of this infernal heat, captain. An inspection is not necessary. They look well turned out; good effort, sergeant major!" Washington was using all his skills to put the soldiers at ease.

In the NCOs' mess tent that night an excellent meal was provided with beef brought by Mr Washington, who was dining with the captain and his fellow companions. The sergeant major had been expressly invited to dine with the big men. This was a considerable breach of mess etiquette but Mr Washington had made the request personally. "Can't have three of us to just one of you, captain, can we?" Thus the clever politician had carefully isolated the two British soldiers from the colonial militiamen.

Three men had accompanied the politicians, and they were employed entertaining the soldiers. Much whisky was supplied, and Peter became wary of the true motives of the three. It was as he had suspected – to see how loyal the company was from the Crown's point of view. Phrases like 'we Americans', and of course 'Our taxes should be to advance America not to pay for the lifestyles of the British aristocracy, don't you think?' laid bare their motive.

Peter was careful not to drink and impair his judgment. Others were not so circumspect. As the evening wore on, with tongues loosened by liquor, he found out that many of his comrades were thinking similarly: What were the British doing here? American taxes for the benefit of Americans! Were the authorities from Virginia inciting revolution in a British Army camp?

It was not long after Washington and his entourage swept out of the camp that Nathaniel Smith and one Bartholomew Biggs, both men of staunchly loyalist persuasion, spoke with the captain.

"I joined, sir, outta loyalty t' the King," began Smith. "So did Biggs 'ere, sir, but what we heard last night was pure treason, nothing but. What say you, Biggs?"

"Indeed, sir, if I hadn't 'eard it meself I'd not be convinced enough to stand afore you and tell it, sir," said Biggs, an easy southern drawl rolling off his tongue.

The captain was at a loss for words. *Could George Washington be part of a separatist movement? Impossible,* he thought. But he knew the men before him were not given to falsehoods; what would they have to gain?

"Men, we must find out those who would be part of this dastardly scheme, but with as little fuss as possible. Each of you and any others you can trust must name those who speak treason. I will consider then, once we know the extent of the rot, how to cut it out. Thank you for your frankness and loyalty. Now go, there is much to discover." The disturbed career officer dismissed his men and turned to his trusted sergeant major, Bill Morrell. "Prepare to get news to the governor, Mr

Dinwiddie, in Richmond. We will need help in dealing with this. Who can you trust to send?"

"The quartermaster, sir – Pearce. He's British-born and much attached to the Fitzsimmons family, whose loyalty is unquestionable, sir."

"Good idea, Morrell. It won't seem strange for him to leave the camp at short notice – procurement trip, what? See to it," said Hardy.

Before long Peter Pearce was on his way to the governor's seat in Richmond. The thoughts in his mind would not have pleased his captain. He had resolved to make a detour via the Fitzsimmons Estate so as to fully inform his employer. In these turbulent times a man had to tread carefully. *I 'ope the master is of the same opinion as me,* he thought.

Mrs Fitzsimmons greeted Peter in her usual familiar way. "Peter, how nice to see ya'all." She almost sang her slow, southern drawl. "What is so urgent to bring you here; are you discharged?"

"Ah, no, ma'am, unfortunately not. I am to deliver a message to the governor, but I thought the master may wish to know of its content, ah, before I deliver it," said Peter in some discomfort.

"You take some risk, Peter," she said solemnly. "I would be happy to pass the message on. My husband is out at the west block with Mr Blackley, the new estate manager."

"May I then borrow a good horse and ride out to meet him, ma'am? Mr Fitzsimmons may wish t' instruct me in some way or other," Peter's attempt at hiding his true reason for needing to see his employer scarcely fooling the intelligent woman seated before him.

"I appreciate you wish to see how my husband stands on the current situation? No, don't answer. Take my stallion, Blade. You are horseman enough to handle him. Climb Windy Ridge and look for the men clearing the land. Like as not that is where you will find my husband. Oh, and Peter, your loyalty has been noted," and with an aristocratic nod, she dismissed him.

It was dark when Peter finally found Mr Fitzsimmons who, perceiving the sensitivity of Peter's visit, invited him to walk with him away from the camp for their discussion. The messenger apprised the tall, slightly balding man, who was a similar age to himself, of the recent turn of events.

"I see," said Fitzsimmons, thinking carefully before replying. "As you are aware relations with Britain have been strained since '65, when the Government imposed the Stamp Act. It seems our leaders in London wish to use the Americas as a cow from which to extract their milk. I, as you know, have been most loyal; that is why I pay you and several others to be part of the King's Virginia militia. You were very wise to consult me on this and your loyalty will be remembered, be sure of that. The fact is that the British Government is losing control here. The House of Burgesses dictates the way of things, the governor merely rubber-stamps their decisions. The members of the house, to a man, see change; this change will be wrought with blood. 'Tis the only thing our colonial masters understand.

"You must, of course, attempt to deliver your message as ordered. We will arrange, however, for you to be delayed. On your way to Richmond you will be arrested as a suspected member of the Sons of Liberty – you wear no uniform and your message is verbal. There is nothing about your person that will prove you are a militiaman. You will be taken to Norfolk and, unfortunately, be put in the town gaol, where you will protest and request to see the governor. I am sorry for this but it is necessary put you out of harm's way for a while. I shall arrange for you to have good food and to be as comfortable as possible. Once this little episode passes into history you will rejoin us here at Broadridge.

"You must leave at first light, but first I must ask, are you prepared to be as loyal an American as you are loyal to me?" The estate owner looked at Peter searchingly.

"Aye sir. England 'as done nothin' fer me but put me in chains fer rowin' a gig. If ye are goin' on the side of the separatists, then so will I. I'd made that decision afore comin' 'ere, sir," said Peter.

"To America then, Peter Pearce," said the landowner, holding out his hand, adding, "No one but you and I must have knowledge of this until it's over, understand?"

"To America, sir," answered a proud new American. Peter Pearce.

That was how Peter Pearce found himself in a Norfolk gaol. No one knew quite what to do with him, and as he had been instructed, he made no real attempt to gain his freedom.

It was months later that the news reached Peter's cell that a Sons of Liberty detachment had attacked Broadridge believing, mistakenly, that the Fitzsimmons family were still loyalist. At the beginning of the American resistance, communication between rebel units was almost non-existent. The attack – more of a skirmish – had occurred at a point near to where Mr Fitzsimmons was alone on horseback, making his way home. He had seen the group of rebels and spurred his horse to raise the alarm at the house. Marksmanship was a strong point in the fledgling rebel army; many of the men had blazed trails westward or had been trappers in the backwoods and mountain that covered vast tracts of the country.

Dropping to one knee, a rebel soldier shouldered his musket and pulled its trigger. The ball shattered the fleeing rider's shoulder, causing him to pull hard on the left rein; his horse reacted by turning abruptly. The rider, in his agony, never saw the low bough in front of him. It took him full in his face, smashing his forehead and driving his nose bone-up into his brain. Mr Fitzsimmons was one of the first Virginian landowners to lose his life in the War of Independence, as it was to be called. He would not, however, be the last American to be killed by his own side in time of war.

The ruse to save Peter from the governor's wrath was known only to him and Mr Fitzsimmons, who was now dead. There was no one to vouch for him and secure his release.

It wasn't until the McCormacks were requiring farm labourers that they visited the gaol and paid the required fine, securing his release.

Chapter 19
The road to liberty

The *Esther May Pearce* had had a hard Atlantic crossing and was now frustrated by light offshore airs as she approached the picturesque southern Irish port of Kinsale. It was from here that three Irish crew members would disembark – two heading to Dublin, the sailing master, Sean Finnegan, to Limerick. They were among the group who had decided to emigrate with their captain, Simon Pearce, to America. They would gather their families together and rejoin the ship in Bristol in two months' time.

Worse than in America, the British rule of Ireland was at best dictatorial, at worst brutal.

England had systematically disenfranchised Irish landowners, replacing them with British aristocracy and paid-off army officers. Catholicism, the religion of the Irish, was repressed, not though to the extent that Henry VIII had achieved at home with the dissolution of the monasteries. When Captain Pearce had declared to the crew his intention to emigrate, offering passage as well as land in the New World to any who wished to go with him, the three Irishmen did not hesitate.

As the afternoon progressed, a gentle onshore breeze developed as warm air over the land rose, making way for air from the sea to take its place. The ship under main and mizzen gaff sails spun neatly up into the wind and anchored in the picturesque seaport. The motion that had accompanied them during the ocean crossing suddenly ceased, as did the creaking of the ship's timbers and the myriads of sounds that emanated from the spars and rigging. The *Esther May* took a well-earned rest.

Next, to Bristol, where those who looked for a new life were released from shipboard duties to return to their homes and put their affairs in order, gather their families, say farewells to those who would be left behind. The rest of the crew were put to work preparing the ship for her final departure from England's shores.

Simon made his way back to Epstein and Sons, the gunsmiths, retracing the steps he had taken with Richard Blackmore 28 years previously. This time his mission was different – he had instructions to fill his ship with weaponry and powder for the Continental Army and fledgling Navy of the Congress. He was now, in effect, a spy, committing treason against the Crown, undercover in his own country.

Old master Epstein had died, but the two brothers who greeted Simon seemed to have changed little in the intervening years. Abraham, the older brother, ran the business side, while the younger Job had developed into a fine artisan and was in charge of production and quality – quality that had made them world famous. Job had developed the breech-loading rifle, an amazing piece of technology that the second Continental Congress had required Simon to procure – as many pieces as possible. The request could not be refused; it was his rite of passage, his passport to the new America. For this purpose they had supplied him with enough gold to ransom a king. As insurance, Michael Johnston, his old first officer, had been sent aboard the *Esther May* again, and the American was with Simon for the negotiations.

"My associates are real keen on your new gun, Master Epstein. How many can you supply for delivery in two months when we sail?" asked Johnston.

Before the gunsmith could reply, Simon added, "You both have to understand that this is a matter of the utmost delicacy and must be handled in secret."

"Gentlemen, I can assure you of the utmost discretion on our part. We manufacturers and merchants of Bristol – and indeed from most of England – are heartily sick of the war. The banning of trade with the Americas has hurt us all, so many of us are in sympathy with your cause. In answer to your question, Mister Johnston, we have had prior warning of forthcoming orders for our product, through the offices of none other than Mr Benjamin Franklin, who is, we understand, now in France. We have therefore taken it upon ourselves to stockpile a large number for just the eventuality you now suggest. Our price is eighteen shillings per piece delivered to your ship." Abraham Epstein didn't bat an eyelid at the exorbitant price he was asking. His customers could hardly go elsewhere now, could they?

Simon asked to be excused and drew his first officer to one side. "Michael, they are asking too much. What was the amount Congress agreed?"

"We'll take it, sir. Our orders are to conclude the business quietly. If we bargain too much they will be less keen to sell to us quietly," returned Michael.

"Aye, I guess so, but let's try them," suggested Simon. "Ah, gentlemen, we could take say ten thousand units if the price were to be sixteen shillings per piece, as well as field pieces, powder and shot," he suggested.

The elder Epstein looked at his brother and sighed. "An order of this size is of course most valuable to us, but the risks are great. Let us agree to meet in the middle, honour then preserved – a price of seventeen shillings per piece, sirs?"

Both Simon and Michael held out their hands.

"The first shipment can be made tonight – cash on delivery, as usual, captain?" asked Abraham Epstein.

"Excellent," replied Simon.

The two seamen slaked their thirst on the return to the ship at dock on the Avon River. On the short walk to the ship from the public house Michael Johnston became uneasy. "We are being followed, captain. I wonder if we have been discovered?"

"Yes, I saw them; two swarthy types – Spanish or Portuguese I think. At least they don't look like servants of His Majesty George the Third. This could be interesting."

The two men reached the safety of the ship and went below. "I'll give a couple of the men some money; they can scour the docklands and see what they can find out about our two friends."

It was not unusual to see dark-haired, olive-skinned people in any English seaport town, the progeny of the would-be Iberian conquerors of England. Many a ship from the ill-fated Spanish Armada had been wrecked after being separated by a southerly gale on the west coast of Cornwall, the Bristol Channel, Wales and Ireland. Some got to the

Hebrides before succumbing to the treacherous waters of which they had little knowledge. Consequently many Spanish seamen found new homes in the isolated communities that clung precariously to the bays and inlets of this iron-bound coast.

Bristol, a busy seaport and commercial centre, had many. It was easy, therefore, for Carlos Jesus Horta and his companion Miguel Maria Bautista to mingle without suspicion in the bustling, cosmopolitan crowd. It was when they spoke their origins became obvious, although in the years since the Battle of the Mona Passage they had learnt English all but fluently.

On their eventual return home they had spoken with the highest officials at the Spanish court and had been fully debriefed. They asked leave to find those who took part in the attack and kill them. The King of Spain had personally approved the young officer's request of a roving commission of revenge, such was His Majesty's anger at the loss of most of the treasure fleet.

First had been Roberto Da Silva two years after the battle. The great ally of Sir Richard Blackmore had been cornered when leaving his favourite brothel in Lisbon, soaked with wine and in the stupor of a man whose carnal desires had been satiated; Roberto was in no condition to defend himself against two much younger, determined attackers. He was found, hands bound, and gagged, with his manly parts removed; his attackers had watched their prey bleed to death.

Now, many years later, they had finally caught up with a major beneficiary of the Battle of the Mona Passage.

Simon Pearce had assumed the position of first officer after George Partridge had retired from the sea, many years before his captain. Partridge had returned to his hometown of Great Yarmouth, home of the North Sea fishing fleets. A widower, he lived by himself in a small cottage, next to the King's Arms public house, where he and his seafaring friends spent much of each day. His apparent wealth had made him popular, in a perfunctory sort of way.

One Monday he failed to take up his normal seat at the head of the table. After a week the landlord and some of his friends broke down the door of his cottage – the sight they were greeted with made them gag. Men who had seen the effect of the cannon ball showering a gun deck with flying splinters turned away in horror.

George Partridge was lying on his back in the parlour, each limb, including hands and feet, had been surgically removed from his body; his putrefying facial features displayed the agony he had undergone. The sheriff had been called, nothing was found in the following investigation except the public house's cleaning woman had observed two strange, dark-looking men on the quay the day before poor George Partridge had disappeared.

Carlos and Miguel were discussing the situation in a rented room on the western side of the Avon River. Miguel spoke in his native tongue. Carlos, the leader, chided him. "Speak Engleesh, my friend; it is safer, no?"

"They saw us. What should we do now?" asked Miguel, the smaller of the two.

"As much as it displeases me, my friend, I think this pirate will get off with little pain. We will have to deal with him from a distance. The ship has mounted an armed guard. These men are seasoned fighters – there is no way we will get to deal with the Captain Pearce in a fitting manner while he is on board. He visits the Ship Inn on River Street for his evening meal, always accompanied and with an escort. We will have to shoot him on his return. There is a flat rooftop opposite the hotel; I will be on it with two loaded muskets. Your job is to make a disturbance in the street a little further down. This will give me more time to shoot as the captain is distracted."

The powerfully built Carlos added, "We've waited a long time for this, *amigo* – the last one. Let us finish what we started long ago. To our fallen comrades."

The two men drank their strong brandy in silence.

Two nights later Simon Pearce was returning with Michael Johnston from the Ship Inn, replete after a fine meal of roast beef and vegetables. As they left the light of the doorway, two men from the *Esther May*'s crew fell in five paces behind, each carrying a brace of pistols and a sabre.

As they walked, a small handcart, seemingly out of control, crashed into a wall 30 paces in front of them. As Carlos Horta had predicted, the group stopped momentarily; he took aim and slowly squeezed the trigger. Seaman Brian Matheson had seen movement on the rooftop. Shouting to his companion, he threw himself at his captain, tackling him to the ground, shielding him with his own body. Davy Jenkinson drew both pistols as the musket was fired; he aimed at the flash and returned fire, his quick reaction bringing a satisfying grunt from the rooftop.

The musket ball had entered Brian's bicep, passed through it and entered Simon's abdomen, a fatal shot had the ball not been slowed down by its passage through Brian's arm. The double charge had rendered both men hors de combat. Michael reacted instantly. Grabbing Matheson's pistols he said, "You hit him, Davy; let's get the bastard."

Thus both Simon and Brian were left to tend each other's wounds without protection.

Carlos swore softly. "Jesus, Mary, Mother of God, bastardos!" He had been lying on the flat roof in the classic marksman's pose, a minimal target, particularly for a pistol. One ball had struck a metal plate covering some rot on the gable of the roof beside him. The ball had ricocheted off the plate into the flesh of his backside – in no way a fatal wound but exceedingly painful. Its position rendered him helpless to stem the flow of blood. He tried but could not stand. *Where is Miguel?* he thought, knowing the answer. His accomplice would be leaving the area as ordered, his job done.

The executioner rolled painfully onto his injured buttock – sitting on it would help stem the flow of his vital juices. He picked up the second musket. Like a wounded beast he waited for his foe to attack; now he was the prey. "I will take one more *bastardo* Engleesh with me, maybe the two!" he grinned, drawing a wicked 12-inch dagger which he laid strategically beside him.

The shots had woken the neighbourhood and help had arrived for Simon and Brian. No one saw the slight figure of Miguel Bautista melt into the darkness, his emergency plan to finish his partner's work abandoned in the hue and cry.

Michael had found a rope snaking down from the roof from which the shot had been fired. "If we climb over that wall the man on the roof will surely kill us if he is not himself already dead. We will wait for help."

Davy reached into a satchel by his side and pulled out a glass ball. Smiling he said, "Reckon this'll see t' the bastard, sir?"

"Great God, Davy, that'll shred him. Stand on my shoulders, light the fuse and heave it onto the roof," said Michael enthusiastically.

The Spaniard heard the grenade before he saw the spluttering fuse. In great pain, he rolled back on his front and crawled towards the deadly weapon. When his hand reached the glass ball the lighted fuse had passed the neck, and he gripped the grenade in an attempt to throw it back at his attackers but it exploded, showering him with shards of flying glass, his hand, arm and head disappearing into a bloody pulp. Carlos Jesus Horta's vendetta was over.

A slightly built man of dark complexion was seen by the guard stationed on the Avon Bridge. A hurrying man had stuck in the mind of the soldier who had stood a thousand night guard duties. Miguel Bautista made his way back to the room he had shared with Carlos at Mrs Amie's rooming house. Reverently he produced a stained green baize parcel from its protective covering. He stood small statues of Jesus carrying the cross, and of Mary, on the small chest of drawers and lit three candles; these he placed on his makeshift altar. He prayed he would live, he prayed that his friend would return, he prayed for guidance – he was used to Carlos making his decisions for him.

Simon and Brian had been taken to the naval infirmary just as soon as the port captain had been informed of the situation. Simon was still on the list of naval contractors; he was well known and liked by the authorities in Bristol who would have finished the job started by Horta, had they been aware of his recent persuasion.

Brian's wound, although severe, was not life-threatening as long as infection did not set in, in which case the surgeon would have to remove his arm.

Simon's case was different; the ball had lodged in the area below his stomach and had to be removed, a dangerous operation, as his intestine stood the chance of being ruptured, giving rise to infection and certain death. The surgeon was one of the most experienced in the navy; had this wound occurred in a battle at sea he would have given Simon little chance of recovery – he would have been carried to the dreaded orlop deck of his ship, the place most feared by seamen in time of battle, the place where the pain of injury was augmented by the surgeon's saw and knife.

The ball was removed successfully, the patient still partly unconscious from laudanum he had to imbibe to dull his senses. When he awoke the next morning, the pain in his gut was as if he had been kicked by a horse. As his eyes focused, a naval lieutenant stood before him, obviously relieved that the famous captain had not died on his watch. The port captain had ordered an officer to be available as he woke.

"Lieutenant Dunwoody, sir, at your service. Captain Richardson's compliments, sir. The second attacker has been apprehended. He has been, ah, questioned, sir, and what a tale he tells. It seems he and his accomplice have been assassinating all those they could get to who took part in the Battle of the Mona Passage – an amazing story indeed, sir. If you will excuse me, sir, I will report to the captain that you are awake."

Simon pondered through waves of pain. *These men have been hunting me for 27 years. How many of my old shipmates have died at their hands?* He passed out with the effort of using his brain. The oblivion was extended by a rising fever; it was touch-and-go whether he would survive. He would say later that in short periods of lucidity he saw Isabella and his children praying for him; he was convinced it was their love that pulled him through.

During Simon's convalescence Michael Johnston took care of departure preparations – the guns were stowed in brandy barrels deep in the bowels of the ship, all ballast was removed and replaced by cannon, the loading done in secrecy. The authorities must not become aware of their change of allegiance.

The British Government at the time was keen for as many loyalist families as possible to move to America, thereby reinforcing pro-British sentiment. They offered free land grants to those who were prepared to undertake the arduous journey. Ostensibly the *Esther May* was being refitted for the purpose of transporting these migrants. Alterations were made to the accommodations to allow for women and children on board. The captain's quarters had been extended to accommodate his wife and four children; a small cupboard-like space had been built for their governess.

It was the end of September 1775, some four weeks later than originally planned, that the *Esther May* was finally at sea, her bows pointed on the course that would eventually lead to their new country. Simon looked with nostalgia at the Isles of Scilly as they slipped by to leeward, a sight he had seen many times. *Would he see his birthplace again,* he wondered. *How were his aunt, cousins and the uncle who disapproved of him so?*

"Full and bye, sir, wind east'nor'east and steady; course south by west captain," called Sean Finnegan. "An' if I may suggest, soir, your coat? 'Ers a might chill, an' it will chill down some more afore night."

"Mister Finnegan, am I to be swaddled this entire voyage? My wound is healing well, the sea air is good for me, so away with your fussing, man," answered Simon in mock annoyance. He was still disturbed by the rapid change of events. England, his homeland, was soon to be his enemy. Could he really run out his guns for America? His crew had all sworn they would, if so ordered. He had tired during the two-hour second dog watch he had insisted on standing, and it was not without some pleasure he went below for the night. They had taken on board a trainee apprentice officer – Neil Farmiloe, grandson of old John Pearce's sister, Margaret Farmiloe – so he would not be required to stand a watch.

Sean smiled as his captain left the deck and began the evening ritual of dead-reckoning navigation, mainly to instruct the young Farmiloe boy – always good for a trainee to be able to check his arithmetic with a bearing from a fixed point of land.

Biscay was its usual October self. The wind had been offshore, however, if rather fresh. Michael Johnston had ferried his captain ashore at his home village of Machico on the nor'east coast of the island of Madeira, while Michael, as usual, took command for the sail to Puerto Funchal.

Having not seen her husband's ship enter and leave, Isabella was surprised when Simon appeared in the entrance of Casa d'Ouro. She ran towards him and was about to embrace him when she stopped, concerned, and asked, "'Usband, you are 'urt, no?"

"Do not be alarmed, my dear. I am healing well. My, you look magnificent." He took her gently in his arms, hardly believing he was back with his beloved again. "I have much to tell, and we have little time. I shall not be parted from you for so long ever again."

She led him to their main living room and sent instructions to the cook to prepare food – the master had returned. Satisfied all was in order, she turned to Simon and asked him to tell his tale.

"I trust, my love, that in my absence you have not changed your mind about America?" he said and let the story slowly unfold.

"I am 'appy, but not 'appy with the little time I 'ave to prepare," she scolded. "But, my love, you 'ave not 'ad all the excitement to yourself! The old governor was so corrupt that my brother 'ad to remove 'im from 'is position. It was a difficult time, but Juan was finally able to prove 'ow bad 'e was. Juan is now acting governor of the island; 'e will be able to look after the estate until it is sold. We should go to Funchal soon and let him know what is 'appening; 'e will be sad to see us go but will be 'appy to 'ave contact with the new America. 'E always talks of it."

Isabella finished her story by which time the children had returned from their day in the hills. Simon spent the evening discussing plans to leave the island and their future prospects in America. He did not inform them of his decision to join the American independence movement; this he felt would be dangerous – after all, Portugal was England's ally, and the children had been brought up half-Portuguese, half-British.

Simon's eldest son Juan was on the island, having completed his medical studies in Lisbon. A young man of great intelligence, he opened the discussion with his father later in private.

"The situation is unstable in the Americas, Father; you have purchased land in the south, which, if I understand correctly, is the rebels' stronghold. Where will our alliances lie? With the British who are strongest in the north, or with Congress who are more or less in league with the rebels?"

Knowing well his son's adroitness he decided to tell him the whole story. The young man listened quietly.

"It is as I had supposed, Father, and I believe you to be right in the course you propose; however, I have some misgivings in leaving my country and family, knowing that in the immediate future I will be considered a traitor, as will my brother and sisters. Have you considered that?"

"Yes, my son, the situation is difficult in the extreme. I have thought hard on the matter and believe the American people are right to disown their colonial masters for all the reasons we have discussed. I had hoped to remain neutral but in all conscience can no longer do so. You are 21 years old and are free to decide for yourself whether to join the ship or not."

"Thank you, Father. I shall inform you of my decision soon, but I urge you to give Carlos, Juanita and Isabellita the same choice. It will ease any tensions that may later arise if each of us have made the decision for ourselves," answered Juan wisely.

"I will discuss it with your mother," said Simon, uncomfortable with the idea that his children may choose not to be part of the new venture.

At the governor's mansion in Puerto Funchal Simon faced his brother-in-law. He knew Juan Mendoza was a highly astute politician, of considerable intelligence. He needed him on his side, a position that may not be easy to achieve if Juan discovered the truth. As they drank the finest Madeira wine, Juan listened to the story.

"I know, brother-in-law, that for some time my sister has 'ad the desire to leave the island, and of course you have good lands in America. I can see the attraction of a new start in a New World, but the country is at war, your lands are, if I understand correctly, in an area held by the rebels. Do you not think it wiser to wait until the outcome of the conflict is determined?" The man who had befriended Simon some 28 years before paused to allow him to complete his story.

"I believe that I must make my mark now, Juan. We will go to the safety of New York first. I shall purchase a house in the city, and we shall live there until things quieten down," answered Simon. The lie that had come so glibly to his tongue sounded lame.

Juan continued, "I think, my friend, you do not disclose all to me, no! But I think it is best this way. As you know I will do everything in my power to make Isabella happy, and indeed you too. I will purchase Casa d'Ouro from you if you so desire. This can be done secretly; we just let it be known that you are away for a while and will return and that I am appointed guardian of your interests. As things are settled in America, I can announce that I 'ave become the estate's new owner. Simple, eh. But not so simple is the price; what do you 'ave in mind?"

Simon had given the matter considerable thought and had come to the conclusion that to get his cash out now would be safer than to await a possible sale at a later date; he therefore offered his brother-in-law an exceptionally good price, in gold, paid before departure.

"I will not dwell on your motives for offering so good a bargain, brother-in-law; I shall simply accept graciously. I think it good that Portugal will 'ave friends in the Americas, with Benjamin Franklin 'aving 'is tongue in the ear of the French court, also the court of Espanha. I do not think our British allies will be long in control of their American colonies, eh! But know neither France nor Espanha 'as given up their ambitions in your New World. Any assistance they give it now will 'ave a 'eavy price later on, so be careful."

The use of 'your' indicated that he was not fooled as to his brother-in-law's true motive. Juan poured a larger than normal measure of the superb vintage Madeira, and the two men drank solemnly to seal their agreement.

On Christmas Day 1775, the *Esther May* was mid-Atlantic, the trade winds a modest 12 knots, hardly ruffling the long, slow swells. The ladies had bedecked the ship with colourful ribbons and items from their wardrobes, some of which had seasoned seamen blushing. Isabella and some of her ladies had relieved the ship's cook from his galley and had set about creating a feast for the 110 souls – almost double the ship's normal complement – who were crammed into every possible space aboard. Much wine and grog was imbibed, the weather being fine with a steady wind; but a handful of crew were needed to keep the ship on course. Among those was the first officer.

Late that afternoon a sail was sighted on the horizon far to weather. Simon was keen to identify the vessel – were she to be French or Spanish, they could be attacked. The ship was safe from British or American interference – they had arranged a special signal to be shown should a rebel privateer hove into view.

"Mister Johnston, I would be obliged if you would go to the maintop personally and see if you can identify the sail; see also if she is making to intercept us. She has the weather gage of us and could easily run us down if she is fast enough. We will begin to make sail slowly with the hands who have not been drinking; I will order the festivities to cease." The captain looked over the port quarter - not yet visible from the deck - she must be ten or more miles away.

"She's a man-o'-war, all right. Don't look British t' me, sir; seems to be holding a reciprocal course, not converging, but she could close tonight. She's quite large; must've caught up while we have been under short sail during the celebrations. I think we can outrun 'er under full sail, sir," said the first officer, panting due to his recent exertions 100 feet above the deck.

"We shall wait till dark; run no lights and come to weather four points. We'll attempt to get to windward of her and make our identification. Having taken the wind gage from her we will be able to get clear easily. I've no wish to fight with the families and most of our worldly possessions on board. Not to mention sufficient weaponry to outfit an army." The captain looked worried as he scanned the horizon.

As soon as the masthead lookout lost sight of the intruder in the oncoming twilight, Simon set about his plan. "All square sails off her, Mister Johnston; rig topsails on the gaff main and mizzen, set the fisherman and staysails forward, and the flying jib. I would prefer to pass ahead, downwind of her - less chance of them hearing us. Double the lookouts and order the ship silent. Have the ship's boys aloft too - they can run messages to avoid the lookouts having to shout," ordered Simon.

He removed the telescope from his eye and looked over his ship. With the wind forward of the beam, she heeled taking water onto the gun deck. This point of sailing was her fastest, the wind speed increased by the ship's forward momentum. No square-rigger could compete, as this would be their worst point of sail; the ship became alive and still had the ability to point yet two points higher. At this speed they should pass ahead of the pursuing ship; a collision, however, was not out of the question. It was a tense time.

The *Esther May* rushed forward, her bow wave a welter of white foam. Suddenly the other ship appeared out of the starlight; a frenzied yell from the foretop lookout broke the order of silence, the lookout rightly judging there could be insufficient time to send a runner. "Ship fine t' larboard, collision course!"

It was too late to run in front of her so Michael Johnston ordered, "Two points to windward, harden the sheets." The ship heeled further and slowed.

The alarm was raised on the other ship as the *Esther May* thundered past her stern, not 20 yards clear. "No need to wait around to identify her now, sir. I see the white of the tricolour on her ensign; she's a large French frigate, 40 guns or more. I wouldn't wish to exchange broadsides with her. You certainly made the right move, captain," said the first officer.

"Quite right, Mister Johnston. She's more than a match for us. Fall off, get the wind a point forward of the beam; she'll know she can't get near us on that course. Ben Franklin must have brought the French in sooner than expected," mused Simon. "She will have seen our British colours and will not wish to let us inform the British Admiralty of her presence. We had best not wait to argue the point with them; besides, there may be a whole battle fleet out here. Keep the lookouts manned; let's change our flag to be sure."

So it was that the *Esther May* wore the rebel American flag for the first time.

Juan Pearce was first to comment. "I agreed to join you, Father, as did all of us, but flying that flag brings home that we are in effect stateless persons. We fly a rebel flag, we are nobody in the old world."

The *Esther May* shaped a more northerly course than usual and was well to weather of the frigate by morning. The lookout, however, saw two more sail astern. They had had a close shave; there was indeed a French fleet abroad on the Atlantic. *They could be reinforcements for the French Caribbean squadron, or reinforcements for American rebels,* Simon thought.

All was quiet for the following week as they skirted the Bahaman islands and shaped a course for the Chesapeake Bay, where Simon expected British ships to be blockading. He would either have to approach the blockading ships flying British colours, then make a run in after nightfall - this course of action would declare to the Royal Navy that he was a traitor before he had gained the security of being amongst his new countrymen – or he could try to make contact with American forces further down the coast, or on the Delaware, and be instructed the best way to proceed.

Whatever he did, he had to avoid discovery by the British as long as possible.

Chapter 20

Independence

The *Esther May* made her way slowly towards the coast, her landfall amongst the sand islands and bays that protected the Carolinian coast for 200 miles, just south of Cape Henry, the southernmost entrance to the Chesapeake Bay. Michael Johnston had suggested it prudent to find out the current situation before making a declared landfall – they had, after all, been away for ten months; much would have transpired in that time.

Pamlico Sound is a dangerous maze of channels and sandbanks but Michael, having sailed these waters, was confident he could navigate the ship safely so long as he had good visibility. They first had to navigate past the treacherous cays and shoals that guarded the entrance. Having spent his youth and early seamanship training in the area, Michael was the best pilot the ship could hope for as they entered a narrow, unmarked channel. Now, finally out of the grip of the two-knot northward flowing Gulf Stream current, they made steady progress in a light, easterly breeze across the open waters of the sound.

"Take command, if you please, Mister Johnston. I will assume your role in attending to the handling of the ship," then in a whisper Simon added, "Take good care of her, eh."

"Aye aye, sir." Michael acknowledged his captain then concentrated on his pilotage. "Two leadsmen in the chains, if you please, bosun, and the best man you have for a foretop lookout. Watch for a headland to open to larboard as we pass the first headland. The water shallows as the headland opens – we will need to begin a steady southward turn on my call."

All on board were on edge, the usual chatter absent. Deep water men feel ill at ease as the depth decreases; the passengers, also feeling the tension, remained quiet.

"All hands to the sheets on Mister Johnston's call. Harden up!" ordered Simon.

"By the mark seventeen, sand 'n shell, shoaling fast," called the leadsman, the fine line with its odd array of differing attached marks telling him the depth by feel as he retrieved it. A hole in the bottom of the lead is filled with tallow to which small amounts of matter stuck; this told him the nature of the seabed.

"Is it safe, 'usband?" asked Isabella nervously.

"Er, yes, my dear, as safe as it can be, entering a strange bay for the first time. We are in good hands with Michael as our pilot. I would be obliged, madam, if you would join the other ladies. Your presence will be a calming influence on them," said Simon, uncharacteristically requesting his wife to leave him while he worked the ship.

"By the mark, twelve 'n an 'arf," was the leadsman's sonorous call.

"Deck there, second headland clear four points to larboard," called the lookout.

"By the deep, nine 'n an 'arf," called the leadsman.

"Bring her up to wind two points, Mister Finnegan." The first officer had asked that the Irishman's firm hands be on the wheel during the final approach.

"By the mark, nine," the leadsman called.

The *Esther May* was carving through the tranquil water of the sound, her wake, ripples and small whirlpools all that gave testament to her passing. She was now a mile or so from the second headland, the shoals to leeward obvious due to light water colouring; a strip of darker water showed the channel, as a road, before them.

Michael knew the deep water was but 100 yards from the headland, and the wind would become fickle as they approached it. "Stand by your sheets and prepare to go about if we are headed. Un-cat the kedge anchor, Mister Thomas. Stand by to drop quickly. Hand the topsails and fisherman; if we ground, let's not drive her on too hard," the pilot's many orders preparing the ship for every eventuality.

"By the mark, seven," was the monotonic call from the chains.

Then a more urgent, "By the deep, five, shoaling, quick sir!"

The *Esther May* required two fathoms – 12 feet – of clear water to pass.

"By the deep, three," called the second leadsman.

"We must tack; the flood is pushing us over the sandbank. Helm up, quickly, lee ho," called Michael. The ship became upright as she passed her bows through the eye of the wind, thus her keel became a few inches deeper. As a ballerina slipping from her points, the ship ground ungracefully to a standstill.

Michael looked at his captain as if to ask if he was to continue. Simon remained silent, confirming his pilot's authority. "Get the longboat overboard; tow the kedge to the other side of this channel, off our beam. We have another hour or so of flood tide. Quickly now, we'll soon be off the sand."

The cutter was halfway across the bay when a musket shot rang out; Simon took out his glass and saw three boats laden with uniformed men pulling from the beach. *We are sitting ducks,* he thought.

"The ensign, sir. We're flying British colours. They're American militia, they think we're on the other side," said Sean Finnegan racing to haul the offending flag from the mizzen gaff. Then to Davy, the ship's boy, "Get me the American flag, lad."

Before Sean could hoist the new flag, the somewhat undisciplined American soldiers had fired further shots at the longboat. The coxswain, one Jim Dawson, a 40-year-old seaman who had been with Simon for 12 years, was fatally hit in his face, the ball rendering his features unrecognisable.

As soon as the new flag was fluttering boldly from the mizzen, a shout to 'cease fire' was heard. The three American boats pulled cautiously towards the *Esther May*'s cutter, muskets and pistols levelled at her crew.

"What ship, and from where bound?" called a tall man, with the weathered features of a backwoodsman wearing a traditional brown buckskin jacket, his authoritarian call identifying him as the officer in charge of the unit.

"The *Esther May Pearce* out of Bristol via Madeira," called back Bryn Thomas, the bosun.

"Well, I'll be," exclaimed the man. "I'm mighty sorry for shooting on y'all. Thought y'all was Royal Navy in a ship captured from us! John Crockett's the name, captain. Carolina Rifles. We've been awaitin' yer. Welcome to America!"

"Some bloody welcome," said Sean morosely under his breath.

The kedge was laid, and with the extra manpower added by Captain Crockett's men at the capstan, the *Esther May* was soon afloat again. With the last of the flood assisting, the ship was towed into a small, deep cove; here she was out of sight of any passing, nosy Royal Naval ship.

That evening a feast was prepared on board for all hands; their American friends supplied a sufficiency of fresh meat shot in the woods nearby. The ship, bringing the finest of Casa d'Ouro's cellar, supplied welcome drink for the men. Isabella had to avert her eyes at the abuse the precious liquid of her homeland was getting at the hands of these rough, now friendly men.

"Well, Cap'n Pearce, y'all 'avin' been away fer s' long I'd better get yer up to date with the way o' things," said Crockett.

"Please do, captain. We sailed from New York in April last year. Not much current, certainly accurate, news was available in Britain. Though I must add that the American cause is well supported by the working and merchant classes; it is they who suffer through the loss of trade that is a direct result of the conflict. There are many who will support an America that is self-determining, back in the realm of King George," answered Simon.

"That's mighty good to hear, sir. The Redcoats here do not seem to hold the same sentiments," answered Crockett. "The recent acts of parliament have added a backbone to a resistance that was previously sporadic and dispersed. You know that the first Continental Congress was held in September and October '74? It was declared that the raft of British parliamentary acts was illegal. Acts such as the Quartering Act - where American homes were required not only to house the British Army, but to feed it at their own expense - were unacceptable. The intolerable, coercive act, designed to curb the power of local government, was the thin end of the wedge. The Regulating Act, were it to be obeyed, would virtually disband the Massachusetts Assembly, banning them from all trade except with Britain.

"In direct contrast to the British tyrannies was the declaration by Congress that asserted the right of all Americans to security and property. In some areas the British Army has been ordered to enforce the new acts, precipitating open rebellion to British rule. A detachment of Redcoats was sent to Concord, Massachusetts to take the fort and munitions dump there; this was destroyed at the cost of 14 of our men dead. Paul Revere, Sam Adams and Bill Dawes all escaped. As the British were on the long road back to Boston, 250 of their number were killed or injured by ordinary people, not even known sympathisers, as they retreated.

"The now illegal Massachusetts Provincial Congress has ordered 13,600 American soldiers from all over New England to be mobilised. They besieged the British in Boston City; they are there to this day.

"In May, Ben Arnold and Ethan Allen took Fort Ticonderoga in New York on the Hudson. The place was loaded with cannon, guns and powder, far more than the British took at Concord. This pretty lot was dragged to Boston with ox carts. We are now in a state of open warfare."

"In May last year, at the second Continental Congress," continued Crockett, "the general was made commander-in-chief of what is now the Continental Army of America, after the battle of Bunker Hill, where our men were ordered not to fire till they could see 'the whites of their eyes'. Those mad Englishmen advanced up that hill twice; thousands of Redcoats died. Had we not run out of ammo their third attack would have failed. As it was, we had to face 'em with nought but fixed bayonets. The Redcoats were much better trained at this, and they took the hill. We lost 400 to their 1,000, but included in our losses was General Warren – he was worth 200 ordinary men.

"The Congress has had one more attempt at reconciliation with old George the Third. They sent him a petition asking for his help in gettin' his jackass parliament to see sense. He didn't even read it; instead he declares we are in a state of open rebellion.

"So Congress declares it will take up arms. The American Army is formally brought into being and so is the American Navy. I guess y'all will be navy men soon, yer hear," Crockett said laughing. "The navy's base is Norfolk, Virginia; it's there yer t' report 'n unload, by 'n by."

"The Frenchies said back in December they would help us agin the British. This thing is getting big." Crockett slurred his words slightly due to his intake of the wine, the power of which he was unaccustomed to. Corn whiskey was more to his constitution's understanding.

"We encountered French ships on the Atlantic; I wondered what they were about. They were far too far north to be headed for the French Caribbean," added Simon.

"That George the Third's one stupid king, if yer ask me. After they repealed the Stamp Act, things quietened down; many people wanted to stay part of 'is empire. If he had seen sense he would have known that to try to strong-arm three million of us from three thousand miles away would be all but impossible. 'Ad he gave a bit then all could well be different. Too stuck up, if you ask me; pride is a powerful thing, but it often works against us, I reckons," continued Crockett, showing his penchant for being a bit of a campfire philosopher.

"What of the British Navy, captain? Will we have a blockade to run to get into Norfolk?" asked Simon.

"Their navy's at full stretch; they ain't got the ships nor manpower to fully blockade all our ports. We plan to create a diversion near Cape Charles, the northern entrance to the bay. A small schooner will make her way round Cape Henry, to the south, and escort y'all in. We'll ferry a couple o' men an' horses across this sound tomorrow. It's 90 miles to Norfolk – two days and a night, and the same back. You put to sea tomorrow; wait ten miles south of Henry for the schooner. If you don't make contact return here for instructions, sir."

It was the first time Crockett had called Simon 'sir'.

He was about to make comment when the American handed him a buckskin pouch. On opening it he found three pieces of parchment, one addressed to Michael Johnston, officially commissioning him as captain, Continental Navy of America.

The heavier document was a requisition order, requisitioning the *Esther May Pearce* to be placed into the Continental Navy of America, her new commander, Captain Michael Johnston.

Simon looked aghast and annoyed at the assembled company. Had he gone through all this to have his ship taken from him?

"Read the third document, please, sir. It would have been better had you read it first," said Michael.

Captain Simon Trefarthan Pearce,

You are hereby commissioned commodore in the Continental Navy of America.

Commander,

The southern arena at Norfolk

Attached was a fourth document, a promissory note granting him eight thousand American dollars, should his ship, the *Esther May Pearce*, not be returned to him in a satisfactory condition at the cessation of hostilities, the payment of which being conditional on Captain Pearce's acceptance of the aforementioned commission. Signed Eske Hopkins, Supreme Commander, American Naval Forces.

Simon showed the papers to Isabella, a look of uncertainty in his eyes; she smiled and spoke sombrely.

"To be a commissioned officer in the American Navy must make you an American, no? So, then, are the children and I. It is one thing worth being parted for, to fight for our new country's independence, my love."

"Well said, madam," said Michael as the two friends clasped each other's shoulders.

"I suppose you have done your work well, Michael, bringing me to the American cause. Let us make this America a place for all to triumph – equal opportunities for all. Ladies and gentlemen, charge your glasses. A United America – freedom for all who live within her."

At the first of the morning ebb on a windless Sunday, the American soldiers towed the *Esther May* from her snug moorings to Pamlico Sound. A further mile on, clear of the land and heading toward the pass, they entered the sound. Then northward on the light breeze and the Gulf Stream. The ship's new captain was nervous; he had worked the ship to make an offing on numerous occasions before, but this time it was different – now he was the captain. The responsibility for her safety and all those aboard now lay on his shoulders.

Simon went below; for him it was strange also. As commodore he supposed he was ultimately responsible for the success of the journey, but the details as to how that success was to be obtained now was the responsibility of another. "Ah, my dear, I see you are awake. You are well, I hope?"

"Yes, 'usband. I am well, and 'appy. We are at the beginning of something very big, very grand; 'ere our family can grow secure, without the need to be well born for success. It is something special you do to fight for such a thing." Isabella was in a reflective mood and totally behind her husband's choice.

"It was this very situation, the taking of sides, which I sought to avoid. But it is impossible to avoid the unavoidable. You, as ever, are ethically correct. I, once a pirate, am now a senior officer in the navy of our new country. I find some difficulties seeing myself in the role. Thankfully Sir Richard taught me well," answered Simon modestly.

The windless conditions continued until the afternoon when an onshore land breeze sprung up providing enough speed for steerage. The *Esther May* should be at the rendezvous precisely on time, at dawn.

Light grew on the eastern horizon; the watch changed at eight. It was cursed cold, and those who had been on deck from four in the morning went below, hoping the cook had provided something warm for them to eat before a spell in their hammocks.

Captain Michael Johnston surveyed the water ahead; they were barely making steerage way in the fickle remnants of a sea breeze. A fine mist dampened everything and reduced visibility to under a mile. The schooner, their pilot, if she had put to sea at all, would be standing still, the current against her equalling her forward velocity. He would need to get much closer to shore to be able to anchor if the calm persisted. Should he not, he may well drift into a blockading frigate or sloop of war. Perhaps they should head back to the cove, but they would have to repeat the exercise later. He longed to ask Simon his opinion; in the end he did.

"To anchor for the night is, I believe, the best course. You may have to cut it free if the wind comes from seaward, or if we are seen by the enemy." The British Navy his enemy! Simon found that, still, a concept hard to grasp fully. *What would Sir Richard Blackmore think of it?* he wondered silently. He had died mysteriously six years before. In the light of recent events it was probably at the hands of the two Spaniards, Bautista and Horta.

Having worked the ship inshore on the dying land breeze, Michael gave the order to anchor off the coast in some 20 fathoms. Sails were stowed, and the ship's company officers, men, women and children waited through another long, cold winter night. At least their position was known; no need for constant attention updating it. All eyes strained in the starlight to see anything that might move.

A weak sun finally peaked over the horizon; the foretop lookout called, "Sail ho."

Anxious people strained to sight the ship.

Michael went himself to the crosstrees and saw the ship, her masts showing above the mist in his telescope eyepiece. "Damn her eyes," he exclaimed. "That's no schooner, she's square-rigged – a warship, I've no doubt. Call action stations. Master gunner load the bow chasers. Mister Finnegan warp the anchor to our stern. We are as steady as a rock at anchor here, and the other ship is but stemming the tide. She's a British warship, I'm sure."

Just then a cannon's muzzle flashed on the approaching vessel, the ball falling harmlessly into the sea 200 yards ahead of the *Esther May*. "What do you think, commodore?" asked the new captain.

"Twelve pounder – at most, a sloop of war, I would think," said Simon. "Our twenties have twice the range. Load the second salvo with chain shot once we have the range. Rip the spars out of her."

The *Esther May* had been turned 180 degrees as she snubbed to her cable, now made fast aft. Her powerful forward guns could now be brought into action. Her ranging shots were true – two holes were seen in the warship's foretopsail. The next salvo of chain brought down her foretopmast. With the resulting loss of power the sloop started drifting backward on the current, away from the *Esther May*, yet pointing for her, her remaining sails providing insufficient power to stem the tide.

"Boats, sir, they've launched their boats. The crazy bastard wants to board us!" said Sean Finnegan in amazement.

"Cut and buoy the cable; head for her while we have range advantage and hit her hard. Load the larboard guns and run out every second gun with grape and canister," yelled the new captain.

The schooner's sails filled. Sailing to windward made the light breeze increase with her forward momentum; soon they had steerage.

The British longboats were 200 yards from the *Esther May*'s considerable broadside. Loaded as they were, the attackers were cannon fodder, at point blank range. The gun crews were silent as they prepared to witness a fate that could so easily be theirs, had they had a glory-seeking captain as was in command of the British sloop.

The captain felt a hand squeeze his shoulder; looking up, he saw it was the Irish sailing master. "Them poor buggers is just doing their duty. A fair fight is one thing; this would be murder, sir."

Michael looked at the gun deck below him, the gun crews looking up at him. "Fire one ball at the first longboat - that should discourage them. That ship is in no position to harm us greatly; we will be out of her range by now. It is more important we deliver our cargo than attempt to take her as a prize." The one ball did far more than discourage the British longboat; it hit it amidships, totally destroying it. With the glass to his eye Michael saw a few survivors clinging to wreckage.

"Let's get away from here; the survivors will be picked up by the others," said Johnston. The loneliness of command settling upon him, he seemed to stoop and age instantly. The commodore answered his questioning eyes with a tiny smile, acknowledgement enough to signify approval. Still, he had just killed at least five men - enemy yes, but was it right?

The schooner didn't materialise until they entered Norfolk roads, where she was to be seen hard aground having misjudged the tide in the lack of wind when leaving for her rendezvous. The *Esther May* was quickly warped to a berth alongside the main town quay, the first on board a short, agile man in his forties. He strode up to Simon, hand extended. "Commodore Pearce, I presume. I'm Eske Hopkins. It's sure good to see y'all safely here."

"Yes, it's good to be here, admiral," answered Simon formally.

"We're a might less formal here in America, Simon. We don't have admirals; my position is commodore in chief," said the man in command of the Continental Navy of America. "You won't have heard but General Washington has sent the British running in Boston and is heading back to reinforce New York. Reckons the British'll try to take the city. He's most likely right - he usually is. For you now, let's get y' settled and your passengers ashore. We've been waiting a while for you and your desperately needed cargo."

"I am afraid my injury in England delayed our departure a month. Are we to unload here, sir?" Simon was not yet comfortable with the first-name terms offered by his superior.

"Norfolk is a long way from where the cargo is needed. I'd kinda like t' get the guns t' New York, that's where the next fight'll be, but it's much safer t' sail up the bay and unload north of Baltimore, go overland t' Wilmington, then on barges past Philadelphia and unload at Trenton. I'm awaiting word as to which route to take. I favour the slower, safer route, but the army needs these guns now." The commodore was not about to risk all to save a couple of weeks, although a day too late and the fledgling American Army may not need them at all; this thought he kept to himself.

It was decided that part of the cargo – the rifles and smaller pieces – would go by the commodore's route of choice. The larger cannon were urgently required by General Washington, as he prepared to meet the British Army at New York. A daring plan was hatched for the *Esther May* to approach at night, carrying the weapons to defend the city directly to where they would be needed.

Simon turned to Michael. "I am told the doctors have suspended me from active service for a while; it's going to be strange to watch you sail away. I'm trans-shipping to a riverboat with most of our passengers. We will head up the Potomac to Alexandria and our new home; it will be good to settle the family before beginning my service. Good luck, Michael. You will do well," he said, extending his hand to the *Esther May*'s captain.

"Thank you, sir. I am fortunate to have sailed with you. I have learned a lot." Then the two men shook hands.

Simon turned to the wind-sculptured face of the ship's sailing master. "Well, Sean, how long is it now – 29 years? All this time you have looked after my back well, old friend. When all of this is over you have a home to return to. Martha and your nephews Seamus and Billy will live with us until a house can be built; we will take good care of them. You have always taken but half of your due payment for services. You have never asked what has become of the rest; why is that?"

"Well, soir, what would an ol' Oirish lad like me do wit' a whole lot o' money, 'cept waste it on the drink. T' be sure, yer better at looking after it 'an me. I know where to go if I need some."

"Well, it's time you knew what your money has done for you. There is, of course, the land; I have ordered a house to be built on it – I bought 30,000 acres of prime land, Sean. A hundred is yours. I suggest you invest in getting the land cleared for farming as soon as manpower becomes available. There is an entity, started in 1756, called the American stock market, where people can invest in American business. The businesses use the money to grow, and pay the investor – you and I – a dividend, a cash return on our invested capital. At the present time you have an equity, that is, a shareholding value of over $30,000 – you are a very rich man, Sean. You don't have to go to sea again. I can get you transferred from the ship. Come with us and your kin to set up your home." Simon was almost pleading for Sean to step off the gangplank and walk away with him.

"My, that's a powerful lot o' money, soir. I'm a wonderin' what an old bog Irishman would do wi' all that. I cain't even count that 'igh. I'm mighty grateful t' ye for th' botherin' wi' it, soir, but I'll ask one more favour of 'e. Young Billy 'n Seamus, soir, them's bright lads. I want 'em t' 'ave the best education money can buy, soir – 'ave I enough fer that?" Sean asked innocently.

"Sean, you have enough income to fully educate 50 young men and not spend your capital. Rest assured, I will start the boys at school as soon as we settle," answered Simon, smiling.

"Fifty boys, y' say, soir," said Sean thinking. "Well now, I reckon I've an idea how best t' spend some o' that money, fer in the name o' Jesus, me an' Martha can't use it all. In Limerick, me 'ometown, be lotsa bright young boys livin' the life o' dogs under the English. Could it be arranged that some o' them could get away over 'ere an' get educated, soir? Reckon it'd be a 'elp t' America too, gettin' all those keen, bright young uns?" the guileless man asked.

"Why, Sean, that is the most wonderful idea. I have set up a trust in England so my Roseland properties can be used for the good of the Pearce and Farmiloe families over there. We could set up the Sean Finnegan Trust in the same way; the money – income, that is –could then be used to benefit those whom you wish to help. Even after your death people will know of Sean Finnegan; it would be a fine tribute to your life."

Simon was again in awe of this seemingly simple man – his friend had cut to the essence of America, philanthropy that would invest in the young minds of the country. "I will make a similar trust available to young Cornish lads."

"Fer now, soir, I'll give young Mister – sorry – Cap'n Johnston an 'and on this trip anyways, not t' mention watchin' the back o' young Carlos. We 'ave still got t' rid our lands o' the British. Them bastards 'ave destroyed ol' Ireland; reckon they've got t' get through me afore they destroy America."

Sean turned as his new captain ordered towing boats to take up the strain; they would tow the ship into the ebbing tide.

Simon stepped ashore and without a thought unfastened the final spring line as Captain Johnston called for shore warps to be cleared. He watched, a single tear in his eye, as his ship, named for his grandmother, slipped steadily away, his son Carlos, who had elected to remain with the ship, giving him a final wave. *So much of my life sailing away,* he thought.

* * *

Simon had secured passage on several catboats for the combined families' travel. The wide, shallow-draft vessels, whose masts were at the front of the foredeck, would take them some 160 miles up the Chesapeake Bay, into the Potomac River and north-westward to their new home.

The voyage would take three days, as they could not sail on the shoal-ridden waterways at night. The women slept under a small doghouse structure. The facilities were primitive – Isabella complained about the latrine, a makeshift plank above the stern boomkin, around which canvas was rigged for the sake of modesty.

It was special for Simon as he was able to spend time with his remaining three children. Juan was a full-grown man of 22 who, much to his father's displeasure, had showed little interest in seafaring. Instead he had been encouraged by his mother, who had an abiding interest in medicine, to study to be a doctor. He had graduated from medical school in Lisbon the year before with honours.

As the catboat made her way gently up the river, the sea captain spoke to his eldest son. "What think you, son, of this move our family has made?"

"From me, Father, you have will have no arguments. Three years in Lisbon dealing with an education system controlled by court and kingly whims was enough. I am persuaded that America is an excellent place to begin my career. I thank you and Mother for taking such a bold step. Isabellita is not so well convinced. The glitter of court, coming out and all the husband-hunting intrigue – to this she is, unfortunately, unlike Mother, strongly attracted.

"Brother Carlos, well at least in him you have the son who will be able to take on your business. He yearns for the sea. At 18 he feels cheated that he has been made to complete his lessons before being on a ship's deck and will now be very happy. He is a born doer of things like you, sir. He will learn quickly." Juan turned, watching the shoreline slip by, fascinated but knowing life afloat was not for him.

Simon moved to his wife sitting with their first daughter. "Juanita, what of you, my rose petal. What do you think of our new country?"

The 19-year-old looked up at her father. He was deeply shaken, as he saw for the first time in the twilight all the things in her demeanour that had attracted him to his wife in the first place. Isabella moved simultaneously, and the faces of the two women were framed in a flicker of lamplight; they were as sisters, stunningly beautiful, the younger having the intense, intelligent eyes of her mother.

"Father, I am well pleased for an opportunity to have a life of my own, not dictated by a society that sees women as perfunctory housekeepers, tools of men. I too wish to study, as has my elder brother; I wish to attend university. Do you think this will be allowed for a female in America, Father?" The young woman was clearly highly motivated.

"You may be the first, my darling, but your father will not stand in your way," Isabella said, answering for her husband and firmly putting forward her point of view.

"It has always been books with you, has it not, my sweet, so I am not surprised. You are so like your mother, she whom I cannot deny. I will do my best to see that all my family become that which they most desire." He put his arm around his two lovely womenfolk, wondering how, even in America, his daughter's ardent dream could come true.

They were silent now on the crowded riverboat; soon sleep overcame them.

In the morning of the last day Juan gave his father a pamphlet entitled 'Common Sense'. "This, sir, you should read. Mr Paine declares for independence from royal rule; he is highly critical of all monarchy, a position I also hold. It states succinctly that what is happening in France, and about to occur, in America can and will happen in the rest of the world. A new world order; about time, don't you think?" The tall young man smiled, leaving his father to his reading.

Peter Pearce was at the landing he had had built on the family property at Alexandria, to meet his cousin and the families he had brought with him to America. He had been very busy and was proud of his achievements. The main house, the design for which Simon had had sent from his architects in New York, was all but complete. Peter had taken it upon himself to proceed directly with the big house. During a lull in fighting many tradesmen were available for the work. All but the servants' quarters were complete, some 12,000 square feet of living space ready for habitation.

"Peter," exclaimed an amazed Isabella, "you 'ave made 'ere a miracle, 'as he not, Simon!"

"Indeed, Peter. I am astonished at your accomplishments; they are tenfold that I could reasonably have hoped for. Show us around. We have some 25 people to house until we find accommodations. What do you suggest?" asked Simon.

"You and your family can occupy the west wing upstairs, we will raise tents for the men and boys, the womenfolk can share the other bedrooms and perhaps the formal drawing room. We'll cope, with the help of our excellent housekeeper, Mrs McNab. She has been laying in provisions for quite a while," said Peter, in his element, organising.

"I shall go to the kitchen to 'elp while our bags are taken to our rooms." Isabella, never too proud, went off to find the indomitable Helen McNab. It was here that Isabella met Dorothy Pearce, Peter's tiny Scottish wife. The two women were to become firm friends.

After the evening meal Simon opened a bottle of wine from Casa d'Ouro and drew Peter and Juan to a corner where they could talk. "Peter, we are truly in your debt. In just one year you have turned a wilderness into an estate. What of the political situation in these parts, and what of the war?"

"We are at a crossroads here in Virginia on the west bank of the Potomac. Much commerce now uses the roads since the Royal Navy blockades the entrance to Chesapeake Bay. Much of the land hereabouts is owned by expatriates from many countries and of more than one generation, so the feeling is mainly pro-independence. The Second Congress ordered that all colonists with British loyalties be disarmed; many have left for Canada. They also opened up all ports to foreign trade, but more importantly, a committee headed by Mr Franklin and Thomas Jefferson has been formed to draft a constitution – a declaration of independence is to be expected soon. You have arrived at a most interesting time, the very turning point of American history," beamed Peter, very proud of his part.

Chapter 21

War

Simon Pearce was in his office in the naval dockyard, Norfolk, where Eske Hopkins had given him command of naval forces in the southern region. Reporting to him was a courier corporal with astonishing news.

"Three British warships have entered the bay at Fort Moultrie in an attempt to regain control of the place and provide a base for the British in the south. Major Davidson, sir, had his guns at maximum elevation; the first salvo severely damaged the frigate *Swiftsure* – she went out of control and drifted onto a sandbank where our guns pounded her to pieces. The British, having rescued the survivors from the wreck, anchored out of range. That night we were awakened by a general alarm. The British had come ashore to try and take us from the land. The major had thought that might happen and had loaded the guns with canister and grape; the poor buggers didn't stand a chance! At the same time a small barge loaded with powder was let to drift between the two other ships. The explosion caused many fires and much damage. The ships slipped their cables, leaving many of the shore contingent stranded. The senior officer was captured and is being brought here by sea, sir."

"Thank you, corporal, and well done. I will organise food and a bed for you. Please attend this office at eight tomorrow morning and return with our reply to the good major."

A *newsy day,* he thought as he reread a general dispatch from operational headquarters, the contents of which was a mixture – on one hand a serious setback, on the other momentous news to the aspirations of Americans.

To all officers commanding units of the Continental Army or Navy:

Be advised that a large British battle fleet has arrived and taken control of New Jersey and New York. It comprises some 30 ships of the line and 300 support vessels. We understand an army of 30,000 men under General Howe has landed. General Washington requires all available troops to join him. Naval units and privateers will attack any shipping, other than our allies, with a focus on seizing them and their cargoes. Should capture be impossible, they are to be sunk.

You are formally advised that the French Government has pledged us support to the tune of $1,000,000. Further, Louis XVII is in negotiations with Spain to send a joint battle fleet to our aid.

Be it also known and celebrated that on the 4th of July, in the year of our lord 1776, the Continental Congress of the thirteen states of America formally ceded from British rule with a unilateral Declaration of Independence. Each said state will form its own legislature for the purpose of local government. These state bodies will serve the Federal Congress of the United States of America. Godspeed!

Now we shall see if we can stand alone. I wonder what price our allies put on assisting us, thought Simon, remembering his brother-in-law's parting comments when as they left Madeira. He imagined the opulent Imperial French court at Versailles … a million dollars would hardly be a dent in their purse. The extravagances of King Louis and his queen, the beautiful if not too bright Marie Antoinette, would cost France a million a day!

Commodore Pearce ordered all his captains to report at three that afternoon.

"I have written orders for each of you here, but in essence they are the same; you are to pass them on to any ship of ours you meet. We are few and can in no way engage the enemy in open battle, but we are able to outsail 'em, are we not?" The men nodded solemnly. "Most of you have a similar background to myself. The kind of fighting we are being asked to undertake is little more than we have been doing all our lives, so let's get on with it!

"Further to the direct order, I want you to take as many extra crew and officers as you can accommodate so you will have the manpower to stay to sea when you have taken a prize. Each of you has a designated cruising area – stick to it! The three small schooners – *Albatross*, *Windhaven* and *Sprite* – will act as couriers, bringing information back here and passing on new orders. Any questions?"

"Yes, sir," said Davy Dawson, captain of the large brig *Mayfly*, which at 1,100 tons was the largest ship in the southern squadron. "Now the British have a huge fleet at their disposal, won't most cargo carriers be escorted?"

"Indeed, Captain Dawson, many will, but you are to avoid open battle with escorts. Be like the mosquito – in fast, draw blood and run before you are squashed. We have some time while the British are busy at New York. We must hit their supply lines hard – remember, every ball or pound of powder has to travel 3,000 miles to get here. Every bit we liberate kills one of theirs instead of one of ours!

"Put to sea as soon as your ships are fully supplied. Good luck. Captain Johnston, remain, if you please."

Simon looked at Michael. *Command has aged him, as it does to all of us*, he thought. "You did very well on that trip to New York. The merchantman you captured carried much useful cargo; you have been mentioned in dispatches. May I ask your opinion of my son Carlos?"

"He did you proud, sir. He boarded our prize with Sean in close attendance, yet it was Carlos who saved his protector from harm. We thought we had them subdued when several rallied; your son was the closest and at one time fought off two attackers with his sword. He dispatched one as the second turned his attention to Sean, who had his back to the melee, guarding those who had surrendered. With quickness I've never seen before, Carlos reversed his thrust and split the man from crotch to belly. I had been worried, having my commodore's son to care for; the lad's years of training with the sword have made him a great asset, sir." Michael's enthusiasm for Carlos was obviously genuine, pleasing the commodore.

"Thank you, Michael, it seems history does indeed repeat itself. I am worried too for Sean – he must be 55 if he's a day. Do you think he should be paid off? He surely doesn't need his sailing master's pay," said Simon.

"I am more than happy to have him aboard; his experience is truly impressive, but as you say, he is getting slow these days. He is still so strong and sees himself as our protector. To dismiss him would destroy him, sir. Could not some sort of training position be found for him here?" asked Michael.

"Yes, indeed. When you return I will have something arranged. If you get a prize put Sean in charge of bringing it in," added the commodore.

"Aye, sir," said Michael as he turned and left the room.

The *Esther May* beat steadily sou'sou'east after rounding Cape Henry, Johnston keeping close inshore as the sou'westerly easily allowed him to do. The inshore route kept them out of the northbound Gulf Stream and in the southern-going cold Labrador Current. By morning they would be in the area where the two oceanic rivers met – Cape Hatteras, their cruising station – ready to pounce on any merchantmen transporting goods to the British.

Cape Hatteras is part of a line of cays and islands, shoals and sandbanks off the Carolina coast; it is one of the most dangerous areas in the world for navigation. For the wily privateer or naval ship preying on passing traffic, it was a veritable honeypot. The cape itself provided an unmistakable landfall for ships having made an Atlantic crossing; it was also the best departure point for those whose final destination was a city in the northern states of America.

They made their way slowly southwards, passing the dreaded cape on the inside of the Diamond Shoals. The captain's local knowledge was critical as they manoeuvred through a narrow channel and anchored close to a passage south of the island that formed the cape in Pamlico Sound, just north of their recent point of entry. Lookouts were set as the ship was settled, snug for the night.

At daybreak a sea breeze gave them a good offing, and before long they had weathered Diamond Shoals.

From aloft came the lookout's call, "Sail ho! Two of 'em."

The *Esther May* shaped her course to intercept the second ship. As they approached, a third, smaller sail was sighted, her ensign identifying her as a British sloop of war. These small ships were designed to be the eyes and ears of the fleet and therefore not heavily armed. They were highly manoeuvrable but unable to point close to the wind like a schooner. With the offshore wind the Americans had the wind gage.

Realising the danger, the sloop piled on canvas to be in a position to defend the transports.

"Clear decks for action, load the bow chasers with chain shot, run out port battery, load with ball," called Michael to the gun captains, an earlier feeling of nervousness now put aside in this time of decision-making. He called his officers for a pre-battle conference.

"Sean, you have done this many more times than I; your advice will be most welcome. The escort is hard on the wind and is no threat while we are to windward of the convoy. We shall run for the first ship and damage her rigging then run across her stern firing into her poop and with maximum depression, to disable her steering.

"The escort will attempt to engage; we will avoid this by staying between land and the transport. Our objective is to capture a transport, not do battle with the Royal Navy, but we must neutralise the sloop before we can board the transport. They will attempt to engage us as we pass to fire on her stern. They will have to tack twice to reach the battle and will still be to seaward of the transport, which we will use as a shield until the right moment. As the sloop approaches we will tack and rake her with the starboard battery. The sloop is then further downwind so we retain the wind gage of her and are heading back to our real target. Carlos, get your topmen aloft and brail the royal and tops'ls at the moment they turn. Don't wait for the order. We will then be ready to beat into the wind. Mister Tomlinson, as first officer, take command of the ship. Please refer to Mister Finnegan regarding all manoeuvres; he knows the ship. I will direct the gunnery personally. Any questions?"

Michael Johnston smiled as he went forward – he loved those huge bow guns, which had decided many an action for them before it had really started. "Reload the leeward gun with ball, Richards. I want a ranging shot."

"Aye, cap'n," said Dirk Richards, the gun captain. He was an old hand who had been a ship's boy with Sir Richard Blackmore. Trained by Gunner in the old days, he was one of the best gun layers afloat.

"On the crest, lads, hold it – fire! Reload with chain," yelled Michael.

A call from aloft, "No waterspout; must 'ave it 'er hull, sir."

"Prepare to fire, on the crest – fire!" The roar of the 20-pounders obliterated all communication as the men sponged, loaded and fired. Each shot was aimed by the ship's captain.

The transport's main topmast crashed to her deck, her ability to sail to windward now seriously impaired. Michael ran back to the quarterdeck, having given orders to Richards to fire at will but lower his trajectory so as to hit her hull. Although she struck her colours, there was insufficient time to board and take her; the sloop *Petrel* was coming to her aid.

It was now time to shake up the Royal Navy. With their prey impotent, the *Esther May* wore ship and powered towards the sloop of war. Richards again waited for his ship to mount a wave crest and began his bombardment. Ten rounds of crippling fire had severely damaged her adversary's rigging before they were themselves in range.

In the main top of His Majesty's sloop *Petrel*, muskets were being fired, and a swivel gun loaded with grape was brought to bear. An unlucky ricochet hit Carlos in his thigh as he was climbing down the starboard ratlines. Intense pain shot through the boy as he hung from the rope ladder, unable to move, his right leg useless. They were now, since leaving the cover of the merchantman, exposed to enemy small arms fire. Sensing a token victory, the British musketeers concentrated their fire on the lone, exposed rebel sailor, and another ball hit the boy's left leg.

"Carlos!" was all he heard as a big arm circled his waist and hoisted the pain-racked, now inert figure onto a broad shoulder. The few moments' climb to the deck seemed like a century as ball and shot whistled around them. Suddenly the barrage stopped as the ship responded to the order to bear away thereby shielding the pair descending from aloft.

Sean laid the unconscious son of his best friend in the bunk of the captain's cabin. He did not ask permission – there was no need. Only when his charge was safe did he succumb to his own wounds, slumping to the floor. The officer's messman, Bert Norris, doubled as ship's surgeon. He had seen the spreading red stain below Sean's left shoulder. "Steady, Sean lad," said Bert.

"See t' th' boy," said Sean hoarsely, in obvious pain.

Carlos opened his eyes as Michael Johnston entered the cabin, alarmed at the extent of blood on the cabin sole.

"How is it, Norris?"

"The boy, sir, is nay so bad. The ball passed clear through 'is thigh 'n gone; the second's but a bad graze. Lost a lotta blood though, 'e 'as. But Sean, sir. That's something else, way outta my league; the ball's deep in 'im," answered the steward, somewhat shakily.

"We should break off the engagement," said Michael, thinking out loud.

"Ney, sir, neither Sean nor I would wish that. You're a hair's breadth off victory. If you can spare Norris to help us, we can wait while you finish the job," said Carlos.

The young Pearce, showing no sign of his intense pain, even managed a wan smile. "A large whisky if you please, Norris. For medicinal purposes only, of course," he added, smiling.

"Look after them, Norris. I'll prepare to take the rear transport; it's heading for home anyway. If anything changes, call me," with which the captain turned, his mind already working out the next engagement.

"Mister Tomlinson, we must be able to communicate as one in the next attack. Mister Thomas will take the role of sailing master in all but matters of navigation, which you will undertake."

Michael called for all those of rank to stand about and understand their part in his audacious plan. "Gentlemen, it is my intention to take both transports." He watched as his words drew anxious glances from his men. "We shall rake the rear transport as before, not to inflict much damage, but to shake them enough to make her crew more willing to surrender. Once we have slowed her we shall not inflict more damage, but as we overhaul them I shall offer them the chance to surrender and head for Norfolk. The first transport is not going far with the mauling we've given her. Their escort will not be able to help with her damaged rig. We are still to weather of them."

Carlos felt more than heard the recoil of the bow cannon as they closed upon the merchantman. "Sean, can you hear me?" the lad asked over the din.

"Aye, lad, I can 'ear 'e," answered the sailing master through a mask of pain.

"Thank you. I thought my career at sea was to be short-lived," returned the boy.

"Nay, laddie. Ye'll be 'ammerin' the British fer a while yet, I'll be bound."

"How are you? You've lost a lot of blood," said Carlos.

"Norris says I'll live if I get this ball outta me. The longer 'tis there, less chance I got. Norfolk be two t' three day away; reckon someone's gonna 'ave to dig fer that ball," whispered an exhausted Sean.

The *Esther May* had soon run down the slow, heavily laden transport, which, under the threat of the *Esther May*'s broadside, had surrendered as instructed. The second ship, instead of attempting to run, having seen the agility, speed and firepower of the American, sat quietly hove to not far away. A boat was sent to search the captives, the second of which was Dutch. The Netherlands was never a friend of England, so they agreed to sail to Norfolk and unload her cargo without resistance. Their price was to be allowed to leave with their ship intact.

"Agreed," called Michael. "I'll put a pilot aboard you, then make for Norfolk. I will follow you closely, so no tricks."

A prize crew was put aboard the first British transport. They found that half the crew were happy to join the American Navy, as its good treatment of crews was well known. Offered the chance of a new life in a free land, all but their captain accepted. In three days the *Esther May* had secured two cargoes of war supplies, one prize ship and 50 willing seamen. Now it was time to leave – no point in losing it all to a cruising British frigate. The vanquished *Petrel* had to watch all this happen, unable to make way to windward due to her shot-out rigging.

Five men held an almost comatose Sean Finnegan, the occasional whimper finding its way through his whisky-induced stupor. "I can't find the damn ball," said a frustrated Michael Johnston, then, "Ah! A hole – it's gone through his shoulder blade. Turn him. Careful lads."

Michael probed as gently as he could at Sean's left shoulder. "I feel it," he said triumphantly. Knowing what he had to do next, he took a swig from the bottle himself. He knew little about anatomy, so with trepidation he made a cut in his patient's back. It took a second cut before he could insert the long forceps that Juan Pearce had left on board. The young doctor had left instructions that every instrument was to be boiled in water before use. Blood and gore seemed to try and hold the instrument deep in Sean's body. Suddenly it released, and the forceps holding the ball exited the wound with an audible 'plop'.

Again Juan's instructions to the officers given during the long Atlantic crossing facilitated the attempt to save Sean's life. "Boiling water, Norris. Hurry man, I need to dress this side then turn him again and clean the entry wound."

Two days later the motley little squadron rounded Cape Henry and made its way up the estuary into Norfolk. Carlos Pearce, sitting up in the captain's sea cot, was seriously concerned, oblivious to the pain in his legs. "Sean, Sean, keep awake."

The captain had said earlier that it was essential he be kept lucid – another lesson imparted by Juan.

"Aye, lad. I'm not goin' anywheres. Yer father's got some papers fer me t' sign afore I takes my talk wi' St Peter." Grey and drawn, Sean's features were racked with agony as he coughed.

Bert Norris came into the cabin with two cups. "Brewed some tea fer 'e, Master Carlos," he said, handing a steaming mug to the boy. "Now, Sean, try this; it'll 'elp w' yer waters."

The small man cradled Finnegan's large head as he held a cup steadily at the sick man's lips. To Carlos they looked like a two-headed gargoyle, but for the tenderness Bert was showing. He said with mock sternness, "I'll not 'ave 'e die on my watch, if 'e please, Mister Finnegan."

The ship's motion had ceased. A barely audible burbling came from her wake as the willing boatmen towed her to her berth.

Michael Johnston burst into the cabin. "Carlos, Sean. Juan is here, praise be to God – on the quay. Someone's watching over ye, lads."

There was a slight jerk as the ship's momentum was dissipated by the spring lines put ashore; a moment later Doctor Juan Pearce was in the captain's stateroom. He quickly examined his protesting brother. "It's Sean who needs you, brother. I can wait; I fear he cannot."

After attending to Sean, Juan turned to the assembled company that included the Commodore Southern Naval Command, Simon Pearce. "I'll not say things are well for him, but he has a chance. Michael, you have done a fine piece of work. I would have been proud of it myself. The fact that he is still with us is entirely due to you."

"Nay, doctor, 'tis due to your lessons that Sean is as he is," returned the *Esther May's* captain.

"The reason Juan is here is that Congress has approved funding for a maritime training establishment here at Norfolk. It is to cover all facets of the maritime military, including medical procedures. Juan here is to train our people in the art of doctoring. For this reason alone he is here in so timely a manner to help our kin," said Simon.

"Now if you please, I need space for my patients. My brother can be taken ashore after I have redressed his wounds. Sean will remain until I determine it is safe to move him and when we have made suitable arrangements ashore. Father, on this note we will need a cool room that has been scrubbed from ceiling to floor with soap and boiling water, after which no one is to enter. The slightest hint of infection will kill him." Simon left to see to his son's orders personally, marvelling at his competence.

Portugal was years ahead of the rest of Europe in the field of medicine. In the early 1430s a fleet of strange ships had appeared in the Mediterranean. These ships had come via Cairo from fabled Cathay, a land so advanced they had found the mariner's Holy Grail – the ability to calculate longitude at sea – 300 years before any Europeans had. They had accurate charts of the oceans produced by earlier voyages that totally debased the Catholic Church's assertions that the world was flat. These charts were graciously given by a strange, slant-eyed admiral to all the courts that would accept them. It was said Vasco da Gama had copies aboard when he made his amazing discoveries. The Chinese visited Brazil, the generator of Portugal's riches, before coming under the influence of that country.

The Church also made an initial stand against the medical science brought by the strangers but secretly set up a sect to research the new technology. Eventually a school for medicine was formed in Lisbon where much of the advanced methodology taught had been handed down from the Chinese. The most important of these was cleanliness in dealing with infection.

"How is it, Sean?" asked Carlos as he sat beside the bed of the old sailing master, having hobbled from his own room on crutches made by a seaman to Juan's design.

"T' be sure, lad, I've bin a sight fitter. I know I've got a bit o' the infection like. Yer brother won't let on, but I know I 'ave. Still, I got the papers fer me trust done, so all will be well enough if I go." Sean looked seventy-five.

"I'll have none of that, man. You're not going anywhere! You've me to train as an officer and many others. Father is putting you in charge of the training of the navy's navigators - you're the best, he says, and America needs you," said Carlos emphatically as his father strode into the room.

"My friend, my son, momentous news! On the 4th of July the Continental Congress disbanded to become the Congress of the United States of America. Their first act was to issue a Declaration of Independence from Great Britain. Both France and Spain are to send a fleet to balance the huge British fleet that arrived at Sandy Hook recently."

A smile struggled to the lips of Sean Finnegan, comfortable in the knowledge that his trust would bring to America a commodity more valuable than gold: strong, willing young men who with a good education would continue to build this free land. *What were those words Simon had read from the declaration?*

'We hold these truths to be self-evident, that all men are created equal, that they are endowed by their Creator with certain unalienable Rights, that among these are Life, Liberty, and the Pursuit of Happiness.'

Aye, that'll do me 'n mine, thought Sean as he passed into a feverish slumber.

At New York, in his initial offensive, General Howe had pushed Washington off Long Island; his victories grew until the Continental Army withdrew from the Hudson River southwards. It is historically accepted that had General Howe pursued Washington after the battle for New York, the War of Independence could have ended in a British victory. But for some reason - possibly weakness on Howe's part - he didn't. So the fledgling American Army was allowed to regroup in the south and grow.

Chapter 22
Isabellita

"You are too young to be courted. Your father would be furious were 'e 'ere! You put me in an intolerable position, young woman!"

Isabella Pearce looked into the dark pools of her youngest daughter's eyes seeing things she did not wish to see – herself at the same age standing before her father Dom Diego Mendoza, governor of Madeira, and her brother Juan. Her pleadings then received a similar response as hers now to her daughter's entreaties.

"Mother, you drag me from my home, half across the world, to what you say is the land of the free, but am I, your daughter, to be allowed some of that freedom? No. I am to be locked up in this – this barnyard – and told I am too young to fall in love. I might ask, Mother dear, at what age did you fall in love?" Isabellita finished, her dark eyes flashing dangerously.

"Captain Davidson is a nice young man, of that I am sure, my dear. 'E is, eh, 'andsome and well born. But 'e is nine years older than you, an experienced army officer, if somewhat young for 'is rank. 'E will be in the thick of the fighting and 'as a considerable chance of being killed or seriously wounded; you could 'ave a broken 'eart before you even reach an age to marry. It is you I'm thinking of, my darling. Your 'appiness is everything to me. Please listen to me," pleaded the girl's mother in despair.

"It is as you say, Mother. Robert may well be one of the many men to fall before this beastly business is over. They are all fighting for our freedom as much as their own. Is it not for us women to give them a haven from the horrors of war? Should we not tend to their tired bodies and cannon-shocked minds? And pray to the one true God that they will return to us?

"We are not asking that we be married; besides, I am not of age.

We are asking that we may meet, under supervision if you so insist. Maybe Robert will take more care in battle if he knows he has a lady-love waiting for him. Please, Mother, please. At least allow him to go to Norfolk and speak with father?" Her passion now spent, Isabellita sank to her knees and sobbed.

Weakened by her daughter's proud performance Isabella capitulated. "If Captain Davidson 'as the time he may go and speak with your father," she answered, exasperated.

The trip down the Potomac was a lot faster then the upstream voyage. A small gig-like boat with two teams of oarsmen covered the distance, assisted by the current, in two days. It was a somewhat worn and dishevelled army captain who stood before the commodore naval forces, southern region.

Simon smiled to himself, while outwardly presenting a stern demeanour. He had heard that a young man had been calling on his daughter and had made enquiries as to his character and background.

"Sir, I am the eldest of three brothers. Our father is a lawyer and a founding member of the State Government. We are not inconsiderable landowners. Should, at the appropriate time, you consider me worthy to become your son-in-law, Isabellita will be very well provided for. For now all I ask is that you allow us to get to know each other, that you give your permission for me to court her. She will be treated with the utmost respect, I assure you, commodore." Robert finished, and standing to attention he looked the epitome of character, a man a father would be proud to have join his family.

"Captain Davidson, Second Virginian Rifles, I understand? I have heard some good things about you, young man. General Washington has mentioned you in dispatches, has he not?" Simon liked the young man before him but could not resist playing his game.

"Yes, sir. I was so honoured," answered the captain.

"It says well for you that you omitted to mention that fact when pleading your case, sir. I have discovered often what a petitioner does not say tells the most. I will not go so far as to allow you to formally court Isabellita. You may, however, visit her and communicate with her in writing. I know the risks you run. It's bravery such as yours that will produce victory for these United States. I also know that you may never be able to marry my daughter, such are the fortunes of war. In one year's time she will be sixteen and one half. We will consider formalising your relationship at that time." Simon rose and clasped the American by the shoulders. "In the meantime I look forward to hearing more about you, captain.

"Ah, you will be unaware of two serious reversals in our fortunes. Last month on Lake Champlain over 80 of our gunships were totally destroyed by a similar number of British. Hundreds of our men have lost their lives with others, thank God not all taken prisoner, and the naval base at Newport, Rhode Island has been captured by the enemy. Our maritime forces are scattered far and wide and cannot seriously confront the British.

"Now be off, your company will be waiting for you. I am afraid time will not allow you to return to Porthellick to take your leave of my daughter. I will see to it that any letter you may wish to write is delivered to her with the next mail. To where are you posted?" asked the commodore.

"Philadelphia, sir. I am to rejoin General Washington there, and thank you, sir, I will not disappoint you." Robert Davidson saluted the commodore.

"I may be of service to you, captain. I have a small schooner sailing on the tide. She is to gather reconnaissance as to General Howe's movements. She will sail up the Delaware and be able to put you ashore within striking distance of Philadelphia. It will save you many days," said Simon.

"I am most grateful, sir, and, ah, I love Isabellita, sir. I thank you again for your confidence in me," said the captain as he turned and left.

* * *

Five days later Captain Robert Davidson encountered the American Army after its retreat from Trenton.

He learned that General Washington, against his own better judgment, had allowed the officers at Forts Washington and Lee to make a stand. The combined force of British and German mercenaries captured both strongholds with the loss of 600 men and over 2,500 taken prisoner.

Robert rejoined his company in Philadelphia, and finding that the American Army was encamped further south on the Delaware, his 120 men marched to join it. In the absence of any formal attachment of his unit to a regiment, he reported directly to the general's staff tent.

On hearing his name, General Washington strode out to greet him. "Captain Davidson! By all that's holy, it is mighty fine to see you, not to mention your fine body of men.

"Sergeant! See to it that Captain Davidson's unit is accorded the finest hospitality we can muster. Billet them as well as we can manage in these straightened times. Now, Davidson, please come with me; your arrival is most timely."

The two men sat in the general's war room – little more than a standard issue, round sleeping tent. The general began.

"Morale here is at a low ebb, captain. I have many men whose enlistment will shortly expire. With the recent reversals I fear up to half the existing army will not re-enlist. A conundrum indeed as the Congress has just voted me the funds to increase the size of the army, yet I cannot hold the men I have! I have called a parade at eight o'clock on the morn. I want your unit to be my honour guard. Have them look as good as you can, Davidson. I need to impress this rabble, with which I am supposed to beat the biggest standing army the British have ever sent overseas. I intend to promote you to major. I will make this announcement at the parade. I will also announce the two other companies that will complete your regiment and invite them to stand with your men. Do you have an officer to replace you as company commander?" asked the general.

"I do, sir. Lieutenant Boyle, sir. The men respect him, an officer who leads from the front, sir," answered Robert without hesitation.

"Good! I will announce Boyle's captaincy at the same time. I apologise for the dramatics, major, but these are difficult times. Had that bumbler General Howe followed us after pushing us out of New York, he would have totally defeated us. I had but 3,000 men to face him. Praise be to God he believes he may get a negotiated victory, a foolish assertion. One more detail before you retire – I plan an attack, an incursion I am confident we will win. Prepare your men well, major. Your unit will have a key part in the endeavour. Now goodnight to you and good fortune." The great man shook Major Davidson's hand, an almost unprecedented gesture.

"Goodnight, general, and thank you, sir," said Robert, turning as he left the tent.

"Thank you, sir," said Charlie Boyle as the newly appointed major passed on the news of his subaltern's promotion to captain.

"You've earned it, Charlie, and you'll continue to do so. The army is a shambles, and it falls to the likes of us to repair it; train the men hard. As General Howe winters in comfort in Philadelphia, a-drinking and a-wenching, we will prepare for him; this respite could well be the turning point in our bid for freedom." Robert dismissed his junior, who was also his good friend.

The army, such as it was, was mustered on a wheat field that served as a makeshift parade ground. At eight precisely, General Washington and his entourage rode onto the field. The general continued alone on his white stallion to the front ranks to cajole the soldiers in front of him into re-enlisting. He then proceeded to hand out honours to individual soldiers and officers. "To Captain Robert Davidson of the Virginian Rifles, the Congressional Medal of Honour, in recognition of his bravery at the Battle of Fort Moultrie. He is hereby promoted to major."

After the general's dramatics, he repeated his call for those present to re-enlist for the duration, or three years, whichever came sooner. The men spoke amongst themselves and one by one stepped forward.

"Shall we formally enrol 'em now, sir?" asked a staff officer.

The general replied, "No, captain. Men as these need no formality to keep them to their duty; they are Americans!"

The cheering was testament to one of Washington's greatest victories, for without a credible army, the title 'general' is a hollow one.

* * *

It was a freezing December day on the Delaware; the Army of America had its back to the river that was frozen over enough to prevent the army crossing by boat, but insufficiently to carry them on foot. The general had a group of divisional commanders in conference in his war room; Major Robert Davidson was one of them.

"You will see, gentlemen, the element of surprise is crucial to our success, which is why we shall make our attack in the early hours of Christmas morning. The targets are mainly Hessians. Germans like to celebrate; we should encounter no severe opposition. Are there any questions? No. Good, then let us be about this business."

Two thousand five hundred of America's finest soldiers recrossed the Delaware following channels broken in the ice by other soldiers not taking part in the raid. That night they attacked the Germans at Trenton. The action was over in an hour. Robert had encountered the Hessian commander, one Colonel Rall, as he stumbled unbelievingly into the street to see his men being slaughtered or led away. As he raised his pistol a shot rang out, fired by one of Robert's sharpshooters. The insolent man was dead before he hit the ground. By nightfall Washington had achieved his much-needed, if minor, victory.

"Major, if you please, the general would speak with you," said a staff lieutenant, breathlessly.

"Ah, Davidson, a good day's work, my boy, but not as yet done, I fear. General Cornwallis is preparing to march on us from Princeton – he has 7,000 men; if they attack us here, with our backs to the Delaware, we shall be undone. However, a new road has been prepared by the river; we must leave soon, go around Cornwallis and attack the garrison he has left behind at Princeton."

* * *

A week later the Americans, lead by their general, defeated the British at Princeton. General Washington was in an ebullient mood. On more than one occasion he had observed Major Davidson in action and was 'utmost impressed'. It was his regiment's pride and the men's total commitment to their young commander that prompted the general, somewhat impetuously, to again promote the young officer in the field.

"Can't have a regimental commander with a mere major's rank!"

Turning to his aide-de-camp he continued, "Record the promotion to Lieutenant Colonel of Major Davidson, if you please.

"I have another assignment for you, colonel. Report two weeks from today. I understand there is a young woman who would be mighty pleased to see you, sir! Make good use of the time; after this you will be away quite a while."

The two actions secured much-needed supplies and two all-important victories. The British retired to Philadelphia to sit out the winter. Their commander-in-chief had given the Americans yet another chance to develop and train the army that would be put against him. They entered the recruiting season with some successful strikes for the cause.

* * *

It had taken four days before Colonel Davidson's horse trudged wearily up the long driveway to Porthellick, the Pearce estate. Situated as it was on the southern side of the Potomac River, it required the crossing of both that body of water and the Delaware to complete the journey. He handed the reins of his horse to a groom at the stables and sighted an old man sitting in the winter sunshine on the porch at the house's entrance.

"Excuse me, sir," he said. "Is the master of the house on the premises?"

"No indeed, soir, himself be on 'is way back to base in Norfolk. The missus be 'ome like, if ye call out. Young for a colonel, ain't 'e?" Then with recognition stirring his tired, pain-racked eyes, he added, "Colonel, now, is it, young Davidson? Then it'll be Miss Isabellita ye'll be a-wantin' t' see, I'll be bound."

The man stood up. Robert was surprised at his size as he made his way slowly into the house.

A most unladylike squeal of delight emanated from the house, then in mock reproach Isabellita added, "Oh, Sean, how could you leave my Robert standing at the door. Come in out of the cold."

"Colonel Davidson is it now? How opportune, and most exquisitely unexpected. I do not recall inviting you to my sixteenth birthday this

Saturday. Now everyone I care for will be here. Oh, Robert, it is so wonderful to see you. I am so proud. You must have served the cause exceeding well."

"I, eh, have been lucky, Miss Pearce; in the right place at the right time. I seem to have the general's favour – he knew of your birthday, of that I'm sure. But you, my love, you look radiant; I cannot begin to express how good it is to see you." He yearned to rush forward and hold her to him. How many times in the last eight months had he been in the position to lose his life or be so severely injured as to make him totally unattractive to the magnificent young woman?

"Robert, be seated. I will call Mother." With which she turned and ran up the broad staircase, betraying the girl that lingered within her.

"Colonel, it does my 'eart good to see you. If you 'ave no accommodations, sir, would you honour us by staying in our 'umble home?" Isabella asked with excessive formality. "You will, no doubt, be guest of 'onour at my daughter's birthday."

"I should be delighted, ma'am," said Robert bowing deeply.

Carlos Pearce was seated in the drawing room as Robert Davidson walked in, Isabellita clinging to his arm in a most proprietary manner. He ignored the stout stick that rested on the arm of the chair and stood unaided before the famous officer. Saluting he said, "Colonel Davidson, it is good to see you, sir."

"Carlos, I have heard of your bravery. Please let there be no formality between us. I beg you, address me as Robert." He strode to embrace the man he hoped one day would be his brother-in-law.

* * *

Simon Pearce was tired; he was late as operational problems delayed his departure. He was reminded of his family's heritage as seamen during his trip upriver in a gig similar to the *Horse* of Scilly. He had paid double to each of the oarsmen and had coxed the boat himself when required.

Still Isabella was angry. "Why, 'usband, I 'ave your new coat and breeches to 'ave fitted, and it is already the day of your daughter's birthday! You 'ave put on many pounds since you now sail a desk, no? I will 'ave to alter these myself."

"I am sorry, my dear; it is the war," he added in feeble defence.

"The war - all I 'ear is war! You men, you plead to dislike it, but no, in reality you love it; but for now you 'ave to consider a delicate situation 'ere at 'ome. Your daughter wishes to become engaged to the dashing young colonel, a match I now fully approve of. Yes, I know she is too young, but you could insist on a long engagement, as my father did with us, if you feel it necessary. What you think, my dear Simon? When we were young we 'ad to spend much time apart; was this bad for us? Besides, the times are 'ard on young lovers; at least let him leave with 'ope that 'e will one day reach 'is 'oly grail." Isabella stood as her seated husband looked up into her dark, determined eyes.

"I agree, my dear. Should the colonel ask for Isabellita's hand, I shall agree, perhaps not so long an engagement would need to be insisted upon - time enough to meet his family, and of course, an allowance for the fortunes of war." Simon answered his wife smiling, his sternness an act, a game with his beloved wife.

The party was an enormous success, the men mostly in dress uniforms, the civilians in amazing finery. Sean Finnegan had been promoted to the rank of captain to suit his role as a training officer and looked a little uncomfortable wearing the dress uniform and epaulettes of that rank. As ever it was the womenfolk that dazzled. It was as if the court at Versailles had been transported to the comfortable colonial mansion of Porthellick, their Marie Antoinette being Isabellita Consuelo da Mendoza Pearce.

The butler, one Marco Fernandez, who had been major-domo to the Pearce family on Madeira, called for silence. Simon Pearce - freebooter, privateer, landowner, seaman and now a fleet commander in the Navy of the United States of America - stood.

"Dear friends, old and new. It is with the greatest of pleasure that I welcome you to our home for what is a most important occasion, especially so to me, as I have missed so many milestones in my children's lives for the following of my profession as a seaman. It is a double happiness that I find myself before you today not only as the proud father of the most beautiful girl in my world, but also to announce her betrothal. Yes, she is young, and yes, I would have things somewhat less hurried if the times allowed, but our turbulent lives are linked to these United States of America, for her very survival is at stake. One of the most successful officers in our young army has done this family and, of course my daughter, the great honour of asking for her hand in marriage. That officer is Lieutenant Colonel Robert Davidson, regimental commander of our own Virginian Rifles."

The applause was deafening, and it was some minutes before Simon could continue. While waiting he gestured for the couple to stand on the makeshift stage alongside him; a more handsome couple it would be hard to imagine.

"So, my friends, in the absence of Colonel Davidson's family, we have yet no wedding date or further details to impart other than a year will pass before the wedding bells are heard. Colonel, I welcome you to the Pearce family."

Simon stood down allowing the newly betrothed to be centre of attention.

"I cannot believe that on the morrow I must be gone. How I will be able to leave, I know not. To know your love for me is now a real and tangible thing will make the months ahead bearable. I shall endeavour to take as much care as I am able to be returned to you whole and hearty." As Robert finished speaking she kissed him with such a passion he was shaken to the core of his being.

"Look away, sir, if you please," said Isabellita. She reached under her skirts and, sliding a pink garter from her left leg, she continued. "As you know, I would give you all before you leave, but as you have so gallantly said, all is what you will live for. Take this intimate token of my love. Our engagement rings will alert the world as to our intentions; this will be a reminder of mine." Her eyes smouldered as she passed him the tiny band.

They talked all night in the drawing room, falling asleep in each other's arms just an hour before the dawn.

Breakfast was a solemn affair. The entire family had risen early to bid their soon-to-be son and brother a warm farewell. Isabella had her arm around her daughter saying firmly, "Men! If the world were run by us women, war would 'ave no place."

"Indeed, Mother, but what a dull place in which to live, if manliness were to be driven from our beaus," she answered wistfully as her beau thundered at full gallop into the morning mist.

* * *

Charlie Boyle was delighted at his friend's return. Charlie had long realised that Robert, although three years his junior, was a better officer than he could ever be. He was, however, of that rare breed that could accept the situation without malice or ego. He had therefore become the ideal subaltern. "By my oath, it is a sight for sore eyes y'all are, colonel," he exclaimed as Robert entered the tent they shared.

"So, Charlie boy, what have you done with the regiment since I have been away?" The colonel was straight down to business.

"Training goes well; the general has seconded five seasoned Prussians to us, one lieutenant and four NCOs. The men baulked at their methods for a while but could see the benefits; they wanted to surprise you on your return, sir."

Charlie had spent an hour explaining details when Robert held up his left hand. "You may see I too have some news," he said, displaying the ring on his left hand. "Commodore Pearce has accepted me as his future son-in-law!"

"By all, that is great news, sir. I have hoarded our share of the rum taken from the Germans on Christmas Day. With your leave I shall invite all officers to drink your health tonight and make sure the men have spirits to do the same," and he left the tent to make the necessary arrangements.

General Washington had disclosed to Robert, on his return to the camp after his leave at Porthellick, that intelligence suggested a large force of British were to push out of Canada clearing the way to the upper Hudson River, their mission to disable the American fortifications and forces along the river in order to link New York with British Canada. This would greatly aid the British in supplying the war. General Benedict Arnold had entreated with Washington to send him some specialised troops, especially marksmen, as these could be used to devastating effect on an enemy travelling by boat in the narrower reaches of the river.

Washington had said to Robert, "You are one of our best trained regiments, most suited for Arnold's purpose. Your orders are here; you have a long journey. Godspeed."

246

The next morning it was hard to imagine the drinking that had gone on the night before as the regiment paraded before their commander. Robert rode first in front of the lines of men, then dismounted and spoke in person to men he knew and was introduced to many he did not.

Robert addressed his regiment – four companies – some 600 men. "I have received our orders and must say that an arduous task awaits us. We will leave this place in five days; we are going for a bit of a march. I call on you all to remember what we are fighting for and the reason we are separated from our loved ones. It is to secure a freedom that the enemy, who lives on the other side of the known world, would deny us. King George thinks only of empire; his men are far from home. Let us send them to hell or back where they belong!"

A mighty cheer arose from the regiment, turning the clear, cold morning to a foggy one with the heat from their breath.

* * *

It was many weeks' hard march before the Second Virginia Rifles joined Generals Gates and Arnold but not, as planned, at Fort Ticonderoga.

The main defence on the Hudson had been lost to the British General Burgoyne – abandoned without a fight when the British with great energy dragged cannon up Sugarloaf Hill. Once operational, the battery overlooked the seemingly impenetrable fort. One hundred and twenty-eight cannon were lost and scores of Americans taken prisoner.

A highly dispirited American Army had also deserted Fort Edward and had taken up positions at Stillwater, 30 miles north of Albany. It was here that Robert and his men finally joined the northern army after a march of near 600 miles.

General Benedict Arnold was highly enthusiastic and one of Washington's most effective field commanders. In April that year he had inflicted a considerable defeat on the British at Ridgefield, Connecticut.

The general strode out to meet the Second Virginia Rifles. "By all that's holy, your regiment is a sight for sore eyes, colonel," he said, shaking Robert's hand. "I will have your men billeted and let them get settled. You, I require for an immediate briefing; please follow me."

The general motioned for the young colonel to be seated, poured whisky for them both and began. "We have had several setbacks; indeed Ticonderoga was a difficult decision. I don't agree with General Gates on many things but in this he was right. The enemy have been forced to leave the fort with a large garrison. Burgoyne is no fool – he wouldn't want us to take it back easily and have us in control of his supply lines. But he is now 800 men weaker; this is good for us! Their advance has slowed dramatically since they left the waterway – a mile or so a day I understand. I need your men to harry them, shooting from cover and reducing their ability to travel. They will have to confront this skirmishing; when they do we will strike hard. How soon can your men be ready?"

"A good dinner, a night's sleep and breakfast, and we can deploy. The men are restless with lack of action; this is just the sort of thing they are trained for, sir. I bring you some good news. General Howe has embarked most of his force in New York and sailed south – to the Chesapeake, we think. This means that Burgoyne will have no chance for reinforcements. He must have hoped to meet Howe on the Hudson, and with only a few divisions left to garrison New York, there's little chance our opposition will be relieved." Robert could see the relief this news held for Arnold.

"Come with me. General Gates must hear this directly from you," Arnold added.

"... so, sir, we should now begin the offensive in earnest." Arnold was keen to get on with things; his commander-in-chief was more cautious. The two men were known not to like each other.

"What do you propose, my dear general?" said Gates with a derisive tone.

"We have intelligence that a column of German mercenaries have been detached from Burgoyne's main column. Our tactics of cutting trees to slow them as we retreat has worked well. They are desperately short of supplies and pack animals. We believe the Germans are to attack Bennington to steal what they can. We must hit them before they reach town. The local militia will set up a defence a few miles outside the town; the Virginians can have at the enemy from the cover of the woodland, staying in reserve to support the locals." Arnold sat back observing Gates's reaction.

"Colonel Davidson – fine work, by the way – you have travelled far and carefully to bring your people to us in fighting condition. How thinks you of the good general's idea?" asked General Gates.

"Thank you, sir," said Robert. "I believe General Arnold is right. We have to stop them resupplying at Bennington. A surprise attack will seriously weaken Burgoyne's main force as well as depriving them of supplies. They won't know yet that Howe is not coming to their aid; it may pay us to inform them of the news. Realising they are on their own and will have to rely on extended supply lines and foraging, they will slow further. They will now have to bring supplies from Canada to reach their army." Robert finished and was pleased to see the commander had taken his words seriously.

"Gentlemen, I agree. Let us proceed; this is an opportunity we must not miss. General Arnold, please see the, ah, enemy are informed of their situation. Washington said you were good, young Davidson. He was right." Gates, ever careful, could see a change in the tide of his war. He was trying to gain the confidence of the up-and-coming star who had the commander-in-chief's ear.

The German column trudged slowly along the muddied track, footsore and weary. They were carrying what seemed to the Americans an impossible load in their packs. A detachment of Virginian Rifles, posing as American loyalists, waited on the road; they convinced the German Colonel Baum of their loyalty to the British. When the Crown troops encountered a band of American militia they took up positions ordered by Colonel Baum, but hovered at the rear. When the fighting began, the men who had been posing as loyalists, fired into the backs of the Germans.

Robert's men then attacked each flank – he personally shot the German commander through the chest. Bayonets and sabres were viciously thrust into soft flesh, rifle butts smashed limbs and skulls as the Germans, dispirited and tired, fell back. A huge Hessian charged Robert, bayonet levelled at his chest; he parried the blow but the momentum of the big man, combined with his state of fury, drove them both to the muddy ground. Robert's adversary drew a long, wicked knife, and from his position astride the young colonel, began exerting massive downward pressure, that would inevitability force the blade into his adversary's chest. Robert realised with trepidation that the German was stronger than he. The dagger continued its downward path, resisted by all the strength he could muster. The Hessian was so consumed by rage that he hardly felt Charlie Boyle's sabre sever his head from his body, just as the dagger first pierced Robert's chest.

"Watch out behind!" yelled Robert over the din of battle, as he struggled to get the headless man off. Charlie stumbled as he turned to see another big man bearing down on him; his bayonet would have run him through but for his stumble. Robert sprang upward from a crouch position, using all the power his legs would provide, thrusting his sword clear through the man, who died instantly, a look of disbelief on his tortured features.

"That makes us even," said Charlie, nursing a wound in his arm.

A second column of Germans came trudging through the rain. Having marched for 16 hours they were no match for the Americans, who had fresh reserves not used in the main battle. The Americans attacked the desperate men with vigour. Of the entire force of 1,200 some 900 men were destroyed, and much weaponry was taken.

Robert was discharged by the surgeon, with no more then a deep cut where the dagger had entered the muscle around his heart. "You were lucky, colonel - another inch and we would not be speaking now," said the surgeon.

"No luck at all, doctor. Captain Boyle over there saved my life. The wound he now endures is his reward. How is he?" asked an anxious Robert Davidson.

"The captain has a nasty tear in his left arm. I hope not to have to amputate. We will dress and clean the wound regularly; if infection sets in, I am afraid the captain must fear the worst. I understand, sir, you are betrothed to Commodore Pearce's daughter?" said Martin Dansig, the chief surgeon northern forces.

"I am so honoured, sir. Why do you ask?"

"Doctor Juan Pearce, as you know, is his eldest son. He has been giving seminars for field and naval surgeons - I was fortunate enough to attend. A truly gifted doctor; his knowledge is amazing for one so young. He has introduced the notion of cleanliness as a major factor in fighting infection and the use of disinfectant made from pine sap. You are to be part of what is emerging as a great American family," the doctor added without reservation.

* * *

"Excellent," exclaimed General Gates to the assembled regimental commanders, having previously debriefed the Virginian Rifles. "I now believe we shall be able to take them; no more retreating, eh. The tide of this war I think, gentlemen, changes in our favour. We shall dig in here at Stillwater and await the enemy whose only chance of some success is to reach the main Hudson River at Albany. To achieve that he will need to beat us in the field. Prepare well. With the recent reinforcements we shall, for once, have superior numbers to the enemy!"

General Gates, who was known as 'Granny Gates' due to his indecisiveness, now believing the field would be his, was prepared to move, much to the relief of the far less cautious Benedict Arnold.

Gates finally gave General Arnold permission to attack, an order the latter deemed given far too late. The British were settled in their attacking positions in three columns, the centre of which Burgoyne lead personally.

The Virginia Rifles were positioned to be able to fire into the enemy's flank, causing terrible slaughter. The British just kept coming, their red uniforms showing brightly, even in the poor light and rainy conditions, their famed bayonets glinting wickedly. As the centre column reached American lines at Freeman's Farm, the hand-to-hand fighting began.

Robert was in the rear due to his injury and was able to view the terrible conflict from relative safety. He had never seen such slaughter. The constant cackle of musketry was often drowned by roaring cannon loaded with canister and grapeshot. "How can any living creature survive here?" he said to no one in particular.

The colonel saw British pickets advancing in the gathering gloom. Forward, he called to the two reserve companies of Virginians under his direct control. Robert's men advanced, firing as they moved from cover. The result was fifty Redcoats lying still on the ground; the accurate fire had killed all their officers and NCOs; his losses four dead, with nine receiving injuries sufficient for them to have to leave the field.

The battle continued, the Virginian sharpshooters high in the trees causing havoc. As night fell the action ended; the British Army had lost a third of its strength. Loyalists, Indians and Canadians, who had enlisted to serve the British, melted away into the forests, perceiving a major rout, the deserters further weakening an almost spent force.

Throughout the night both sides remained in position. The British had to listen to the cries of their wounded out in the darkness; they were unable to assist them due to the sharpshooters. The howling of wolves added a macabre twist to further rattle the men's nerve.

The following day, General Burgoyne was informed by those field officers capable of service that the condition of the exhausted troops made it impossible to carry out the bayonet charge he had designed. The attack was therefore postponed.

Later Burgoyne was advised that a long-awaited counter-attack was being made from New York. The garrison had finally been reinforced sufficiently. They were making a push upriver to clear the Hudson of all opposition. This operation was successful leaving only the American Army at Stillwater between the British northern army and the reinforcements advancing up the Hudson.

Hearing that an American force had retaken Fort Ticonderoga, Burgoyne decided to attempt to reach Albany by going around the Americans entrenched in Stillwater. The opportunity to retreat to winter in the northern fortification was no longer open to him.

As the days passed, any opportunity to leave the field with honour was removed by the constant sniping and attack from an enemy who knew they would eventually win.

With his army exhausted and in retreat, and too far from the advancing reinforcements, Burgoyne made the decision to sue for terms, and on the morning of the 17th of October the British and Germans marched out of their lines to surrender their arms at the American camp, ending a five-week action. General Burgoyne handed his sword to General Gates at Saratoga; the British Army of the north was no more.

Gates and Arnold began a push down the Hudson, stopping at West Point where Arnold would be left in command. The British were forced back to New York. The Virginians were released and sent back south to assist Washington - much to the relief of Colonel Davidson who had wedding plans.

Chapter 23

Carlos

A much-wearied naval lieutenant raced his horse the final 300 yards to the great house, Porthellick. Carlos ran into the house, nearly running into his brother-in-law, Colonel Robert Davidson. "What news of my sister, sir?" he asked.

"I am informed all is well with both mother and child. Your nephew Michael was born two hours ago. The women are fussing up there but I am sure they will allow you to see them," answered Robert, grinning broadly.

Isabellita and the colonel had been married the year before on her seventeenth birthday, a most memorable day for the Pearce family. It had been a double wedding with full military honours.

The second bride and groom were Carlos Pearce and Sally Antoinette Dufresne, a young woman from an old-established southern family, which had emigrated from France when that country was still the area's colonial master.

The Dufresnes hated the British as they saw the Americas belonging rightly to France, if not to Americans. They were strong supporters of independence, using their influence in their erstwhile homeland to secure as much help for America's cause as they could. Their lobbying at the court of Versailles greatly assisted Benjamin Franklin in his work, trying to secure for the new country help from the capricious French king and queen.

Seeing his lovely wife, Carlos ran up the stairs, raced to her and embraced her. "You are well, my love? What news of my sister?" he added breathlessly.

"Ma darlin' man, it is wonderfully unexpected to see ya'all. Isabellita is just fine, y' hear – fine an' dandy. I think she's sleepin'. Peek in, the baby's there too." Sally Antoinette's drawl was warm and comforting.

Carlos could not believe the serenity of his sleeping sister, signs of the exertions of childbirth all but gone, all evidence of the birthing cleaned away. The baby boy mirrored his mother.

Quietly leaving his sister to rest, Carlos returned to the drawing room where he found his brother-in-law deep in conversation with his father. "That traitorous swine, when I think how we all worshipped him at Saratoga, and now this! Ah, Carlos, join us please."

"Benedict Arnold has turned traitor, Carlos. He almost got to hand West Point over to the British. Been giving Clinton advance warning of General Washington's intentions for nearly a year now. I wonder how many American lives he has cost," Robert said angrily.

"I wonder, indeed," said Simon, for once out of his naval uniform. "Our reversals over the past year have been a huge drain on our resources; Arnold's treachery will have played no small part in these events. Now General Green has replaced that procrastinator Gates, we should begin to achieve some results against Cornwallis here in the south."

Carlos was amused at the beginning of an American twang in his father's voice.

"For sure we are leading the British a merry dance down here," continued Robert, "but their tactics have changed. Being short of supplies they are stealing food from the local population. Here at Porthellick you are off the beaten track, sir. Some terrible things have been done in the name of intelligence gathering. Why, just outside Charlotte, near Spartanburg, a church was burned with the entire population of the village locked inside. As the men broke windows in an attempt to push their women and children out of the smoke and flames, the Redcoats were ordered to shoot them. The pretext for the ghastly incident was that there were collaborators among the congregation. The swine of an officer in charge is known – his days are numbered, mark my words." The determination on his brother-in-law's face reinforced this fact.

"What of you, son? We haven't seen you since the English raid; tell us of John Paul Jones capturing a British frigate in English waters; that'll set the bees a-buzzing," commented Simon.

Carlos began his tale. "We left Boston in August; a fair passage across the Atlantic was had, fair but awful cold. Captain Jones had decided to sweep south in an attempt to intercept loaded merchantmen leaving for New York. We encountered but small ships between Fastnet Rock and Land's End. We attacked and sank them.

"Before daylight the next day, foretop lookout saw a stern light. The captain decided to close for a dawn attack. We were favoured by the wind gage. All was ready; we were perfectly positioned. We were about to attack when masthead saw a sail to weather of our target. They had seen us and were bracing their yards to intercept us. She was soon identified as a 40-gun frigate – our 24 twelves were never going to match 40, half of which were eighteens.

"Our plan was to run down the merchantman, our original target. Slow her, go about and, using her as a shield, try to hit the frigate with our bow chasers. All went well but for a lucky shot from the merchantman that took out our mizzen topmast. The frigate came on, all guns blazing; it was only the captain's seamanship that kept the old *Kitty Hawk* afloat. We turned on the wind heading for the frigate, firing our bow chasers; we had little time, as we were sinking. Rounding up smartly we grappled the frigate, firing our guns one last time before abandoning ship. Our people were boarding the frigate, when the her guns roared again just six feet away as we all left our sinking ship.

"Many of her crew were still manning the guns; we had boarded with our entire ship's company. First clearing the decks with grenades, we had an early advantage; this was soon diminished as the gun crews joined the hand-to-hand combat. We had no choice – 3,000 miles from home, taking the ship was our only hope of survival. Two hours after boarding, the ship was ours. We put the survivors ashore in a cove on St Martin's in the Scillies and sailed home. What a sight! A British frigate under American colours sailing into Boston Harbour."

"And now first lieutenant, I see," said the commodore.

"I am advised my captaincy but awaits a suitable vessel to become available, Father. Is this why I was transferred to the southern command?" enquired Carlos.

"Your promotion to captain, my boy, is still to be confirmed," said the commodore sternly. "You are to accompany me back to Norfolk. In two days we shall head downriver. The French are landing south of Yorktown, supported by a large battle fleet. I believe Cornwallis to be overconfident; this is our opportunity to gain a decisive victory in the south. Robert, I am afraid you will need to accompany us; a commander of your stature is sorely needed."

"Of course. One night with my family is far more than most men have had this past year." The 27-year-old colonel, with a prematurely lined face, left the room – the sound of his son's awakening had alerted him. He would not waste a precious second of the short time he had been allowed with his wife and son.

* * *

Carlos was in awe; he had never seen a fleet of ships of the line before. Towering above the waves, two- and three-deckers stretched from horizon to horizon. With the auxiliaries and frigates nearly 3,000 guns lurked behind their gun ports. The British fleet, while outnumbered, were still a formidable force.

Carlos's charge seemed puny in the company of these giants. *Thistle* was a bald-headed gaff schooner barely 200 tons, built a privateer by a group of loyalist merchants from New York; she had been captured by the American Navy a month before in an action near Bermuda. Captain Jones had given the command of the prize to his talented first lieutenant. Carlos Pearce had his first command.

His job was communications; to this end, his first officer and five seamen had been seconded from the French Navy. Pierre St Martin was not from the aristocracy; however, he knew the Dufresnes of Burgundy, ancestral home of Carlos's wife's family. The two men got on well to start with. However, St Martin was 30 years old, had been in the navy since he was 15, and became annoyed at the naval practices of his young captain, whom he deemed had been given the command due to family position, something he thought was not done in America.

Thistle danced around the ships of the line like an antelope in a herd of elephants. She had been called to the flagship of the French Admiral Le Comte de Grasse for orders. The British fleet had been sighted. It was the year of our lord 1781; on the 5th of September battle commenced.

Thistle's orders were to run down the line flying flags of instruction for each unit of the fleet. She would read any signals the ship's captain wished to convey to the admiral and pass them on.

The two British divisions were a considerable way apart. Admiral de Grasse decided to concentrate his force on the forward of the two under Admiral Graves. The ensuing battle was a complete success for the French fleet; they severely outnumbered Graves, who was further separated from Admiral Hood's division, and was badly mauled.

Lieutenant St Martin and the other French sailors aboard *Thistle* cheered as they saw their countrymen achieve victory over the British Squadron. "A signal from the flagship, captain. 'Return to port' is the order, sir."

Carlos could hardly believe his ears. The French fleet could now attack the rest of the British fleet, resulting in the wiping out of the British naval superiority in American waters. "This is madness," he shouted. "Let's finish the job, for God's sake!"

Thistle's crew watched as the French tacked and made their way back to their anchorage in the mouth of Chesapeake, leaving a patrolling squadron to deter any further British attack.

"Captain, look yonder; an enemy frigate with damage, I tink," called the French lieutenant.

"Yes, I see her, we will harden up and rake her. We could take her as a prize, should they be as immobile as they seem," said the young captain.

The French fleet had caused considerable damage during their brief encounter. Three large ships were on fire, and several had sunk. *Thistle* sailed through a sea of wreckage and broken pieces of ships. Many bodies and parts thereof were floating or hanging on pieces of wreckage.

Some hearty souls cursed the schooner's crew as they passed, the captain deaf to their cries as he approached his target.

Thistle's single bow gun lay several shots across their prey's topsides. Carlos noted that her starboard guns were run out - whether they were trying to lure him close enough to deliver a crushing broadside, or whether the gun crews were busy trying to save the ship, he could not determine. A large group of men were busily engaged cutting away the fallen mainmast before the wreckage caused the hull to be damaged.

Handled beautifully by Carlos, *Thistle* approached from far enough forward to be out of the frigate's arc of fire; she was not able to manoeuvre, therefore little threat. "Master gunner, we will run across her stern; fire as you bear."

Six guns raked the frigate's stern as *Thistle* passed at point-blank range, when smoke belched from a cannon on the frigate's quarterdeck. Not being able to depress the gun sufficiently, the British iron flew high, holing the mainsail.

"They need luck to hit a spar," said the captain as he put *Thistle* through the wind and hove to on the frigate's quarter, where they poured shot onto the position of their only gun able to bear, setting fire to the after-structure.

Carlos called across the narrow stretch of water separating the two vessels, his guns ready. "Captain, HMS *Hyperion*! I offer you the chance to surrender and make for the bay. Should you refuse it will be my painful duty to sink you."

The British captain, a veteran of dozens of actions, stalled. "I see our fleet is unable to assist us, and we are at your mercy. Do you intend to send a prize crew aboard?"

Carlos, realising that an attempt at close combat would be futile, as the frigate's crew outnumbered him three to one, replied cheekily, "Would that I could enjoy your surrender personally, sir, but will on this occasion resist taking that honour. Strike your colours, hoist a truce and run in your guns. When that wreckage is clear, make for the bay under foresails only. I shall take up position astern of you; should you not comply within five minutes I shall rake your stern till you do."

Thistle sat menacingly across the frigate's unprotected stern, all waiting in tense silence. Was David indeed going to capture Goliath? The wreckage from her fallen mainmast drifted in her lee, as exactly on five minutes Carlos began his systematic bombardment of their much larger adversary. After the second salvo the frigate captain's play for time had run out. Now free of his encumbrances he could set sail and smash this arrogant puppy. Alas, he knew that by the time he was under way, the much more manoeuvrable schooner would have disabled his steering.

Thistle stopped firing as the flag of truce fluttered at proud *Hyperion*'s masthead; a huge cheer went up from the victor. Her forecourse, topsail and topgallant crackled in the freshening sea breeze. As instructed, the proud Royal Navy frigate headed into the hands of her enemy. *Thistle*, not a hundred yards astern, was like a hound harrying a lion.

Carlos flew the American flag alongside the French tricolour, thereby acknowledging the ally's major part in the action. Once anchored, a French senior officer came alongside in a ship's boat.

"Captain Pearce, I 'ave come to escort you to *Hyperion*. Admiral Le Comte de Grasse 'as reserved you th' 'onour of receiving formal surrender from 'er capitaine."

In a never-to-be-forgotten moment, the most junior captain in the American Navy received the sword of one of the most experienced captains of the British Navy.

Sir Bartholomew Norrington, senior post captain in His Majesty King George III's Royal Navy, spoke solemnly as he handed over his sword. "I trust your fledgling navy has not many more of the likes of you, sir. Had you allowed me a few minutes more, the tables would have turned, but of course you knew that. You could have killed many more of our people from your position. You have honour as well as skill, sir."

"Thank you, sir. When the hound harries the bear, sometimes circumstance will favour the hound," answered Carlos graciously.

That evening a grand dinner was held aboard the French flagship. Simon Pearce could hardly contain the pride he felt for his youngest son, seated beside him at the admiral's table. After some wine the admiral said, "I think the tide is about to change, commodore. Once we see to Cornwallis in the south, your war will be close to won. When your America is secure, send your son to France – our navy will add polish to 'is skills, eh."

"A great honour, indeed, Admiral de Grasse. Thank you," answered Simon.

"Carlos will 'ave my personal patronage, commodore," with which the admiral turned to General Washington, who sat at his right hand, discussing the next move, now the British fleet had been subdued.

Later that evening Simon turned to his son. "Well, my boy, you have made friends in high places. The admiral suggested that we might give you the *Hyperion* as your next command. Couldn't do that, of course. Nepotism is rife in our hierarchy – I won't be part of it. Besides she will be under repair for many months after your taking her apart. I'm going to give *Hyperion* to Michael Johnston, Carlos. He has experience of square-rigged warships from his time as an undercover agent while an officer in the Royal Navy. That, of course, leaves the *Esther May* without a commander; I wonder who would be best to captain her?"

The commodore grinned widely as he shook his son's hand. "Keep a good eye on her, son. With luck, you'll be captaining her in peacetime soon."

Carlos hugged his father in a most Iberian fashion. He had no words to describe his joy. The father and son drank their Madeira in silence, contemplating the time they could return to their families. Thinking of Sally Antoinette, Carlos reached into his jacket pocket and produced a crumpled letter addressed to him in his wife's careful copperplate. "Excuse me, Father, this was handed to me as we went aboard the flagship. May I?"

"Of course, my son. I'll bring the candelabra closer so you can read," said Simon.

Dearest husband,

I pray to God that this letter will reach you before you put to sea. All the talk is of a great sea battle between our allies, the French, and the British fleet. I know you must do your duty but pray, take great care, so you return safely to us.

Yes, my darling, I am with child and pray our baby will have a father to grow up with.

Your loving, proud and happy wife,
Sally Antoinette

"Father! Your second grandchild is conceived. Sally Antoinette is with child!" exclaimed an excited Carlos.

Simon beamed. "God yet again shines his light upon our family. Congratulations, my son."

Carlos was aboard *Thistle* packing his personal gear, awaiting the arrival of the *Esther May* from Boston. A knock at his cabin door brought him back to the present. "Enter."

A large man ducked to clear the doorway been built for the average sailor man.

"'Tis a sailin' master y' be a-needin', I hear, captain?"

Sean Finnegan held his cap in both hands in front of the young captain, in the same humble way he had done in the presence of Richard Blackmore 35 years before, the glint in his eye still as bright.

"Sean, you look well. Wonderful to see you. Does Father know you are here? I thought he had you teaching at his new nautical college?"

"Aye, soir, that was what 'e 'ad in mind, but me, well I ain't no college type, now am I? Never been to a school in me life. I'm a sailor man, s'all I know, an' nobody knows the ol' *Esther May* likes I does, do 'em?" said Finnegan.

Carlos weighed the proposition up in his mind: the American Navy was sorely short of trained, disciplined officers. He came to a decision. "Welcome, Sean – subject to my father's approval. You will be our lieutenant navigator, training officer, on the condition that you are not a front-line officer. You are primarily aboard to instruct whomsoever they give me as crew – no risk-taking, none, do I make my point clearly?"

"Indeed ye does, soir. Thank 'e," answered Sean.

"With the training officer title we will sort of fit into my father's plan, eh," said Carlos smiling. "Glad to have you aboard, old friend."

Within the week the *Esther May* was despatched to join the allied fleet offensive of Yorktown. The British General Lord Cornwallis had been dismayed at the British fleet's loss off Chesapeake. He was now trapped –with his back to the York River he was a sitting target. Yorktown was mercilessly shelled from the sea and unable to break out landward as General Washington had reinforced his army to 17,000 men, almost double the British force. The American policy was to shoot officers first, and marksmen were deployed to this task, greatly reducing the enemy's ability to retaliate.

The *Esther May* reached the battleground in half a day, the noise of continuous bombardment audible during the entire voyage. It was a scene impossible to fully describe.

"I can see our lines," called Digby Taylor, the new midshipman. At just 13 years of age his excitement was being tempered by a brutal reality. "Poor Yorktown, my family came from here. I hope they got away before this all began."

"Our part in this is purely to observe and report to naval headquarters. After the powder and shot we carry for the fleet is unloaded, make to flag, awaiting instructions," ordered Captain Carlos Pearce.

As the trans-shipment of munitions was taking place, a 'hurrah' was heard above the din. "White flag, soir! Cornwallis has surrendered!" yelled Sean Finnegan. The crew went wild with excitement.

It was a cool day – the 19th of October 1781 – as Robert Davidson and other senior officers of the American Army were at the head of their regiments observing the British Army. As it marched out of Yorktown, minus weapons, a band played 'The world turned upside down', which was apt for an army that had not known major defeat before. General Washington rode up to Cornwallis and received his sword.

Five days later the *Esther May* was sailing back to Norfolk with news of the victory when they espied a number of British ships in the mouth of the Chesapeake Bay. Carlos prepared his ship for action. This proved unnecessary as they were in the process of turning and heading back whence they came. It was made known later that an army of 7,000 under General Clinton had been despatched to relieve Yorktown. They were returning to New York now the battle for the south had been lost.

Yorktown was the last major engagement of the War of Independence.

Chapter 24

Doctor Juan Pearce

Juan was tired, bone tired. He had been dispatched to Yorktown to attend to American wounded. "To think we won," he thought out loud, startling a nurse who was standing nearby.

The scene in the military hospital was desperate. Not much was left standing in the town after the continued French naval bombardment; the hospital was part of a church whose spire had been demolished. A gang of militiamen had worked feverishly to make temporary repairs to the roof using sail canvas. Men with limbs removed, men delirious with fever, blind men, deaf men, men whose nerves were so shattered by the noise and what they had seen that they could not function. A sea of blood-soaked bandages was the first impression a visitor got when they entered the nave, which served as a hospital ward. And these were the lucky ones – they were alive.

Anxious people arrived in a steady stream looking for comrades or loved ones. Those who found who they were looking for eventually left, the same stunned look of horror on their faces. Those that found no one left sullenly, to continue their search elsewhere.

Slowly the worst cases were being evacuated. After two weeks the young doctor had more patients die before him than most would in a lifetime.

At last, relief.

"Dr Mark Fredrickson at your service. Where shall I start, Dr Pearce?"

The man who had just introduced himself to Juan was an experienced, old-school military sawbones, not yet acquainted with the rules of cleanliness Juan had imposed. Help, however, was help.

"Cleanliness – clean – all must be scrubbed ..." Juan awoke with a start, to see his mother at his bedside. "You were dreaming, my darling. I 'eard you from the 'all; you are not unwell, I 'ope?"

"I am fine, Mother. It's a dream that recurs; even the smell of putrefaction is present. I am fine now, thank you." Juan sat up holding his mother's outstretched hand.

"I will 'ave your breakfast in 'alf an hour," Isabella said, brushing a wayward lock of hair from her son's forehead.

Simon was at the table and greeted his eldest son warmly. "When is it you have to return to the university, Juan?" he asked.

"Next week, Father. I shall take up my new position as head of surgery at the end of the summer recess. After years of training doctors with little formal study, medicine is now a degree course," answered Juan.

"Well, brother, you must be one of the youngest professors in the country. My sincere congratulations! When, pray, will your grand University of Pennsylvania allow us women into its hallowed halls?" asked Juanita testily.

"That, sister, is as you know, out of my control. Pennsylvania is the first school of medicine in the United States. It is young – but 17 years old. My college in Portugal had a history dating back to the thirteen hundreds. Having had several female monarchs they are more liberal there. Perhaps you should consider advancing your education in the land of our birth?" answered Juan, avoiding the question.

"So, we are the New World, a new country, the land of the free, and yet only men are deemed of sufficient intelligence to attend an institute of higher learning! What indeed have we improved upon? What is new here? All you can suggest is that I return to the old world to further my education, only because I am a woman." Juanita was angry and it showed. The 25-year-old had a fiery temper, sufficient to scare away most potential suitors.

"The law is the law, my dear. Your brother cannot change it," stated Isabella. "Look at your sister – she has a wonderful life with Colonel Davidson, our fourth grandchild on the way; she is 'appy."

"Mother, I am not and never will be some man's baby factory! I have a brain, a good brain, and I have skills, do I not, brother?" said Juanita, appealing to Juan.

"My dear Juanita, you are probably among the most learned, medically well-read person I know in the entire country. Women are simply not allowed advanced study, so you will not be able to obtain a practising certificate. As I have said before, do formal nursing and midwifery. In this field you will at least be able to be of benefit to womanhood. It is the only way as yet, dear sister," said Juan.

"Father, Juan is right. I shall go to Lisbon and try to enrol. Grandfather Diego is now there and has influence; he will help," and the handsome young woman rose and hurried out.

"It is poor that our new country does not give women the same rights as it does men. We still support slavery, and while religious freedom has been proclaimed, bigotry within the denominations is fierce. I think our daughter is right – we have come so far to be little further ahead in personal freedoms." Isabella carefully folded her napkin, and following her daughter, left the men to speculate further.

"It is what it is, and my sister must abide by it," said Carlos. "She angers me when she talks so. It is as if she puts herself above other women. Sally Antoinette is a cultured, intelligent woman. Does she hanker for things that are not to be? No, she is a wife and mother and proud to be so. Is that not right, my dear?" said Carlos.

"Indeed, Carlos, I am a proud wife and mother, but I kinda agree with Juanita – society would be better served with women being educated." Sally Antoinette looked boldly into her husband's disapproving eyes.

"She is packing," said Isabella on her return to the family table. "I shall give her a letter of introduction, and of course Father will assist her. She will seek passage from New York when the winter gales abate. With Britain declaring an end to hostilities last February, she will be able to trans-ship there. One blessing is Cousin Peter has agreed to sail with her as far as England. He says he wishes to see the Roseland again and visit family."

* * *

Juanita had been gone two months when the family gathered again at Porthellick in the Alexandrian hills, by the Potomac River.

"Now, all rise and fill your glasses for tonight's toast. As you all know The Treaty of Paris was signed on the 3rd of September in the year of our lord 1783. Our great country is from now on officially a sovereign nation," said Simon Pearce. "I give you the United States of America," he added beaming with pride.

Juan Pearce walked along Spruce Street and onto the campus of Pennsylvania State University, the first non-sectarian state government college in the Americas. He was recognised by many of the faculty, as well as being greeted by students as he walked towards the office of the provost. On his way were the faculty apartments where he would be living during the academic year. He entered and announced his arrival to the faculty housekeeper, one Bernadette Smithers, a fine woman widowed by the war.

"Your rooms are aired and ready, professor. Here is your key. I shall clean and change linen once weekly; please advise me of the most convenient time, sir."

"Thank you, ma'am," answered Juan, as he left the building to pay his respects to the Reverend John Ewing. On the way he passed a statue of Benjamin Franklin whose concept the institution had originally been, and who had proposed the original provost, Reverend William Smith, in 1765.

"Professor Pearce, wonderful to have you on board. I'm a great admirer of your work on sterilisation of wounds. As a mathematician I like clean, orderly processes. I see a great future for this school in the discipline of medical science. You will see from your teaching schedule that you will have ample time for research. I pray that you will use it well." Reverend Ewing beamed at his new faculty member.

"I am greatly interested in that research time and I do indeed intend to use it well, reverend. Thank you," answered Juan.

"There is a point, a delicate point, I wish to discuss with you. This is a non-denominational college; religious differences are welcomed by most of us. However, as a Catholic, you will find the occasional, shall we say, disgruntlement from some of the old school. I ask you to inform me if things get out of hand in any way. I will not tolerate sectarianism on this campus. Where, may I ask, do you stand on the matter, professor?"

Juan spoke earnestly. "I, sir, as you say, am Catholic born. My father is converted Church of England. I am not deeply involved in the church but attend occasionally, as my mother taught us. I have a non-sectarian point of view myself. I could happily give praise to God in any sanctified place."

"Well said. As you know, we perform non-sectarian devotions here on campus. While not a requirement, it would be, ah, advantageous were you to attend," replied the reverend. "Please make yourself at home. Here is a file detailing your duties and curriculum vitae of your students. Again, welcome. Please sit with me at dinner this evening." He extended his hand, closing the interview.

* * *

Six years later Juan Pearce, his wife Rebecca and four-year-old daughter Anna arrived at Porthellick for the 4th of July celebrations of '89, an affair that was also to celebrate his father's fifty-sixth birthday. Nestled in a bend on the Virginian side of the Potomac River, the mile-long driveway was lined with a variety of trees from evergreens to deciduous. Juan's mother had planted the trees so she could see the change of seasons as she drove along to the mansion. The colourful changing seasons were one of her favourite things in the new country.

"How much land do we have here, Father?" asked Carlos, at breakfast the day before the party. He was now the only member of the Pearce family still holding a commission in the Navy of the United States.

"A mile square is near a thousand acres, son; the title shows some ten square miles," Simon answered. "I have allocated some to Sean and Cousin Peter and sold some to those of *Esther May*'s crew who wished to settle here. I believe there is approximately eight and a half thousand acres left. Why do you ask, son?"

"As you know, there will be great developments in this area, the new capital city is to be built on the District of Columbia site donated for the purpose by Maryland. Our family lands will hold immense value as the centre of the country becomes hungry for expansion. Your choice of site purchase was fortunate to say the least, Father. What plans do you have for the land's future?"

"Ah, you are thinking ahead, Carlos, as am I. Our lands to the north, closer to the new District of Columbia, are at present being surveyed into parcels of ten acres; many new titles will be issued. When the time comes we can sell some parcels to fund building projects on others. As the new city grows it will need to lease many buildings to house its staff. As a Burgess man on the Virginia State Legislature I was aware of Maryland's desire to create the new capital in their state. I have made a few strategic land purchases adjacent to the District of Columbia. The family is well provided for, have no fear, son," answered Simon.

"My admiration for you as a father was always immense; as a seaman you have given me a target to aim for. It seems as a businessman you are equally excellent! I too have had some small success in our new venture," announced Carlos.

His father looked slightly uncomfortable listening to his son. "Thank you for your praises. I had a good teacher in Sir Richard; I have merely attempted to follow his good example with my children. Now what of China?"

"I have, as you are aware, just completed my second voyage to Canton since the *Esther May* was returned to us after the war. Father, China is exotic and wealthy. Its history dates back 4,000 years. They are on one hand the most advanced civilisation on earth, on the other, they are backward. They simply have not taken advantage of the enormous knowledge gained in the fourteenth and fifteenth centuries. Think of it, they could calculate longitude in the 1400s and made long sea voyages in huge fleets. It is rumoured that they landed here in America. Some Indian tribes talk of slant-eyed foreigners coming amongst them from across the seas. Now they are isolated from the world and only allow foreign trade through Canton.

"We cannot get enough of their goods landed here to satisfy the demand! Silk, porcelain, spices, medicines, every item of luxury you can imagine. You have seen the figures showing the returns on our Chinese trading. These will pale into insignificance if we were to set up a trading house in Canton and not only supply our own ships, but those of others without connections – connections we now have. I have made a deal with the court-appointed trader of the province in which Canton is situated. Over and above the trading tithe imposed by the court in Peking, we pay Li Hung-hsu a personal tribute calculated on the same basis as the emperor's tithe. I know you will hate paying off officials, but in China it is the way government officials make their living - they get little from the emperor's purse." Carlos handed his father a sheaf of papers.

Continuing, the trader pressed home his case. "Father, my report gives all the details of my proposed expansion. Please read it so we can discuss it further while the family is here."

Simon flicked through the papers and stopped, surprised. "You name Robert as the head of our proposed trading post in China? Would you have your sister, nephew and niece move to the other side of the world? This will make your mother less than happy, methinks."

"They would be living in the old Portuguese trading town on Macau in most comfortable circumstances. The British, French and Germans are all well established in the city and have embassies there. We would be the first trading house of American origin. I understand the British have set up an international school to educate the children of expatriates. Robert has hinted he would be interested. Since the army was largely disbanded he has been bored; my sister's husband is no farmer," answered Carlos vehemently.

"We shall talk again once I have studied these. Now let us greet your brother's family. I believe it is they driving towards us this very moment," said Simon Pearce, carefully putting the sheaf of documents into his desk drawer and locking it.

Later, after dinner, the family sat together in the drawing room. The large space was crammed with extra furniture as the whole family was present.

"'Ow is university life, Juan?" asked Isabella.

"It has been a most interesting experience, Mother. I fear, however, I am not ready for a teaching career," Juan replied.

"Tell them of the recent offer made to you, Juan," Rebecca suggested of her husband.

"Yes, my dear, I had so intended. Rebecca and I were honoured to be invited to President Washington's inauguration ball - it was, as you may imagine, a glittering affair. During the evening I was requested to attend a meeting with Mr Rory Douglas, President Washington's chief of staff. Mr Douglas was most kind in reviewing my career and offered me a post on the president's staff."

"Post, what post?" asked his father, showing no little impatience.

"Juan has been given the position of inaugural secretary of health!" burst out Rebecca in an uncontrollable show of pride. "He will work hand in hand with President Washington."

For a moment the gathering was stunned to silence. Slowly Simon got to his feet and applauded his son; the rest of the family soon followed suit. Juan sat uncomfortably as his family lauded him.

When they stopped and were again seated, Juan added, "I have been honoured by the president, but it is to this great family that I owe the opportunity. President Washington later spoke with me and recounted the many deeds that the Pearces and Colonel Davidson have performed for our great new country. He was kind enough to refer to my work on medical hygiene and was most concerned should I need help in the political arena, offering his ear whenever I may need guidance in that field. So I accepted. We shall move to New York forthwith, where the government ministry of health is to be temporarily."

Fireworks exploded, the colourful display taking the edge off the activities. Memories of war the explosions brought tumbling back to the men at the party sent some scurrying for cover.

Another matter disturbed the hostess that night. She had received a letter from Juanita many months before announcing that she would be leaving Portugal on the British ship *Harrier*. It was due to have docked in New York six weeks previously, plenty of time to reach Porthellick before the party.

Simon sensed his wife was disturbed. "You are worried, my dear. A late spring gale could have delayed them; the ship may have had to put into Antigua for repairs. The sea does not necessarily keep to the schedules set by man; she is her own mistress. Fret not, my love, Juanita will be with us soon."

The next day all those in the house stayed abed late. Sean Finnegan, now a septuagenarian, was sitting in a rocking chair in the morning sun. He greeted the courier. The letter was from Martin Dempsey, Pearce Shipping's agent in New York. Sean looked long at the package, weighing it carefully in his hands. He was uneasy; it was unusual for a single letter to be delivered on its own this far from town. It was addressed to Mrs Isabella Pearce; it could only contain news of Juanita.

Sean waited until the mistress of the house came into the morning room. Coffee was ready. When Isabella was seated, her cup full of the steaming, ambrosial liquid, she became aware of Sean.

"What is it?" she asked.

"It's ... a ..." his voice trailing off as he handed her the package and sat down beside her, a most uncharacteristic gesture.

Isabella opened the package with a rush, her eyes pleading that they might read good news of her beloved daughter. Once read, the letter fell from her trembling hand, and a powerful sob racked her body. She simply stared at the floor. A servant rushed to bring the master, who arrived on the scene. His wife was the very picture of desolation. Sean picked up the letter and handed it to him. He read it and his expression grew serious.

It is my painful duty to inform you that the British ship Harrier *has so far failed to make contact, either here or in the Caribbean. Please do not give up hope, as you will well know there are many variables when undertaking a sea voyage of this extent. The ship has, however, been officially listed as missing.*

I will keep you informed, and be assured I shall pursue every avenue of enquiry.

Your humble servant,
Martin Dempsey

The flamboyance of the night before, the achievements of the Pearce clan, paled into insignificance with the news of the missing ship – not just any ship but the one that had been carrying their sister, their daughter. Breakfast was barely touched, the children sensing something was wrong – apart from Carlos and Sally's new baby, Imogene who demanded attention continuously.

Juan was first to speak. "I think we should consider the positive – missing is not dead! She will turn up."

The family that had crossed this ocean dozens of times between them simply looked at the academic; the looks were from a deep knowledge of the sea. The wives who had waited many times for loved ones to return were also silent. At the very best Juanita was in great danger; at worst, they would never see her again. A ship was not posted missing lightly.

"I shall be in the best position possible when in New York to pursue enquiries. Be assured, I shall leave no stone unturned."

Juan and his family bade goodbye to his mother and father at the columned entrance of Porthellick. They looked old and grey, far older than their years.

In his study, Simon sat behind his large oak desk. The papers Carlos had given him were laid out; he had reached a decision. The new butler, an Englishman named Davies – who had previously served as butler to the Duke of Monmouth but had taken the opportunity to stay in America after the war – ushered Robert and Carlos into the sombre, book-lined room.

"Robert, have you considered the implications on your family should you take up this position within the Chinese business and discussed these with your wife?" asked Simon.

"I have, sir. We are in agreement that it would be a most interesting experience to travel to the Orient. Neither of us has had the chance to travel outside the United States and open our minds. It is a most welcome opportunity – there are few enough of these for retired army officers. We both welcome it. My father is also keen to put capital into the venture on my behalf, if you would be so kind as to consider it." Robert's words were spoken with authority, of one used to commanding.

"Carlos, how do you feel about sharing the company with your brother-in-law?" asked Simon.

"I am more than at ease with the proposition. It is far better to have senior members, nay, vital members, of our company as family with a vested interest. I propose the shareholding is one-third you, Father, one-third to me, one-third to the Davidsons. With the extra capital I would purchase two more ships; this will bring my year two income projections into year one, and we will recoup our initial investments in two years. I would also begin the importation of opium for the medical sector, as requested by brother Juan." The three men shook hands.

Simon then spoke to his son. "I wish you to be head of the firm. I have the farm and property development to work on. I propose to be non-executive chairman of the board; you must be managing director

273

as you have knowledge of the business. We should appoint Robert's father to the board. He is a talented legal man and can keep an eye on the Davidsons' investment."

"I am honoured, Father, but your guidance will always be welcome. Robert, how say you?" stated Carlos.

"Everything said has my approval. I can hardly attend board meetings while in China, can I. I assume I have a seat on the board when I am in America?" asked Robert.

Both Carlos and Simon agreed.

"I'll set the lawyers to work then," said Simon closing the subject. "Gentlemen, there's much to do. It will keep our minds off Juanita."

Part Three

1786–1799

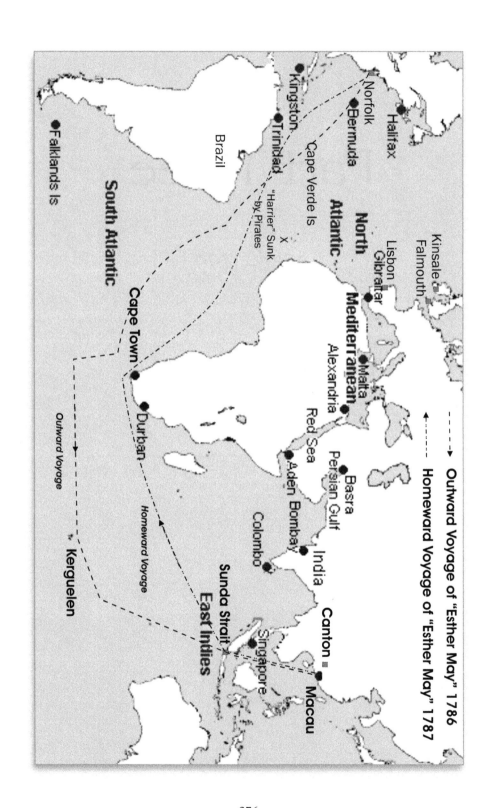

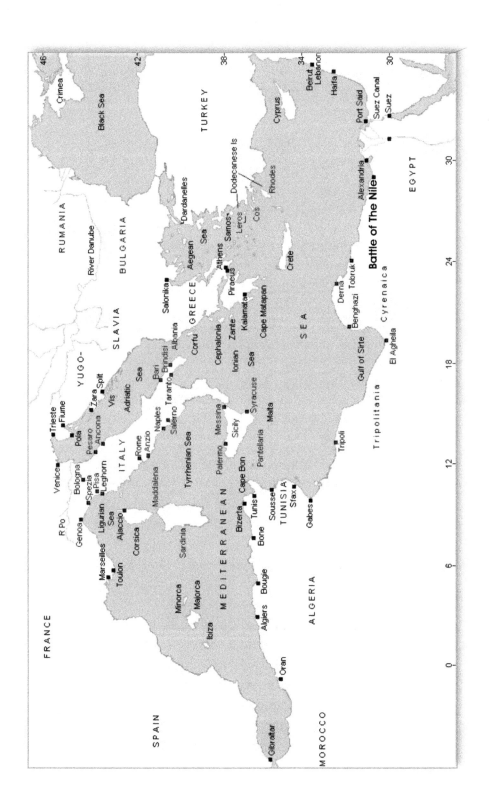

Chapter 25

Voyage to the Orient

The *Esther May* worked her way around the South Atlantic high pressure area seeking the southern ocean westerlies to give them a fair passage for a Cape Town landfall. The crew and passengers had suffered in the doldrums, where it had taken the ship 17 days of light, contrary winds, in intense heat, to cover 600 miles. At one point Captain Carlos Pearce ordered a bosun's chair rigged from the main yard so the passengers could be dunked in the cool water, a practice that had to cease when large fins were spotted by the lookouts, stealthily approaching the ship.

At latitude 40 degrees south, 20 east, she picked up the first puffs of the westerlies that prevail in the Southern Ocean. The cooler air revived the 68 souls on board, and the ship, wind fair on her port quarter, became the living thing she was meant to be.

A wild north-easterly storm caused the ship to take a track far to the south of the Cape of Good Hope, any chance of a few nights' respite and the possibility of resupply at Cape Town evaporating the further south-east they were driven. When the westerlies finally resumed, the course to Cape Town would have required many days beating to windward. Captain Pearce called the ship's officers and Colonel Davidson to his cabin, now much reduced in size to accommodate their two families.

Carlos spoke to the assembly. "Gentlemen, we are now so far to leeward of Cape Town that it would be imprudent to attempt a landfall there. We shall therefore take advantage of the westerlies to make our easting. Our landfall will be the westernmost part of the Spice Islands, avoiding the Dutch East Indies if possible, due to the ridiculous tariffs they impose on ships not in the employ of the Dutch East India Company. Should our situation deem it prudent, or if we need repairs, we can reverse this decision.

"I am informed that our supplies are adequate to reach our destination, with prudence and mild rationing. We shall rig awnings and set water butts up on deck to collect water later during tropical downpours. At our current average speed of 170 miles per day we should arrive at the point where we head north in 20 days. Robert, please give the ladies my apologies for the inconvenience; they and the children will not be subject to rationing, other than water for washing – that, I am afraid, will cause them much inconvenience. Are there any questions?"

"Aye, sir," the first officer, Daniel Carter, spoke up. "I'm mighty concerned with that split in the maintopmast. During the blow it has widened and deepened; we cannot fly the fore-topgallant – even the topsail's a risk. I was hoping to make the repair in Cape Town."

"Cannot a temporary repair be made at sea, Mister Carter?" asked Carlos.

"Ney, sir. In this here Southern Ocean the seas are too big; we'd lose lives for sure, sir. There's one possibility, sir. I was in these parts en route to Sydney when we passed an island near 20-mile long, and high. If we could find a lee and anchor two days, the repair would be done in safety."

"You're right, the island is called Kerguelen – can't be more than four days' sail, if further south than I care for. We would be able to replenish our water casks as well. The island is, as you say, most mountainous. We should find it with ease."

The night before their estimated landfall, sail was shortened – Carlos did not want to run into what was in fact an archipelago of islands in the dark. Even so, it was hard to keep the nimble vessel under six knots in the 25-knot following breeze, a mere zephyr in these latitudes. The eastern sky lightened and not ten miles to the nor'east lay the island. They quickly wore ship then headed for the centre, where a bay with a deep fjord running inland, with waterfalls running into it, was found. Carlos had misplaced his landfall; he would have preferred to approach from the north where more anchorage options in shallower water were said to be, but he had no choice in their landfall, being too far to the south.

Under fore and aft rig, the *Esther May* beat past the southernmost headland. They passed a fjord where the katabatic effect from the surrounding highlands doubled the wind speed sending the ship racing towards a far shore. A little later the sea was calm, and the crew could enjoy a steady sail before tacking into a cove at the head of the bay. Just as the anchor was let go, a call from the masthead had all looking landward.

"Smoke to the nor'ard."

"That's most strange, these islands are said to be uninhabited," exclaimed the captain. "Send a boat's crew ashore, Mister Carter; they had better be fully armed. Let us concentrate on the foretop repair. I want to be away as soon as it is complete. Whilst ashore, see if it is possible to take on some water to augment our supplies."

"Aye, sir," said Dan Carter turning to give the orders. William Hardacre, the ship's lowest ranked officer, was put in charge of the shore party. He chose Michael Pratt, the ship's gunner, as his chief NCO. Pratt picked a crew of experienced fighting men to man the shore-bound cutter.

"We'll take a couple o' casks in case we gets the time for a-fillin' of 'em, soir." Pratt's soft Worcestershire twang was not to be confused with weakness; one look in his eyes showed he was a man not to be trifled with.

"There's a mite bit too much surge on that boulder beach, Mister Hardacre. We dunna want t' wreck the boat," said the experienced gun layer.

"How's that beach to port? See the protective point at the western end? Let's try there; it's a bit of a march back, but it's sand. What do you think, gunner?"

"Aye, Mister 'Ardacre, that be best spot for sure."

With the boat safely ashore, a stream was found on the other side of the sand beach forming a protective spit between fresh and salt water.

"Three of ye remain 'ere. Fill the casks from that stream o'er yonder, and guard the boat; th' rest o' ye, let's go," and the burly gunner started along the beach. They climbed a rocky point between the landing place and 'boulder bay'. From their vantage point they saw what appeared to be some sort of village 500 yards to the east, inland from the beach. They could see no sign of life, so they proceeded with caution – years of skirmishing and hand-to-hand fighting experiences had sharpened their senses.

They circled the camp and approached from all corners as one. They rummaged through the three rude huts cunningly woven from branches and covered with what remained of flax sailcloth. Then they became aware of a low moaning which seemed to float down from the heights above them. Signs of recent habitation were everywhere.

Meeting at the centre of the triangle formed by the huts the men exchanged details of what they had found.

A seaman named James spoke up. "There's a path leading up t'wards that sound, sir, over 'ere."

"This smacks of a camp of shipwreck survivors; you'd think they would be running t'wards us, not hiding! What is your opinion, Mister Pratt?" asked the young lieutenant.

"Aye, soir, could be. We best be on our guard, though; thar cain't be a host of 'em. Let's head on up the track, get us a look see. I'll lead if yer like, soir," said Pratt.

"Please do, Pratt," said the young officer, again deferring to the experienced man.

After twenty minutes' steep hike, Pratt stopped, sniffed the air, and turning back to the others said, "Smoke – not far away, I reckons."

The chanting noise grew, rising and falling softly on the wind. The gunner looked over a rocky abutment and withdrew hastily. "Good God," he whispered, "there's five of 'em. One's a woman – seems t' be leadin' some sort o' pagan ritual. The odd thing is, she looks European! They must've been up 'ere since we hove into view 'n don't know we're on the island."

"'Ow should we proceed, gunner?" asked the young officer.

"We're armed and outnumber 'em; we should just march in. If any try t' run, I'll fire a warning shot, after that just wing the runners. Ready lads – go!"

The gunner's warning shot had the men, all of whom seemed to be of a dark complexion, fall flat on their faces. The woman, however, stood calmly, a wry smile on her beautiful face, showing no fear.

"Madam, we are American sailors from the schooner *Esther May*. We mean you no harm," said the boy officer with embarrassment.

"What a coincidence. I shall be very pleased to board your ship and meet with your captain, sir." She spoke with an attractively accented, otherwise perfect English. "Leave these people here for now – they won't attempt to harm you. I will issue instructions for them to remain at the camp." The strange, dark olive-skinned woman was obviously the clan's leader.

She spoke to the four men in some unintelligible dialect; they rose and moved off slowly down the path. She then went into a small cave, emerging a few moments later carrying a small bag.

The boarding party, led by the strange woman, moved off. She said nothing more whilst en route to the ship but held herself erect, calm yet.

"Cutter's returning, sir; they've got a passenger," called the ship's lookout.

Isabellita and Robert stood with Sally Antoinette and Carlos at the gangway as the visitor stepped on board.

Isabellita cried, "Oh my God," and fainted.

Carlos, eyes bulging with incredulity, was speechless.

The woman spoke first. "Oh, brother, it is you! When I heard the ship's name I prayed you may be in command," and she ran forward and embraced him.

"Juanita, dearest Juanita. How in God's name ...?" Carlos cried.

"It is a long story, brother dear," then seeing her sister reviving she knelt down and hugged her, both women a flood of tears.

"Dearest Juanita, how have you come to this godforsaken place?" Isabellita asked.

"Oh, dearest sister, I long to tell you, but first, brother dear, can you send a party ashore to apprehend my fellow castaways. They appear calm and in control, when in fact they are dangerous pirates. I turned myself into a figure that inspired awe in them, as the only form of real protection. As is usual with superstitious people in isolated circumstances, they came to believe I could commune with the spirits of this place. I became their prophetess; this is all that saved me from a death which, after use at their hands, would have been a merciful release." Juanita looked tired and drawn. "Can you give me a place to rest, I am faint with all this excitement."

"I will take her to my bed, Carlos. Let us leave this godforsaken place and its inhabitants to rot!" and Isabellita took her sister below.

"Aye, sister, do. We will await her full story before I decide on the fate of the others ashore. Mister Carter, how long until we are ready for sea?" asked the captain.

"Another day should see the work completed, sir."

"Very well, but I want an armed watch kept while we are here. Break out the weapons, if you please. I do not wish to be subject to a surprise attack from that vermin ashore. Colonel Davidson, Mister Carter, my cabin in ten minutes, if you please, gentlemen."

The captain left the deck after a quick look aloft, where he could see the new topmast being carefully swung into position.

The reduced space that was the captain's quarters seemed crowded with just the three men. The women had stowed their luggage well, but it still occupied half the available space, the smells associated with their womanhood transforming the usually male domain into more of a floating boudoir.

"I must apologise for the unseamanlike aspect to my cabin, gentlemen. Being with my lovely wife has its drawbacks," said the captain smiling, if somewhat embarrassed. "I have asked you here to discuss what I deem a dilemma. It would appear from what my sister has so far said regarding her companions on the island that she was brought here by force in some way. If this proves to be the case, what are we to do with them?"

"Leave them to rot would be my suggestion, brother-in-law," answered the colonel.

"Yes indeed, Robert, that would be the simplest way, but I fear some legal implications would follow that course of action. It is a fundamental law of seafarers that shipwrecked sailors, regardless of their actions, are cared for. If it is believed that they are in some way an enemy they may be restrained and dealt with by the proper authorities. Also to leave them roaming wild here is to put the next ship that has need to stop at risk. This, in all conscience, I cannot allow. You being a senior officer in the United States Army Reserve means I can abrogate my responsibility somewhat, by passing the dealing of this situation to you, especially as my own sister is the victim; however, this would put the possibility of some later prosecution on your head should, in some unlikely event, an action be brought."

"Fear not for me on that account, brother-in-law. Let us hear Juanita's full story then decide an appropriate course of action," replied Robert. "In the meantime if you, Mister Carter, would be so kind as to put forward, under my command, the best dozen hand-to-hand fighting men you have, I shall prepare them for a sortie ashore to deal with these ruffians. I agree with the captain; they cannot be left to roam freely."

Robert, pleased to have the possibility of action to contemplate, left with the first officer to organise his shore party.

Somewhat rested, Juanita joined the family for dinner, and having heartily enjoyed her first civilised meal in nearly two years, began her tale before Carlos, Sally Antoinette, Isabellita, Robert and Daniel Carter – he was the only one present outside of the family. The company sat spellbound as her tale unfolded.

"My ship, the *Harrier*, left Lisboa somewhat later than anticipated. She had taken on a special consignment requiring delivery to the Cape Verde Islands, so it was not until September that we finally cleared Lisbon harbour. The diversion was a most troublesome lengthening of our voyage, but as it was by royal decree, we had to accept it. I had a wonderful time when we stopped off in Madeira and could have been tempted to stay as the governor offered me a doctorial position in the new municipal infirmary. I was, however, most homesick and desperately wanted to return to be with the family – a decision I was soon to regret. Our voyage was initially uneventful until we approached the latitude of our destination, when the weather took a turn for the worse. This, combined with what I could see was a navigational error, put us far to the south-west when Cape Verde was sighted. In the thunderous storm we were unable to reach even Praia harbour on São Tiago Island in the south, let alone São Nicolau, our original destination.

"We beat back and forth in the lee of the islands, but the old *Harrier* was not able to make progress into the wind. We prayed for a shift, anything but the due northerly that pushed us southward. We hove to but we were now far away from the small shelter that the islands had afforded us. We were pressed further southward. When the foremast gave way all pretence of making ground was abandoned. The wrecked foremast acted like an anchor, holding our head into the wind as we waited for the storm to end. Our pumps were manned 24 hours a day, but were slowly losing the battle; the violent weather opened poor *Harrier*'s seams. When it looked as if all was lost the wind abated, and the next day we wallowed in the residual swell. Our exhausted crew were attempting to make some order from chaos when a sail was sighted. Making for us, with its triangular sails it looked at first as if it could be a caravel and our hearts rose, only to be broken when a lookout identified them as Barbary Coast pirates, among the most despicable and bloodthirsty villains on the sea.

"Captain Henry drew the three women to him and ordered that we be given a loaded pistol each. 'Dear ladies,' he said, 'it is my painful duty to offer these weapons to you, not as a means of self-defence, more a means of self-destruction. Those who will soon be locked in a life or death struggle with us would capture you as slaves to be sold on the markets of Arabia, where women of fair skin fetch a high price. You must decide whether to accept this fate or take the course these pistols afford you. We will of course hope to avert this necessity by fighting in your defence against what is a numerous enemy. Should we fail, you will have to choose.'

"The battle was fast and furious, our exhausted crew no match for the fresh, strong foe. In a moment of thoughtlessness I discharged my pistol into the head of a man attacking poor Captain Henry's back while he was engaged in combat with a huge Nubian. I was quickly restrained, as was Polly Marchent, one of my female companions. The third, Annette Wakefield by name, took the captain's advice, put the pistol barrel in her mouth and pulled the trigger, the awful sight a normality amid the dead and dying sailors.

"Young and strong were herded with the two of us onto the pirate vessel; the others were left on *Harrier*, it seemed, just to drift – but no! As we pulled away from her sides the pirates fired cannon at her waterline, the survivors left to drown in a merciless ocean.

"We were taken below decks; the pirate crew touched us in the most unseemly manner but caused us no injury. Polly and I were brought before the captain – his name was Mahmood; our condition was one of dread and trepidation. A more unseemly personage it would be hard to imagine. He was of light brown skin heavily marked by the smallpox and tattooing, an awful scar joined his left eye socket to the crease of his mouth, and the grin with which he greeted us was as if from the dominions of Lucifer. To our surprise he spoke Portuguese quite well for the ruffian he was.

" 'What a find we have here,' he said. 'A fine price you will fetch in the markets if you choose to live. For your choices are few! You can attempt to harm yourselves, or choose not to eat, in which case I will consider you not worth my protection and hand you to the crew as, eh, entertainment. Or you may be assured of my protection if you keep yourselves in good condition so you fetch a good price. If you are bought by a wealthy Muhammadan you will be treated fairly well and have a life of comfort. So decide, for now you will be locked in a small room for which only I hold the key. I shall watch carefully beware.'

"Polly and I were incarcerated in a small cell with not the slightest privacy. We spoke that night and agreed to do as the captain had ordered, for now at least, and await a change of fortune. The days were interminable and the nights cold as we headed south. I marked on the cell wall as each day passed to keep a track of time. After ten days we turned eastward, and the ocean swells grew in height and distance, so I perceived we were in the Great Southern Sea. On the twelfth day we made a turn to the north amid a rising wind and confused sea conditions. Soon a storm of a far greater ferocity than that which had disabled *Harrier* forced us to run eastward before it, all sail taken in.

"That night a huge wave broke over the stern of the ship; all those on deck were swept away or injured, but for the helmsman who battled to keep our stern to the seas. The captain rushed on deck to view the damage. It was then I informed him that I was a trained doctor. He looked me in the eye then unlocked the door. 'See what you can do for the injured. You,' he said, indicating Polly, 'help her.'

" 'We are badly damaged and unable to take these seas other than rear end on. There is an island not far away; we will attempt to land there. Can you help them?' Mahmood said, pointing to the nine men under an awning in the shelter forward of the poop deck.

"I said, 'I have no equipment and no medicine, but I will do my best. Do you perchance have opium on board?'

"He looked at me hard and long and decided to trust me and said he would get some for me. Now I could at least alleviate their pain.

"Evil though he may have been, Mahmood was a fine seaman. He brought the ship to anchor up in the deep bay to the west. Of an original complement of near 50 we were reduced to a mere 19 uninjured men with six under my care; almost 30 had perished. The odds had turned a little in our favour.

"My group of injured became quite friendly and protective of Polly and me. As they improved they ensured that the others did not harm us. The situation became dangerous, as our group broke away from the crew that remained with the captain. One day Mahmood came to me with a proposition: 'We have here a stalemate, one that can only end with one group killing the other. I suggest we put your group in the ship's boat and let you go ashore. I will give you weapons and such supplies as I can. My men already believe you to be a witch so it will be easy to convince them to put you ashore with those of your group who wish to go. They would never allow you to leave here with us; fear of the unknown weakens the strongest of men. You will be castaways, but alive – what do you say?'

"I answered yes, not knowing if my dominion over our six would hold. We left that morning and rowed as far as we could to be away from the remaining pirate crew. They up anchored and left soon after.

"Mahmood was right – those who remained considered me some form of priestess, building a place for Polly and me in the hills by that cave. Polly had become my acolyte by this time. I simply became what they had created in their minds. Polly, poor thing, went slowly out of her mind. One morning she was gone – as was one of the men – the thought of rescue sometime in the future no longer worth her hanging on to.

"The five remaining brought me food, and I created a service that was as near to a Christian one as I dared. During the years I have been here I have acquired a considerable knowledge of curing plants and herbs. I trust I may be able to collect these and bring them with us, brother? They will be of considerable help to medicine."

Juanita ended her fantastic tale, her audience in awe.

"And you are – unharmed, sister?" asked Isabellita.

"Yes, and intact, if that is your meaning," replied Juanita.

"Those ashore, do they pose a threat to us?" asked Robert.

"Not if I go to them peacefully. If you take a raiding party they will fight," replied Juanita.

The next day the colonel and a group of sailors escorted Juanita ashore. "Wait here. I will bring them. Stay in the open and try not to look too aggressive, please!"

It was an hour before Juanita led her group of survivors to the beach. Her precious plants and a few possessions were gathered. The castaways didn't look back as they were rowed to the *Esther May* lying snugly to her cable.

With her new foretop secured, the *Esther May* spread her wings towards the east, the Spice Islands and the island of Macau.

Macau was a Portuguese trading place, where the intricacies of trading with the Emperor of China had been developed for 150 years. Many nations were vying for the lucrative trade now. The *Esther May* was but the third American vessel to land here. She would not normally be welcome; her captain's aristocratic Portuguese heritage, however, opened the way.

Tired-looking after her eventful 13,000-mile voyage from the Chesapeake, the *Esther May* was warped into the waterway behind Macau itself. She slid into the calmness, off the town of Santo Antonio.

Carlos had some difficulty in persuading the authorities to take custody of the five castaways from Kerguelen; however, as in the time-honoured manner, a case of American corn whiskey made them more amenable.

Isabellita was amazed; the churches, houses and wharves made them imagine they were back on Madeira or, for that matter, any Portuguese seaport town. Yes, she thought, *she would make a home away from home for Robert and Caroline here.*

This was journey's end for her – only men could land in Canton, 70 miles away, the only mainland trading port open to foreigners in China.

Chapter 26
China trade

It was some weeks before the Pearces and Davidsons were settled ashore. The womenfolk - Isabellita, Juanita and Sally Antoinette - organised an army of Chinese tradesmen to transform the 100-year-old colonial mansion into a suitable home, two separate wings affording each family privacy while the communal areas offered companionship in the strange land.

The *Esther May* soon completed the 70-mile hop to Whampoa anchorage, on the great Pearl River, situated 13 miles south of famed Canton, or Guangzhou in native Chinese. Trade goods were checked for damage, samples readied for the scrutiny of buyers.

Whampoa anchorage, merely a wide, deep bend in the river, was full of shipping flying every flag of every trading nation in the world. The *Esther May*, however, was the only one flying the American Stars and Stripes at that time. The great full-rigged ships of the larger European nations lofted it over the smaller brigs and barks of Holland and Denmark. The *Esther May*, while a most handsome vessel, was among the smallest at Whampoa that season.

Once secure, Carlos sent word upriver to the merchant Yamqua, an honourable '*hong* merchant' with whom he had dealt on his previous visits. A comprador was hired to keep the ship supplied with her daily needs. In his position as interpreter, it fell to the comprador to deal with the bureaucracy that wielded considerable power, not least in dealing with port officials and their levying of taxes. The most difficult to deal with was the representative of the emperor - it was his job to exact 'tribute' from the traders. Tribute was a compulsory gifting process, as His Imperial Highness was far above the day-to-day business of trade. Should the tribute offered be too little, the ship would wait for days before proceeding to offload its cargoes. The interpreter would carefully judge an amount he believed would suffice – including a commission for himself. The offer of tribute would then be made.

Carlos had hired a local river junk to trans-ship his trade cargo. However, from past experience he knew the Chinese merchants preferred to deal in cash – this was his main stock-in-trade. When this became known the bureaucracy moved a little faster, and within a week Carlos and Robert were making their way the final 13 miles upriver to Canton itself.

The city seemed to be perched on an endless hill; buildings most strange seemed to climb upon each other like the trees of a forest reaching for sunlight. It was a walled city that was very much out of bounds to *Fan Kwae* – foreign devils, as westerners were known to the insular Chinese.

At the river's edge was an area of approximately a quarter mile square housing the 'factories' or *hongs*. On this strip of land the *Fan Kwae* lived and did their business, effectively quarantined from all but the official traders. Here no western women were allowed – this rule meant that Isabellita would spend many weeks separated from her husband, as he would be protecting the company's interests in the *hong* district. It was essential that Robert create a good impression on the trader Yamqua, their only link to the goods they desired. He would place their orders and ultimately decide on the quality of the product they received. Robert had spent weeks prior to departure learning the intricacies of porcelain and silk, the most sought-after Chinese products in the United States.

Yamqua had arranged for a private viewing of samples of the products he was offering. Robert spent a considerable time examining each porcelain piece and bolt of silk, while the merchant sat on a mat sipping tea from a finely made cup, seemingly disinterested, as his client went from piece to piece.

"A fine selection, sir. Some excellent pieces," he ventured only once.

Robert and Carlos eventually separated those suitable from the rest.

"Velly fine choice. It is thees you have chosen, I myself would choose." He waved his hand to an assistant who opened the door to two coolies waiting to bring in a large box carried on handles. "I tink it now good to show best, yes? As the honollable captain and colonel seem know lubbish from good. Ha ha," Yamqua continued, laughing at his own little joke.

"Thank you, Yamqua. We want only the best, but we also wish to commission sets with American designs for our next voyage. The colonel here will oversee the progress and, of course, issue payment as deliveries are made," replied Carlos.

"Now I give a list of stock for you take now," said Yamqua, putting an abacus behind each sample set to show the number of cases he could supply of each item; added to these would be cases of tea to completely fill the holds of the *Esther May*. He was impressed by the extent of the purchases and indicated he would return after inventorying the trade goods offered. Once a value for the cargo was agreed, a cash difference could be struck to conclude the deal.

"Can we trust him?" asked Robert when they were alone.

"Yes, I believe we can. He sees in us an ongoing stream of business, especially as we are setting up a 'house' in Macau. Once he puts a final price on the stock we will review it, and after a negotiation we make a deal. You will be able to get much better prices for the goods we will be ordering as they will have six months to produce them before the *Yorktown* arrives. I estimate at least twenty per cent better than when we buy from stock, as there is a great deal of competition here from the large number of ships eager to fill their holds. Remember the golden rule: never be in a hurry – the faster you want things, the higher the price, and the slower the process will be."

"I've much to learn, Carlos; I trust I will meet the company's expectations."

"You will; you did well today, Robert. In Macau there is a canny old devil called Dom Francisco Garcia – he is known to my family in Portugal; he will guide you. Meanwhile we wait for our price."

It was three days before the merchant asked to meet again. During that time the two Americans busied themselves gaining as much knowledge as they could. They spoke with other traders and ships' captains. When they drank their tea, a precursor of any Chinese meeting, they felt they knew what the figure should be. Yamqua was well aware of their enquiries. A neat inventory of their cargo was presented to them written in Chinese characters and therefore unintelligible to them. At the bottom of the page was a number in English – $4,087 – this was the difference the trader required after their goods had been accounted.

"Thank you, esteemed sir," said Robert. In a well-rehearsed gesture, he suggested he and his companion should leave and, showing as little emotion as his well-trained, card-player's mind could muster, he added, "We will return with our answer at the same time tomorrow, if that suits you, sir?"

The Chinaman stood and nodded stiffly; it seemed he expected an answer straight away. "Ah, tomorrow. I will keep this stock in your name until then," he said, bowing more deeply.

The two Americans bowed and left.

"That was a bit hard, Robert. The offer is almost exactly what we expected. We could have done the deal then and there."

"Indeed we could. I just want to establish some rules around here. In the morning we'll counter offer, not so low as to insult him, but enough to let him know we won't let him have too much cream, eh!"

Carlos slapped his brother-in-law on the back and laughing said, "I see we have picked the right man for the job here," whereupon they proceeded to pursue a growing American tradition – drinking straight corn whiskey.

The next day with Yamqua, after tea was finished, George produced a copy of the document that the Chinese trader had proffered the day before. They had, however, had their comprador go through the document carefully the night before. The number at the bottom was about twelve per cent less than the one put to them. Yamqua looked long and hard – for a moment they thought they had lost their bid – then the trader picked up a brush and changed the figure again and passed the document back to the traders. It was almost halfway between his offer and their counter.

Robert stood and said solemnly, "Agreed."

Each side bowed and the merchant clapped his hands. Rice wine was served in the finest porcelain cups either of them had ever seen. These and two complete sets were presented to them as gifts by their hosts, with a hint of a smile.

Both men, while pleased with their new company's first transaction on Chinese soil, were not totally satisfied.

"We did all right, but it will be better next time," said Robert.

It was three weeks before the unloading of the ship was completed. They made the final payment of dues, leaving Robert to finalise the details. Carlos had the ship weigh anchor then, moving swiftly on the ebb tide, set course for Macau.

Isabellita Davidson had found her way quickly into the somewhat stuffy atmosphere of Macau society. It was an expatriate town with one concern – trade with China and Japan – therefore the heads of trading houses were often away securing the best quality goods for shipment home. Only the established traders with a trading house here or on nearby English-dominated Hong Kong island made the large returns sought by all. The ships that arrived to trade without connections would be palmed off with rubbish, made to wait for officialdom to grant them the required permits and made to pay high fees.

The Garcia family had been trading in the East Indies and the Orient for near 200 years; they had been established in Macau for more than a hundred. Dom Francisco Garcia was the current head of the Garcia trading house. At the ripe old age of 81 he still held the reins of command firmly in his hands. Both his sons had returned to Lisbon, ostensibly to work the homeland branch of the family business, but in reality it was to escape the iron control of their dominating father. Only the grandson had remained, learned the business and was the heir apparent to the House of Garcia in Macau.

Dom Francisco had taken a shine to Isabellita and her two children, as had his wife. His second wife, Katarina, at the age of 60, some 20 years younger than her husband, was the eldest daughter of Isabellita's uncle. She had been widowed when her husband had been killed by natives in the Portuguese territory of Brazil.

Katarina had assisted in all aspects of the setting up of the Pearce-Davidson residence in Macau, as Dom Francisco had been most effective in procuring it for the Pearce family. The beautiful residence, situated on Aomen Bandao, or the Península de Macau, was built as any grand house in Lisbon, before they were mostly destroyed in the earthquake. The house was perfectly suited in its location and aspect – warm in winter, yet offering protection from the burning summer sun, with its wide verandas and covered pergolas. Isabellita's daughter, Caroline, now 12, was cared for by an old Portuguese governess who had lived in England a number of years. She spoke fluent English and was of course able to instruct them in their mother's native tongue. They had left 14-year-old Michael in America under the guardianship of his grandparents until he turned fifteen, when he would enter the United States Navy as a midshipman.

Dom Francisco's heir, José, was not a happy man. He was concerned about their business. His grandfather seemed to have lost sight of his priorities. Yes, José himself liked the polite American colonel who had been decorated with so many honours in the War of Independence, and he agreed that a man of such military accomplishment would be an asset to the community should the British, Germans, French or the money-hungry Dutch cast proprietary glances at Macau; but for the grandfather to suggest that they assist in schooling the colonel in the intricacies of business dealings with the Chinese, and even that the two houses work jointly in the Japans, was too much for the young man.

Robert Davidson had chartered a seagoing junk so he could visit Canton as he pleased. He was returning as fast as the cursed winds would let him; he dare not be late. Isabellita, after three months of tradesmen and organisation, had arranged the date the Davidsons and Pearces would present themselves officially to Macau society at their home on Saturday. The gala party was also the launching of the Pearce-Davidson House, to create the right impression, critical for the American venture to be successful. It was with some relief that Robert's ship dropped her anchors in the waterway between Macau and mainland China, just a day before the party.

The first hint that all was not as it should be was when several prominent people sent servants with their apologies – they would not be able to attend.

It was Juanita, who had remained in Macau when offered a position at the infirmary of the Convent of the Sacred Heart, who got wind of what was afoot. The mother of a child she had treated – Marta Lopez, the wife of the assistant governor no less – confided in her out of gratitude.

"I believe the cause of the absenting families is a story some have heard – untrue, I am sure – that your family's fortune is based on ill-gotten gains from piracy. Even that a member of your family was, ah, executed. Someone in this town does not want your family established here. We are typical expatriates, a bunch of rumour-mongers and snobs. You need to be careful, my dear," said the child's mother.

"Well, Marta, I thank you for your candour. Like many dangerous rumours, there is a grain of truth in the assertion. My father was once a privateer, honoured by the King of Portugal for actions against the Spanish. Now, of course, the Spanish are allies, so his actions of 40 years ago could be misconstrued if taken out of context. Do you by chance know the originator of this ... story?"

"Yes indeed, as the originator spoke to my husband on the matter. He was somewhat loath to attend your event himself, but I insisted because of the fine work you are doing in helping our son with his breathing ailment. Be careful of José Garcia; that is all I can say," said Marta.

The family was stunned by Juanita's revelation.

"José! Why that's a ridiculous suggestion, sister. The Garcias have been wonderful to us. Why, it was Dom Francisco's introduction to the mother superior that enabled you to work in the hospital as a doctor," exclaimed Isabellita, not a little distraught.

"I know, dear, but Marta Lopez would not have spoken to me for no reason; she's not like that. Besides, José has spoken no lies, just not the complete truth," returned Juanita.

"I see it now!" exclaimed Robert. "On my last trip I was led in a fruitless direction in some cases by leads given to me by José. I will speak with him at once!" He turned to leave but was restrained by his sister-in-law's hand.

"Robert, I urge you not to be in direct confrontation with José. We cannot allow Francisco and Katarina to lose face over this; we must be subtle in our handling of the matter, you understand, Robert."

"Yes, I agree," said a cool Isabellita. "Let us charm those guests who have agreed to attend, and perhaps, as the opportunity arises, let them know the full story of our family's history."

"I have an idea," said Robert turning to leave the house to seek out Dom Francisco.

"And I, too, have a plan, dear sister," said Juanita.

José Maria Garcia thoroughly understood the business of trading with the Orient. He was 32 years old and as yet unmarried. It was for this reason that old Francisco would not hand the company over to his control.

"Marriage brings stability and a sense of purpose to a man. Children offer the reason for a future, young man," he had said on several occasions. It was rumoured that José liked boys; there was no proof, of course, but why else had he resisted the attempts of so many young girls to lure him to the altar?

"Why, Doctor Mendoza-Pearce, charmed to see you again," said José with a genuine smile as Juanita was shown into his office. The Garcias lived but a short walk from the Pearce-Davidson residence.

Juanita was instantly aware of the man's charm; she had felt this before; besides, he had called her doctor. Although she held that qualification, most men believed that a woman should not hold that post and only addressed her with her title when they were in need of her services. "Senhor Garcia, I wonder if I may speak with you on a matter of some importance to me?"

"My dear doctor, I would be delighted," he answered.

"During my training in Lisboa, reference to oriental medicine was often made. It is accepted that in the fourteenth century the Chinese covered the globe, mapping and charting as they went, did they not? Our own great navigators have referred to sea charts and maps made by these early adventurers. They first discovered the great Portuguese colony of Brazil.

"While I am interested in navigation, it is medical knowledge that most interests me. It was for this reason I was so pleased to be able to work at the convent hospital as I could study oriental medicine while practising there. I have been much impressed by the Chinese healers' use of herbs and their knowledge of drugs and opiates. I wish to know more, especially of a procedure known as acupuncture. This involves the insertion of tiny needles; when placed in strategic positions about the body I am told the results can be dramatic."

"Indeed, doctor, they are," replied José. "I have benefited from this treatment myself. I damaged my elbow and had been in pain for many months, then on a trip to Canton my comprador noticed and asked if I would consider a Chinese solution to my problem. I was born here and in many ways I am as much Chinese as Portuguese, so of course I agreed. He smuggled an acupuncturist out of Canton city. You understand that only Chinese authorised by the emperor may have anything to do with *Fan Kwae*, as they call us. The man came at the risk of his own life.

"I speak mandarin so I was easily able to detail my symptoms to the man. As you describe, he inserted tiny needles in my body, nowhere near the site of my discomfort. The needles caused no pain except when he rotated them and an intense heat was felt. The results were emphatic – the pain left me. I had three more treatments, took some herbal medicine and that was the end of that." José Garcia was most emphatic as to the benefits of Chinese medicine.

"To hear this from a man of our culture, such as you, only confirms my desire to study Chinese medicine. I believe it will be of great comfort to many Americans. My brother is the Secretary for Health in the United States Federal Government. I will have an ear in high places to get oriental methods known and adopted there. Can you help me access practitioners in these specialities? Both Europe and America will be large markets for the herbs and medicines, and the house of Garcia as well as Pearce-Davidson could benefit greatly."

"I see you have an enquiring but commercial mind, doctor, and, if I may be so bold as to say, the mixture of Anglo–Portuguese blood has made you a most enchanting person. But there are many difficulties in acceding to your request, the main being, as I have said, that it is against imperial edict for Chinese to mix with outsiders – us. I am, of course, intrigued –nay, excited – being a trader, as to the commercial implications of your suggestion. Our two houses' budding alliance could, I now see, have considerable beneficial implications. Not the least of which is that I shall – of business necessity of course – have to spend much time in your company."

Juanita felt as she had never felt before. She had always been a passionate student, with no time for romantic alliances; she was a 34-year-old virgin. The handsome, charming man, who but a few moments ago had been a target, an enemy, had metamorphosed into the object of her most intense feminine desire.

"Eh, mm, y ... es, er ... yes," she stammered. "I would enjoy that. Now please excuse me, sir. I must prepare for the party. You will be attending, I presume?"

"Eh? Yes ... of course," said José, reversing his earlier decision.

"I shall save a dance on my card for you," said the stoic doctor as she fled, blushing as might an 18-year-old bride.

"What on earth did you say to him, Juanita?" demanded Isabellita at breakfast the morning after the party. "José simply gushed over us for the whole evening, talking of a firming of bonds between the House of Garcia and Pearce-Davidson and of your fabulous idea. Francisco and Katarina were seemingly as unaware as were we of this warming towards us that José was now embarked on. But I saw a glint in the old man's eye. Tell me, sister, or I shall die of frustration. Have you fallen under this man's spell?"

"I don't know, sister. I blushed in front of him like some moony adolescent. I am a medical professional, but I can't describe the symptoms, let alone the cure."

"I, sister, know both, and I think the cure may be well known to you, even though you may not admit it."

"Why, Isabellita, what are you saying? You are disgusting!"

"A little lewd maybe, darling, but right, no? I think the problem we discovered last night might soon dissolve, if you allow yourself to be the woman you truly are, under your doctor's disguise. Oh, dearest Juanita, I am so happy for you. If you can have a tenth of the happiness I have with Robert, you will be the second happiest woman on earth."

Just two days later José arrived unannounced at the Davidson home. "I wish to see Doctor Mendoza-Pearce, if she is available, please," he asked the servant who answered the door.

The Chinese answered in Mandarin, which she knew José would fully understand. "The doctor is due home soon, sir. Would you care to wait in the drawing room?"

"Thank you, I will."

A few moments after he was comfortably seated he heard the unmistakable swish of a lady's skirt.

Standing and facing the door, he bowed courteously as the lady of the house entered.

"Senhor Garcia, the maid told me you were here. My husband is away, as you know. May I be of help?" asked Isabellita, already knowing whom he had asked for.

"Thank you, madam, but it is your sister I have called to see – a matter of business, I assure you. No doubt she has told you of her plans to study Chinese medicine? I have some good news I thought to impart to her in person." José's normal calm was shaken under Isabellita's piercing gaze.

"I think, sir, I shall remain for the sake of propriety, if you do not mind?"

"Of course, madam, as you wish, but I assure you there is no need."

The tall, immaculately dressed man looked uncomfortable.

The door opened again, and Juanita swung into the room, unaware of the two already seated.

"Ah, sister – and Senhor Garcia – what a nice surprise!"

"Senhor Garcia has some news for you, Juanita."

"I see. Perhaps the gentleman would care to impart his news to me in private, sister dear."

"That will not be necessary, my dear doctor. I have come to inform you that my sources have located an acupuncturist willing to see you and discuss his art. Only because he is a humanitarian and wishes us all to benefit from his skills is he prepared to take the risk. He knows you are a woman – this was a difficulty. If, however, I remain with you, as indeed I must to interpret, he will pretend I am the doctor, not you, and thereby he will save face. I trust this somewhat convoluted arrangement will be acceptable to you?"

"Thank you, Senhor Garcia. I am not the least offended. In other countries we accept the indigenous customs. It would seem the Chinese are as afraid of women as are Americans."

"Please call me José, and I may use your given name?" he asked, now more in the manner of a suitor than a business partner.

"Of course, José."

"You are welcome to accompany your sister, senhora, if you wish," he said with some irony.

"Thank you; that will not be necessary." Juanita answered the question for her sister. "At my age I am far beyond the need of a chaperone."

Looking miffed, Isabellita was inwardly delighted.

"Very well, we sail tomorrow on the afternoon tide. I shall send for your luggage at ten. Good day, ladies," and the Portuguese trader stood, bowed and left.

"You shall take a housemaid or I shall ask Robert to forbid you to go, Juanita."

"Oh, Isabellita, please don't get all moralistic with me. I don't want or need a maid. Save Robert the embarrassment of me defying him, were he to be so foolish to attempt to stop me. Sister, please, I am a doctor. I have quite recovered from my earlier vapours. Yes, I am attracted to José as I have been to no other, but I am a big girl and will take my time."

"Be careful, my dear, he is a powerful man, and he is head over heels in love with you. Love and lust are hard to differentiate in the beginning."

"I will, don't worry. I spent three years on an island warding off the advances of savage men. This one will be easy," said Juanita, embracing her sister, a faraway look in her eyes as if she didn't quite believe her own words.

Chapter 27

Home

The *Esther May*, having returned to Whampoa to load her traded goods, slipped her moorings at Whampoa anchorage for the second time, heading first to Macau. Colonel Davidson was quiet during the last meal in the ship's main cabin, somewhat restored to its normal proportions after the extra passengers had been offloaded. He was thinking aloud.

"I now feel the full responsibilities of my position as resident director."

"Indeed, brother-in-law. You are wise to take it seriously, but surely commanding a regiment in the army was a much greater test of your skills?" replied Carlos Pearce.

"Yes, but very different – there I was a commander, in a position of life-and-death control, as you have on your ship. In commerce, one has to be more persuasive, more subtle – a far more tenuous situation."

"Fear not, Robert, I have seen you in action. You did well with Yamqua; the Chinese respect a good negotiator. The company can rest easy with you at the helm here. I will, if I may, charge you with one more responsibility, as you are head of the house in Macau. As you know Juanita has chosen to stay to study oriental medicine. Please keep a weather eye on her for me."

"I will, of course, assume the role as head of the family in your absence. I fear, however, that your lovely sister is beyond any counselling a mere soldier can offer. I will take all care, but not responsibility. I am sure you understand, Carlos."

"Yes, I understand you completely," he answered.

The meal was finished with little more said.

The captain felt his ship heel to the nor'west monsoon; it was late in the season, time to depart.

The *Esther May* thrust her bows past the islands of Coloana and Taipa, into Macau's main anchorage where, much to Isabellita's chagrin, her brother planned to stay but one day. "I must insist, brother, that you wait until after the weekend party I have organised. Everyone will be in attendance, including the governor."

"Sister, dearest sister, I simply cannot. The monsoon is almost over; we have 1,500 treacherous miles to sail before we pass through the Sunda Strait and clear into the open Indian Ocean. A day, let alone a week more here could condemn us to a month's longer voyage just to clear the Eastern Archipelago. As it is the return voyage, which I plan to make without stop, it is 130 days – one third of a year!" argued Carlos.

"You will have Robert beside you. At the party it will be good for his standing in the community to be seen as the sole head of the House Pearce-Davidson in the Orient."

Isabellita saw the determination in her brother's face, her seafaring family's roots giving her the understanding she required to press him no further. She simply hugged him.

"I will go now and pay my respects to the governor, my sweet, and ah, apologies. Please ask Sally Antoinette to be ready to board tonight; my longboat will await her at the quay."

* * *

That was 12 days ago – 12 days that saw the ship working her way through the islands between Sumatra and Borneo, into the Java Sea. The monsoon had almost ceased, the winds were fickle, navigation extremely difficult.

"Work her as near to Java as is safe, Mister Carter. We will be in the best position then to work the shifts through the strait. If the nor'wester holds we will be on the lee coast, but in clearer air," ordered the captain.

"Aye sir," called the first officer. He was as tense as anybody, knowing only too well how dangerous the passage they were about to make truly was.

Two days later they were becalmed at the eastern approaches to the Sunda Strait itself. They were, however, covering ground on the current that had reached a peak of one and a half knots, courtesy of the northerly monsoon that had been blowing for three months. The sun beat down, and spars creaked as the ship rolled gently to a slight swell.

"Prepare the anchors, bosun, and put over the longboat. Leadsman to the chains," called the captain. "We've two hours or so of a fair tide. I want her in soundings before the turn or you'll be at the oars all night," he finished.

As the tropical night descended a zephyr, a mere gasp of humid air, induced a sluggish rippling in the sails. The exhausted men in the cutter found energy enough to cheer as the weight on the towing hawser lightened.

"Breeze abaft the beam, cap'n," called the bosun. "Will us clear the headland, sir?"

"Aye, methinks we will; the tide's on the turn; it'll push our bow clear. Leadsman, call if we are in soundings," Carlos shouted.

"No disrespect, sir, but wouldn't anchoring be a safer plan?" asked Daniel Carter.

"Aye, but if the monsoon picks up in the morning we'll be anchored on a lee shore. I'd rather be moving if there's a breeze. We'll beat through then tack on the north side, lee bowing the tide. Double the watch, if you please. Plot our dead reckoning. I'll sail the ship," decided Carlos.

It was a long night, but sunrise showed the Sunda Strait to the east; 12,000 miles of open sea lay before them. Landfall was made at the Cape of Good Hope, but they continued on. They entered the Caribbean Sea between Trinidad and Grenada, on through the Mona Passage where Carlos's father had so successfully attacked the Spanish fleet 43 years before. They were soon in American waters and a day out of the Chesapeake. A hundred and seven days had passed as Cape Henry slipped astern. All were weary; the captain had pushed his crew hard.

"Mister Carter, you will assume command and take the ship on to New York after a couple of days' rest. I shall head up the Potomac with my wife to our home."

Carlos and Sally Antoinette trans-shipped to a packet for the last part of their voyage, longing to see their children.

A spacious carriage was waiting at the private dock, which serviced the Porthellick Estate. Carlos's eyes watered as he recognised the young man striding towards them. "Jonathan, by God you've grown; you're a man, my son!"

"Hello, Father. You've been nearly a year and a half away – at my age one tends to grow."

Sally Antoinette hugged her son, unable to speak.

Carlos thought a fraction too long. "Fifteen, isn't it now? And yes, I see so much more of your mother in you – French, Anglo and Portuguese – you will break some hearts in your time, my boy, I'm sure."

As Carlos hugged his son, he noticed an almost imperceptible reluctance on the boy's part.

"It's good to see you, Father," he said stiffly.

"Where is your sister, lad? I'd have thought she would be here with you."

"She is in Washington, sir. Imogene is starting some new finishing school or other, so she will not yet know of your arrival. I have sent a messenger to inform her," Jonathan answered.

"Of course, we've been at sea three and a half months. I'm surprised even you are here. Let's get along, son. Your mother and I shall be glad to sleep on a stable bed tonight," and they set off in the carriage, expertly driven by his son, to the homestead.

"You are quiet, my boy. Is all well?" asked Carlos.

"Yes, Father, but I have some news. I ... I am not sure if you will be pleased."

"Well, spit it out, boy, or Mother and I will never know, will we."

"I have been invited to do my midshipman's training in France, sir," blurted the boy. "The current Comte de Grasse, your own sponsor's son, has personally invited me. It's a great honour."

"Well, yes, my son, but have you considered the consequences? England and France are close to war. You may well be on the French side and America may side with the British." Carlos was trying to maintain a cool demeanour; he was a wise father and knew that to appear outraged would drive his son from him.

"Indeed, sir, it is possible, but unlikely. I ask you, who is our ally? England, who has tried to subjugate America, or France, who came to our aid in time of need? France, with whom you yourself fought and was honoured. Have I not got French blood in my veins? Mother is a Dufresne, is she not? I have spoken with Grandfather Dufresne; he believes that Napoleon Bonaparte will prevail in Europe because of his anti-royalist policies. America is anti-royalist, is it not? Did not the British Crown attempt to impose its tyrannies on us? Father, the countries of Europe are sick of hereditary monarchies. France and her soldiers are champions of the poor," the boy finished with a flourish.

"Yes, indeed it does, Jonathan – by executing the nobility. It is amazing that the younger de Grasse remains a power in the French Navy. Most of its experienced officers come from the upper classes, and most of them have fallen foul of Monsieur Robespierre and found themselves under *Madame la Guillotine*'s knife," returned Carlos, searching for a way to dissuade his son from his proposed course of action.

"Father and Mother, this I know. Some injustices have been perpetrated in the name of *La Révolution*. Any time people throw off the yoke of their oppressors, innocents suffer; a mob is a mob. Napoleon has brought the mob to heel, Father. Paris is now a safe place to be.

"I can see you are displeased, Father, but please think on it. I am due to leave in two weeks. Grandfather and Grandmother Pearce have organised a ball at Porthellick this weekend. Uncle Juan will be home from Washington. He will, I'm sure, tell us of all the latest developments in Europe. The party will now double as a welcome home party to you too! By the by, Mother, Imogene has missed you terribly, as she has you, sir. It is not my place to say, but I hope you will be home for a good time. She needs you."

The rest of the journey passed quickly, as Jonathan detailed what had transpired since his parents' departure 18 months previously. Both father and son carefully avoided further discussions on the subject of the boy's imminent adventure.

Sally Antoinette had remained quiet during the ride, but much had been going through her mind. She would support her son in his ambitions to join France.

"Immy!" yelled Jonathan excitedly, the man fleeing for a brief moment as the boy returned. Both carriages had arrived at the door at the same instant. Carlos and his wife were reunited with their family.

"Imogene, is that you? You are even more beautiful than your mother, if that could be possible. You could be sisters but for your brown eyes. By God, it's good to be home. Both you and Jonathan have become adults in our absence." The proud father's eyes moistened.

"Wonderful to see y' home safe 'n sound, sir. Tea is served in the drawing room, if y'all please." Carlos, never one for formality, strode over to the major-domo and clasped his hand.

"Thank you, Henry. You have looked after them well, I see."

"It is my job to do so, but thank you, sir." The large Negro would have been seen to blush but for his jet-black skin.

Later, when alone in their bedchamber, Carlos held his wife's hands and looked sorrowfully into her eyes. She pre-empted his question. "Not tonight, my love; tonight is for us," and she slipped out of her already loosened gown, standing before him, naked.

The subject of Jonathan's career move was again avoided, as a carriage arrived from the main house, Porthellick, soon after breakfast. Carlos leapt from the table at the sound of his father's voice.

He embraced his mother first. Isabella Pearce was now 60, but her looks were of a woman 20 years younger. "My son, it is wonderful to see you. As 'andsome as ever, isn't 'e, my dear Sally Antoinette."

"I think so, Mother-in-law – very definitely still the handsome man I married."

Simon Pearce grunted slightly at his son's bear-like hug. Carlos noted he seemed taller than his father, where in fact they had always been the same height.

"You grow no weaker, my boy, I see; by all, you look very well. The voyage does not seem to have tired you?"

"It was long, Father, so very long. My mind is a mite more wearied than the body. You, sir, you are well?"

"No, he is not, Carlos," answered Isabella for her husband.

"Be still, woman, don't go rumouring. It's nothing but a bad chill," interjected Simon.

"Pneumonia is no chill, Simon. Juan 'as been quite specific; you must stay warm and rest at 'ome." A line of worry uncharacteristically creased her face. "'E should not be 'ere, stubborn man that 'e is."

"Let us sit. Henry, please bring coffee," ordered the mistress of the house.

"What of the voyage, son? How do things stand? And I look forward to Juanita's story in detail, if you are ready to speak now, son."

"Yes indeed, Father." Carlos gave an accurate if relatively brief description of the past 18 months, omitting only some business matters that would be for the board of directors of the Pearce-Davidson trading company. At the end of his lengthy talk he asked, "And what of matters here? I am advised that plans are laid for Jonathan's imminent departure?"

A silence overtook the room, ending only when the major-domo coughed, asking if any of the company required more coffee.

Once the cups were placed on the tray Simon broke the heavy silence.

"In your absence, we, the family, decided that the offer was too good to pass up. Jonathan has decided to follow in your footsteps and start his career in the navy of France.

"We are all aware that to progress in our American Navy it is an advantage to serve first in a larger organisation. That is, in France, Spain, Portugal or of course England. We were considering Portugal, as we discussed, before you left. Jonathan understands the language quite well.

"Then came the opportunity, some three months ago, when Le Comte de Grasse was on a goodwill voyage to America. He came here to dinner and, well, things advanced from there. Le Comte's squadron is due to leave New York soon; Jonathan is invited to sail with them. It seems logical, following, as it were, in his father's footsteps," said the patriarch.

"Am I to understand that a final decision has yet to be made?" asked Carlos.

"In your absence, Carlos, I was asked to assume the role of head of your family in this matter. The lad is keen to go, and if I understand correctly, his mother agrees that the French option is best. Le Comte assured me personally that he would keep a firm eye on Jonathan. There are still risks, of course, as there are in our service. The bloody British are taking able-bodied seamen off our ships at sea and pressing them into the Royal service. I see no future in an alliance with England."

"And you, my wife, are in agreement with this?" asked Carlos.

"No mother wants her son to become a warrior. Would that he could be like Juan and wish for a non-combatant career, but this is not the case. He is part-French; if he intends to have a naval career, why not begin it with France? He could join the next ship we have sailing to the Orient, but the lad wants to start his career as a naval officer – for why, it is beyond me. A year or two with the French will not harm him, as it did not harm you. If he must become a naval officer I believe this will be good for him." Sally Antoinette looked stern.

"It seems a *fait accompli*; pardon my poor French," replied Carlos. Then turning he added, "It may seem to you unfair that I am not as enthusiastic for this adventure as you may like. But as this company knows I have first-hand experience in the French Navy. For me, it was not the wonderful adventure that you desire. Especially now as their navy has not the skilled leaders it once had, due to the revolution. Had I been here at the start of this direction you have taken, I would have done my best to dissuade you. I have arrived too late for that. I will simply wish you *bon voyage*. God go with you, my son."

"Thank you, Father. I will make you proud."

"I'm sure the men will wish to discuss business; let us leave them to it, Mother," said Sally Antoinette.

"Jonathan, come with Grandfather and me to the main house. It will be good for you to begin to understand the business that you will partly own one day." Carlos noted the pride in his son's face and knew he had hit the right chord.

"Uncle Juan, it's grand to see you," said Jonathan greeting his uncle, noticing a rather large man in a black coat who kept his gaze firmly on the government health secretary.

"You are a fine sight to behold, nephew. Excuse me a moment."

"Withers. This is my home – you need not be paranoiac for my safety here, man! I have arranged for you to board with Jonathan's family; the house is only a few minutes away from Porthellick."

Dr Juan Pearce had been President Washington's health secretary for several years. He should have known better than to try to displace the man whom the president himself had picked as his bodyguard.

"Thank you, sir. I'm sure something closer can be found. I shall sleep on the veranda if there's nothing else." As ever, the ubiquitous Withers was not about to let his charge out of earshot.

"As you will, Withers, as you will," said Juan in exasperation.

Withers gave a curt bow and stationed himself at the door.

"Uncle, where are my aunt and cousins?" asked Jonathan eagerly.

"On their way, my boy. I have come from Philadelphia where I was sent by the president. The secretariat for health is in New York, where, as you know, we reside. The family are travelling by sea, a prospect your Aunt Rebecca and the girls will not relish. I am impatient for the city to be completed in the new District of Colombia. I am informed that the total move from the government's eight current locations will not be till 1800."

"Your new house overlooks the river and the city. It is in a magnificent position, Uncle."

"I am impatient to see it. With your grandfather in charge, I'm sure it progresses well."

"With your leave, Uncle, I am eager to know how our government views the wars between Britain and France."

"Of course, my boy, and so will your father and grandfather. I will freshen up at the guest house and be over soon. I will speak with you all together then."

"But sir, do I have your support?" interrupted the boy, unable to conceal his impatience.

"Look, unofficially our government leans toward revolutionary France, even though it was poor Louis who supported us in our struggle against England. But post-revolution France is a frightful place. I am not entirely comfortable with a nephew of mine throwing his life into the hands of a people in such a radical state of change, such as the French are."

"But General Bonaparte is winning; he will calm them. General Washington made the transition from soldier to president. Bonaparte will, I believe, do the same," said the impassioned young man.

"We will speak later, Jonathan. I have told you my concerns," said Juan with some edginess.

The boy had to curb his eagerness further as a carriage complete with three armed outriders swept up the drive. Rebecca Pearce and her daughters Anna, Isobel and Constance alighted and walked elegantly up the magnificent entry stairway of Porthellick.

Juan ran down the steps to embrace his beloved wife.

"Sir, such a display, and in front of the whole household! I am sure you shame me," said the elegant woman mockingly.

Juan was soon awash with petticoats and lace, as his all-female family enveloped him.

Jonathan was temporarily distracted as he gazed upon Anna. The tomboy he once climbed trees with had become a stunningly beautiful young woman, now fourteen. A smile covered his lips as he remembered the pledge they had made to each other whilst high in the oak at the rear of the family house. *Would Anna remember?* he thought.

Imogene joined the group, and they were soon swept away with the cousins' laughing and giggling, the young women briefly becoming the adolescents they truly were. Jonathan left, wishing his only male cousin, Michael – who had by now been a year in the United States Navy – had been there to even up the male-female ratio.

The house was ablaze with light. Over a thousand lamps and candles in the mansion were supported on the outside by fiery torches and braziers that glowed brightly, fanned by a light spring breeze.

By nine the company had dined, and Simon Pearce, standing a little unsteadily, rattled his crystal glass with a spoon. "Ladies and gentlemen, a moment of your time, if you please. I will try not to bore you, but this gathering was firstly as a farewell to my grandson, who is following his father's footsteps and becoming a junior officer, on secondment from our own navy, in the French Navy. He has been asked by the son of our family friend, Le Comte de Grasse, to sail with him on his command, the *Tonnant*, a 74-gun second-rater. It is of great importance to our navy that our young officers gain experience in large ships of the line and fleet management. Jonathan has a great opportunity to learn. Learn well, and Godspeed, Grandson."

The crowd burst into applause. Jonathan was well pleased as his eyes fixed upon those of his cousin Anna. She was clearly very impressed, as her flushed face betrayed.

"And now we have a second reason for a party. My son Carlos and his lovely wife Sally Antoinette have returned safely from the Orient having established great things, not the least the rescue of our beloved daughter Juanita." This announcement brought the house down. "A very timely arrival, son, if I may say so. You have saved me the cost of a second party."

The company laughed politely at Simon's joke, before he became serious.

"The Royal Navy boards our ships at sea and abducts our seamen. This they consider their right! Could it be that, as yet, England still believes it has dominion over the United States? I am sure, friends and family, that, should England not be so involved in the war with France, the guns of the Royal Navy would be aimed, once again, in our direction, the Redcoats we all helped push into the sea would be landing on our shores. I am proud, yes, oh so proud, that the Family Pearce is totally committed to strengthening our country's position, be it through commerce, military training or high government office. Now I propose not one, but three, toasts."

"My daughter Juanita. Captain Carlos and Sally Antoinette Pearce. Midshipman Jonathan Pearce."

After the chorus a second well-known voice was heard.

"Indeed sir, you and your family have done this country proud. I offer a fourth toast. Raise your glasses, ladies and gentlemen: The Pearce family!"

The company turned, silenced by the presence of none other than General George Washington, the first President of the United States of America. The august personage had been invited but was not expected. The company burst into applause.

"Thank you, thank you. Halfway through the second term of my presidency, I am in awe as to the achievements of our country. It is families such as yours who make this land strong, and I am proud to say you are not alone – there are thousands such as you, may God be praised. As Commodore Pearce described, Britain is now well occupied, as is France. The outcome of these wars in far-off Europe will certainly decide whom we must protect ourselves from in the future. The stronger we become economically, the stronger will be the military we can build. I pray that this military will be a great enough deterrent. The European nations have fought for centuries. A strong American navy will deter them from venturing to our shores. Let them squabble, and while they do, we shall grow wise and strong."

The president's speech brought the company to its feet, cheering and applauding.

A place at the head table was being hastily set. When asked what could be brought the president confided that he had visited Mrs McCorkingdale, the housekeeper, for a light repast before entering, as the modest man didn't wish to interrupt the banquet.

The grandeur of the occasion had tired Simon Pearce. After the president had left, Juan once again became the doctor he was and ushered his father, protesting, to his bedchamber.

"Father, I believe that you have suffered a mild stroke recently, a form of seizure in the brain. You have been lucky, it was a mild event, and you are only slightly debilitated. A major event could paralyse you, rob you of your speech or worse, kill you. I have spoken with Mother. Although she insists she wishes to care for you, she has agreed that a medical person should live at the house to administer the medicines I shall prescribe. Nurse Patricia Smith-Harley has worked with me; she is excellent and has agreed to take the position. I trust you will not be against her appointment?"

"You all fuss so. I am tired, yes. Something has occurred that I should be careful of, yes; but I'll be damned if I'll become an invalid at your behest, son or no son!" roared Simon.

"It is my wish also, 'usband," said the soft melodic voice of his wife. "I 'ave no wish to be a widow, alone – yes, alone – for I would never seek nor accept another. Listen to your son and to me, please. The situation will be temporary, I am sure, but while there is a risk I wish to 'ave skilled 'ands close by. I insist."

Unable as ever to resist Isabella's pleas, Simon capitulated. "As you wish, but it is to be a temporary arrangement, agreed?"

"Agreed, only until you are fully recovered," answered Isabella.

Juan was due to leave the day after next. He and the family were to return to New York.

"Why does Jonathan not travel with us? He can lodge with us while he prepares to join his ship," said Juan.

"Would you deprive me of a last day or so with my son?" asked Sally Antoinette.

"Mother, please, it would be grand to sail with Uncle Juan!" implored the boy.

"Of course, selfish of me, but let us spend this last night together as a family, your father, sister and I."

"Surely, Mother, as you wish. I will take leave of Grandfather and Grandmother."

The Pearce family rose early the morning of departure to wish Juan's family, and of course Jonathan, a good journey. Used to goodbyes and long separations, the farewell was not outwardly emotional. As the riverboat slipped her moorings and swung to the tide Carlos put his arm around his wife's shoulders. She wept, but only once the riverboat had turned the bend.

Chapter 28

The Roseland

"By the powers vested in me, I hereby christen this child John Joseph Hooker Pearce."

The Wesleyan chapel at Philleigh rang with voices as those present sang 'Oh God our help in ages past'. The minister handed the child back to his mother who beamed with pride at the congregation. She offered a special smile to the Michael Davidson who had recently arrived from Washington in the Americas. The upright young naval officer was a grandson of the Pearce family's favourite son, Simon.

Michael, resplendent in his United States Navy lieutenant's uniform, was in England on board the USS *Saratoga* – an unfortunate name for the first official peacetime goodwill visit of an American warship since the peace of 1783, as it was at Saratoga the British General John Burgoyne surrendered his army to the rebel Americans in 1777.

Jane Pearce, Michael's nearly 90-year-old great-grandmother, was quick to engage 'the American', as he was called locally, in conversation in the modest Wesleyan chapel grounds once the service was concluded. There were things that needed to be said to clear up the future of Penpeth Farm. "'Twere a fine thing t' see 'e at the service, Michael. Yer grandfather would 'ave been right proud of 'e. Will 'e be stayin' with us at Penpeth, my 'ansome? Speakin' o' Simon, did 'e say as to what 'e wants to do with 'is landholdin's 'ere on the Roseland?"

"Thank you kindly, Great-grandmother, but you have many staying with you at this auspicious time. I have booked lodgings at the Roseland Inn - it's but a brisk walk to the farm. As to the titles, ma'am, I have some papers here from my grandfather that I am sure will interest you and the family. Perhaps we should meet later to discuss them with everyone?" The young man's American drawl rolled lightly off his tongue.

"'E must join us fer dinner, me 'ansome; all in'erested parties will be there," answered Jane, still well in command of her faculties despite her age, and having buried two husbands.

"I will. A fine new great-grandson you have there. Good day to you, ma'am," Michael said as he lifted his hat then turned to leave.

Later that evening in the parlour at Penpeth Farm, the elders of the Pearce family gathered in some discomfort, because of the smallness of the room, to hear what Simon proposed. As legal owner of the two farms, added to the original Penpeth holding, he was to a large extent in control of the Cornish branch of the family's landholdings.

After the pleasantries were exchanged, Cyril Pearce, grandfather to the newly christened baby John, and tacit head of the sprawling Pearce family, addressed Michael. "I unnerstan' that 'e 'ave some news fer us, lad, regardin' the wishes o' your grandfather, our cousin Simon's thoughts on the ownership o' this fine piece o' Cornwall we sit 'ereupon?"

Michael extracted a large, sealed folder from under his uniform coat. The company's eyes followed its progress from the coat to the parlour table.

"Ehm, I presume, sir, that the enclosed should be passed to you," he said as he pushed the folder towards Cyril.

More light was hastily brought, and Cyril held the document at arm's length. "Hmph, er, ehm ..." These and other unintelligible sounds escaped his florid mouth as he struggled to come to an understanding of the letter's contents. "It says Simon wants all the property put in a trust, whatever that may be, for the benefit of the Pearce family as an 'hole, it says."

"May I be able to offer some explanations here?" Michael injected.

Looking around at the blank looks of the assembly, Michael continued. "Grandfather wishes that the property be placed in a legal entity called a family trust, to ensure the property will continue to be used by, and the profits used for, the benefit of the Pearce family. No individual can ever take it from the others. Also, importantly, it means that death duties payable to the government on a property title-holder's death, are bypassed, as a trust is in perpetuity – I mean, does not die, so to speak. Grandfather passes his role as trustee to one he nominates in his will. You will see, Uncle Cyril, you are appointed trustee; one other, yet to be appointed, will handle administration of all the trust's affairs. A further appointment should be a legal expert, a lawyer well versed in English law. He should probably be from outside the family unless a suitably qualified person is available from within."

"The Trefarthans are distantly related to your Uncle Peter's side o' the family by marriage. Our lawyers are Smithers, Trefarthan and Trefarthan of Truro. We'll need 'em to look at this anyhow. We can go in on the morn if it suits 'e, lad," said Cyril.

Michael nodded his assent adding, "The sooner the better, as far as I am concerned, as I must rejoin my ship in three days, thence a transfer. I am being seconded into the Royal Navy."

"There's also the matter of arrangin' John Joseph's midshipman's berth in the navy – old George Trevarthan's the man fer that. We'll meet with him tomorrow. " Cyril finished speaking and passed a flagon of mead around the men in the company, first giving himself an ample glassful. The women sipped tea.

"And what of ye, young Michael, goin' in the British Navy for a while, is it?" asked Sidney Pearce.

"Indeed, sir. When the *Saratoga* leaves for America, a number of officers, myself included, are to join ships of the Royal Navy to gain experience in ship and fleet handling. I am honoured to be joining Admiral Nelson's flagship, HMS *Vanguard*."

Early next morning, Cyril and Michael left Penpeth for Truro, where they met with the family lawyers.

George Trefarthan had married Elizabeth Farmiloe, Margaret's daughter from St Just. He had been in legal practice for near 50 years and was somewhat of a stick-in-the-mud.

Michael was therefore disturbed when George suggested himself as the potential legal member to the proposed family trust.

"With the deepest respect, Mr Trefarthan, while your experience is obviously immense, are you not of an age where retirement should be more on your mind than the taking on of new, onerous responsibilities? My grandfather's instructions were explicit, in that a long-term solution to the protection of the assets be arranged," said Michael.

Unused to the directness of Americans, George Trefarthan spluttered so as to hide his indignation. "Young sir, you are concerned as to my age, is that it?"

"Ah, yes sir, I am. May I suggest your son, Mr Archibald Trefarthan, as the trustee, with you, sir, as adviser. This, I'm sure, would fulfil my grandfather's requirements," suggested Michael diplomatically.

The wily old lawyer accepted, thinking that the valuable business would at least stay with the firm. They would also retain some control over the valuable Penpeth property, a point uppermost in his mind. "If you so wish, young sir. An excellent compromise, don't you think, Cyril?"

"If ye says so, George, so be it," answered the farmer.

"Grand, I shall review the papers with Archibald and prepare our suggested alterations, if any," said the old lawyer.

"Can this be done today, if you please, sir? I believe there requires little change as Grandfather's lawyers are fully versed in English law. I apologise, but I must leave to rejoin my ship very soon. As I have power of attorney, I am able to sign and complete this business, as instructed," asked Michael.

The two men stayed at an inn near Cathedral Square. They would meet with the lawyers again at ten next morning.

Michael had asked his uncle to relate to him the circumstances of his Great-uncle Peter's death, and that of his wife.

"'Twere mighty sad, that'n, lad. Peter decided t' stay a year or so – it were near 40 year since he were transported. Would 'ave bin '88; 'im and Dorothy were off to Scilly t' catch up wi' the family. 'Eadin' back t' Falmouth direct instead o' Penzance as were usual, them got caught in the wors' spring gale in livin' memory. The ol' packet sprung a leak. Unable t' weather the Lizard they tried t' wear ship 'n 'ead back, when she broached in the trough of a mighty wave – the Lizard light keeper saw it! Nothin' nobody could do; she rolled over and sank wi' all 'ands. We got Dorothy's body back, buried in chapel she is, but ol' Peter weren't never not seen agin." Cyril looked grey in the reciting of the sad tale.

That evening Michael invited the extended family to the New Inn where a fine Cornish roast dinner had been prepared. He did not want to be a burden on the Roseland people.

The evening was going extremely well when a young man entered the inn and surreptitiously spoke to several of the men at the table. Cyril attempted to engage the young man in polite conversation. As several of them stood, doffed their caps and left, Michael asked his great-grandmother what was going on.

"Ship, me 'ansome. Some poor ship's aground, I'd reckon."

"And our men are going to the rescue?" asked Michael.

"Ye could call 'er a rescue, more like, ah, salvage, I'd call it; yes salvage be more like it," answered the ancient woman.

"Should I not join them, lend a hand?" asked Michael naively.

"I think ye in uniform might be a mite conspicuous lad. No, there'll be many a hand at the beach this night. No place for a young officer 'bout t' join Lord Nelson, no indeed," said Jane smiling.

His business with the solicitors successfully concluded, Michael was on his way to rejoin the *Saratoga* the very next morning. As his coach crested the rise heading east, he could see much of the coast. A large bark was lying on her beam ends a mile east of Portscatho. *Funny,* he thought, *that no one spoke again of the luckless ship or her crew.*

The carriage made its way over the crest of the final hill and began the steep, dangerous drive down to the ferry, over the River Tamar, out of Cornwall into Devonshire. The sight before him was magnificent as both the Channel and Mediterranean fleets were in port.

Ships of all sizes from cutters and yawls to the mighty 100-gun, three-decked first-rates. Literally hundreds of masts and spars rose from decks of ships that had been to the most far-flung corners of the earth, increasing the mighty British Empire.

There was one man who stood between England's plans for commercial and colonial domination of the known world. That man was Napoleon Bonaparte, the brilliant Corsican general who had conquered most of Europe in the name of France.

The French Revolution had seen the advancement of many more ordinary folk as *la belle France*'s aristocracy was put to the guillotine. Ordinary citizens, sick and tired of aristocratic domination, had flooded the city streets in blood, in a frenzy of republican fervour.

If the French could see this, they would concede that Britain ruled the waves, thought Michael, as his mail coach carefully negotiated the steep road down to the Plymouth waterfront.

Later Michael was in the great cabin of the *Saratoga*, taking his leave from Captain Dwight Daniels. "You have been an excellent second lieutenant, Michael. I am sorry to lose you. You are the future of our navy, so learn why these accursed British are such a power on the seas and come back in one piece to tell us. There's something big brewing, real big. Boney's cooking up something in the Mediterranean; he wants to weaken British supply lines to India. It's only the navy that stops him. You are about to witness a turning point in history, my boy, under the command of the greatest naval strategist the world has ever seen."

"Aye, sir. It's a great opportunity."

"Learn, Michael. Learn. America may well have to fight the British again. As you know, the Royal Navy is desperately short of trained seamen; they have been pirating manpower from our ships at sea and those of other nations. Why, as you look out yonder at all these ships y'all are looking at, many will be manned by many American seaman, pressed into the King's service. Congress will only put up with so much. We're hoping the French will take some of the sting out of the British, giving us time to build our defences."

Commander Daniels rose and shook Michael's hand. "I knew your father when he was in the service. Do as well as he, and the navy will be well satisfied. Remember, ears and eyes open, mouth firmly shut. All right?"

"Yes, thank you, sir. It's been grand serving under you. I will do my best." Michael left the cabin and made his way to the cutter waiting, oars raised at the chains.

The *Saratoga* was one of the American Navy's newest and largest ships. Carrying 52 guns and a crew of some 300 men, she was as a minnow to a pike compared with *Vanguard*. Michael climbed up the companionway, past three decks of closed gun ports and onto the main deck. He stared at her mainmast which was three feet thick.

The officer of the watch, a lad of 19 and the ship's most junior lieutenant, greeted him warmly. "Welcome to the *Vanguard*, sir," he said proudly. "The captain and first officer are ashore, sir. I have been accorded the task of introducing you to the ship and some of the crew. Do you wish to refresh yourself first, sir?"

"Thank you, no, lieutenant. I will be delighted to embark on the induction as soon as you are able. I am Michael Davidson, lieutenant, United States Navy."

"I am the sixth lieutenant of *Vanguard*, sir, Martin St Jerome, at your service," he said, eagerly commencing his tour of the mighty warship. "She was laid down in 1759, but remained incomplete until thirteen years later, when in '78 she finally went to sea as a flagship. Admiral Nelson recalls seeing her moored on the Thames awaiting completion when he joined his first ship, aged twelve."

As they walked slowly forward from the companionway the young lieutenant continued. "*Vanguard* is a second-rater, carrying 74 guns. On the lower gun deck are 28 twenty-pounders, and the upper deck has 28 twelves. Eighteen various guns are to be seen on the main deck, poop and fo'c'sle. The ship is 227 feet long on deck, 51 feet in beam and has a draft of 21 feet. She is 1,370 tons berthen, and our complement is 767 souls, including yourself, sir." The young man finished his breathless recitation with obvious pride.

"Excellent, Martin, thank you. How long have you been on board?" asked Michael.

"Since '94, sir. I've been through the recent refit as clerk to Mister D'Arcy, the first officer. I am well acquainted with the ship and will be happy to be of assistance any time you require. Ah, here is Mister Sexton, our bosun. May I leave you in his care for a while? I have to make the noon log record. Please present Lieutenant Davidson to the bosun's mates, Mister Sexton."

"Have you the time, Mister Sexton?" asked Michael.

"Indeed, sir, 't'll be me pleasure." The bosun was clearly not used to being asked 'if he had time' when being given an order. *Americans! Different, may be*, he thought, *but still a bloody officer.*

Later, as Michael strode the quarterdeck, his head struggling to remember the names and ranks of the dozens of men introduced to him, he began to realise what an enormous undertaking running a ship of this size was. Not to mention caring for her people in the tight confines of the gun decks. He couldn't imagine how the entire crew could muster on her deck at one time. Just to think of feeding 760-odd men twice a day made him giddy! He stood before the huge double wheel, the helm that guided the giant. Suddenly he realised that soon he would be in sole charge of the ship as a senior officer of the watch, directly under the eye of Admiral Nelson, somewhat daunting after the *Saratoga*, a mere 42-gun fourth-rater of 620 tons berthen.

His reverie ended when Martin St Jerome called to him from the main deck. "Captain Berry will see you now, sir."

Michael walked towards his destiny – a good first impression on his new captain, Nelson's flag captain to boot, was important. Most Royal Navy officers did not like Americans, calling them colonials and treating them with suspicion and distrust. Michael hoped fervently that Captain Berry was not of that ilk.

Michael knocked on his captain's door and waited; the marine guard eyed him with suspicion – he was wearing his United States Navy uniform.

"Enter," came the command from within.

Michael took a deep breath, sent a quick prayer aloft and opened the door, his six-foot frame bending deeply to clear the doorway and deck beams designed for much shorter stock.

"Davidson, is it?" asked Captain Berry.

"Yes, sir."

"Good Celtic name. Where are your roots?"

"Cornwall, sir. St Just-in-the-Roseland and the Isles of Scilly. I've just seen the area for the first time. Very beautiful, sir."

"Good, yes good. Many a fine seaman hails from Cornwall, that's for sure. You're tall, young man. I suggest you keep well away from Admiral Nelson – he is … ah … not at all tall. Yes, keep well to leeward of him. I've read your record, sent by Commander Daniels; he thinks highly of you. From a seafaring family too, I see?" Captain Berry skimmed the detail.

"Yes, sir, my great-great-grandfather was on the *Association* with Sir Cloudesley Shovell."

"Indeed. Wasn't the sailing master, was he? Should have been hung if he was."

"No, sir. Bosun's mate."

"Good, he wasn't responsible then. My tailor will be aboard shortly. You will need an English officer's uniforms; can't have the

Frogs thinking America has declared with us, eh? Have ye money for that lad?" asked the captain. "It will cost ye some three pounds for two working and a dress uniform – and shirts of course."

"Yes, sir, I have. Commander Daniels ordered that I report to you in my American uniform, sir. I trust this is in order?"

"Yes, yes, now sit ye down, man; ye'll damage my deckhead bashing it with your head like that. Let me give you some advice. Learn our ways and learn quickly; the admiral is a stickler. You need to hit the deck running, knowing what yer doing, understand?"

"I'll do my best, sir."

"Let's hope your best is good enough. We will be under way any time now. Know our terms and names of the ship's parts so our men can understand ye. Marine!" the captain bellowed. "My compliments to the first lieutenant. Ask him to join us."

Captain Berry returned to writing his report, ignoring the junior officer before him. Michael gazed around the cabin which had been made much smaller to accommodate the admiral's quarters. The captain's quarters on his father's ship were far more commodious.

After what seemed an age the first lieutenant knocked and entered. "You required my presence, sir?" said an immaculately attired officer, with that distinctly affected accent of the British aristocracy.

"Yes, thank you. This, D'Arcy, is your new fourth lieutenant, an, eh, American – Michael Davidson. The *Vanguard*'s first lieutenant, Lord D'Arcy Monmouth. You will simply address His Lordship as 'sir' on board, d'ye understand?" stated Captain Berry firmly.

"Yes, sir. Pleased to meet you, Lord Monmouth."

"You will be if you're a good officer; you certainly won't be if you're not," said the aristocrat haughtily.

"Take him with you, D'Arcy. Introduce him to the other officer; he's to see the tailor once he's done."

"Aye, sir," snapped both subalterns, who saluted and turned to leave, a gesture totally lost on the captain – he had returned to his never-ending report writing.

"Take two days and learn this ship, Lieutenant Davidson. You can join the larboard watch and be excused daylight watch-keeping while ye get orientated. I will examine you at the end of that time, understood?" said the first lieutenant gruffly.

A week later the admiral was piped aboard. When he was introduced to the ship's officers, Michael wished, for the first time in his life, that he was a foot shorter, closer to the height of Rear Admiral Sir Horatio Nelson.

Later that night, crowded into the admiral's day cabin, the great man addressed his officers. "As you have probably determined we have orders to reinforce the Mediterranean fleet. We will join the commander-in-chief Vice-Admiral Earl St Vincent – the first British fleet in that sea since 1796. From there we shall take control of the water from Bonaparte and the French fleet. We sail on tomorrow's tide. *Bon voyage*, gentlemen."

The admiral's lapse into French drew a titter from the company, once he himself had laughed at his own joke.

Continuing with uncharacteristic humour the admiral added, "Better station the fourth lieutenant at the mainmast in action. With his height the Frogs will have him quickly if he stands on the quarterdeck."

Michael blushed, but found the presence of mind to speak. "Thank you for your advice, sir," and saluted the man so small of stature yet so grand of deed. The company, including the taciturn Captain Berry, laughed. It seemed the ice was broken.

Michael was in awe of the massiveness of his ship's mast, rigging and timbers – they were a sight to behold. But it was the size of her sails that impressed him the most – acres of white canvas. The *Vanguard*, as flagship, was at the centre of the line, with seven ships of the line ahead and seven more behind. Five frigates accompanied the fleet, two scouting ahead and two abeam of *Vanguard* ready to convey the admiral's wishes wherever and whenever he needed them. The fifth frigate patrolled at the rear of the fleet. There was little chance they would be taken by surprise.

Lookouts were doubled as the fleet passed western France; escorts had sighted their sails and would inevitably report that a fleet was at sea headed south. Biscay was unusually uneventful, and the fleet anchored in Gibraltar without mishap.

During the voyage Lord D'Arcy Monmouth had steadily pressed his fourth lieutenant and found him all a superior officer could wish for. Apart for his disregard for the rigid discipline customary on a king's ship, Michael Davidson proved a fine seaman and navigator. He had the ability to continually update the ship's dead-reckoning position in his head. Like some diabolical futuristic machine, he came to the plotting table ready to plot the fleet's positions whilst his fellows would struggle, using pencil and paper.

The first lieutenant was no great navigator himself, but he knew one when he saw one.

They made their way down the Spanish and Portuguese coasts well offshore to avoid detection. A difference of opinion regarding the fleet's position occurred some days after sighting Cape Finisterre; no sun sights could be taken for a few days because of cloud cover.

The first officer whispered to his captain, "Mister Davidson puts us here, sir, 30 miles to seaward of Cape Trafalgar. If he is right, and I believe he is, we should come on the wind now or have a long, slow beat eastward to Gibraltar."

It happened that the admiral agreed with his flag captain as to the fleet's position, which had previously been handed to him by Michael. The frigate *Argus* was despatched to confirm. She returned five hours later having sighted the cape. The fleet was ordered hard on the wind, which shifted at sunrise, allowing an easy ride into port.

The admiral's barge was launched immediately the *Vanguard* came up hard to her anchors. Sir Horatio and Captain Berry repaired aboard the admiral of the fleet Lord St Vincent's flagship.

In the somewhat more relaxed atmosphere created by the absence of the senior officers, the first officer bade Michael join him in his cabin for a glass of port. "You were bang on man. How do you do it, Michael?"

"I guess I've been at sea all my life; navigation has always fascinated me. Our family's ships have been using chronometers for navigation for decades before Captain Cook proved Henderson's chronometer in his circumnavigation. I've a head for numbers, sir; they talk to me, paint pictures for me. It's numbers I do best."

"I've spoken to Mister Fitzgerald, the sailing master, and had it approved by the captain. The sailing master determines the ship's position by dead reckoning, I want you, Michael, to help with astronomical observations. This is unorthodox, but orthodox would have had us at sea three more days than was necessary."

"Thank you for your confidence, sir. I will enjoy being part of the navigational effort."

The young American was becoming more impressed by the British aristocrat each day of sailing with him. If numbers were his thing, then getting the best performance from his men was Lord D'Arcy Monmouth's, a man only five years his senior. They smiled as they sipped the fine port wine, as close as life on a man-of-war would allow.

Chapter 29
Battle of the Nile

Captain Berry was in a foul mood. He hated shipboard life in port, and they had been at Gibraltar several months awaiting orders, that is apart from two missions, one to Toulon and a raid to Corsica, the latter an attempt to annoy General Bonaparte, whose birthplace the island was. It was hoped that the raid would tempt the wily general to make a rash move, but he had far greater plans afoot.

For many months Napoleon had been moving an army, brigade by brigade, to the shore towns of the Mediterranean. To the casual observer they looked like a reinforcement, but Bonaparte had a much more cunning plan.

The British raids did not, as had been intended, initiate a responsive chase by the French Navy.

"The men are getting lazy, gentlemen," Berry said to his officers and senior NCOs. "Crack down on them. I received permission from the admiral to undertake an exercise in seamanship on the morrow; wind and tide should be fair. We shall shorten the anchor cables at first light and beat deeper into the bay, to a position near town, thus making revictualling speedier. We will be under the eyes of two senior admirals and the entire fleet. I need not remind you, I am sure, that any breach of discipline, incompetence or slacking will be severely dealt with. Any questions?" Captain Berry would brook nothing less than a flawless performance from his crew.

The chorus of, "Yes sir", was somewhat tentative.

"You gentlemen had better be more enthusiastic at dawn. Dismissed. Monmouth and Davidson remain." The first and fourth officers stood as their colleagues left the room.

"I've got that useless third Hargreaves a berth on Admiral Earl St Vincent's flagship as an arse-licker of no real import. At least he

326

won't be aboard here to disrupt the work of real seamen. Davidson, the first officer has recommended you for promotion over several well-connected juniors in the fleet, and I am inclined to agree with him. How say you, sir, are ye up to it? You will shift from the upper gun deck to the mainmast in action - might be a little exposed for your liking, eh?" chided the captain.

"I will keep my head down, sir, and thank you, sirs, for you confidence. I believe my skills are more aptly used in seamanship and navigation than gunnery," answered Michael.

"Your first opportunity then is on the morrow; be firm, the men will test you. Particularly Hodges, the bosun's mate at the mast. I note you tend to be light on them - the American way, what? But here, Davidson, we will have it the British way, the Royal Navy way. I do not favour officers carrying a rope's end as a starter, so you are expected to report slackers. I trust I am understood?"

"Yes, sir, crystal clear," answered Michael.

"Good, you both may leave."

"Thank you, D'Arcy, I had no idea," said Michael.

"I have been trying to rid myself of that idiot Hargreaves for a year; your promotion suits me well. But you may have cause to regret your new position by tomorrow night. The captain is hell-bent on flogging someone; I hope it's not you who will have to report that person. They don't flog in your navy, do they?"

"No, indeed not. My grandfather, when commodore, was instrumental in banning the hideous practice," answered Michael.

"I too hate the use of the cat. Beware on the morrow or your promotion may be short-lived." Lord D'Arcy Monmouth looked with some pity on his American colleague. "To avoid trouble you need to have the men on your side. They know what this exercise is about. But do you have the time?"

"May I relieve Hargreave's watch tonight, sir?"

"You may indeed, but you will be on deck for two watches as we have to ship in your replacement as yet."

"I can cope with that, sir. I need the time with the men," said Michael.

"As you will, then." The first officer turned and left with a smile of contentment.

At eight bells, Michael began his second watch with his new crew, at the end of which he would have been on deck for eigh hours. He caught sight of Hodges who moved towards him.

"Congratulations on your promotion, sir. Anything I can do fer 'e, sir, just ask."

"Thank you, Hodges, yes there is. You may escort me over the main rigging, put the hands to work checking every detail so it is correct for the morning. I will meet each of them at their station."

"It's pretty dark aloft, sir. Perhaps it'd be better done in daylight," replied the heavy-set bosun's mate.

"I've a lot to learn before dawn. I don't want to let you all down now, do I. It would look bad if a man was flogged for a mistake I have made," replied Michael.

"Aye aye, sir; as you wish, sir." The older, more experienced man felt this American would do, after all.

A tired but alert Michael Davidson stood to his position as the second anchor left the seabed. With the foretopsail aback, the cumbersome vessel swung as predicted. Michael called to loose the main topgallant, as the sail was sheeted home; the foretop yard swung its full arc – about 160 degrees. The manoeuvre was flawlessly performed; the captain stood emotionless as if perfection was the norm.

She slid slowly on her first tack, making a bare 20 degrees into the wind. Never did a single knot ship speed seem so fast as the dock, a mile distant, got closer very rapidly.

"Prepare to go about!" called the first lieutenant. "Helm up, by the lee."

Vanguard swung slowly across the wind, at first Michael thought too slowly. The light breeze finally put the foretop aback, allowing Michael's crew to reset the main topgallant on the new tack. It was dangerous, a slight mistake, a shift in the wind, could put the sails aback, driving her out of control stern first into another anchored vessel.

The tacking manoeuvre was performed five times when Michael's maintop lookout called, "Deck below; shift approaching, 45 to larboard." They had to tack again and quickly.

The shift had allowed D'Arcy Monmouth to con the ship to her new allocated anchorage without further tacks. "Furl sail, drop the bower anchor," he called.

"All too easy, Mister Monmouth," said the captain. He was about to leave the quarterdeck when a cry from the chains indicated something was amiss.

"Anchor fouled in the hawse," was the cry from forrard.

The second lieutenant, George Ferrier, called, "Drop the kedge quickly, for God's sake, or we'll drift astern and not have swinging room."

The kedge, a considerably smaller anchor than the main bower, seemed to skip.

"More warp, more warp. Move, move," Ferrier called.

At last the ship's bow swung to the wind.

"Interrogate the anchor crew, Mister Monmouth. I'll have those to blame in my cabin once the ship is secure."

"'E's happy now he's got some poor bastard to flog," said Hodges within Michael's earshot.

"And you'll be alongside him at the gratings, Hodges, if ye don't mind your tongue!" retorted Michael with more determination than he felt.

"Aye, sorry sir," answered the bosun's mate, angered at being shown up in front of his men.

A poorly made temporary lashing had failed to part as it should have, thus causing the anchor cable to kink and jam on the hawse. The culprit was a pressed man, brought aboard in Plymouth prior to the fleet sailing. It was but his fifth time taking part in anchoring the huge warship. He was brought on deck, having been sentenced summarily by the captain to two dozen lashes. Once the ship's company was assembled, the man was stripped to the waist, tied to a hatch grating, shaking uncontrollably. Bosun's mate Morgan, nicknamed the slasher, untied the cord of a red baize cloth bag, which held the dreaded cat-o'-nine-tails.

"Commence punishment!" called the captain after reading the articles of war to the ship's company. They were, as always, required to witness corporal and capital punishment, as a deterrent – the sight of a man's skin being lashed from his bones tended to be quite effective in that endeavour.

Morgan, a large, well-made man, swished the cat in the air a few times before bringing its nine lead-tipped leather thongs hard on the sailor's back. The man screamed through the gag in his mouth, as nine red welts appeared on his skin. 'One' was called, then 'two', 'three', and on the cruel scene went. At sixteen Michael shuddered. As he felt something hit his face, he realised it was a piece of the man's living flesh. It was all he could do not to move, as to do so would have brought the wrath of the captain down upon him.

At last it was over. The man, now mercifully unconscious, was cut down, the 24 lashes multiplied by the nine thongs had removed most of the skin from his back, his shoulder blade bones on view in the sunlight.

Michael vowed he would never accuse a man of anything that could bring this barbaric punishment down on him.

The mood on the ship was sombre, relieved only when a sloop of war entered the anchorage with dispatches from the Admiralty in London. Their orders were to proceed to sea, hunt down the French fleet and finally, capture Napoleon Bonaparte, who was using the fleet to cover an amphibious landing somewhere in the Mediterranean theatre – but where? This was the burning question confronting Rear Admiral Sir Horatio Nelson, that warm spring day of 1798.

* * *

"Gentlemen, your attention please." Nelson brought the meeting to order.

The company consisted of the captains and sailing masters of *Vanguard*, *Minotaur* and *Defence* – all 74-gun ships of the line – as well as those in command of three of the fastest frigates on the navy list. Most junior among this top-brass company was Michael Davidson, his navigational skills earning him his place.

"We have become aware that Bonaparte has been gathering a large force along the Mediterranean coast in France and Italy. His fleet at Toulon is ready for sea. What is his target? I hardly think he will be heading west into the guns of our fleet. So it is to the east his ambitions lie. The Directorate of France cannot deal with his popularity at home; he has been almost too successful in subduing Central Europe, and his popularity with the masses has made him too dangerous, politically, to allow him home for long. They are sending him on an expedition far enough away to remove him from the limelight, yet do us harm. Britain is the only nation opposing them now, so while they remain expansionist in policy, their plans will be to the detriment of England, that is for sure.

"We will sail close to the Spanish coast. Now we have finally beaten them I foresee no possibility of any opposition. What is left of their fleet is on the Atlantic coast. We will head for Toulon and discover their intentions. Keep close, only five cables distant, so my signals can be seen. *Minotaur* shall be in the van, with *Defence* at *Vanguard*'s rear. The frigates ahead and to landward shall patrol up to 30 miles from the squadron, with the third ready to return and report to the admiral of the fleet the moment we discover anything."

No questions were asked for the little man simply raised his eyes from the chart he was using to describe the manoeuvre. "Should we become separated we shall all meet off northern Sardinia and regroup. Thank you, gentlemen, we sail on the morning tide."

The fleet covered the length of the Spanish coast without mishap. At Barcelona it headed east-north-east into open water for the 200 miles to Toulon. Halfway across the Gulf of Lion, old Jack Smithson, the sailing master, looked aloft anxiously; the wind had backed to a cold north-westerly, the sky clear.

"What concerns you, Mister Smithson?" asked Michael.

"Mistral, sir, the cursed mistral, and we're in for a good 'un. See 'em mare's tails up high? Better give the bad news to the captain – gale afore nightfall, I reckons." Thirty years at see had taught Smithson the signs, good and bad – these were bad.

"Hand the main course and spanker; gaskets good and tight, if you please," Michael called as he went below to report to Captain Berry.

"We'll be blown clear across the Ligurian Sea if this builds as Smithson suggests, and I concur. Under bare poles we'll make five knots, sir," reported Michael.

As Captain Berry was reporting to the admiral, a loud cracking sound was heard.

The first lieutenant knocked and entered the admiral's day cabin without waiting for an invitation. "Main t'gallant's blown its gaskets and taken out the topmast, sir; the debris has carried away the foretopmast in its fall. The wreckage is swinging wildly; no man would survive aloft to cut it away unless we can stop the rolling."

"Set a storm staysail, and bring the wind abeam; signal our intentions to the fleet, Mister Monmouth. Set a course for the rendezvous, if you please. We must not further damage the fleet."

The admiral displayed no emotion but calmly looked back at his chart, adding, "Yes, make for the lee of Sardinia – it means having Corsica as a lee shore but we will have plenty enough sea room."

Vanguard anchored alone, damaged and vulnerable in the shelter offered by San Pietro Island. The next day repairs were under way as the other two 74s anchored protectively either side of the wounded flagship. The frigates were not seen again; however, one had returned to report to the commander-in-chief. Earl St Vincent, correctly fearing time to be short, dispatched ten ships of the line to reinforce Nelson's squadron, with orders to find and destroy Bonaparte's fleet.

Intelligence was obtained from a trading ship that Napoleon had attacked and taken the island of Malta, leaving the island heavily garrisoned. The French were five days ahead of them.

"It's Egypt, by God. Yes, that's his target. From there Bonaparte can attack our supply lines to India! Set course for Alexandria, Captain Berry. Signal the fleet." Nelson looked calm, his decision made.

The British fleet arrived off Alexandria to find the harbour empty – no French fleet had been seen.

Nelson ordered the fleet northward. "It's the devil's luck I have," Admiral Nelson complained to his flag captain. "Where is that cursed Bonaparte?"

Two nights later Michael Davidson was officer of the watch.

"Black as the insides of a whale," the sailing master said to him.

"Deck below, a light t' port," called the maintop lookout. All eyes strained to find the elusive if not phantom light.

"Where man? Can ye still see it?" yelled Michael.

After a short silence the man replied, "No, sir, it were but 'n instant."

"Double the lookout, bosun, if you please," Michael ordered, going below to report to the captain.

"You've doubled the watch?"

"Yes, sir."

"Then carry on, Mister Davidson. We're not chasing ghosts all over the ocean. If we had a frigate we could investigate," said Captain Berry returning to the comfort of his wide sea berth.

Bonaparte realised that the British had passed him in the night, having got to Alexandria before him. When his scouts had discovered Alexandria free of a battle fleet he ordered an immediate invasion. The Ottoman Empire, Britain's allies, then controlled Egypt.

* * *

It wasn't until five weeks later that Nelson obtained the information he required. He had passed the French that night of the light sighting; his enemy was now in control of the north of Egypt. With Bonaparte having arrived the day after Nelson had left Alexandria and sailed north, Admiral Sir Horatio Nelson was not a happy man, but at least now he knew where his quarry lay. Had he attacked the fleet with their lumbering troop transports at sea, the invasion of Egypt may have been foiled, possibly with the capture of Napoleon, thus altering the course of history.

The captains of HMS *Alexander* and HMS *Swiftsure* reported that a fleet of transports were anchored at Alexandria. The absence of the French battle fleet surprised the admiral, and then he stabbed his finger at the chart. "Thirty miles westward, gentleman – Aboukir Bay is the only place they could be. Make all speed; we will be there mid-afternoon with this fair breeze. The flagship will take the van."

"Deck below! French fleet ahead, anchored in line of battle," called a lookout.

"Battle stations; signal the fleet. We have the wind gage of 'em, by God," called the little admiral excitedly. "We shall attack now. Call that young American navigator of yours, if you please, Captain Berry."

Michael Davidson stood before the flag captain, the admiral and his adjutant lieutenant. Totally overawed by the weight of brass before him, he awaited their pleasure.

"Lieutenant Davidson, I believe Admiral Comte de Brueys has presented us with a golden opportunity. There are extensive shoals extending from Aboukir Castle point at the west of the bay. From my observations, the French line begins further away from the shoals than the French admiral believes – far enough to allow the passage of some of our ships ahead and inshore of the leading French ship, *Guerrier*. We will thus have the opportunity to bombard each of the enemy's ships from both sides at the same time. Further, the enemy is not moored with hawsers from ship to ship, so not preventing us from breaking their line. You have observed the situation from aloft. Am I correct in the positioning so far?"

"Yes indeed, sir. I believe you to be correct."

Michael had come to the same conclusion – the French had left the gaps the admiral had suggested.

"You have spent your life sailing the Chesapeake, Bahamas and other shoal waters, have you not?"

"Yes, admiral, I have."

"Good! British officers get testy when sailing in confined waters; I want you to go aboard the lead ship as pilot. Join Captain Hood on *Zealous* – he has the honour of first blood. Here are his orders in my hand; go with God, young man."

The admiral moved the conversation to *Vanguard*'s part of the action. She, with two other ships, was ordered to attack the megalithic, 120-gun *Orient*, Admiral de Brueys's flagship.

Michael was quickly lowered to a gig, which raced across the water so as to cut off her target, the 74-gun HMS *Zealous*. It was no mean feat for Michael to scramble aboard the racing ship. Once aboard he handed his orders to Captain Hood.

"You'd better be as good as the admiral believes. I care not to hand my ship over to a bloody colonial who may harbour French sympathies. Put us aground, sir, and I'll shoot you personally."

Ignoring the captain's comments, Michael addressed the assembled deck officers. "What is your draught?"

"Seventeen feet, sir. We have the shallowest draft in the fleet - it would be why the admiral picked us to lead," came the answer.

"I would like to con the ship from the foremast crosstrees, if you please, sir, and have a leadsman call from both starboard and larboard," Michael requested.

"As you will. Mister Fredricks!" Captain Hood called out to his first officer. "Have a midshipman stationed at the foot of the mast so he can repeat the lieutenant's directions, and have as many of the gun crews as you can spare to help at the sheets and braces until we are in action."

Michael climbed to the fore crow's nest as *Zealous* raced towards the enemy. Shot from Aboukir Castle flew harmlessly overhead, as did that from *Guerrier*. The shot was erratic and poorly aimed, as many of the ship's crew were ashore on foraging parties, stripping the countryside of water and food. Napoleon had taken almost all of the fleet's supplies to feed his 31,000-man army.

Michael had an excellent view of the upper Aboukir Bay the instant he was aloft. He saw an outcrop protruding from the main shoal that was hidden from deck level. "Port fifteen, no twenty," he screamed.

At speed, the lumbering *Zealous* responded quickly enough to miss the rocks just four feet under the water.

"Captain Hood, keep her high, if you please. There's a sunken rock fine to starboard; once we pass it, the bay opens. We will have 300 yards from the enemy line shoreward before we would ground," called Michael coolly.

"Thank you, Mister Davidson. Your arrival at our masthead was indeed timely," the captain replied.

"Fire broadside," called Captain Hood, now in his element as he positioned his ship abeam of *Guerrier*. "Hand sail, prepare to anchor. She's swinging and can't hit us. Attach a warp from aft so we can position ourselves."

Insufficient time was available for all the captain's commands to be completed before the ship had passed its prey. The anchor, however, grabbed hold just ahead of the next French ship, *Conquérant*, which became heavily engaged by *Zealous*. Hood's spring lines to his anchor cable allowed him to take the anchor's strain from either end of the ship. This allowed him to position the ship so her guns at point-blank range would cause devastating fire. The French ship could not get her attacker in her sights, being anchored fore and aft.

The second British ship in the line crossed and anchored in front of *Guerrier*'s bow, set up as was *Zealous*, before pounding her quarry to submission. Many of the French captains were still aboard the flagship at conference. They were totally surprised by the attack, which Admiral de Brueys had thought would not come till daylight.

Surprised, confused and undermanned, the French fleet could do little. Having attacked with the wind behind them, the British ships simply destroyed one anchored enemy after another. It was simply a matter of moving along their line – they encountered minimum retaliation. Undamaged French ships to the east of the battle were unable to up-anchor and assist their companions, as they were downwind.

While attacking the French flagship *Orient*, Nelson was wounded on the forehead; blood flowed so heavily he thought he might die. He handed command to his flag captain, Berry, who now had the responsibility of the entire battle as well as fighting with his own ship. After examination by the ship's surgeon and the application of several stitches, the admiral returned to his quarterdeck.

At nine in the evening, just five hours after the conflict began, Nelson had control of the battle. The French flagship was well ablaze. An hour later she disintegrated as the fires reached her powder magazines. The explosion caused flaming wreckage to set fire to other ships within a 500-yard radius. Nine hundred men had perished in a heartbeat.

A dazed young sixth lieutenant aboard the aptly named French 74-gun *Franklin*, struggled to his feet, around him his shipmates lay either dead or grievously wounded. He saw no other officers standing; the captain had been decapitated by chain shot. His ship's first officer, pinned by a massive splinter to the mainmast stump, babbled incoherently, blood dripping from his mouth. The 21-year-old was struck dumb by the carnage around him; body parts lay scattered like autumn leaves dripping their liquid gore onto sun-bleached decks, a picture surreal to his young eye. He looked over *Franklin*'s port side and saw her aggressor sitting quietly to her anchors, guns quiet, waiting for his ship's final submission.

A marine, no older than him, severely wounded and bleeding to death, held his loaded musket towards the officer. The intention was obvious, but through his mask of pain, he was still a French marine – he would not surrender.

The youngest officer of the ship sensed his comrade's last wish. Taking the weapon he crouched behind the bulwark and surveyed his ship's attacker. Slowly he raked the British warship with his clearing eyes, coming across her name in gold leaf just under the cat head. 'ZEALOUS' he read clearly.

A movement in the rigging of her foremast caught his attention – it was an officer, his white pantaloons showing clearly in the glow given off by burning ships. Yes, he was alive; he moved temporarily out of sight. Then – again – the leg, encased in its telltale white sheath. The young officer raised the musket. Something told him to stop, but he was focused on retaliation. In the heat of the moment he squeezed the trigger as he had done on many occasions before. His aim was good; the enemy officer fell back into the crow's nest.

The reply from *Zealous* was as swift as it was devastating. Captain Hood ordered a further broadside loaded with canister and grape shot, aimed high so as to sweep *Franklin*'s decks. The hail of lead scythed across unprotected open decks, killing and maiming. Had regular ball shot been fired, the young French officer would have been blown to pieces; the bulwark, however, had sufficient stoutness to withstand grape. Blood ran down his face from a graze where a ball had ricocheted into his place of cover. He was numb and tired, all resistance savagely smashed out of him. He, as the highest rank standing, brandished a white cloth in submission.

As her enemy was now totally subdued, a boat left *Zealous* with a boarding party to take possession of her prize. Fires were put out and the living brought onto the main deck.

"Bring that officer back with you, Mister Jones. He's the only man of rank left alive; he must surrender the ship officially to Captain Hood," said *Zealous*'s second lieutenant.

Soon after, they brought the frightened prisoner aboard.

"Your sword, if you please. Your name and rank for our record," asked Hood.

"Jonathan Pearce," said the man, handing the captain his hanger.

Captain Hood was taken off guard. "Are you English, by God?"

"No, sir, I am American," said the young officer in the tattered French naval uniform.

"Then, sir, you have a countryman aboard this ship – one Michael Davidson. He, however, has the decency to wear the uniform of the Royal Navy!" The captain watched for any emotion. He was surprised at the amount he received.

"Michael Davidson! A tall man of 22 years, sir?" asked the shocked French officer.

"Ah, yes. You are acquainted with him?" asked Captain Hood, his suspicions aroused.

"Y ... yes, sir – he is my cousin! Can I see him? We were close as boys growing up," said Jonathan.

"I was just apprised of his condition. He was shot by a sniper from your ship. It was that shot that caused me to order the final broadside. The sniper's ball shattered the lieutenant's knee. I am afraid amputation was the only option the surgeon had. He is recovering but not yet conscious. He's fortunate our surgeon is the best in the navy," said the captain. "Guard, lock him below. I shall have Michael's condition relayed to you. When the surgeon deems it wise, you may visit him," and Jonathan was dismissed.

Jonathan, the lively, vibrant young man, scion of the Carlos Pearce family, had shot his cousin and brought him to death's door. This fact he omitted to mention to his captors. Had they known him they would have seen his features twist and change. Once in the privacy of his cell he sobbed himself to sleep.

A faint dawn showed in the east at four am, after which some sporadic fighting resumed. Several French ships were run ashore, the only option other than surrender, further fighting being deemed foolish.

The British 74 *Bellerophon* had run aground on the spur identified by Michael Davidson earlier. The dawn found her damaged but not yet past saving. She was eventually expertly extricated from her dangerous position on a lee shore. While at anchor she was attacked by a French frigate. The ever-busy Captain Berry saw her situation and rushed to her aid, crippling the smaller ship with a single broadside. She could not, however, prevent two 74s and two frigates under Admiral Villeneuve escaping to seaward. To attempt to engage such a force without support would have been death for the ship and her crew.

For the rest of the day the British fleet were kept busy plucking bodies from the sea; for every Englishman there seemed to be a dozen French. Survivors were rounded up and made prisoners of war.

The fleet was to remain at Aboukir Bay for two weeks. Nelson then split the fleet, leaving five ships to hold the bay. The prizes were made as seaworthy as possible while the ships too badly damaged were set fire to where they lay. *Zealous* had suffered only one death and little damage; she was sent as escort with the convoy of prizes, first to Gibraltar then on to England.

Most of the captured French sailors were released ashore under strict parole that they would never again take up arms against England. These terms were soon broken by Napoleon himself, who formed them into an infantry unit. Without support from the sea the French ambitions in the Middle East were largely thwarted. It was many years before the remnants of the *Grande Armée* of the East returned to France, beaten – half their number had died. Napoleon left the army to others and headed home. By the time their remnants finally reached French shores, he had France firmly in his grip.

The Battle of the Nile was considered a turning point in the war. The French fleet would not see battle with the British again until Trafalgar.

Zealous rolled steadily westward, the summer calms impeding the fleet's progress. The progress of a certain injured crew member, one Lieutenant Michael Davidson, was good. Aided by his cousin, he hopped around the deck with assistance from a shoulder crutch made for him by Jonathan.

During daylight Jonathan was given the freedom of the deck, where he would spend time with Michael, tending to his every need. At night he was locked in steerage with a few other French prisoners the British had decided not to release. As the young man lay in his bunk, one word went constantly through his mind – amputee. Michael was an amputee, and he had caused it. He became drawn and tired through lack of sleep and self-mortification. It was a long way home; could he keep the terrible secret from his family once back at Porthellick?

Chapter 30

A family divided

The cousins were given leave to disembark the ship at Gibraltar. Jonathan's all-consuming feelings of guilt only increased when Michael had begged his captain to release his cousin as a prisoner of war into his parole. All Jonathan had to do was swear not to rejoin the French.

In the great cabin of HMS *Zealous*, the young man swore.

"Gentlemen, I swear on the Bible not to take arms again with the French against England." At this point he broke down and snivelling he added, "I am, however, guilty of a crime my conscience can no longer contain."

"So, young man, what is this heinous crime to which you wish to confess?" asked Captain Hood.

Looking at his cousin who had so gallantly stood for him, summoning all the resolve he could muster, he told his tale. "It was I who fired the shot that injured you so grievously, Michael. Oh, to God that that last salvo had killed me; alas, it is not so. I am to blame for this act of war that has your situation so."

Captain Hood was a wise old sea dog. Well renowned for being firm but fair, he was one of the navy's most liked captains. His men never shirked, they fought for their captain first, England second.

"Regrettable, yes, and an attack on an officer of His Majesty's service is a serious offence. We must, however, temper this by recalling the situation we were in. The Royal Navy was attacking the French fleet, an act of war! You were, for whatever reasons you may have had, on the side of our and your cousin's enemy. Should the situations be reversed and the French had won, I could see from their point of view that your action in continuing to fight under heavy disadvantage being worthy of the highest recognition. What say you, Lieutenant Davidson?"

"I agree, sir. Jonathan did not know who he was firing at, and his target was an enemy officer. He did not even know that I had been selected for secondment to the Royal Navy; he thought I was still an American naval officer. It was I who had considered the possibility of Jonathan being on board one of the ships we were engaging. My cousin acted as his duty demanded, sir." While Michael said the words, his face showed confusion, a fact noted by his younger cousin.

"This is not a matter to warrant further investigation from the Royal Navy's point of view. You must reconcile this matter yourselves; an unfortunate matter, indeed. On behalf of His Majesty's service, I commend you, Lieutenant Davidson, for your service in recognition for which I have recommended a decoration. Here are your honourable discharge papers and your cousin's release document, with its conditions. You are hereby cleared to join the American-bound Portuguese caravel, as is your wish. Goodbye, gentlemen, and good luck."

Both boys saluted, saying simultaneously, "Thank you, sir," and left.

The caravel made good time, passing the Canary Islands after seven days; the ship was now in the trade winds with a bone in her teeth, the wind on her starboard quarter. The cousins had not been in serious discussion regarding the injury since that day in Captain Hood's cabin.

One sunny afternoon, ten days out, after Michael had checked the ship's position, he sat beside Jonathan and spoke quietly in an effort to relieve the tension between them. "Cousin, I can see holding this incident close to your heart has caused you much torment; the pain is as the written word upon your face. I agree totally with Captain Hood – fate has dealt us a cruel blow. I am clear in my mind you are guilty of nothing. I can wish it hadn't happened; I am grateful it was not the marine who held the gun – had it been so, my wound could have been fatal." Michael could see his words fell on closed ears.

"Would that I could sever my own limb, that it could repair yours; alas, it cannot be. I am sentenced to watch as you hobble on a crutch while I still can run as a deer. I understand completely what Captain Hood said, but it changes nothing – I injured you, the means are of no consequence. It just won't leave my mind." The anguish on Jonathan's face gave evidence to his inner pain.

Just then the ship's priest, who was standing by, moved to join them. "My son, I 'ave 'eard what you 'ave said. A confession before God will 'eal you - you are of the Mother Church, I understand?"

"Yes, father, we are," answered Jonathan, "and yes, I will be happy to take confession with you. But even if God forgives me, can I forgive myself?"

"Cousin, it was an evil twist of fate, not an act intended to harm me. You have nothing to be forgiven for; there is no misdeed to answer for," persuaded Michael.

Jonathan turned a tired face that looked much older than his 21 years towards Michael. "You are generous to a fault, dear cousin, and believe me I fervently wish your words were enough. Do you not see what looking at you in your condition each day does to me? I did this to you, I did it, the circumstances will never alter that."

The caravel *Santa Maria* berthed at Manhattan docks. A runner was sent to the Ministry of Health, to inform the Secretary for Health that his two nephews had arrived. Soon the two young men had forgotten their cares being once again reunited with their family.

Their three female cousins pestered the boys and treated them as heroes. Anna, Jonathan's childhood sweetheart, excitedly announced her engagement to a young New York doctor. She noticed a darkness in her once fun-loving if dramatic cousin. But he would not be drawn; the boys had made a pact to keep the accident a secret from the family.

After a few days Uncle Juan spoke at dinner. "I have some good news, Michael. The department has been funding research at Harvard on the development of artificial limbs.

"I understand that some great advances have been made in the last year or two; I have made arrangements for you to attend a clinic the day after tomorrow - political position has some advantages. They are going to see if you are a suitable candidate for a trial of the latest device. It is truly amazing, most lifelike."

"That's wonderful, darling. It will be good to have some good news to impart at Grandfather Simon's birthday. It will be a grand affair; the whole family will be at Porthellick for the first time in years. Your mother and father should arrive from the Orient any day, Michael, as will Juanita and her new husband. Our two young heroes will make quite a splash." Rebecca Pearce, the epitome of a statesman's wife, eased the tension in the room.

"I am hardly a hero, Aunt; my side lost the most decisive naval battle in modern history," said Jonathan, barely able to hide his anguish.

"You fought for your country, young man. Be sure, that is heroism. America cannot remain immune to war forever, though many believe our isolation secures us just such immunity. When you return to naval service here you will have much to share from your time with the French – as will Michael from the British. Mark my words, we will have to fight either Britain or France once their current squabble is decided, do you not agree, dear?" said Rebecca.

"As a cabinet member, I have heard nothing of sabre rattling. But I understand preparations to defend our country are well in hand." Juan would not be further drawn.

"Well, young man, you were with Nelson at the Nile! They are saying it was the most decisive battle of modern times. What are your thoughts?" asked Dr Archibald Watts, the head of Harvard's prosthesis programme, turning once again to examine Michael's stump. You are lucky, young sir. Those naval surgeons are mostly untrained butchers. The way the man has stitched a flap of skin over the stump has prevented infection and given us something reasonable to work with. Having used your navy peg leg, you have hardened it nicely. We will only have to make minor trimmings."

Michael flinched visibly at the thought, his memory recalling the shocking feel of the surgeon's saw as it cut through his living flesh above his shattered knee, while he regurgitated the majority of the rum he had been forced to imbibe by way of anaesthetic.

Seeing his patient's alarm, Dr Watts said hurriedly, "Fear not, young man, opium is in common use here; you won't feel a thing."

Watts then produced an artificial leg with a knee and ankle joint made of metal. "You will be the first of many to test the 'Runner', as we call it. We are working on a model that can attach your own tendons to the knee; the research for this is not yet complete. But even with this prototype you will walk – it will be over to you as to how well, but from what I see of you, you will work hard at it, I am sure."

"Indeed I will, doctor. My cousin's sanity is as much at stake as my ability to walk. I must be walking in five weeks. We have a large family gathering, and I intend to walk with my new leg."

The doctor could see Michael was determined, but cautioned, "Ah yes - I would have thought four months would be required, but we can but try. If you devote all your time to the project, but not inflame your stump, who knows? I will measure you today; come back Friday for a fitting."

At Porthellick the news of his grandson's injury had had a bad effect on Simon Pearce. Since his heart attack Simon had grown frail.

"Madam," Simon said to his nurse indignantly. "I will travel to New York and visit my grandsons; neither you nor my dear wife will prevent me. Am I not still master of my own house?"

"Sir, it would be most unwise for you to undertake such a journey. Jonathan will be here next week, and I hear from Dr Juan that Michael is doing well and will follow soon. Please be content. By the time you got to New York, the family would be headed here," reasoned the nurse.

"Besides, darling," his wife interrupted, "the 'hole family will be moving soon. Juan's department is one of the first to relocate to the new capital. The family will be living three miles away. Be patient, my love." Isabella's dulcet tones affected her husband of nearly 50 years as usual. "Besides, Juanita and José will be here soon with a new grandson we 'ave yet to see. Will you be away risking your life and miss their arrival?"

"I am the head of this house in name only, madam," Simon said gruffly. "Your logic, my dear, is impeccable as usual, damn it."

Three days later, Juanita, the daughter they had last seen eight years ago, before she had been given up for dead, entered the family home, followed by her sister Isabellita and Colonel Robert Davidson.

"Mother, you look so well. Father, I can see they are taking good care of you. How are you feeling?" asked a concerned Juanita.

"Never mind about me! Let me hold you, girl - young woman, I should say," exclaimed the delighted patriarch, tears filling his eyes. "And this young man must be José."

"It is a great pleasure to meet you at last, commodore. Our families have joined not only very successfully in business, but as a family also."

The tall, dark stranger bowed deeply to Isabella and kissed her hand.

"Ah, a true Portuguese gentleman. America is full of gallantry, sir, but you wear your ancestry as a cloak. I am sure I know your grandmother," said Isabella in Portuguese.

"It will be my pleasure to converse with you as to the home country at your leisure, madam, although apart from school I have spent little time there," José replied in their mother tongue.

"And this is our son Miguel. Greet your grandparents, my son."

The three-year-old moved forward on his father's cue, bowed deeply and said, "My pleasure to meet with you, Grandfather and Grandmother," delighting the entire company.

The next day the Davidsons arrived with Jonathan, who, while delighted at his cousin's progress using his prosthesis, was still noticeably reserved.

It was a further week before Robert, Isabellita, Caroline and Michael arrived. They had just got off the coach from New York. Michael was as anxious to see his grandfather as Simon was to see him.

Simon held on to his grandson in an emotionally charged hug.

"See, Grandfather, I can walk as well as any man, and the next generation of artificial limbs will have me running as fast as any of you."

Simon was unable to speak for fear of betraying himself.

Eventually Isabella, looking worried, suggested he sit in the drawing room. "Michael can talk of the sea and war while you rest, my dear."

"Yes, Grandfather, it will be good for me as well. This tin leg makes me sore," added Michael, now seriously concerned at how Simon looked, so drawn and tired.

"You all fuss horribly; I am fine. Besides, we have two of the best doctors in America in the house, as well as the excellent Mrs McNab," said Simon.

He did, however, allow himself to be seated beside his grandson and looked relieved for it.

It was when Carlos, Sally Antoinette and the Davidsons were left alone together that tension became apparent. Many things were left unsaid of their sons' participation in a battle that had changed the world.

It was fortuitous that José chose that moment to appear in the doorway. "Senhor Pearce 'as asked if you gentlemen would be available for an informal discussion as to our company's position in China. 'E is in the study."

The men left the ladies and joined Simon.

"The figures I have been receiving are, on the face of it, pleasing to say the least. We have four ships now plying the China trade, and our offices are well established in Macau. It seems America is enraptured with the porcelain and silks we import. The medicines, Juan tells me, are being copied here to good effect. This will, in time, lessen that important branch of the trade. I sense though things look good, we must guard our future carefully."

"Your synopsis is correct, sir," said Robert. "As far as porcelain is concerned, much inferior product is coming in at low prices. We have been forced to mix our cargoes, as there is only so much market for the expensive wares. We are also faced with locally made product, which in turn lowers our returns. The same is happening with silk. Silk worms and Chinese artisans have been imported to California; while the local product will take some years to have a great impact on our operation, have an impact in the future, it must."

Juan then spoke. "I must add that in the field of medicine we are making considerable advances. We grow poppies for laudanum and are creating many new drugs in several growing enterprises throughout the country. But the costs are high, and the imported products are cheaper and better quality."

"Further to this, more and more ships arrive each year. When the Franco-British conflict ends, those countries will be vying for Chinese product again, pushing up our buying costs," offered Carlos. "I believe we should attempt to wrest some of the spice trade from the Dutch - spices are hard to replicate here. We can buy from them but they charge prohibitively; if we could buy directly we would make huge profits."

"That would amount to a declaration of war, would it not?"

"Bonaparte is holding the Dutch in a position of neutrality, Robert, a position which allows them freedom away from Europe. They can use what warships they have to protect their trading fleets, as they cannot use them at home. It would be considered an act of piracy should American ships interfere with Dutch interests in the East Indies. Just this year, on the 1st of February, the Dutch Government nationalised the Dutch East India Company and formed the Army of the East Indies. We would be courting a war and stiff opposition. The American Government may consider it an act of piracy, or so the Dutch will claim," said Juan.

At the mention of piracy a glint came into the old man's eye as he recalled his actions of more than 50 years ago. "A little, shall we say, pressure – unmarked ships well armed? Not an impossibility, think you not, gentlemen?"

"Not impossible but highly foolhardy. Every nation in the world, including our own, would vilify us. Times have changed, thank God! If you wish to continue in this vein I should leave – as a government officer I am grieved to hear this family speak so." Juan stood to leave.

Simon waved him to be seated. "We jest, Juan. It was simpler in the old days," he said with a sigh. "They do not have control of all the islands in the group, do they? Maybe an exploratory expedition?"

"I will look into it," said Robert. "We should all meet again in a week, at the same time, to review the results," said Simon in closing.

"Carlos, I have been worried about Jonathan since his return. Something is on his mind, and it is doing him no good. Have you any idea what it is?" asked Simon.

"Not the slightest idea, Father. I am, as you are, most concerned. I think it possible that because they were on opposing sides at the Nile, Jonathan blames himself for Michael's injury. Sally has tried, and Mother has primed Imogene to investigate, as yet to no avail. I was going to ask you to speak with him."

"Yes, I will arrange it," said a thoughtful Simon.

"Jonathan, it's a beautiful morning. Come walk with me a while," said Anna.

The young man thought to resist his beautiful cousin but, as ever, he was putty in her hands. "It will be a pleasure, my dear cousin," he said with more enthusiasm than he felt.

When clear of the house and its ever-open ears, Anna spoke to her taciturn cousin, beginning the mission entrusted to her by her grandmother. "I cannot believe a man returned from the most famous sea battle of modern times does not speak of his gallantry. Pray, tell me what it was like; it must have been terrible as the great ships drew together, cannons blazing. You met Admiral Villeneuve, did you not?"

"Yes, cousin, I had that honour. Villeneuve is a great man. It is only because of his actions that a part of our fleet was able to escape the trap that fool Brueys put us into," answered Jonathan.

"You speak of the French still as our side; is this how you feel?" the girl asked.

"I have not changed my mind because I am safely with my family. I am one-half French, but a quarter British and Portuguese. I am of the opinion that Napoleon will prevail; he has taken all of Europe, apart from England. America, a sister republic, having thrown off the British yoke, should declare war against England, our common foe. Was it not the French who came to our aid in the hour of need? Did not my father fight alongside Frenchmen to secure our republic for us? Who, in our family, other than Grandfather, are of pure British blood? The swine would have hanged him for flying American colours if they could have caught him."

"I see your views have not moderated at all," said Anna. "My father says President Washington is determined to remain neutral, even though he is bombarded, diplomatically, from both sides, to join the conflict. He believes, as does Father, that once the victor is decided they will try to regain their position in the new world. We must build our strength for then."

"Napoleon is honourable. If we help in his time of need, he will support us, of this I am certain. I spent years in the company of French officers and men. They consider us allies, a sister republic, but wonder where we are in their hour of need." Jonathan fell silent.

"What of Michael?" Anna asked after prolonged silence. "How does he feel?"

"I believe he is in accord with the government's position, and I can't fault him for that. He has little allegiance to Britain; he joined the Royal Navy at the behest of our naval authorities; he was there to learn, and learn he did. He was awarded the King's Medal for valour." The young naval lieutenant regained his pained expression.

"What has come between you two?" Anna asked boldly.

"Would that you could know! Know this, however, I am beholden to Michael for the rest of my life. A conundrum, think you not – the best of friends, family? I will leave stories of that awful battle for him to retell; he was, after all, on the winning side." Jonathan smiled thinly, turned and left. Anna now knew her grandmother had something to be concerned about. She followed, determined to discover the truth.

"So, my dear, we 'ave your story direct from your own lips. It is impossible for us 'ere ever to fully understand 'ow you survived in that godforsaken place," said Isabella once Juanita had finished retelling her story to all the womenfolk.

"Yes, unbelievable," said Sally Antoinette, "but what we are interested in is how you snared that gorgeous man."

Womanly giggles erupted; all gave Juanita their undivided attention.

"It is true that some men are interested in a woman for more than just her looks. José is easily bored as he has a finely tuned intelligence. I am able to talk at his level, understand his business and partake in it, in the medical area.

"We share an interest in Chinese medicine; it is amazing that European Americans have no idea how sophisticated the Oriental peoples are in this discipline. Miles ahead of us. Rebecca, I hope to interest my brother in what we have learned. Have any of you heard of acupuncture? Fascinating field – fine needles are inserted in specific areas of the body where nerves are close to the surface. It relieves pain and cures illnesses – a truly amazing technique – and one I intend to practise here."

"Interesting, my dear," said Sally Antoinette, "but what is he like as a husband and a lover."

Juanita answered, cheeks reddening, "José and I have more to our marriage than mere husband and wife matters."

"Ah, so he's that good! I thought so," said Sally Antoinette with a sly smile, causing nervous laughter to ripple through the group of women.

"Madam, I will thank you to desist from these personal subjects." Saying this, Juanita left the Pearce women to their gossip and went in search of her older brother.

"My dear Juanita, I am most impressed with these discoveries," said Juan. "At some future time I shall arrange a meeting of top doctors, and you can present your findings. I believe first we should secure patents and form a company to manufacture and distribute the new medicines ourselves. I am tired of politics and will not remain under the new administration once President Washington ends his final term next year. We can do a great service to the country by building a great pharmaceutical company. I am sure José would be keen on that, don't you think?"

"Indeed, brother. I am still unable, as a woman, to practise as a doctor in our land of the free. I can, however, run a drug company. Your contacts combined with our knowledge will ensure success, think you not?" Juanita beamed; she could see a clear way of influencing her husband to remain in America.

"So, Michael," said Simon Pearce once pleasantries had been exchanged in the interview with his injured grandson. "You know of nothing that has occurred that would account for young Jonathan's sad demeanour and odd behaviour?"

The young man reddened at his grandfather's intense inquisition. "I ... I am sworn to silence; I gave an oath on my honour, sir."

"Listen to me. You are an honourable man, beyond reproach; that is not in question. Captain Hood said as much in your letter of honourable discharge from His Majesty's service, did he not? Was not this countersigned by Lord Nelson himself?"

"Yes, sir, I am humbled by his words, and of course by the admiral's reaffirmation."

"You are, of course, not in my service. I cannot bring dire consequence as a goad to extracting the knowledge I require from you. But I am the head of this family, and one of its most promising sons has an impediment. I will leave no stone unturned as I seek a cure for this ailing – be sure, no stone at all. You, I believe, Michael, have some information that could allow us to help Jonathan; this we need to know."

"I will not speak, but will remain while Jonathan speaks with you, sir. I shall encourage him to do so."

Simon sent for him. It was a quarter of an hour before Jonathan entered the oak-panelled study.

"Jonathan, please join us, lad. Take a seat. I have been hearing from Michael how the battle unfolded. I would be very pleased to hear your story."

Jonathan had noted his cousin's discomfort as he entered the room and guessed that something was afoot. "I was involved in controlling my gun crews, sir. I remember the terrible noise and was able to understand that Admiral de Brueys had condemned us to defeat by allowing the British to attack us on both sides at one time. When his flagship *Orient* exploded, we were next in line for the firestorm. We were reduced to a hulk in 20 minutes. Half our guns crews were ashore foraging; we had not sufficient men to man the guns and repel an attack from both sides at once."

"An invidious position, indeed. What ship attacked you?" coaxed Simon.

"*Goliath*, sir, and – and, er, *Zealous*, sir," said Jonathan, now deflated.

"*Zealous* – was that not your ship, Michael?"

"Ah, yes, Grandfather – briefly."

"A most invidious position, but of course you would not have known that Michael had been seconded to the Royal Navy, would you? Do you two consider yourselves enemies, is that it?" asked the old man.

"No, sir; at least I have no such thoughts," said Michael.

"It is far more than that, Grandfather," said Jonathan, head in hands as tears started to roll from his eyes. "We had been called to surrender by *Zealous*. I looked around the decks and saw naught but broken bodies and ship's equipment; no officer was alive that I could see. I saw an officer in *Zealous*'s rigging. The musket in my hand rose, as if by its own power, to my shoulder; I aimed and fired."

"So, had your side won you would have been awarded a decoration, by thunder. You did your duty man, I am proud of you!" said Simon emphatically.

"That officer I shot w-w-was Michael, sir," added Jonathan, sobbing uncontrollably.

Simon went pale and slumped backward in his chair. For a moment that seemed an eternity, the two grandsons watched as saliva ran from the corner of their grandfather's greying lips. Then Jonathan let out a terrible groan, putting his head in his hands.

Michael yelled out, "Grandfather," in anguish, rushing from the room, shouting for his Uncle Juan and Aunt Juanita.

"He is gone, Mother," said Juanita, after receiving a confirming nod from her brother.

"I am so sorry, but his heart was very weak from the previous attacks; this one was simply the last straw. Three score years and ten," exclaimed Juan. "He was cheated by just one day."

Isabella, always so strong and proud, allowed her doctor son to hold her as she was racked with violent sobbing. She was soon joined by the other Pearce womenfolk, apart from Juanita, who asked Michael, "Nephew, you were with Father as the event occurred. It would help us if you could describe the circumstances that led up to his seizure."

Michael looked for his cousin and could not see him in the room. He leapt from his chair and ran as fast as his prosthesis would allow, screaming, "No, Jonathan, no!"

There was a full five minutes of frantic searching before Michael heard a single shot ring out. He found his cousin in Anna's arms; she had Jonathan's head between her bosom, her fine lace petticoats red with blood, the barrel of a duelling pistol in her hand.

"I, I ran to him and grabbed the gun he had pointed at his head. He is badly hurt but not, praise God, dead."

Michael saw a savage wound, whose entry was at the top of Jonathan's left knee, shattered flesh, bone and tendon in its path.

He looked at Anna who said innocently, "He has the same wound as you have. How strange."

"He will recover physically and will have the best doctoring available today," said Juan. "It is his psychological well-being I am concerned for. Jonathan will need constant care while his mind deals with the guilt he imagines he should feel. Sally Antoinette, Carlos, I suggest he lives with us while he recuperates. He has a strong attachment for Anna who has volunteered to nurse him. He must not have his feelings of guilt reinforced by other members of the family. I understand that Robert and Isabellita are taking Michael back to Canton. This is partly because of the, ah, accident and Simon's death. They will, I'm sure, get over it, but your son must not be exposed to any negative feelings. A repetition of the attempt on his own life is a strong possibility should his feeling of guilt be reinforced. I shall ask Mother to stay a while too."

Juan, acting as the family doctor as well as the titular head of the family, convinced his younger brother.

"As you wish, Juan. Sally? Do you agree?"

"Why the boy would not be better off with his own sister and family, I fail to grasp. But I agree, in the meantime; you are in the capital, close to the best medical attention in the country. Let us review the situation once our son's limb is healed," answered the desolate mother.

The funeral was a sombre affair with Simon Pearce being laid to rest in the family cemetery that held just one other – Sean Finnegan, who had died at the age of eighty-one. The two comrades-in-arms would now be able to watch over each other for eternity.

It was unbearably close in the drawing room as the family sat while Mr John Smyth opened the sealed envelope that held the last will and testament of Simon Trefarthan Pearce.

After the reading, they sat in shocked silence.

Juan, Juanita, Carlos and Isabellita had been bequeathed their respective houses and land on the family estate, Porthellick, as expected. The other lands, which included valuable parcels on the banks of the Potomac opposite the new capital city – which according to rumour was to be named Washington after the first president and general – and, more importantly, the family businesses, including the China trade shares, were put into a family trust, with Isabella and Juan as trustees.

Carlos was now in a minority position in the company he had developed. He had three shareholders to deal with in Pearce Shipping as well as the Davidsons, to whose side of the family they were no longer favourably disposed, since the truth of Michael's accident had come out. He knew of his older sister's desire to expand the medicinal drug trade and suspected Juan would back her and José. His dreams of wresting the spice trade from the Dutch, and enjoying the fight in doing so, were extinguished.

He sat in silence and planned, saying, "I suggest a meeting of the board at the earliest opportunity to elect a new chairman to replace Father."

"A meeting will not be necessary," said Isabella. "As head trustee, I shall assume the chair for a period of two years – if, that is, my co-trustee is in agreement. The distraction will fill my hours, Juan."

"Yes, Mother, I think you are the best arbiter at the moment."

"We will expand the board to include each of my children, with Robert, of course, and José," continued Isabella. "Juan will be my immediate deputy and heir should I, for any reason, be unable to continue my duties. Thereby each of the grandchildren will be represented. This family must stand together; we must not let a simple twist of fate tear it apart. We shall work together in the interests of the Pearce family, the Finnegan Trust and the health of America."

Isabella, always the strong supporter of her husband, assumed his role with eloquence and ease, her firm hand a comfort and a counter to any dangerous thinking within the family.

The new matriarch would see peace once again on Pearces' ocean.

BIBLIOGRAPHY

Bowley, RL, 2004, *The fortunate islands*, Bowley Publications, United Kingdom.

Isles of Scilly Council and Museum, 1999, *Shipwrecks & maritime incidents around the Isles of Scilly*.

Isles of Scilly Council and Museum, 2007, *Poor England has lost so many men*.

Downer, M, 2004, *Nelson's purse: The mystery of Lord Nelson's lost treasures*, Corgi Books, London.

Hibbert, C, 1990, *Redcoats & rebels, the war for America 1770–1781*, Grafton Books, London.

Lubbock, B, 1924, *The Blackwall frigates*, James Brown & Son, Glasgow.

Rodger, NAM, 2005, *The command of the ocean: A naval history of Britain 1649–1815*, Penguin Books, London.

White, P, 1997, *The Cornish smuggling industry*, Tor Mark Press, Redruth, Cornwall.

Wright, E, 1965, *Fabric of freedom*, Macmillan & Co., London.

Maps

Emerson Kent, American War of Independence map, www.emersonkent.com

Gordon Smith, www.naval-history.net

Encarta, English Channel

Internet (in date order)

http://www.aboutbritain.com

http://en.wikipedia.org/wiki/Cornish_pilot_gig

http://www.islandlife.org/forts_gsy.htm

http://www.smuggling.co.uk/gazetteer_sw.html

http://en.wikipedia.org/wiki/Cloudesley_Shovell

http://www.hmssurprise.org/Resources/SIR_CLOUDESLEY_SHOVELL.html

http://encyclopedia.thefreedictionary.com/Spanish+War+of+Succession

http://Madeira-islands.com

http://www.madeira-web.com/PagesUK/Machico.html

http://www.madeirawine.com

http://www.madeira-web.com/

http://swashbuckler.co.nz/?Realpirates

http://kipar.org/?piratical-resources
http://hegewisch.net/?blindkat/thrown_grenade.html
http://www.historyplace.com/unitedstates/revolution/revwar-77.htm
http://www.ushistory.org/declaration?doc/index.htm
http://sandy-hook.com
http://www.history.com
http://www.americanforeignrelations.com/O-W/
http://www.let.rug.nl
http://www.americaslibrary.gov/

CPSIA information can be obtained
at www.ICGtesting.com
Printed in the USA
BVHW041137240320
575838BV00007B/211